Lilith Adams Series

Blood Lily
Rose of Jericho
The Lotus Tree
Ghost Orchid
Wormwood
Hellebore

Novellas in the same world

Draga & the Savage: Dragobete
Draga & the Savage: Dracul
Draga & the Savage: Corvinus
Draga & the Savage: Țepeș
Draga & the Savage: Snagov

For more information about permission to reproduce
selections from this book, write to
Permissions, Jenny Allen Books,
872 Stoverstown Rd., York, PA, 17408

Manufacturing by Ingram Spark.
Book Design & Interior Formatting by Jenny Allen
Editing by Jenny Allen
Cover Art by Blondesign and © held by Jenny Allen.

ISBN: 979-8-9928592-0-1

Jenny Allen Books, York, PA 17408
JennyAllenBooks@gmail.com
www.JennyAllenBooks.com

Your mental health matters. Some may find this to be a checklist of endorsements, but for those who have triggers, please read this list carefully.

Trigger Warnings include but are not limited to:

Graphic violence & murder
Body investigation/horror
Brief mentions of child sexual assault & murder
Mentions, explanations, and instances of torture
Violent night terrors/nightmares
Near-death experiences
Execution
Night Terrors
Mentions of warzone casualties
Sexual content
Gun violence
Execution
PTSD
Survivor's guilt
Grief & Loss

The **988 LifeLine** provides 24/7 free and confidential support to people in crisis via phone call, text, or chat. 988lifeline.org

SAMHSA (Substance Abuse and Mental Health Services Administration) offers 24/7 free and confidential treatment referral and services 1-800-662-HELP

The National Domestic Violence Hotline provides 24/7 free and confidential help. You can chat at thehotline.org, text "START" to 88788, or call 1-800-799-SAFE

Rose of Jericho
Soundtrack

Scorn – Portishead – page 16, paragraph 5

Flight – Lifehouse – page 58, paragraph 2

Sabotage – Beastie Boys – page 134, paragraph 2

Colour Me In – Damien Rice – page 148, last paragraph

Don Abandons Alice – John Murphy – page 174, paragraph 3

Hearts' on Fire – Passenger – page 203, paragraph 3

Anger and Disdain – Jack Trammell – page 223, paragraph 5

The Grudge – Tool – page 250, paragraph 7

Don't Look Around – Mountain- page 278, paragraph 6

Baron Samedi – Spiritus Mortis – page 291, paragraph 4

Shadows Alive – Daniel Davies – page 326, paragraph 2

The Sound of Silence – Peyton Parrish – page 353, paragraph 1

Climbing up the Walls – Radiohead – page 380, last paragraph

Saturn – Sleeping at Last – page 401, paragraph 7

Praise for Rose of Jericho

"Better than the first! I am officially hooked on the Lilith Adams Series! The action and twists and turns in this book kept me on the edge of my seat and turning the pages! It wrung every emotion out of me. Jenny Allen is a fantastic writer, painting vivid, heart palpating and emotional scenes with her words. Andrew Cohen has made his way into my heart alongside Chance! Do yourself a favor and read this unique series! These are characters that will stay with you."
- Jennifer Saviano, *Author of the Saviors MC Series*

"I am absolutely in love with everything about this series: the plot, the characters, and how the story is developing. Trust me, Buckle up babe and hold on because it keeps getting better and better page by page. I honestly cannot get enough of this fresh and different take on the world of the supernatural."
-Sammi Dyer, *Reviewer*

"Please secure your seatbelts before reading this book. wow! It was a whirlwind of plot twists and turns that I didn't see coming. When I thought I had something figured out - NOPE! Nope, not even close. I loved that. This was a well-plotted and thought-out book. I don't feel like there are any loose ends that need to be answered.."
-Amy Hildebrand, *Reviewer*

"Seriously this is brilliantly written, fast paced, and so much action it gives you whiplash. It leaves you on the edge of your seat and eventually in tears, not wanting to stop reading just in case something you want to happen does. To me that is the art of a very talented writer. Not many books have done that to me, but this one did. I've gone through every emotion possible, so well-done Jenny. You did something many authors have failed at."
-Ann Daniel, *Reviewer*

Praise for Rose of Jericho

"Rose of Jericho didn't transition the story from Blood Lily, but seamlessly bled the story across the pages to book 2. I once again found myself invested in the new and old characters, hoping some would die horrible deaths while others realized their value. On the next to the last page, I was struck by something Lilith said, "Find the people who hear your voice even when you can't, and never let your love for them be mediocre." I'm going to carry that with me for years to come."
-Kristy Hurst, *Reviewer*

"This was truly one of the most action-packed stories I've read in a while. When something happened, you thought everything would kind of even out and then get into something else later on, but it was…one. thing. after. another. So, if you want to truly sit on the edge of your seat and never know what's coming around the corner….read this series!"
-Marissa Hux, *Reviewer*

"The 2nd book in this series definitely did not disappoint!! It was a fast-paced and jaw-dropping read from beginning to end. I can't wait for the next chapter in the crazy lives of Chance and Lily!!"
-Michelle Beck, *Reviewer*

"What a fantastic heart-stopping, no-time-to-catch-your-breath, absolute rollercoaster ride! I was completely enthralled with Lilith maneuvering her way through a couple of nights in hell. I feel like I didn't get a chance to catch my breath. And POOR COHEN. He takes my heart in this one. His growth and the light shined on his past just makes me love him! What an absolute binge-worthy read, and I cannot wait for book 3! Well done!!"
-Emily Davis *Reviewer*

Rose of Jericho

Jenny Allen

Jenny Allen Books
York, PA 17408

Chapter 1

In only a week and a half, Lilith's life had gone from boring routines to a whirlwind of torment reminiscent of an absurd plot in a horror movie. Nine days ago, she'd investigated the staking of an emo kid who thought dental caps and black fishnet made him a vampire. The mundane case seemed like a vague memory from a past life. Only hazy remnants persisted—piles of empty takeout boxes, black candles, mainstream vamp books, sloppy black paint, and the crude wooden stake protruding from his chest.

The life of a contracted CSI for the NYPD Major Crimes Unit wasn't as glamorous and exciting as the endless parade of cop dramas on TV. Until recently, chasing suspects, surviving gunfights, and participating in interrogations had been rare anomalies. She'd investigate unusual scenes, submit her report, and move on.

Contrary to popular belief, people tended to stick to their job descriptions. DNA analysts didn't traipse through crime scenes, and coroners didn't take down perpetrators. That was Hollywood fantasy, along with the inappropriately low lighting used to ramp up the drama.

Ninety percent of the time, she had felt useless, a safety measure against the remote possibility of a publicity nightmare. The real vampire community consisted of small civil groups spread across the world, too smart to resort to territorial angst. Still, it only took one case, one story, to put them in danger. One slip could reveal them, and the world had a lengthy history of persecution. But understanding her job served a vital role hadn't made her *feel* useful.

When she'd stood in that dead kid's apartment, she had wished for a genuine mystery to chase, a purpose for her forensic talents. How naïve. The age-old lesson of the Monkey's Paw haunted her now: *Be careful what you wish for.* She had learned about the universe's perverse sense of humor the hard way. Although she'd gotten what she asked for, everyone around her had suffered the consequences.

She'd give anything to be back in that crappy apartment, testing the blood of a harmless poser in Hot Topic couture with Alvarez chirping in her Bluetooth about Gloria and the girls. *Everything changed.*

Her partner and dear friend, Detective Felipe Alvarez, lay buried in the ground. A madman had murdered her Uncle Duncan and most of his family, and her once-fantastic relationship with her father had shattered into unrecognizable shards. As icing on the cake, a few near-death experiences had left her with the lingering remnants of Cohen's blood, which allowed her to sense other people's emotions.

She glanced down at the black dress from Alvarez's funeral, ripped and torn—a perfect metaphor for her current life. Feeling unsatisfied with work paled when compared to the heart-rending tragedies that had occurred since her stupid wish.

Now, she sat handcuffed in a plane, bound for an unknown destination at the whim of a mysterious enemy. The most unbelievable part was how she'd ended up in this predicament. A monster resembling a Marilyn Monroe impersonator with crippling vocal cords had abducted her, assisted by a platoon of SWAT-style henchmen. Of course, that had happened *after* a six-hundred-year-old abomination destroyed her life.

If it weren't true, she'd laugh hysterically. It sounded like every scandalous talk show's idea of a Golden Ticket. Somehow, she didn't think her father's plan to go public included a circus of dysfunction run by ratings-junkies.

Sadly, this wasn't a bizarre movie plot, the imaginings of a lunatic, or Reality TV on steroids *and* LSD. This madness had become her life. It had changed her world forever, and she couldn't take back her Monkey's Paw wish.

An average person would panic, fight, and scream if abducted, but she didn't see the point. The private jet flew ten thousand feet above anyone who would care. Besides, she had done those things for the first two hours. Now, she sat bored, tired, and numb with only her guilt for company.

Her olive eyes scanned the cabin for the millionth time, resting on the three anonymous henchmen. Two of them sat silently across the aisle in matching first-class seats, facing each other like deadly bookends. The third man paced back and forth down the aisle. To her immense relief, the ear-splitting bombshell remained out of sight with the other flunkies. *Thank the fates for small miracles.*

Once again, she studied each guard for some clue, but they all wore black tactical gear and matching vacant expressions. She saw no name badges, nothing unique to differentiate them. They were merely characterless fixtures with stun rods, something she never expected to see outside of *Demolition Man.* Although they resembled cattle prods more than sleek batons with cool sound effects.

"So…how is your henchmen's benefit package, or are you independent contractors?" The men stayed still as stone, staring straight ahead, without a single flicker of movement. "Does conversation cost extra? I think there's a twenty in my pocket…" *Nothing. Guess I don't rate in-flight entertainment.*

She had at least expected a glimpse of anger, considering three of their squadmates had died in the ambush. Instead, only calculated caution lit their eyes. Nothing personal. Either they weren't a close-knit team or had mastered the military mindset, conditioned to view themselves as expendable. Most likely, their detachment resulted from a mixture of both.

She sighed and slouched into her seat, readjusting her arms. The handcuffs kept digging into her wrists. *Dammit. Who could throw this kind of arsenal at us, and why would they?* Nothing made sense.

She had no enemies besides Ashcroft, who was now a smoking corpse. She seriously doubted anyone cared about his death. He hadn't won any awards for teamwork. In the end, none of it mattered. Knowing wouldn't change her situation.

After running out of things to distract her, she finally rested her gaze on her fellow inmate. Conflicting feelings roared to the surface. Even unconscious, Chance Deveraux was insanely handsome in his black button-up shirt and matching slacks. They accentuated his six-foot-three, lean yet muscular frame in a very enticing way. Soft stubble covered his firm jaw, and subtle hints of auburn infiltrated his chestnut hair, which made him genuinely irresistible.

A pained sigh escaped her lips as she studied him like she would an intricate puzzle, one she may never solve. Chance Deveraux, bodyguard, friend, guardian, partner, a knight in shining armor, boyfriend. None of the labels fit, and yet they were all true.

A torrent of tumultuous emotions pulsated under her skin, the precise reason she had avoided looking at the man handcuffed to the seat across from her. However, she couldn't avoid dealing with the jumbled mess in her head any more than she could escape the stale, recirculated air.

Everything concerning him was raw, unpredictable, and tenuous. Their romance, or whatever it was, blossomed amid the most horrific moments of her life. *Can one intense moment in an alley be called a relationship? Can anything real be built on such dire circumstances?* Of course, none of those questions had ever occurred to her until the monster in stilettos had waltzed into his apartment.

Although Chance had admitted to holding a torch for her the past thirteen years, everything had escalated in a few days. They never had time to discuss what would happen next. After the agony of Felipe's funeral, she'd found herself too overwhelmed and burned out to broach the subject. The scariest part of things developing so fast was that they typically ended just as quickly, at least in her limited experience.

When the demoness had strolled into his apartment, wrapped in a skin-tight dress, she'd forced Chance into mindless adoration by shrieking like a circular saw cutting through metal. Then, with one piercing note, she'd knocked Chance out. He'd been unconscious ever since. The happy smile still plastered on his face served as a reminder of those gut-wrenching moments.

At least the handcuffs kept her from slapping the blissful look off his face. She didn't have a valid reason to be angry. It wasn't his fault the woman had some power over him, but it still *felt* like a betrayal, and he was all she had left.

Amid her chaotic thoughts, he groggily opened his eyes, and she braced herself. He attempted to lift his hand, but the restraints stopped him short. That's when his hazel eyes snapped wide open with alarm and confusion.

"What the hell?" He glanced up, and for a moment, his face softened into an expression that made her blush. Concern flooded his eyes as he caught sight of the cuffs restraining her. "*Mon cherie*, are you okay? What's going on?"

She shifted in her seat again, uncomfortable and defensive. Perhaps it stemmed from her reaction to the slight Cajun accent in his deep voice, or perhaps she felt guilty for wishing she could slap him in the face.

Then again, maybe another relationship on rocky ground was too much. After her father and Gloria, what would happen if she leaned on Chance, relied on him, and he changed his mind, abandoned her? What if she never lived up to the fantasy he'd formed in his mind over the past decade?

The memory of his glowing adoration when the banshee sang haunted her, and she swallowed the lump of tears in her throat before answering his question.

"Well, while you were napping, our captors gave us matching jewelry." The harsh tone wasn't intentional, but her illogical war of emotions put her off-balance.

The frown deepened as his head tilted to the side inquisitively. "Is there something *else* I missed?" His warm eyes studied her. She knew he sensed every emotional fluctuation, which left her both flustered and irritated.

How can I answer his question? I feel betrayed because he made moon eyes at some creature wrapped in a Marilyn Monroe costume who could command his attention with her voice? The concept sounded insane, and she didn't have any right to be upset. Still, with logic on vacation, her erratic emotions remained in control.

So, she did the only thing she could, pathetic as it may be. After pulling on a tight smile, she lied through her teeth. "No. I only want off this plane."

He crooked a skeptical eyebrow and settled into his seat, eyes never leaving hers.

"I've been on a plane with you before, remember? You were the one lecturing me about staying calm and controlling my fear of enclosed spaces. You're radiating a million things I can't pick apart, but none of it feels related to a fear of flying. So, *amour de ma vie,* what's wrong?"

His concerned stare bored into her, piercing through all the protective layers of sarcasm and wit she naturally wrapped around herself. He knew she was holding back, thanks to the demon blood that had saved his life. However, a dozen reasons could explain the dominating notes of fear and apprehension. She only needed one he'd believe.

With a weary sigh, she twisted her wrists, trying to find a position that didn't pinch her skin. There wasn't one. *Did the cuffs suddenly get tighter, or is that my anxiety?*

"I wasn't handcuffed to the seat and flanked by armed guards last time." She couldn't tell if he bought it or not, but he changed tactics.

After glancing at the bookend henchmen, he focused on her again. "Can you tell me what happened in my apartment? The last thing I remember is two mercenaries jumping you."

She cocked an eyebrow, unable to hide her skepticism or surprise. "You don't remember *anything* else?"

Micro-expressions of confusion littered his face as he studied her carefully—nose and forehead scrunched, lips pursed. "Uh, I get the impression I'm missing something major?"

Before she could temper her reaction, a smartass snicker escaped her mouth. Something major was a *definite* understatement. She had never believed in the supernatural or the paranormal. The irony wasn't lost on her, but vampires weren't inherently superhuman. Most of the mythology consisted of nothing more than media hype, some of which the vampire community itself had perpetuated.

Now, her logical brain was working overtime to rationalize *another* new supernatural creature. That made four in roughly a week between Cohen, Coffee, Ashcroft, and this banshee.

It wasn't difficult to imagine how humans would react to vampires coming out to the public with her new perspective. That type of fear typically led to discrimination and violence, not necessarily in that order. She sure hadn't experienced anything positive with her newfound knowledge, and she *certainly* wanted to put a bullet in the banshee's head.

Chance ignored her and closed his eyes to focus. "I remember a struggle…and a voice." His eyes flashed open with bewilderment as he squinted at her. "Were you singing?"

She clamped down on a bitter laugh. "Uh, no. I only participate in redneck karaoke. Thank you very much." When he still appeared confused, she clarified. "You know, singing at the top of your lungs in the car, shower, any place you're completely alone?"

"Quite an image." The grin crossing his lips held a slight heat, and then it dissipated. "Okay, so who was singing? Or am I going crazy?"

She opened her mouth to tell him all about the bombshell but closed it. She couldn't explain, not now. The last thing she wanted to do was blame Chance for something beyond his control. If she started talking now, with her frayed nerves and fragile psyche, he'd sense every undercurrent of betrayal she was trying to suppress.

He stared at her expectantly. The longer she took to answer, the more suspicious he would become. With no other option, she blurted out the only thing she knew would derail his train of thought. "They have Gregor."

Chance flinched at the unexpected declaration, his brow furrowing. "And you didn't think to lead with that? How do you know? Is he on the plane?" He twisted in his seat, trying to scan the cabin.

The gruff tone made her bristle, and she glared at him irritably. "First, you *just* woke up, and I'm telling you now. So, drop the attitude." A small part of her felt guilty for scolding him when her smartass sarcasm was in overdrive, but then…she didn't precisely have control over her mouth right now.

With one eyebrow raised, he settled back into his seat, jaw clenched, eyes tight, and waited for her to continue.

Lilith took a cleansing breath, trying to wrangle her erratic thoughts. Alienating Chance wasn't a move in the right direction. She needed his help. When she finally continued, she managed to lose the edge in her voice and imitate some semblance of normalcy.

"Whoever our mystery guys work for snagged Gregor in Knoxville. Timothy called me while I was in the elevator and said Gregor never got off the plane."

Chance nodded thoughtfully as his unfriendly stare melted. His hand rose to comb through his hair until the cuffs stopped him short. He growled in frustration, and she suddenly remembered the flight to Tennessee. The man had nearly knocked over a middle-aged woman to get off the plane.

Thankfully, Chance released a long breath and shifted to a more comfortable position. As curious as she was about the stun batons, she didn't want to experience them first-hand.

"Then, Cohen called." Mentioning the detective's name made him sit in a rigid line, rapt with attention. Not only would she never label them friends, inferring they were warmly neutral was a stretch.

"I couldn't understand much because. The connection was spotty. But he said *they got to Gregor* and told me to run. Whatever this is about, Cohen knows something."

Chance clenched his jaw while stretching his neck from one side to the other in good-ole-fashioned anger. "Why am I not fucking surprised?" After a slow exhale, he glanced back up at her with a calm facade she knew wasn't real. A clipped coldness still infiltrated his voice, though. "Cohen told us the FBI closed the case, and his family had no idea about Ashcroft, Gregor, or anything else. I mean, come on. He calls your cell, and a second later, I'm jumped by guys from the henchmen union?"

"It doesn't look good," Lilith admitted. The FBI wouldn't use a mercenary squad to detain them, and they wouldn't employ a supernatural creature, either. Cohen's family made the most sense. He told them they possessed limitless resources and would mercilessly protect their secrets.

Then reality hit her. If she was right, a single piece of the puzzle alone could damn them, even if they chose one randomly from a hat. Gregor had killed off an entire family line of their species, Ashcroft had risked public exposure, and Cohen had revealed specifics to them, including their blood's healing properties. As if that wasn't enough, Chance was suffering a rare side effect, which allowed him to draw energy from people like an emotional suckerfish. For her, the effect dwindled quickly, but they had no idea if it was temporary or permanent for Chance.

Amid her internal rambling, she noticed the expression on Chance's face. It immediately derailed her train of thought, stopping it cold. A twinge of anger tightened his eyes, targeted at her, which made no sense.

"What?"

His jaw clenched again, not as tightly, but tension pulled at every muscle. "Why didn't you listen to him?" The question seemed calm and reasonable, but her confused frown abolished his restraint. "Dammit, Lily. What the hell were you thinking? The cab was right outside! Why didn't you run?"

Chance released an aggravated sigh when she merely stared in shock.

Did he really just ask me that?

His hazel eyes fixed on her cuffed wrists, and he growled again.

Her mind stuttered, unable to comprehend his fury.

"Are you serious?" After everything they'd endured in Tennessee, she had never expected him to bash her for running into the metaphorical fire and saving his ass. *Okay, perhaps that is an exaggeration, but A for effort.*

His eyes closed for a second, and when he opened them, they bored straight into her. "Yes, I'm serious. Cohen told you to run. Whether he's on our side or not, you should have listened. You could have escaped."

With her heart thundering in her chest, she snapped. Now that she finally had a valid target for her pent-up anger, she proved he wasn't the only one who could lash out.

"Oh, no. Don't you fucking dare. You are dead wrong. If they know where you live, they sure as shit know where I live. The odds were better with you upstairs, not that I stopped to think about that rationally."

Lilith sucked in a rattling breath to steady her quaking muscles as she surged from simple anger to pure fury. *Chivalry be damned!* She refused to let him railroad her for doing the right thing.

"Do you really believe I could ever see running as an option?! You would have done the same thing, so don't lecture me!"

"It's *my* job to protect people, not *yours*." He instantly snapped the words with steel-like certainty.

Her howl of laughter hung in the air like a bitter cloud. "I'm sorry. Do I need a super-secret bodyguard union card to give a shit about people? Fuck. Do you think if I ask nicely, the guard will knock you out? I think I prefer you unconscious right now." Out of the corner of her eye, she spotted a smirk on the pacing man's face. At least someone found things entertaining. She sure as hell didn't.

Chance stared at her, slack-jawed, while she studied the closed window to hide her tears. This whole thing felt like a nightmare. Fighting with him wouldn't help their situation. All it did was shred her insides. They needed answers, leverage, something, anything but this.

"Shit. I'm sorry, *mon cherie*." His Cajun accent thickened as the words escaped with a deep sigh. But when she finally tore her eyes away from the window, the tight pull of his jaw and stiff posture said he had more on his mind.

Great.

Part of her found his offer to play nice tempting. Unfortunately, that wasn't the part in control.

"But..." She fixed him with a glare while he tried to appear confused. "Finish what you want to say. Let's hear it."

"And I thought Gregor was stubborn." The man smiled.

Damn him. The enigmatic expression chipped away at her animosity, but she dug in her heels and held on. "Cut the crap. This entire night has been a total disaster. Alvarez's funeral was enough trauma for one lifetime. Do you really want to add to it by being dishonest?"

Chance studied her, an internal battle raging behind his eyes. He seemed calmer, not that she could say the same. Her heart raced like a rabbit on a case of five-hour energy drinks, maybe two.

Lilith was starting to think Chance would never answer. He just stared at her.

Finally, Chance shifted in his seat with a resigned sigh. "When those men busted through the window, my first thought was, *At least Lily is safe*. I could handle whatever they threw at me as long as you were in the cab, heading to your apartment."

Chance glanced over at the bookend thugs, twisting his wrists against the cuffs. It quickly became apparent that he didn't feel comfortable having this conversation in front of an audience, but he reluctantly continued.

"When I heard your voice, everything changed. I wasn't fighting for myself anymore. I was fighting for you." He leaned back, gazing at the ceiling as if it held all the answers. "I was terrified I wouldn't be able to save you. I didn't…"

The haunted tone in his voice abolished the remaining vestiges of her anger. She tried to hold on to it like before, but the rage slipped through her grasp like grains of sand. Then, the panic sank in as her conflicting emotions bounced around her brain like ping-pong balls stuffed with dynamite.

"Chance, from the moment we stepped foot on the plane to Tennessee, we've been a team, and not because of the…" She faltered again, uncertain how to label things. "… the romantic stuff. You need to stop viewing me as a client and start seeing me as a partner. Can you please drop the white knight complex? It doesn't change our situation."

"*Mon cherie*, please." After the pleading words, he sighed again with an edge of frustration. "You don't understand what I'm trying to say. It's not my *white knight complex*…it's you."

Lilith flinched and tried to swallow the sudden lump of tears in her throat. His words felt like an accusation, as if *she* should apologize. He kept talking, but it was all white noise for a few seconds as she struggled to reassemble her fragile psyche. For most of her life, Lilith had relied on her logic, and now it had failed her.

"God, Lily. I've waited so long, thinking the day would never happen. I can't lose you, not now. That sense of panic doesn't come with a side order of rational thought. With you, I can't be objective, which is what I need in a fight."

Thankfully, he wasn't waiting for a response because what could she honestly say? *Thank you? I'm sorry? Fuck you? What the hell do you expect me to do?*

The silence seemed to stretch on forever. Chance gazed at the ceiling with a faint blush to his cheeks. Perhaps he was trying to figure out what to say or why she hadn't said anything. Maybe he was silently cursing himself for speaking at all.

Lilith didn't trust her instincts right now. She couldn't even decipher Chance's expression, a talent that had become second-nature. Usually, she didn't have to think about it. The translation of people's micro-expressions just popped into her head. She read faces like a book. But currently, her head was filled with white noise and panic.

Lilith kept searching for the right words, any words, but came up empty every time.

Finally, Chance leaned forward as far as the restraints allowed with a puzzled expression. After a quick sideways glance, he lowered his voice to a conspiratorial whisper. "If this is Cohen's family, why go through all this trouble?"

The abrupt subject change soothed her jangled nerves. It gave her something concrete to work on, something that required cold logic. Handling emotionally ambiguous moments of vulnerability didn't fall into her wheelhouse. She'd always felt like someone attempting to defuse a ticking bomb in oven mitts.

"How do you mean?"

"Why send a private jet? Why risk a kidnapping? Cohen told us that if they got wind of things, they'd kill us. So, why aren't we dead?"

"Well, I prefer our current state of alive and breathing. Thank you."

"Smartass." His frown slowly transformed into a sinful smirk. "You know what I mean. One assassin could have taken us both out quietly with a few sniper shots from a rooftop or by rigging a fire in my building. They have the resources to make it happen."

"I don't know. Perhaps they like to handle things personally or want to discover precisely what we know. It's impossible to say with my psychic powers on the fritz." She dialed back her sarcasm from scathing to playful by some miracle. Her default defense mechanism was sharp-tongued humor, but she didn't want to keep slipping into that mode. Chance deserved better, and it wouldn't help them.

"Seems like an awful lot of trouble." As strange as it sounded, that was the most optimistic thing she'd heard all day. If the demons wanted something, maybe they still held a bargaining chip.

"By the way, how did they knock me out? I don't hurt anywhere, and I'm not groggy from a sedative." He shifted back into his seat and stretched.

Out of one awkwardly painful conversation right into another. Awesome. The subject kept coming back around like the worst white elephant gift ever. Still, he needed to be prepared, no matter how much talking about it hurt.

"There's a woman on the plane. She was in your apartment." Her brain fumbled for a reasonable explanation for something she barely believed herself. "I don't know who or what she is, but she's dangerous."

A curious sensation tickled over her skin, which hadn't originated from Chance. A side glance across the aisle revealed the minions watching them for the first time. *Damn.* They hadn't seemed the least bit interested in anything else so far, not even when she'd mentioned the call from Cohen. Of course, she probably shouldn't have said anything in front of an audience, but too late now. She didn't need to dig herself any deeper by advertising what she knew about the mystery woman, which admittedly wasn't much.

Chance picked up on her observation, nodded in agreement with her unspoken conclusion, and changed the subject again. "Did you see where they took us? What airfield?"

"Nope. The blacked-out windows made that a futile effort." She shivered, remembering the awkward car ride with the Marilyn impersonator inspecting her like people studied intricate diagrams. "When we got to the runway, I didn't see any signs, only the plane. It's private, but if they can afford a squad of goons, a private jet on a remote airfield isn't surprising."

She glanced over at the guards, but again, their blank faces showed nothing. They didn't care. *Weird.* The only response she had elicited centered on the woman who had accompanied them. Perhaps she fascinated all men, even her own. The thought didn't improve her mood or their odds. Loyalty consistently outweighed money as a motivating force.

"Lily, I apologize. I shouldn't have gone off on you." One more unexpected turn in the conversation, and she could file a claim for mental whiplash. "It's just…this night didn't go exactly as planned." His mouth quirked in a half-hearted smile.

"You mean you *didn't* order the dangling SWAT team? I think if you were trying for the Cirque du Soleil, you dialed the wrong number." She summoned up a playful smile, and he chuckled before relaxing into his seat. The oppressive weight finally began to lift from her shoulders.

An easy grin slipped across his lips with a familiar glint of smartass humor. The combination had always intrigued her. "Well, you know, I started to dial that number but figured what the hell? We haven't had enough excitement since we got back to New York. A man can't fall back on the old standards when he's set the bar so high. Who wants dinner, roses, and clowns when you can have martial arts, guns, and hostage situations? Romantic, right?"

His Cheshire cat grin warmed her right down to her toes, and, for a moment, she felt like they were someplace else. In nine short days, his flirty wit had begun to feel like home, a balm for her wounded emotions. No matter how infuriated or embarrassed she was, she loved him—a simple fact which refused to be ignored.

"Eh, well. I hate clowns anyway. They give me the creeps." She visibly shivered, which wasn't a complete act.

He crooked an eyebrow and grinned like a kid in a candy store. "Oh, really? A clown phobia, huh?"

"Noooo. An extremely strong *fear*, which is not the same thing. A phobia is irrational. Getting spooked by grown-ups in primary face paint parading around with creepy voices is *not* irrational. It's entirely legitimate."

"*Killer Klowns from Outer Space* or *It*?" He settled in with a glowing confidence she hadn't seen since that first morning in Miriah's apartment. Apparently, they both needed the comfort of familiar banter.

"*It*. I had nightmares for three months straight. I *still* can't walk over open storm drains."

Chance burst out laughing, and she even heard a faint snort from the human statues across the aisle.

"Okay, now how is *that* not irrational?" he asked with a smirk.

"Hey, stranger things have happened. In New York City, anything could live in those sewers, ready to strike at your ankle." She kept her serious expression screwed in place...barely.

"Yeah, like the enormous killer crocs?" He coughed the words through uncontrollable laughter.

"Don't be silly," Lilith chided.

Chance wiped at his eyes, still grinning at her stern expression.

She waited until his amusement settled into sporadic chuckles, maintaining her chastising frown. "They can't fit their giant jaws through the opening."

He howled with laughter, and even the stonelike henchmen sniggered.

"With a reaction like that, maybe I should quit my job and become the first vampire comedian. I could do an HBO special and land a movie deal for a romantic comedy with Gerard Butler." She flashed a cheeky wink at Chance and sank into her seat, a million times more relaxed.

"A Scotsman, huh? It appears I have the wrong accent, *mon cherie*." The twinkle in his hazel eyes made his grin even more alluring.

"Oh, don't you worry." Her lips stretched into a saucy smile as she leaned forward to whisper. "Before Gerard Butler, there was Gambit, a Cajun who could really make a girl swoon."

Chance's warm chuckle filled the cabin and eased the war raging in her head. Everything melted away as she forgot about the fight, his soul-baring confession, and even the handcuffs, at least, for a little bit.

Chapter 2

As soon as they landed, a flurry of activity ensued. The aisle-pacing minion took his position at the exit, eyeing the cabin with a calculated stare. The bookend guards hastily uncuffed and recuffed Lilith and Chance. Much to her relief, there was no sign of the supernatural *thing* accompanying them. Perhaps getting to her feet while wearing a skin-tight dress and stilettos proved too tricky for the banshee.

With her out of the picture, they could shove the guards down and run, perhaps escape. But she spotted several issues with the idea and dying ranked high on the list. They still had their guns as well as stun batons. Lilith and Chance couldn't dodge bullets like Ashcroft.

Besides, they were in an unknown place at the will of an anonymous enemy who had zero problems finding them at Chance's obscure home. They needed to know more before making a move, especially since they had her father. Lilith hadn't abandoned him to Ashcroft's grimy clutches, and she certainly wouldn't ditch him now.

As terrifying as it was, she allowed the men to lead her off the plane while her keen eyes scanned everything. The airstrip lay blanketed in ominous darkness, which obscured any clues to their location.

She recalled Security Officer Coffee telling her that Detective Cohen had moved to Knoxville from a town in Alabama. *Is that where we landed?* She freely admitted Cohen possessed a million faces, and none of them screamed, *Trust me.* The state might merely be part of an elaborate cover story. Of course, even if it were true, that didn't mean his family based their operations in the same state. Speculation wouldn't help, so she refocused her efforts on their surroundings.

A noticeable lack of blinding security lights meant another small airfield. A lone streetlamp illuminated two black town cars. The extended vehicles most likely had opposing bench seats and, hopefully, a minibar. After the hellish day, she needed a drink or *five*.

Chance played it cool, letting the henchmen guide him toward the vehicles with a relaxed half-smile. Sure, he could act like an ass, but he didn't fit the brainless bodyguard stereotype. He wasn't a short-sighted renegade who always resorted to violence when pushed. Beneath his occasionally hot temper hid an intelligent strategist.

Unless it involves me, apparently. His comments on the plane still itched under her skin.

Despite knowing all that, his calm exterior surprised her. Why did she expect him to Hulk out on people? Perhaps because, on some level, she wanted him to. Of course, it could involve a deep-seated reluctance to view him as a whole person, which meant facing a host of scary emotions that threw her anxiety into overdrive.

No. That can't be it. That *is the behavior of an immature preteen not a full-fledged adult...which I* definitely *am...most days.* Her inner monologue didn't sound the least bit convincing.

In the middle of her silent debate, a lyrical tone emerged from the plane. Her heart thumped violently, and her jaw clenched tight as the very first note rang in her ears. The emotional jolt was about as subtle as an Epi-Pen to the chest, and Chance noticed.

"Your chariot awaits!"

Lilith gradually turned with a bitter grimace and stared down the banshee who was striking a pose at the top of the stairs. The lavender dress that wrapped around her voluptuous curves threatened to burst a seam if she made a wrong move. Her platinum blond curls bounced against her shoulders, and somehow, the harsh lighting made her pale skin glow flawlessly while she sauntered down to the pavement.

Awesome. The man-enthralling demon is auditioning for a role in the next incarnation of Desperate Housewives. Lilith's mind blazed with an overwhelming desire to punch the woman's throat. *I'd like to see her try to sing with a crushed larynx.*

Chance caught sight of the hateful snarl on Lilith's face and frowned, completely mystified. His head turned, and for a minute, Lilith held her breath, unsure of what she hoped to see in his face. She prayed it was anything except the blind adoring worship she'd witnessed in his apartment.

Rose of Jericho

Not a single spark of recognition appeared—no adoration, no lyrically enhanced attraction, nothing.

Lilith released a ragged sigh as relief washed over her. *Does distance make a difference, or is she choosing not to pull his strings?* Knowing more about her trick would prove extremely useful.

Chance turned back around and inched toward Lilith with his armed escort. "Who the hell is she, Lily?" His hazel eyes held hers, searching for answers.

Not only had her scowl betrayed her, but Chance sensed every erratic emotion pulsating through the air. Worse yet, he now knew her omission on the plane hadn't just been because of their audience.

Fear rattled down her nerves as her mind raced, trying to assemble some sort of answer. When she didn't respond, he sighed wearily and prompted her.

"You mentioned her earlier, but she doesn't *look* dangerous. Is she a ninja world-famous for chucking stilettos with deadly accuracy?" The sarcastic comment wasn't playful. The iron tone in his voice made her shiver. He *knew with certainty* that she was keeping something important from him, which did *not* make him happy.

Lilith's continued silence only made things worse.

Her throat tightened, and her teary gaze fell, unable to hold his penetrating stare. She needed to tell him. He had to know how dangerous the banshee was, but in her bones, Lilith knew telling him what had happened in his apartment would hurt them both. Between her wounded emotions and his guilt, she might lose him, and her heart couldn't take that loss. No matter how hard Lilith tried, she couldn't force the words out past the lump of fear in her throat.

Beneath the stern aggravation, genuine worry pulled at his features, emphasizing the tension in his body. After a deep breath, she bravely met his green-flecked eyes and pleaded desperately. "Not now. *Please*. I can't." The raw vulnerability in her whisper took him by surprise.

"Oh. You didn't tell him?" As soon as the musical words hit the air, Lilith squeezed her eyes shut while a tear rolled down her cheek. Uncontrollable tremors wracked her body, and she desperately wished they could get in the car. Racing off to their deaths seemed like a more appealing option at the moment.

"Lily? *Mon cherie?*" Heartbreaking concern riddled his voice in the wake of her terrified reaction. She knew he wanted to help her, but he had no idea how, and her refusal to acknowledge him revived his anger.

Lilith didn't want to ignore him, but if she lost her concentration, she'd rattle apart at the seams.

When she finally summoned the bravery to open her eyes, the banshee strolled up to Chance and draped a hand over his shoulder. Whatever her game was, she had chosen not to employ her tricks, at least not yet. Chance was still staring expectantly at Lilith.

Every inch that the banshee's fingers traveled made Lilith's blood boil, transforming her heart-rending terror into rage. She had never considered herself a jealous person, but she fit the description of a territorial Scorpio well enough.

A sudden desire to break every one of her willowy fingers seared Lilith's brain. With a smirk, she wondered if the banshee's screams would be musical, too.

Chance glared down at the woman's hand and then glanced up at her rounded face with a hostile scowl. "If you expect to keep that claw of yours, you'll take it off me. *Now*." The feral growl tingled down Lilith's spine, and she glowed with pride. That was the man she knew and loved. Hopefully, he still felt the same way after tonight.

"Aww, but we had such fun earlier." Her face puckered into a pout as she drew back her hand and turned the oppressive weight of her stare on Lilith.

"My, my, my. He is *feisty*, isn't he?" A conspiratorial grin split her plump lips as if they were two girlfriends sharing gossip over coffee, but a dangerous glint lit her pale blue eyes. Rage boiled over into pure fury as Lilith's fists clenched tight with the obvious intention of punching her in the throat.

Before she could move, Chance intervened. "Feisty?" He fearlessly chuckled at the demonic woman. Of course, thanks to her, he didn't know about her villainous superpower. So why would he be afraid? "If you think *I'm* the feisty one, you sure as shit know nothing about *her*."

He caught Lilith's eyes with a mixture of confusion and ambivalence, which made her heart sink. The selfish need to protect her feelings left him unprepared to deal with the new monster tormenting them, and he didn't need Cohen's blood to figure that out.

"The last thing you want to do is piss this woman off. She's got one hell of a temper." Then he turned his attention to the banshee. "You can ask Cohen about her right hook."

"Oh, you two are adorable!" She clasped her hands together and flashed a dreamy smile at them both. As her eyes drifted to Lilith, the sweet expression slowly melted into something darker, accentuating every malicious line hidden in her face.

"Mm, my *absolute* favorite. I've found nothing more exquisite than utterly destroying every single shred of love and affection between two people." Her mouth curled into a depraved smile, and a soft hum slipped past her lips. Although it pricked Lilith's skin like a thousand needles, the lost look already started creeping into Chance's eyes.

His sly grin disappeared, one tiny muscle at a time, as if his entire personality began to ebb away, and Lilith stood there, powerless, unable to stop it. The banshee slid her pale fingers along his cheek, turning his face toward her, but the grin and venomous chill in her eyes fixated on Lilith.

"Do you think they'll let me keep him? Assuming they leave enough to play with, that is. He'll be an infinite amount of fun. I like it when they fight back. It only makes the surrender sweeter." The demonic woman kept her eyes locked on Lilith as she turned and brushed her plump lips against his.

White-hot fury scorched up Lilith's spine, blinding her in a sea of red. Without a single thought, she lashed out with her cuffed wrists and slammed the chain into the bitch's throat with every ounce of force she could muster. Although the guards immediately shoved her against the car, the bombshell gagged, desperately trying to catch her breath as she crumpled to the ground. Lilith grinned deliriously, reveling in her victory. The sight was now her favorite moment of all time.

Chance shook his head and blinked a few times as the humming abruptly stopped. When he saw her pinned down by two henchmen, he immediately sprang into action. After slamming his fists into the guard beside him, he sprinted for the men holding her with fierce determination.

Before he reached her, the aisle-pacer from the plane clubbed him hard across the shoulders with a stun rod, sending him skidding to the concrete like a pile of bricks.

"No! Leave him alone!" Lilith screamed, but the man jabbed the cattle-prod into Chance's side, watching his body twitch and convulse. "No! Stop! Please!" The man backed up, but not out of pity or sympathy. One of his squad mates ground his knee into Chance's back while he hovered, ready to stun him again if he continued to resist.

Chance's hazel eyes cast about, panicked and unfocused, as the man shoved his face into the pavement. His strangled cry of pain and frustration tore at her heart, and Lilith tried to break free. She kicked and pushed, but the man crushed an arm against her throat to pacify her.

Unfortunately, the commotion gave the banshee enough time to recover. She rubbed at the angry red mark across her pale throat but made it to her feet. A confident animosity filled her eyes as she callously stepped over Chance and strutted right toward Lilith. Each click of her high heels echoed ominously on the open runway. When the woman held up her hand dismissively, the guards backed away, happily abandoning Lilith to escape the splash zone.

With unexpected strength, the bombshell clamped her manicured hand around Lilith's neck and smashed her into the car so hard the steel frame groaned.

Suddenly, all the air escaped her lungs as bright spots danced before her eyes. The world spun in dizzy circles until the banshee's round face loomed into view. The smoldering-temptress facade twisted into a sadistic sneer, which nearly made her unrecognizable.

This is her true face, the monster under the surface, saying hello.

The lilting Marilyn-style voice vanished, replaced by an icy tone darker and scarier than anything imaginable. "Oh, you will pay for that. You think *you* can intimidate *me?*" She leaned in closer with vindictive spite as she studied Lilith, drinking in every ounce of her terror. Suddenly, a confident grin split her full lips, and she eased back, slightly loosening her grip. "Do you have any idea what I can do to him?"

The vengeful words sent Lilith's mind racing through horrendous scenarios that caused her pulse to quicken. Her eyes drifted to Chance, who still lay pinned to the ground, his eyes closed in defeat. Dread tightened around her heart like a vice lined with vicious spikes.

"Oh? You're quiet and docile now?" The woman's head tilted, blocking her view, forcing her undivided attention. Platinum blond curls fell over her pale shoulder while her mouth set in an innocent smile. At first glance, the mannerism appeared cute, but ice-cold malevolence infused her bubbly voice. She reveled in the fear and panic that tore Lilith apart, consuming it…just like Ashcroft.

Then, her voice lowered to a sneering whisper meant only for her. "The next time you contemplate raising your hand to me, I will enthrall him, and he will choke the life out of you. He won't resist. He will beg and plead to kill you merely for my appeasement. He'll watch the life drain from your eyes, inch by inch. Then I'll release him with the memory of turning you into a corpse, which will break every shred of his sanity. It will haunt him for the rest of his long, long life, and I'll make certain he lives as long as I see fit. Do you think fifty years of reliving your murder will be enough to destroy him? A hundred?"

Lilith froze, utterly horrified, unable to breathe as her lungs seized in terror. None of Ashcroft's threats compared to the demon's demented promise. Forcing Chance to murder her and live with the memory exceeded the realm of mere physical torture and death.

Once satisfied that she had seared all the implications permanently into Lilith's brain, the banshee stepped back. The red mark from Lilith's cuffs had vanished, leaving only unmarred alabaster skin. Then, the vicious monster sauntered away to the first town car with a spring in her step.

Lilith rubbed at her throat and slid down to the pavement, shaking and sobbing uncontrollably. As she drew her knees close, she noticed Chance staring at her in absolute bewilderment and sorrow. Although he didn't hear anything, he had experienced every bit of her torment.

She knew the banshee was merely trying to rattle her cage, but it worked, leaving her powerless and defeated. All they'd lived through, all they'd survived, all the impossible situations they'd escaped, only to end up in even hotter water.

The genuinely terrifying element *wasn't* the evil bitch, but whoever held enough power to keep her under their thumb. *What kind of monster keeps a creature like that as an obedient pet?*

Her very core shook with the alarming realization, and when the guards moved her into the second limo, she didn't struggle. Instead, she obediently took a seat between two henchmen while wiping her eyes with trembling hands. She needed to pull herself together, but the banshee's threat dug under her skin, consuming her thoughts.

She kept picturing Chance, as broken and mindless as Duncan, chained in a basement. In the end, her uncle observed too much horror to maintain his cognizance. After witnessing the slow and excruciating torture of his daughter over more than twenty-four hours, he wasn't a person anymore. Duncan died a scratching, raving beast, gnawing at his own limbs for blood. Chance would face a similar fate if the banshee made good on her threat.

"Lilith, are you alright?" The voice didn't have the Cajun inflection she expected. However, the vaguely European accent was all too familiar.

Her eyes lifted to see Detective Andrew Cohen sitting across from her. No trace of the warm, southern charm from his Tennessee cover remained. He more closely resembled a tired aristocrat, defeated and downtrodden. Under her withering stare, his almost-handsome face creased in pure exhaustion.

"What the *fuck* is going on?"

Before he responded, the last minion shoved Chance next to Cohen and rapped his knuckles on the raised divider. As the car began to move, Andrew took advantage of the distraction and ignore her, which only made her boiling hatred rise to new levels.

Anger was a much easier emotion to handle. If she couldn't direct her rage at the terrifying creature in the first car, Cohen would make an excellent substitute. He wasn't innocent, and she had plenty of valid reasons to target him. All the displaced wrath flying out of her mouth resembled a therapist's dream, not that she cared.

"Cohen!" When she snapped, his pale face swung toward her, astonished by the sharp tone. "You need to talk *now*! After one cryptic call from you, mercenaries burst through the windows like a damn Nicholas Cage movie. Then the blond shows up, screeching and shrieking. Of course, while the sound makes my ears bleed, it's apparently a turn-on for *some* men. What *the hell* is happening?"

The last bit caught Chance's attention, and he leaned forward, hazel eyes trained on her without a flicker of amusement. *Crap.* "Repeat that, please?"

During the rage-fueled rant, she'd blurted out the very last thing she wanted to say. Although she fully realized the conversation was inevitable, this wasn't the way she wanted to discuss it, especially not in front of Cohen. Then again, maybe *he* could explain it better without the emotional subtext.

"Ask Cohen. I'm sure he knows more about the evil Marilyn impersonator than I do."

Chance turned his intense gaze on the detective with open hostility. Obviously, he found Cohen a more comfortable target for his anger, too. "What is she talking about? What is that woman?"

Cohen heaved a sigh as he stared into the pale brown liquid at the bottom of his glass with no trace of his typical suave confidence. If their lives didn't rest on his cooperation, she *might* feel sorry for him. Unfortunately, he held the answers they needed. She didn't have time to fluff his ego, and his silence only made her see red.

"Andrew! What the fuck is going on? Say something!"

The detective ran a hand through his sandy hair and drained his glass. Slowly, he raised his cloudy gray eyes. "Welcome to my nightmare. Cheers." The words slurred while his eyes struggled to focus. *Perfect. Not only is he ignoring our questions, but he's also drunk.*

"That's it? That's all you have to say?" When her clipped questions produced no response, she resorted to growling through clenched teeth. "Take your damn balls out of your mouth and say something helpful."

Both Chance and Cohen gawked at her in surprise, but she didn't care. Cohen wasn't the straw that broke the camel's back. He was the final straw added to the enormous pile *suffocating* the damn camel.

Unable to contain her mounting fury any longer, she jumped across the town car and smacked the detective's defeated face. The guards immediately grabbed her and hauled her back, but she kicked and scratched the entire way. *Rules and stun batons be damned.* She needed to wake him up, and verbally attacking him didn't seem to work.

"What the hell, Lilith?" Cohen rubbed at his cheek while unsuccessfully trying to evade her kicking feet. "Damn. Ow! Stop! I'm not the enemy!"

The useless declaration rang false, only enraging her further, and she shook off the two guards. After lunging again, she landed a vicious right hook and a few more kicks. "The hell you aren't! I haven't forgotten the basement when you offered to carve me up like a Thanksgiving turkey. I have the scar to prove it! Where is my father, and what is happening?!"

When the two men pinned her painfully against the leather, she continued to fight.

"Lily!" Chance's insistent shout cut through the detective's wounded yelps. "Stop!"

"No! If he wants to drink his problems away, I will beat the crap out of him until he says something *fucking* useful. I'm tired of his damn games. Why the hell are you defending him?"

"I'm not. I'm defending *you.*" He held her gaze for a significant moment before gesturing at the two henchmen attempting to wrestle her into submission. When she glanced at their faces, the barely contained frustration became obvious. Further action would cause ugly repercussions, which wouldn't help their cause.

"You do not wish to make these gentlemen incapacitate you. It isn't precisely what I'd call pleasant." Such formal language coming from Chance's mouth seemed so paradoxical that, for a second, she merely stared at him in disbelief, and she wasn't the only one. Then, she remembered her father using the same trick to calm people down. Apparently, Chance had picked up a few things over the years.

"You're right. I'm good." After surrendering to the guards, she crawled back into her seat, allowing cooler heads to prevail.

"Where did *that* come from?" Cohen gaped slack jawed as if he'd honestly never seen Chance before. "I mean, thank you for the assist, but typically *she's* the one pulling on *your* leash."

Gradually, Chance turned to face him with the same menacing expression an Alpha wolf would give another predator. Cohen displayed a hint of fear for the first time, shrinking away from him a bit.

"You better talk." She echoed Chance's open hostility, but it wasn't anywhere near as intimidating. In all fairness, bodyguards inherently got more practice than forensic examiners. Scowling at a corpse had never sped up the investigation.

The detective glanced between them while a silent war raged behind his cloudy blue eyes. After a sigh of resignation, he finally spoke.

"Your father is alive, for now. You'll see him soon." The ominous words sent a chill down her spine. "We *all* will."

Well, that sounds even less cheerful.

As if emphasizing the point, his head fell forward, emulating a man on death row about to face his imminent execution.

Perhaps he truly was in the same hot water. His family must be involved somehow. *Did they find out about Ashcroft? The blood exchange? Would the answer make a difference? Probably not.*

Andrew refilled his glass and swirled the caramel-colored liquid, pointedly ignoring them again. It appeared that sharing time was over. Perhaps he merely wished to avoid discussing specifics in front of the enemy. If he shut down permanently, they'd be walking in blind, unable to count on him for anything. The concept wasn't much of a surprise.

Cohen drained his second glass of scotch while Chance continued to glare at the dark window as he had for the past hour. Several times, she caught herself wondering what he was thinking, but not even Cohen's blood would tell her that. The ability to detect his powerful emotions didn't help her understand his full train of thought. The male mind had never been her specialty. She always felt like a cat in a blind panic, tangled in twine, and every attempt to solve the puzzle only made things worse.

At least, in this case, she knew why he was mad at her. She had closed down, refused to talk to him about the musical monster and its effect on her. She didn't want to lie by omission, but she couldn't bring herself to vocalize her feelings either. The fear and embarrassment blocked her throat every time she tried.

Now, she stewed in self-hatred for not conquering those obstacles. If she didn't trust him, confide in him soon, she might lose him forever. Staring at him, she wondered if it was already too late. Was the damage already done? Could he forgive her?

Then, the vehicle rolled to a stop, and she forgot how to breathe. This was it, their first glimpse behind the curtain. The guards quickly exited and began hauling them from the backseat. She expected a grandiose estate squirreled away from the city lights—something befitting an ominous organization. However, when she stepped out of the car, no grand lawns with creepy statuary awaited them.

Of all the possibilities milling around in her brain, a deserted parking garage had never occurred to her. Hiding in the middle of a city seemed ballsy, but she did the same thing.

Several bare security lights illuminated small pockets of the dank structure. The stale odors of exhaust and rubber indicated an underground location that saw regular use. That ruled out squatting in an abandoned building, so their hosts most likely owned the place.

Judging by the sporadically parked cars, it was past their legitimate business hours. To her disappointment, she couldn't make out the license plates. None of them sat at the right angle, and knowing what state they had landed in wouldn't be much help.

She released an enormous sigh of relief when she didn't spot the other town car. She *really* wasn't ready for round three. As fantastic as it had felt to slam her cuffs into the banshee's throat—and it had been pretty damn amazing—the cost outweighed the moment. The monster's threat still rattled around in her brain, making her chest tight and her pulse quicken. She couldn't allow that to become Chance's fate...or hers.

The guards corralled them toward an ordinary blue door, but to her, it loomed in the dim light like an ominous mouth, ready to swallow them whole. Her body vibrated with the urge to stop, kick, scream, fight, bolt, anything, but none of them were viable options. So, she forced her muscles into submission, moving forward, one shaky step at a time.

The minion on the left swiped his keycard over a black box beside the door—moderate security. However, a simple card scanner would run through the number sequences in seconds, granting them access.

The peeling door popped open with a groan that plucked at her raw nerves. Her anxious eyes stared, terrified of what might wait on the other side, but it was only a generic stairwell with a stainless-steel elevator. *No demons. Not yet.*

Another swipe of the keycard and the elevator opened with a mechanical ding. They all shuffled in, a tight fit for six people, especially with the tension hovering around them like a five-ton elephant. A guard punched the fourteenth-floor button, and the metallic doors closed on the utilitarian space.

When she noticed the buttons skipped from twelve to fourteen, she smiled in amusement. *Odd. It seems even supernatural, emotion-sucking demons are superstitious.* The more important observation was the number of floors—twenty. With that many, they had to be in a decent-sized city, somewhere. If she ran with the Alabama theory, perhaps Birmingham or Huntsville?

Her eyes drifted up to the elevator permit's placeholder as Cohen slumped against the wall. To her utter disappointment, the sign merely read, *Permit on File with Security Office.*

When the doors finally opened, the men ushered them into a modern waiting room. An expansive reception desk dominated the space, complete with recessed lighting, shimmering green countertops, and the crisp scent of sanitizer. Oversized, brushed aluminum letters, illuminated from behind, spelled PMIC on the ebony-tiled wall.

She sighed at the ambiguous initials, which provided no help. Of course, understanding what they stood for wouldn't necessarily be beneficial either.

The trio of guards marched them past several corporate-style offices in neutral tones, divided by glass walls. A computer and a phone graced each desk without the slightest hint of personalization. The place might be an accounting firm, a magazine company, an ad agency, an insurance office—endless possibilities.

When they reached the only room with solid walls, the mercenaries unceremoniously shoved them inside and locked the door. A wooden conference table with a scattering of utilitarian chairs filled most of the space. Beige walls matched the ultrathin carpet, with no modern art, inspirational posters, or windows to break the monotony. The discoloration from foot traffic, coupled with the thick layer of scuff marks on the table, showed people routinely used the room. It seemed probable that the business wasn't a hollow front, but a legitimate company.

A pile of suitcases and duffle bags lay haphazardly on the table, and she recognized a few pieces as the only luggage she had left after the hotel fire in Tennessee. Then a thought occurred to her, and she began rummaging through the bags, hoping it would be there. Her triumphant smile widened as she pulled out her forensic case. However, her joy was short-lived.

"Lilith, you *need* to talk to me. What the hell did that woman say to you?" Chance's rigid voice held a clear warning that instantly made her feel guilty. When she turned, he stood there with his arms crossed and his jaw clenched tight.

Shit.

"Chance..." She stepped forward, hesitantly meeting his intense stare, and touched his shoulder. "What she said isn't important. It was just a threat." She searched his eyes, desperately hoping her answer would satisfy him and he'd drop the subject—no such luck.

"No. Whatever she said scared the shit out of you, worse than anything at Phipps Bend. So, talk!"

She quickly recognized the moment as a point of no return. If she denied anything now, it would only result in pointless betrayal. With a defeated sigh, she turned back to her forensic kit, blinking back tears.

"She threatened to hurt you, and you're right. I'm terrified of her. So much so that I physically can't say the words out loud. I need to focus on things I *can* control."

She didn't turn to judge his reaction. Instead, she allowed him to process her confession freely. After a measured breath to hold back the onslaught of tears, she flexed her trembling hands and popped open her kit to frown down at the meager contents. Someone removed all her scalpels, prods, thermometers, and anything else she might use as a weapon. *Bastards.*

Warm hands rested on her shoulders, and then his breath tickled over her neck, instantly lifting a tremendous weight from her heart. "Remember, we are partners. More than that, *amour de ma vie.* You need to trust me and share...later. Deal?" Not all the anger had left his voice, but enough to let her breathe again.

While blinking back tears, she nodded and tossed a bag of cotton balls on the table, still digging through her kit. When she finally trusted her voice not to break, she spoke again. "Are any of these yours?"

As Chance moved around her to investigate, Cohen chimed in.

"This is all extremely entertaining, but not the best use of our time." He lounged at the far end of the table, relaxed and self-possessed—his typical cocky self. And…not the least bit drunk, apparently.

"Well, *detective*…" When Chance growled the title, it sounded like an insult. "… why don't you start talking? Why is our luggage here, and where the hell are we?"

He ripped open a plain black suitcase while snapping the questions and dug through folded slacks and button-up shirts to find two suit jackets on the bottom. Not a single pair of his well-worn jeans or t-shirts hid inside, much to their mutual disappointment. With his hopes for a comfortable clothing change dashed, he shoved the suitcase away and fixed Cohen with a hostile glare.

The detective's mouth curled into a smug smile, and he reached into his jacket to pull out a device about the size of a Bluetooth earpiece. A blue light blinked with the push of a button, and he gently placed it on the table.

"What is that?" She tensed and stepped back, unnerved by his erratic, shifting behavior.

"It's a short-range scrambler." Cohen smoothed the lines of his navy-blue suit and sat taller, reclaiming his sophisticated charm. When he smiled, it held all the southern allure from when they first met. Of course, knowing it was all fake made her trust him less.

"My family bugged every room in this building. As for *where* we are, I'm afraid I can't share that little tidbit of information. It wouldn't help your current situation, anyway."

His cloudy gray eyes moved past Chance and fell on Lilith. "My apologies for the car. I know it upset you, but I know what I'm doing. I need them to believe I am under their control. Trust me. It's our best play."

For a minute, she stood there, stumped. A million questions flooded her mind, but they all came back to the same one. *How can I ever trust him?* While mulling over the thought, she removed a stack of bags, uncovering a small compartment. After a silent prayer, she popped it open, and a tiny key glinted in the light like a beacon of hope.

"Trust you? How can we believe anything that comes out of your mouth, *putain de menteur*?" Chance plucked the question right out of her mind, minus the French gibberish.

Cohen slid from his chair with raised brows and stalked around the table, keeping his eyes on Chance. The public intoxication was all part of his act, and now he appeared... offended. She suddenly wondered what Chance said.

I should have picked French over Latin in college.

"I helped you kill the monster in Tennessee, handled the FBI, and kept Gregor out of their investigation. I saved *both* of your lives and called to warn you. *Pour l'amour de Dieu!* What is your problem?"

"Great. More French." Lilith mumbled the words under her breath, but no one noticed.

Chance surged forward, getting right in Cohen's face, and shoved a finger into his chest. "*You* are my problem. By throwing me in a holding cell, you put her life in danger. She only needed your help because you interfered. If you'd handled the local police, Humphrey wouldn't have shot me, and the FBI would never have gotten involved. And for the record, *Lilith* saved my life, not you. *You* would have let me rot in Phipps Bend. Every complication *you helped us with* happened *because* of you! *Merde!*"

With a growl of frustration, he slammed his fist into the wall to keep from punching Cohen, which showed a lot of restraint. Despite being a skilled strategist, his mindless-Hulk side seemed to emerge every time Cohen opened his mouth.

The detective never flinched. He stood calm and collected in front of the six-foot-three tower of rage and waited for the storm to pass.

"This is all very dramatic but pure fiction. I did not engineer those situations, no matter what you think, Mr. Deveraux. What purpose would I have for such trivial games?" Cohen's blond eyebrow raised with all the cocky grace of his true aristocratic heritage.

Chance leaned over him, and even though he was only a few inches taller, he made every bit count. "Because you need us, or Lilith, at least. *She's* what you want." His eyes hardened with suspicion before he continued. "Either your family is using you as a sympathetic face, hoping we'll confide in you, or you're in just as much trouble as we are. I have no doubt you'll throw us under the bus as soon as you get the opportunity."

Cohen studied his face with no signs of intimidation or concern. His calm blue eyes narrowed as if emotionlessly weighing his options. The sight made her shiver. She remembered the same expression from the basement as he held the scalpel, sliced her skin, and prepared himself for more of Ashcroft's dirty work. He claimed it was merely part of his cover, but she didn't honestly believe that deep in her core.

After a tense moment, Andrew mutely turned on his heel, leaving Chance to frown in confusion. He strolled back to his chair on the far side of the table and slid into the seat. After drawing in a deep breath, he leaned back, crossed his arms behind his head, and finally turned his nonchalant gaze on them.

"You're right. I *could*." Although his statement was unexpected, she didn't have the energy to appear shocked after all the curveballs he'd thrown tonight. "Lucky for me, you have no choice." The slight smile didn't appear gloating, more like he was stating an uninteresting fact.

After using the key, Lilith finally slipped off the handcuffs and rubbed her sore wrists. She stared down at the rough pink scars left by Ashcroft's manacles and shook off the onslaught of memories threatening to rise to the surface.

"We need actual answers, Andrew, not power plays." She motioned to Chance, holding up the key. Reluctantly, he took his eyes off the detective and held his arms out to her.

"Somehow, my family found out about Ashcroft, who and what he was, and everything Gregor did to him. So, yes. I need your help."

Lilith's hands froze in mid-motion as her jaw dropped. "How is that possible? You said no record of his name existed. You researched my family and didn't have a clue. So, how the hell do they know so much?"

He shrugged in one elegant movement, as if her questions were insignificant. "Perhaps they placed bugs. They sent *me* to vet Duncan, and it wouldn't be the first time they took extra precautions on a case they assigned me." The hint of bitterness in his tone meant they had stumbled upon a sore subject. "Then again, maybe Spencer said something to the wrong person, or perhaps my family planted a spy, who knows?" One shoulder lifted momentarily as he spoke—a clear indicator that he had no confidence in his words.

"Or maybe you ran your mouth," Chance snapped at him as she unlocked one cuff and moved to the next one.

"That is ridiculous. Besides, it's a pointless line of questioning." He waved a dismissive hand at them, completely bypassing the typical reaction of outrage.

With a surge of anger, she pulled the cuffs off Chance's wrists and slammed them down on the table. "How they learned about Gregor and Ashcroft might help us determine *what* they know. Perhaps you don't want to admit you screwed up."

He dropped the calm expression and leaned forward with his eyebrows drawn together in anger. "Cute, but we don't have any idea how they got their information. Prattling on with theories won't help. We have a precious window of time until they drag us into the courtroom. Can we please cover something useful? I'm more concerned with them discovering *how* I saved your life..." As his eyes drifted to Chance, they filled with ambivalence. "... and *yours*, as well. Of course, *Lilith* is solely responsible for that, as you so clearly explained."

Lilith fought the overwhelming urge to slap him in his sophisticated face. "So, in other words, you want to figure out how much trouble *you* are in?"

Cohen had the good sense to appear offended...for a moment. Then he settled back, eyes assessing her with the same look he'd given Chance earlier. "Point made."

The drastic change from the man she'd met in Tennessee and the drunk from the town car made one thing quite clear. This was the real Cohen sitting before them, cold, indifferent, weighing every option, and playing to his advantages. He couldn't comprehend the true meaning of loyalty and self-sacrifice, even when he emulated them. He memorized the lyrics but couldn't hear the music.

"I've gone about this all wrong." The apologetic tone rang hollow. She saw past his chameleon-like nature and the layers of condescending sarcasm. To some extent, Chance was correct. Cohen's bottom line would always involve saving his own skin first. "You have questions. Ask away. I'll answer what I can."

Before she opened her mouth, Chance barreled ahead. "Tell us about the woman from the plane." His gaze swung to her as he spoke. Although he still harbored a trace of resentment, he appeared more interested in gauging her reaction.

"Could you be more specific? I wasn't on the plane." The barest hint of a smug grin tugged at Cohen's lips.

With an irritated sigh, she glanced at the demon. "The bubbly blond bombshell who thinks she's the reincarnation of Marilyn Monroe. The one who makes my ears bleed with her dying cat screeches. I believe I mentioned her in the car."

She grabbed Chance's hand with a nervous smile, and his eyes softened with a wisp of gratitude. He deserved answers, no matter how much the subject made her cringe. *In for a penny, in for a pound.*

An amused smile crossed Cohen's face as he relaxed into the chair. However, she spotted tension in his muscles and tightness around his eyes—subtle indicators of fear. "Peisinoe."

"What?" Chance growled impatiently.

"*Peisinoe* is her name." His eyes moved from Chance to Lilith and back again as he waited expectantly.

Are we supposed to recognize the name?

When they returned only blank stares, the demon sighed dramatically and clarified. "No one appreciates the classics. Peisinoe is a siren from Greek mythology."

"She's a... siren?" Lilith stumbled over the incredulous word, but then, why should the term surprise her? Labeling the monster as a banshee was just as unrealistic.

"Well, no. Not *the* Peisinoe. She chose the name. She's a *chanteur d'âme.*"

"What? That makes no sense?" Chance appeared more confused than she did, despite speaking fluent French, the second language in Cajun country. "A soul singer?"

"What, like Aretha Franklin?" An awkward, nervous sound she intended to be a chuckle escaped her lips. Even reverting to smartass humor as a defense didn't help. The siren scared the hell out of her, and she doubted his explanations would ease that fear.

Cohen leaned his elbows on the table as all his jovial humor vanished. "This isn't a joke. I didn't misspeak. Allowing her to leave and retrieve you should impress the seriousness of our situation. She's dangerous, even by my standards. More dangerous than Ashcroft if you get on her bad side. Trust me."

"Too late." She mumbled the words with the siren's threat and his ominous warning weighing heavy on her shoulders. Then she noticed Chance still examining her reactions, and she suddenly felt like a bug under a microscope. With an abundance of nervous energy, she began returning items to her kit.

"What do you mean by *allowed her to leave*? What is she, *exactly*?" His intense focus finally moved back to Cohen, and Lilith breathed a little easier.

"She's one of my species, in a way. Her ability results from a rare genetic anomaly. When identified, they are immediately executed—no exceptions. The council believes they are far too dangerous, and rightfully so." After a brief exhale to steady himself, Cohen continued.

"Their voice is a multi-faceted weapon, as you've already seen. She shares the *pleasant* aspects with men—her sexual preference—while women hear something akin to a banshee screech. Once focused on her intended victim, they fall under her will *absolutely*. No amount of willpower, strength, or fortitude provides the ability to resist. You become her mindless slave, and my kind is not immune, which is why the council executes them."

As the demon spoke, Chance eased himself into a chair, lost in thought. His eyes swung to her as he began stitching together the missing pieces. Micro-expressions of a dozen conflicting emotions clouded his face as he worked through the evening's events.

Focus, Lilith.

She forced her attention back to Cohen, intent on keeping the information flowing. "Wait. Obviously, this woman is not only alive but employed by your family. Why wasn't she executed?"

"That's a lengthy story we do not have time to discuss. It's interesting background information, but none of it helps our cause."

"How does it work?" Chance spoke up again with his own agenda. "Her mind control stuff."

"Peisinoe targets males exclusively. When she sings, the intoxicating melody swims in their veins. She could command them to kneel, jump off a cliff, or even kill someone, and they *will* do it with a blissful smile on their face. It's blind worship." Andrew visibly shivered at the thought, and she didn't blame him.

"Do they remember…being controlled?" As eager as she was to change the subject, she needed to know if Peisinoe's threat was valid.

Cohen nodded weakly. "Typically, no, but if she wants them to, yes."

Lilith swallowed the sudden lump of fear congealing in her throat as her hands trembled.

"That's what happened in the apartment, isn't it?" Chance stared at her with pleading eyes, begging for a truth she could no longer deny.

She merely nodded, not trusting her voice.

"What happened? What did she do?"

With a deep breath, Lilith finally caved, unwilling to lie to him again, even by omission. "She pacified you. I watched the real you slowly disappear as if I lost you to her…and the way you looked at her…" She wiped the sudden tears from her eyes as her voice broke.

After a moment, she exhaled again and continued with determination. "Chance…it wasn't your fault. There was nothing you could do."

Guilt slowly replaced his torrent of emotions as his eyes held hers, the exact thing she tried to avoid. "And at the airfield?"

Embarrassment turned her face crimson as she braced herself. *No lies. Only the truth.* "She took control of you, and…" Her eyes fell to the table, unable to handle the agonized expression on his face. "She kissed you. So, I…I slammed my cuffs into her throat, which pissed her off."

Staring at the scuffed tabletop, she hesitated, trying to summarize the threat into a brief statement. "She said if I attacked her again, she'd make you kill me and then force you to live with the memory." Once she gathered her courage, she lifted her eyes to see Chance sitting perfectly still, white as a ghost, while Cohen appeared incredibly impressed.

"So much for avoiding her bad side. Damn, you picked the wrong fight."

A surge of uncomfortable anger prickled over her skin as her cheeks burned violently. "Thanks. I hadn't noticed."

Andrew cleared his throat, humbled by her sharp sarcasm, and changed the subject. "Anyway. Moving on. I assume you have other, more relevant questions?"

"How did they get my father? I thought you put him on the plane."

"Ah." Cohen's nod meant she had finally asked the question he'd expected to hear first. "After I dropped Gregor at his gate, I received a warning call while heading back through security. I ran, and it took quite a while to lose the tail. I called every contact I had inside, but they all shut me down. When the mercenaries started closing in, I called you." He released a tiny sigh, as if realizing he had forgotten to buy milk. "I should have called sooner."

"Why didn't you?"

Cohen casually shrugged his shoulders. "The initial information I received didn't include you and Chance. It only mentioned Gregor and me. I thought handling it on my own would be less risky. I didn't realize how deep the situation extended until it was too late."

She glanced over at Chance to read his reaction, but he still looked lost, mutely mulling over the events. With a sigh of resignation, she turned her focus back to the demon. "So, what do we do now?"

"My contact only mentioned Ashcroft and Gregor, nothing else. If they find out about the blood exchange…" Cohen locked eyes with her, fear and desperation displayed on his face. Somehow, she didn't think it was fake this time. "It will be a death sentence. Whatever you do, please, keep things in check, both of you. Don't think about using your new little gifts against the guards or anyone else. I know you are still adjusting, but if they sense that, we will all die."

"After all the blood loss, I haven't had that problem, but Chance…"

He finally peered up at the mention of his name and nodded, acknowledging their concerns.

An awkward silence followed, leaving her free to scan the room again. "Do you know why they stopped to pack our things? It seems odd if they intend to kill us. Are any of those yours?"

Cohen merely nodded, deep in thought, trying to piece things together. She still didn't trust him, but he had a stake in their survival, which once again made him an ally…temporarily.

"Can you tell me about your contact, the one who warned you? Do you think they can help us?"

"I'm sorry. I can't fill you in, not yet. When the guards return, they'll take us to see Farren." His voice faltered when he spoke the name. Whoever the man was, he scared Cohen more than the siren, which didn't bode well.

"Protocol dictates they take us to the full council, but they won't because of me. My contact won't be present. We'll be on our own. The less you know, the better for now."

A cloud of impending doom settled around her, an all-too-familiar feeling she had quickly grown to hate.

When she opened her mouth to inquire about this new villain, their armed escort arrived, signaling an end to their conversation. *Time to face the music.* If they found her father, perhaps they might still make it out of this alive. Clinging to hope was all she could do at that point.

Chapter 3

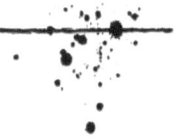

Lilith came to a sudden stop in the doorway, her body unwilling to take another step. The room's sole purpose became immediately apparent—intimidation through extravagant displays of power. More importantly, it worked. The menacing courtroom stole the breath from her lungs, making her feel insignificant and powerless. National leaders and shadowy super-powers most likely forged plans for world domination in this room.

A long table sat lengthwise before the trio, with three chairs awaiting them. Interrogation-style spotlights hovered over each seat, making them about as welcoming as a hangman's noose. Then, her eyes moved beyond the table and sea of soul-consuming darkness to land on the centerpiece of the cavernous space.

A mahogany desk, the width of the room, sat high on a raised dais. Antique spindle legs carved into dragons supported the desk's massive weight, the flames from their mouths curling to form the feet. A lone spotlight focused on a high-back leather chair placed at the center, and the darkened windows hiding the city lights provided a stark backdrop.

Her eyes stopped on an elaborate door in the far corner seconds before the guard shoved her toward the seats. She stumbled forward and quickly slid into the center chair, eyes scanning the area wildly as her heart raced. The room clearly emphasized the organization's terrifying power. This wasn't a minor operation in a temporary office, but a corporation shuffled through a hundred shadow companies that exerted global influence. They didn't hide from the world. They manipulated it. The sudden realization only accentuated her feelings of inadequacy.

She twisted to watch the guard's blank faces as they shoved Chance and Cohen into their seats and lined the wall behind them. The anonymous men seemed more like androids than real people, and it still sent shivers down her spine. Their eyes held no flicker of emotion, no excitement for the coming drama, nothing. Their clean-shaven faces merely stared forward with no spark of human intelligence behind their dull eyes.

"Do they drug them or something?" She glanced at Cohen as he straightened his jacket, eyes firmly fixed downward.

"Or something." He mumbled the words while closing his eyes, most likely preparing to resume his role as the defeated alcoholic.

While she watched, his demeanor changed, muscle by muscle, and she wondered if Chance was right. *What if he orchestrated the events in Tennessee?* Chance adamantly believed in his guilt, and the man confessed as much to Ashcroft.

Then again, perhaps the demon merely acted in ways that garnered him the most favor—a reactionary response. But after seeing how easily he switched roles, she wondered. *Did he expect someone to make a move on her while alone? Did he keep her bodyguard in holding to force a confrontation?*

Chance slid his fingers over the back of her hand, pulling her attention from Cohen. He flashed a soft smile meant to be reassuring, but the tightness around his eyes betrayed his nervous fear. She squeezed his hand tighter, grateful for the anchor. For a moment, she gazed into his warm eyes, wishing she could abolish the lingering shame and regret hiding there.

"*Cher*... I'm... well, I..." Whatever Chance attempted to say died with a creaking sound and confident footsteps that echoed with dark foreboding. Their attention immediately snapped to the carved door as it swung open.

The man who entered the room looked about forty, but something in the way he moved suggested a *much* higher number. Slight specks of gray invaded his ashy brown hair, which he kept short and to the point. His navy suit sported a tailored cut, complementing his tall, broad frame. Although his stature and posture seemed slightly imposing, he didn't look like someone capable of earning Cohen's resentment, much less his terror. He resembled another middle-aged pencil-pusher with far too much money.

However, once the man took his seat and moved his gaze over the three of them, she suddenly understood. The eyes set deep in his angled face shone as cold and soulless as the arctic sky. An indescribable weight of centuries existed in them, enough to make her father look like a petulant child.

They also rivaled Ashcroft's in cruelty, but a distant, intelligent evil instead of blind psychotic rage—an infinitely more dangerous combination. She couldn't goad him into action.

With a puritanical air of power rolling off him in nauseating waves, he inspected them one at a time. Then, his thin lips stretched into a grimace, resembling a knife slash across his face.

Just as Lilith thought her heart couldn't sink to a deeper depth of despair, Peisinoe sauntered into the room like a pet shark swimming through blood-scented waters. She still looked like Marilyn's ghost, but the bubbly persona vanished, sloughed off like snakeskin. With a toothy smirk aimed directly at Lilith, she took her place behind the terrifying man, draping a delicate arm over the back of his chair.

"Shouldn't the entire council be present?" Cohen's shaky voice somehow sounded defiant, which left her wondering how much was real.

The man's cruel eyes narrowed in on Cohen as the silence became uncomfortable. When he spoke, each precisely enunciated word cut through the air like a razor.

"Do you honestly wish to petition the entire council?" He gestured his hand around the room with a vicious, patronizing sneer. "You want to parade them around in front of strangers?"

His long fingers pressed together in a steeple as he leaned over the table. The stark light hit his face in harsh angles, making him even more intimidating. The scene made Lilith's skin crawl as if a thousand centipedes writhed beneath the surface.

"You wish them to bear witness to your crippling ineptitude? Your blatant incompetence? Your despicable cowardice?" His top lip curled in contempt as he spat each insult. She struggled to stay still and not curl into a fetal position. Fortunately, both the man and his pet monster focused intently on Cohen and not on her. Peisinoe licked her full lips while her hungry blue eyes delighted in the sight of him squirming.

Andrew's head hung down as his shoulders slumped forward in surrender. No matter how impeccable his acting skills were, she knew the words cut deep. Farren represented a dominant force of nature no man could stand against, not without damage.

"No, of course not, grandfather."

Absolute shock flooded her face as Chance's hand tightened around hers. Cohen forgot to reveal that little tidbit when he mentioned the man. Although he frequently referred to his *family*, she thought it was merely a turn of phrase, a way of summing up his species or their organization. She didn't realize he meant his literal relatives.

"I don't mean to interrupt…" Lilith felt both surprised and proud that her voice didn't shake when she broke the tense silence. The imposing man's eyes fell on her with an intensity that made her immediately regret speaking. A deep-rooted desire to crawl under the table nearly overcame her, but Gregor deserved more.

"Where is my father?" The demure question took a concerted effort, but their inquisitor's arduous gaze returned to Andrew. The disapproving shake of his head made it clear she wasn't supposed to know about Gregor's captivity. Whatever the reason, she was grateful for the reprieve from his soul-crushing stare.

Once Cohen appeared properly humbled, the disgust left his face, and his eyes came to rest on Lilith again. He seemed disappointed that his grandson spoiled the big surprise. Now, he merely moved through the motions with bored apathy.

"Gregor Adams, as he is currently named, stands accused of atrocities against the council and the community it represents. The punishment for his transgression is death." Farren's voice held a deep undercurrent of old-world accents as he rattled off his prepared speech with all the enthusiasm of wet cardboard.

"His *transgression*? I'm sorry, what are you charging him with?" To her amazement, she managed to ask politely, keeping her inner rage from breaking to the surface. However, considering the demon sensed *every* hidden emotion, her hard-won accomplishment was most likely futile.

She could only hope he appreciated the amount of effort it took. They needed the conversation to move in their favor, and fast. She wanted to get far away from the man and his pet as soon as possible.

Farren raised one thick eyebrow in what she interpreted as an expression of surprise. Either he found her question asinine or ballsy. Neither one seemed very appealing. His soulless eyes pinned her in place as effectively as holding the point of a knife to her chest.

"Your father admitted, in his own words, to brutally slaughtering an entire family line of our species. Then, he created an abomination which exposed us in the process." The scathing anger and revulsion in his voice rang true, especially when he mentioned the *abomination*, clearly the worst offense in his eyes.

Farren took a moment to enjoy their torment as the accusations sank in before his eyes came to rest on Lilith again with malicious glee. "Do you refute any of these claims?" He dared her to try, perhaps even wished she would give him an excuse to dispense more *justice*.

While weighing her options, the glint in Peisinoe's eye told her precisely how her father *confessed*. Farren controlled the ultimate truth serum in humanesque form. One thing Gregor knew, which the cruel man failed to mention, was the blood exchange. Hopefully, they didn't stumble across it and decide to hold it over their heads later.

"Now isn't the time, Lilith. Comply." Cohen's voice shivered. He was right, but no matter how much this *judge* terrified her, lying down like a passive lamb burned in her gut like napalm.

"No, I do not refute that you *literally* described my father's actions." This time, she couldn't hold back the faint traces of rebellion that accompanied her rigid repetition. Recent events may have strained her relationship with Gregor, but she didn't appreciate the black and white assessment of his moral standing.

Farren seemed amused by her spirit as the hint of a smile curved his thin lips.

"If this is about Gregor and his crimes, why are we here? If you expect us to…testify against him…" The demon's thick eyebrows rose again as he turned his fierce gaze on Chance.

"My apologies. I thought the answer would be obvious, Mr. Deveraux. You three are not only witnesses, but accomplices. You helped conceal Mr. Adams' misdeeds and took part in a plot to assassinate one of our kind…"

"Ashcroft was a monster! He wasn't one of you anymore. The creature tortured and slaughtered Gregor's family. He even tried to turn your grandson…" Chance vibrated with a rage so intense that holding his hand became painful, even with her weakened senses, but she held on for his sake.

"Silence!" Farren surged to his feet while his hand slammed down on the table with a thunderous force that echoed through the room. Chance flinched and swallowed his unspoken words. Farren pointed a spindly finger at him, dark eyes hardening.

"*You* are here to be judged, not to judge the actions of others. If you interrupt me again, I will ensure Peisinoe persuades you to remove your own tongue."

Jenny Allen

Lilith's heart jumped into her throat, beating ferociously. The siren's threat kept buzzing in her head as she glanced up at the demon's pet, whose plump lips curved into an excited smile directed solely at Lilith.

Farren eased back into his chair, ignoring the staring contest between Lilith and Peisinoe. Thin hands smoothed his suit, pulling a civil facade over his vicious core while content to let tension fill the room.

"As I was saying." He returned his focus to the trio as he straightened his tie. "You are here so I can pass judgment on your crimes, and, thanks to my incompetent grandson, you know too much."

"Is that the only reason?" Since Farren's outburst seemed to stem from a lack of respect, she kept her voice calm and neutral. She needed to play their cards strategically while they still had one or two in their hand, or at least she hoped they did.

His heavy eyes rested on her for a long moment, most likely recalculating his estimation of her. Speaking up after he threatened Chance meant she was gutsy. The slight lift to his left eyebrow and the downward quirk of his lips suggested the question held merit, which made her feel faintly optimistic.

"Is there another reason you should be here?" His head tilted to the side in mild curiosity. The motion fit his ancient fluidity but seemed at odds with his physical appearance, like an archaic creature stuffed into human skin.

Lilith settled back, folding her arms over her chest in a show of relaxed confidence. Cohen wasn't the only actor on their side of the table.

"Perhaps because of my uncle's book." She assumed all his grandstanding was an attempt to bully them into working for him. There wasn't any other explanation for the luggage. If that was the case, he already succeeded. *Why not cut through the theatrics and get down to business?*

While she studied his reaction, his eyebrows arched, and for an instant, his lips pressed tight together, revealing not only surprise but also desire, which lurked beneath the surface. Farren might have lived for centuries, but micro-expressions were universal and timeless. She didn't need demon blood to read emotions.

"That *is* why you sent Cohen to Tennessee, isn't it?" The moments of silence stretched out painfully. Although the nefarious man didn't fly into a rage, he stopped reacting, content to stare her down mutely. *Is he waiting for me to continue?*

Reluctantly, Lilith swallowed the sudden lump of fear and pressed her luck, hoping for the best.

"It doesn't seem your justice system includes due process, so I'm sure you've already tried and convicted us. If you wanted us dead, your *pet* could have accomplished that in New York City without the hassle of kidnapping and transport." Still no reaction. Farren's face looked like a marble mask, devoid of anything vaguely human. Fear rattled down her nerves, making her hands shake, but she pressed on.

"I only see one reason for bringing us here, luggage in tow, and risking more exposure. You want something. You win. We will do whatever you want without the scare tactics. Can you please just tell us what you want?"

The cackle that rang painfully through the room didn't belong to Farren. Apparently, Peisinoe found her outburst quite hilarious. While the men seemed unbothered, her laughter cut like razor blades, burrowing into her skull. The siren's stoic master held up one hand, and the *chanteur d'âme,* as Cohen referred to her, promptly shut her mouth, though a smirk lingered on her plump lips.

Once Lilith's ears stopped ringing, she peered up at Farren, who scrutinized her with ominous eyes. His long fingers rubbed his chin, weighing his options. Their chess game intensified with every passing second, and all she could do was wait and see if her bold move won the game or cost her everything.

Farren rose from his chair without a single word, lording over the ornate desk with his fierce gaze fixed on Lilith. Her heart raced as she fought not to squirm under the weight of his stare. Pushing him was a real gamble, and judging by the malicious glint in his eyes, she hoped they lived to regret it.

He moved away from the table with regal confidence, stepped off the dais, and strolled across the room. The terrifying man paced, head down, eyes sightlessly aimed forward, as if he had all the time in the world to consider his course of action. The movements seemed so benign, but Cohen stiffened beside her, tremors running through his arms.

Then the demon changed course, and each echoing step tightened her chest. By the time he moved past their table, she could barely breathe. The footsteps echoed behind her, and she twisted to see Farren walk up to a guard. Slowly, his long fingers wrapped around the man's gun, pulling it from the holster as the minion stood at attention. His soulless eyes looked the weapon over, examining it, not because he'd never used one before, but because he hadn't decided what to do with it yet.

While still inspecting every angle of the gun, he nonchalantly wandered around them. A knot of dread blossomed in the pit of her stomach when he stopped in front of her. Her heart pounded against her ribs like a wild animal in a cage, eyes locked on the weapon balanced in his hand, unable to focus on anything else. *Shit. I overplayed my hand, pushed too far.*

When he didn't move, she forced herself to look away from the gun, her gaze rising to meet his stare. Farren's ancient eyes pierced straight through her, pinning her to the chair with their ferocity as her panic bubbled up inside.

"Peisinoe. Retrieve the prisoner." Smoldering anger lurked beneath his calm demeanor, which distracted her from deciphering his words.

Moments later, a strangled moan and the sound of shuffling feet ripped her attention away from the intimidating man standing before her. Gregor stumbled through the door with the siren prodding him forward. A mass of bruises covered his nearly unrecognizable face, bringing tears to her eyes. Blood saturated his blue polo and charcoal slacks, as well as his gray-streaked hair.

The bombshell used her heel to shove him forward, sending Gregor to his knees with a sharp whimper. The distant memory of her powerful father lingered in the back of her mind, a pillar of goodness supporting her life. Until nine days ago, he was her entire world.

The past week proved that image wrong too many times to count. Now, her once regal father was a broken man who welcomed death, a release from his overwhelming guilt. The beating physically depicted how he felt inside since confessing his sins, and the sight cracked her heart in two.

A heavy sigh of exasperation escaped Farren's thin lips. "Get him on his feet, *chanteur d'âme.*"

Lilith fought to keep her mouth shut as the banshee dug her nails into her father's hair and hauled him up like a rag doll. The sudden change in position made him cough violently, and the slight gurgling sound indicated a punctured lung.

Lilith wanted to run to him, but Farren still stood in front of her, mulling over the gun in his hand. In the corner of her eye, Chance white-knuckled the chair, ready to pounce, but held himself back. On her left, Cohen sat still with his head slumped forward in defeat.

Gregor's swollen eyes rolled around aimlessly, as if unable to focus. Finally, they found her, and his sky-gray eyes immediately watered. "Lily?" The rough voice escaped so faintly that she couldn't be sure he said her name at all.

"Oh god, Lily, my girl. I'm so sorry." Peisinoe tugged hard on his hair, pulling a painful yelp from his lips before he fell silent.

"You're right, Ms. Adams." The indifferent tone in his voice scared her more than his anger. "I want something." After wiping her wet cheeks, she forced herself to look at Farren's apathetic face. He harbored no feelings for what he was about to do.

"Although your father verified my intel, you are the one I need..." In one smooth motion, he turned, aimed, and shot Gregor in the kneecap. Immediate shrieks split the air as blood splattered across the floor. The siren's claws held him still, preventing him from crumpling to the ground. "... not him."

Lilith surged to her feet, ready to vault over the table, but Chance and Cohen snatched her arms. "*You monster!*" Her screeched words contained all the venom and hate she accumulated in the past few days as blind rage consumed her. Both men fought to hold her back while she stubbornly continued to struggle.

"Lily, *mon cherie. Please.*" Chance wrapped his arms tight around her and turned to block her view. Gregor's screams of agony still echoed through the room, tearing at her skull, but she relented, conceding to the comfort of his embrace.

"He's trying to push us, Lily. Be strong. I know..." His tear-drenched voice broke as his arms squeezed tighter. "Breathe, just breathe." She couldn't tell if he meant the mantra for her or himself, but they both inhaled deeply and exhaled slowly before turning around to face the demon.

Once Farren had their undivided attention, he calmly strolled towards Gregor. Every footstep cut her like a dagger as her eyes flickered between them. *No, no, no, no!* Her mind screamed the word over and over while the sadistic man flexed his hand around the pistol grip.

When he stopped next to Gregor, her breath caught in her throat, the nervous terror causing her entire body to tremble. He pressed the gun to his temple, and her father flinched away as the hot barrel seared his skin. Farren retaliated by shoving the gun harder against his skull, twisting his neck. Gregor's panicked eyes found Lilith's, willing her to understand a million different things, but he didn't dare speak.

"No! Please!" Lilith sobbed in pure desperation.

"We'll cooperate. Please, there's no need for this!" Chance's feral growl rumbled over her shoulder while his fists clenched.

Farren's face transformed into a malicious grin of victory, but he kept the gun firmly pressed to her father's head. "Ah. So, there is something you *both* want?"

"Stop begging. It won't help." Cohen's tired, almost bored voice ignited a fire in her belly as she peered down at him. He merely sat there, arms crossed, passively observing the show. She wanted to rip the defeated mask off his callous face.

"You fucking coward! Do something!"

The line of his jaw tightened before he finally glared up in righteous frustration, as if she were a petulant child refusing to behave. "And what, *exactly*, would you like me to do? Throw myself in front of a bullet for a mass murderer? I don't think so."

With a snarl of white-hot rage, she kicked Cohen, catching him in the knee.

"*Arête!* Stop!" Chance's strong arms dragged her away from Andrew, who yelped in pain, clutching his aching leg.

When she went still, he whispered over her shoulder, the warm breath tickling her skin. "*You* are supposed to keep *my* temper in check. *Je ne peux vivre sans toi, mon âme sœur*, and you aren't doing your father any favors by losing it."

Although she didn't understand when he dissolved into French, the quivering timbre of his voice said enough. She went limp in his arms, weeping as she struggled to inhale past the lump in her throat. Chance spun her around and sank his hand into her auburn curls, tilting her face up to his. As she stared into his bloodshot eyes, full of tears, the room faded, and the vise around her chest loosened.

"*Amour de ma vie*, whatever happens… I love you, and we will face it together, okay?"

Before she could respond, Farren cleared his throat. When they turned back to face the room, the demon stood next to her father, gun at his side.

"If I *finally* have your attention…"

Chance gripped her hand, and it glowed with a warmth that traveled up her arm as if infusing her with strength.

"Cooperate, and I will allow your father to live… for now, but do *not* test my patience. Your dramatics do not amuse me. As for Andrew…" Farren casually waved the pistol in Cohen's direction with a dispassionate expression as he strolled toward them.

"You can't force the man to grow a spine, vampire. He's never had one, despite my every attempt to remedy the situation." His face filled with contempt, disgust, and a perverse victory that made her stomach queasy. Cohen wasn't her favorite person on the planet, but she couldn't imagine growing up with this monster as a grandfather. Mere survival was a miracle.

As Farren moved closer, he frowned with blossoming confusion. His soulless eyes drifted to Lilith, moved to Chance, and then fell on their entwined hands with a partially formed question.

Suddenly, Cohen surged to his feet and then slammed his palms on the table, jolting Farren out of his thoughts. It was the first time the monster flinched in genuine surprise. Somewhere in the back of her brain, she realized the delay of his hands hitting the table indicated a staged display of outrage, but her jumbled thoughts prevented the realization from sinking in.

"Dammit, Grandfather!"

Farren's hard eyes studied him as if seeing him for the first time.

"I am not some family accident!" Cohen's instant rage exploded like a bomb blast, which sparked out of nowhere. Docile and defeated one minute, livid and defiant the next. Everyone watched, transfixed, as he stared down his tormentor. "There is no need for your bullying tactics. They are reasonable people. If you explain the circumstances, I'm sure they would…"

Farren's hand lashed out in a slap so vicious that Cohen stumbled sideways. Then the sharpness of his ancient stare bored into him, locking him in place like a pin piercing a butterfly. "Always running that mouth of yours." He snarled the words, nostrils flared, lip curled upward in revulsion.

The entire situation turned awkward as he stepped up to his grandson, wrenched him closer, and whispered in his ear. She could guarantee it wasn't to apologize. The scene felt like the result of old wounds accumulated over decades, and merely bearing witness seemed intrusive.

Lilith averted her gaze, leaving them to their family dispute, and her eyes drifted to her father. Peisinoe allowed him to sit for the moment, his right knee still bleeding. Judging by the pallor of his skin, he would go into shock soon. Gregor mutely stared at her, unwilling to break the temporary truce, but all the things he wanted to say swam in his watery eyes.

No matter what crimes he had committed or what death and chaos he had caused through his actions, the man was still her father. Chance was right that night in the car. The past didn't matter. Only the man he became for her genuinely counted.

The events six hundred years ago didn't erase the man who held her on his shoulders when she was three and told her to reach for the moon. He was still the man she entrusted with nearly every secret, the one who made her hot cocoa with extra marshmallows on cold, wintery nights. He was her compass, rudder, center, and she wasn't ready to live in a world without him. *Why didn't I return his calls? Why didn't I forgive him?*

Lilith gazed at her father with apologies in her eyes as he smiled back with love and regret. Chance hugged her close without breaking her eye contact with Gregor, not only to comfort her, but to quell his instinct to attack. His fingers ran through her curls as his head leaned against hers. She knew he sensed the guilt and sorrow strangling her heart, and somehow, the ability to share her pain without voicing it lessened the weight.

Gregor's face softened at the sight of Chance embracing his daughter as a peaceful calm settled over him. He mouthed the words *I'm sorry*, and then Farren's booming voice shattered the intimate moment.

"Get them out of here. I will consult the rest of the council."

"Wait! What about my father?" The words escaped her lips without a single thought, but she couldn't leave him behind, not with these monsters.

"Lilith, no." Gregor shook his head with tears still streaking his bloody cheeks. "Chance, get her out of here. I love you, my sweet Lily." The finality in his shaky voice only made her panic rise.

"Please! He needs medical attention!" Farren continued walking toward the door, ignoring her cries. "Please, you said you'd let him live if we cooperate." The nefarious man's casual gait didn't waver, and desperation wrapped around her throat like a noose.

"Farren! Please, I'll do whatever you want, just please, please answer me!" She couldn't let things end like this. She needed to know her father would be okay, that despite being a demon, Farren would keep his word.

Rose of Jericho

He stopped, standing absolutely still in the middle of the room. While studying the demon's back, she held her breath, hoping and praying he would give the order to release Gregor into their care. Between the severe beating and the gunshot wound, he needed blood and medical attention.

Farren didn't move. He stood still as stone, giving her no sign of his intentions. Then, a split-second pulse of tension across his shoulders sent Lilith's heart racing.

In one swift motion, Farren raised his hand, and a shot rang out, echoing through the room like ominous thunder.

Chapter 4

Lilith watched in absolute horror as Gregor's head whipped back, blood and brains splattering seconds before his lifeless body hit the wall. He slid down in slow motion, smearing the bloody spatter until he landed face-first on the carpet with dull gray eyes.

"There is your answer." Farren snatched Peisinoe's arm and stepped over the body, carefully avoiding the pool of blood. They left the room before Lilith even registered what happened. The moment froze in her mind, unwilling to process the deadly result. Then, as if someone pressed the fast-forward button, reality hit her like a sixty-foot tidal wave of broken glass.

"NO!" Her heart-rending scream ripped through the air until her voice broke as tears flooded her eyes. Chance held her tight, shouting something her brain couldn't comprehend as she doubled over.

The guards rushed forward, trying to herd them out of the room with little success. Chance shoved one of them against the wall with bone-crushing force while Lilith wildly punched and kicked at the others.

When she finally broke free, she sprinted for Gregor. Distantly, she heard the brawl behind her, but her focus narrowed to one thing—her father.

She skidded to her knees and grabbed him, tugging his bloody body into her lap with gut-wrenching sobs. Through the sudden hurricane of grief, a radical and desperate idea sprang to her mind. Her fangs clicked into place immediately. *This has to work.* She couldn't lose her father, not now, not after wasting the past few days angrily ignoring him, unable to handle his blood-soaked past. He needed to hear how much she loved him. Her father couldn't end like this.

As her fangs scratched the surface, Cohen grabbed her wrist and violently ripped it away from her mouth. "What the *fuck* are you doing?!"

Lilith glared up and snarled in his face. "Get away from me!" She wrenched her arm away as her voice broke from the tears and white-hot rage.

"Lilith, you cannot do this!! Even if it worked, you'd be killing us all!" He grabbed for her again, and she screamed with everything she had left. Her hands flew out, blindly shoving him away.

"Fuck you. He's my *father!*" Her screams of anger broke into overwhelming tears as she fought to protect Gregor.

"He's already dead!" Cohen finally got past her blind attacks and slapped her hard on the cheek. Although she reached a new level of loathing, the sudden fiery burn distracted her enough to stop swinging.

The demon grabbed her shoulders and shook her roughly. "Look at me!"

With a deep well of hate and contempt, she scowled up at him.

"What the fuck are you thinking? You can't bring him back. He's already dead. Don't be stupid enough to join him or selfish enough to take us with you!"

With another shriek of outrage, she shoved him away again and stared down at her father's lifeless face, sky-gray eyes staring out sightlessly, the bullet hole oozing. Heaving sobs wracked her body, her soul crying out in excruciating pain as she caressed his bruised cheek. Her father was dead.

She would never see his proud smile, feel the warmth of his embrace, or hear his soothing voice again. *Why didn't I answer the phone and apologize for all the horrible things I said while I still had the opportunity?* It was all over, and she could never make things right.

"*Mon cherie.*" Lilith glanced up at the sound of Chance's tear-laden voice, and his handsome face reflected her guilt and horror, like an emotional mirror. She wasn't alone, and she found some small measure of comfort in that fact.

He bent down in front of her, his hand softly caressing her cheek. "I am so sorry, Lily…" He dissolved into tears as he gently pulled her away from the body and into his arms. His lips brushed her cheek as she wept against his shoulder, unable to summon either the strength or the desire to resist. She had nothing left, only a gaping hole in her chest.

Rose of Jericho

"We have to go." Although Cohen tried to impress a sense of urgency, she didn't care—not about him, Farren, the council, or anything else.

However, Chance heeded his words by sliding his arm under her legs and lifting her as if she weighed nothing. "I'm sorry, Lily." He kept whispering the words as he carried her away from the nightmarish scene. She merely stared despondently over his shoulder at the bullet wound above Gregor's left eye. It stopped bleeding, which meant her father was truly dead, and her life would never be the same.

Her eyes never left him as Chance carried her toward the door. No one spoke. They didn't say where they were going or what was happening. Instead, the mute mercenaries marched them forward as her head filled with white noise, blocking out everything as the door finally closed on the gruesome end of her loving father.

The fatal shot replayed in her mind again—the loud echoing pop, the momentum snapping his head back, the crack of shattering bone, the red mist before the sickening smack of brain tissue against the wall. It all occurred in a split second, but she fixated on every single detail. Her entire universe narrowed to the one defining moment that would haunt her forever.

Too far in shock, unable to cry anymore, she rested in Chance's arms, feeling hollow. One bullet, a tiny piece of metal, killed part of her soul. Since her mother's murder, Gregor was all she'd known. He defined her entire world. Leaving him to attend UCLA on the other side of the country was hard enough. Now she had to leave him forever, a tortured, lifeless body on the floor of Farren's courtroom. She squeezed her swollen eyes shut as her throat tightened around a suffocating lump of guilt.

When she opened them again, the heavy elevator doors closed on the dismal hallway. Chance's stubbly cheek caressed hers, still wet with his tears, but she merely stared unresponsively into oblivion as an awkward silence filled the tiny space.

The elevator chimed, and the henchmen resumed their march forward. The elegant hall, decorated in reds and golds, eerily resembled the hotel in Knoxville. Her lungs seized as the memory of that night flashed through her mind. That evening, her father bared his soul to them, sharing everything, and she rejected him. Now she would never fix things.

She rested her head against Chance's shoulder as the fresh memory of her father's brains on the courtroom wall washed over her again. The scene became an infinite loop of horror she couldn't escape. Other memories wilted in the wake of its dominance each time she closed her eyes, leaving her with nothing else.

Another faceless guard stepped in front of the group and swung open a door, signaling them all inside. Chance carried her into the room, and she passively gazed across a large living room filled with modest furniture in neutral shades.

"Your luggage is on the way up. You'll remain here until the Council reaches a decision." The man recited the words in clipped, matter-of-fact tones. She noticed the tension in the henchmen's face, a faint undercurrent of awkward impatience. He couldn't wait to leave because he had no desire to mingle with the walking dead, the death row inmates slated for execution.

All the guards disappeared with the click of a lock, and suddenly, she became painfully aware that they were alone with Cohen. A surge of fury flooded through her veins with such intensity it burned everything else away. Before she could move a muscle, Chance's arms tightened around her, and he whispered in her ear. "Lily, don't."

"Lilith, what you tried to do was idiotic and…" Cohen's impatient voice sent her hatred spinning out of control, but Chance spoke up first.

"Fucking save it. We need a moment." His low voice held a clear warning, and Cohen quickly raised his hands, conceding.

With a final death-glare, he carried her toward the closest door and kicked it open. Distantly, she wondered how he still supported her weight with such little effort. True, vampires possessed a slight advantage in strength, and she didn't weigh over one hundred and fifty pounds, but she should have felt a muscle twinge or something by this point.

After forcefully slamming the door, he crossed the room and gently set her on the edge of a bed. Then he knelt before her, palms resting on her thighs, eyes searching hers with sorrow as bottomless as her own. It quickly became too powerful for her shock-addled brain to handle, and her eyes closed, sending a single tear down her cheek. A black hole loomed in her chest, consuming pieces of her, even her rage. If she couldn't stop it, nothing would remain, leaving an empty husk in her place.

"I am so sorry." The hesitant yet tender caress of his palm on her cheek tore through the thin skin that held everything at bay, leaving her exposed. An avalanche of emotions exploded from the gaping cavity beneath her ribs, and she collapsed, sobbing.

She still couldn't believe that after all the pain he lived through, all the guilt he survived, it came to a halt, snuffed out by one vicious man's bullet. One hundred and twenty-four grams of metal ended over six hundred years of life. *He is gone. He is really gone.*

"I should have kept my mouth shut!" Lilith screamed as her soul burned in fiery torment. "Why did I push him?"

"Oh god no, Lily." His voice filled with tears, but a quiet strength lurked beneath his words. "*Cherie*, listen to me." His hand caressed her cheek again as he angled his head, trying to look her in the eye.

She pulled away and angrily wiped away her tears because she didn't deserve his compassion or solace. This was her fault and no one else's. "No! Don't lie to me. If I didn't push Farren, if I kept my fucking mouth shut, Gregor would still..." Suddenly, her throat tightened, and she choked, unable to finish the sentence. Her mind exploded into a whirlwind of self-loathing and regret. "How could I be so stupid?"

This time, he moved too fast to avoid, his hand wrapping around the back of her neck, pulling her closer. "No, Lilith!" Strength and conviction filled his voice while he held her gaze. She stared, lost in his deep eyes, and felt his sorrow, pain, concern, and something deeper she failed to recognize.

"He would have killed Gregor no matter what you did. You heard him. They sentenced him to death, *cherie*. Nothing we could say or do would change that."

"Chance, don't." She grabbed his arms, intending to shove him away, but she couldn't. Every ounce of strength ebbed away, leaving her powerless. "He said he was going to keep him alive for now. We could have rescued him or made a bargain, something..."

His brow furrowed in sadness, crestfallen, his heart aching not only with his grief, but hers as well. "Lilith," The tone clearly stated her arguments consisted of nothing but fantasies. "There's no way the two of us could break into this place and bust him out, *even* if we escaped. And you tried to bargain with the man. He had zero interest in making deals, especially not for an admitted killer. If he kept Gregor alive, he would only continue to torture him before doing the same damn thing."

Her shoulders hunched inwards, and she stared down at her hands resting on his arms. He was right, but it still didn't lessen her guilt.

"What am I supposed to do, Chance? I..." The hot tears stung her eyes, but every time she closed them, she saw her father's lifeless face.

Unable to take any more, she screamed in agony as her mind twisted with a million emotions.

"I don't know what to do! Alvarez is dead, Gloria won't speak to me, and now my father is…my whole family is…Malachi, Miriah, Duncan, my mom…my dad…they're all…" The word refused to come out, as if vocalizing it would make all the deaths too real and keep her trapped in the nightmare, never allowing her to wake up.

For a moment, she squeezed her eyes shut, trying to see *anything* except her father's bloody face. When she realized it was a futile endeavor, she opened her eyes to stare down at Chance with the unbearable weight of her guilt. "You should run while you still can. Leave. I'm the angel of death and staying with me means nothing but pain." Her entire body shook as she broke down, weeping.

Through her tears, she watched an ever-changing myriad of emotions ripple over his face, constantly morphing from devastation, to anger, heartbreak, concern, righteousness, and terror, but one thing stood out. Her words shocked him to his very core.

Then, his mouth set in a firm line, and he pulled her off the bed to nestle into his lap. He cradled her face, making sure her eyes met his before he spoke.

"I will *never* run away from you, no matter what happens. I didn't wait thirteen years to abandon you now. All that wasted time while I was content to steal moments with a woman who merely saw me as background scenery, too terrified to tell her the truth. No. I won't allow you to send me away because you're scared. You got pissed at me earlier for inferring the same thing. Remember, you aren't the only one allowed to fight for what they care about."

His words brought a fresh wave of heart-rending pain as tears flooded her eyes yet again. She felt overwhelmingly unworthy of such beautiful devotion. He deserved more than anything she could offer him.

"Chance. Please. I almost lost you once. I can't…I love you, and I just can't…I can't lose…" When her voice broke, she leaned her forehead against his, her chest heaving with each ragged breath. She never cried so much, not even when her mother died, and part of her felt weak for falling apart.

"Shh… Lily." With his muscles trembling, he held her tighter, his breath rushing over her lips in a sigh of immense relief. Suddenly, she understood his fear. The thought of her holding him responsible for not saving her father terrified him but blaming him never occurred to her. Not only did she immediately shoulder all the blame, but there was nothing he could have done.

"I have always loved you, *cherie*. I'm *not* going anywhere. Besides, thanks to you, I'm a little harder to kill. So, you're stuck with me." Chance kissed her with aching tenderness before resting his forehead against hers. The warmth of his arms, his breath, his words, his lips...They all slowly ate away at her heartache.

After another vulnerable kiss, Chance lifted his chin, allowing her to nuzzle against his chest while his hand ran through her wild tresses. Each stroke eased a little more of her panic and grief. For a while, she merely listened to his heartbeat, letting it tame her racing pulse. Finally, she reached the eye of the hurricane, and a quiet calm settled into her sadness.

When he finally spoke, the soothing tones enveloped her in a safe cocoon. "You know, despite our disagreements, I loved Gregor like the father I never *really* had, and I would have done anything to save him, but he signed his death warrant a long time ago. Farren never intended to release him. What you did granted him a clean death and ended his needless torment. You didn't get him killed, Lily, you saved your father."

While caressing his cheek, she pulled back enough to see his face. "Do you honestly believe that?" She searched his hazel eyes desperately. If he didn't truly mean those words, the hollow rhetoric would only make things worse.

"Yes." He clearly stated his answer with no hesitation. He meant it with every fiber of his being, and a weight lifted from her heart. "As soon as Cohen told us what his family discovered..." He faltered, trying to find the right words. "... I knew he wouldn't make it out alive. That night, in Phipps Bend, Gregor was ready to die. The only reason he fought was to save you, Lily."

Tears glistened in his eyes as his fingertips brushed the hair from her face. "He only wanted to see you survive. The guilt of all those deaths weighed heavy on his heart. He didn't want to die, but he was ready. He lost everything."

While mulling over his words, she rested her head against his chest and wept. Then her hands curled into fists as new thoughts flooded her mind. Intense anger rose inside, seizing her lungs until she screamed again in sobbing frustration.

"Why didn't I return his calls? You were right. His past didn't change who he was to *me*. God, he thought I hated him, and I never got to tell him…" The surge of fury trembled and faded until her voice broke. Her blind selfishness cost her precious time with her father, and she had no idea how to forgive herself or if she should.

Chance softly kissed her hair and sighed. "No, Lily. He knew you loved him, and you can't blame yourself. He would never want that. You tried to come to grips with a lot of dark history. That kind of stuff is never easy. No matter what I said or what he said, you needed to resolve things in your own time. You can't predict the future, *cherie*." His arms tightened around her as the soul-wrenching sobs slowly subsided.

"Do you remember what you told me the first time Ashcroft attacked you?"

She pulled back to meet his eyes again, frowning in confusion, unable to dredge up the distant memory.

"You think you're responsible, but you need to stop hogging all the blame. I see this going one of two ways…"

Despite everything, he somehow coaxed a smile to her lips, a feat that seemed impossible. The memory snapped into focus, and she recited the last line. "Either you guilt yourself into a coma, which will get me killed, or you'll become so overprotective that I'll have to kill you myself."

His soft chuckle rumbled through the air, lessening the weight on her heart. When he pushed back the hair from her face again, he stared down with an expression of pure vulnerability. "You can't give up. We still have to figure this out and make it home alive. I need you too, *mon cherie*. Whatever Farren wants, I think your expertise is the only thing capable of bringing us out on top, and I can't lose you either, not now."

Without a single thought, she rose to close the distance between them, capturing his lips in a kiss tinged with tears. He quickly supported her weight as their kiss deepened and the ice in her veins melted, giving way to a smoldering glow. Each caress of his fingertips, every touch of his lips, pulled her out of the darkness, inch by excruciating inch. Her fingers sank into his chestnut hair, reveling in the silky texture as his arms tightened around her. They felt so warm and safe that she finally released the self-loathing, the guilt, and everything else holding her back.

The smoldering glow burst into a roaring fire, burning away all the remnants of her doubt. Her breathy moan washed over his lips as their kiss deepened. When their tongues met, a spark ignited, born from their mutual need to prove they survived that bullet.

Rose of Jericho

With a feral growl, Chance grabbed her hips and surged to his feet. The sudden motion quickened her pulse as she latched onto his shoulders. They both fell on the bed, a mass of intertwining limbs, as his lips brushed along the tender flesh of her neck, leaving shivers in their wake. For a moment, she let the intoxicating sensations vibrate over her skin, making her dizzy.

Then, his lips found hers in a passionate kiss that sent a sudden surge of heat roaring through her. Lost in the blind haze of raw desire, she wrapped herself around him, pulling him closer, drawing in his warmth and light to burn away the remaining darkness lingering in her soul.

His fingers clenched in her fiery tresses when the kiss turned more urgent. Mewling moans filled the air as his leanly muscled body moved against hers in an exhilarating moment that made the world spin. Nothing remained except the feel of his skin, his heady scent, the strength of his hands, the steamy rush of his breath, the deep groans escaping his lips.

A loud, unrelenting knock at the door fractured the moment, and Chance pulled up enough to growl in a fierce voice. "Go the fuck away!"

Immediately, he turned his attention back to her with a powerful expression of desire, making her breath catch. It transcended the blind look of adoration elicited by the siren's voice, and it *belonged* to her, given freely. The realization caused her to hesitate for a second, and she witnessed a twinge of fear seep into his eyes, scared she might somehow still reject him.

Determined to wipe away his insecurities, she wrapped her arms around his neck, pulling him toward her, and kissed him with wanton abandon. Instantly, he melted against her, his tongue caressing hers as the fiery passion enveloped them.

Once again lost in a sudden surge of need, she grabbed his shirt, pulling and tugging, desperate to feel his skin. Her fingers trembled, fumbling with the infuriating buttons, and with a groan of frustration, she tore open the black dress shirt. Then Chance used one hand to pull the rest over his head before his lips found hers again with an all-consuming hunger.

A familiar sense of power infused her, not from an ability to consume his energy but from driving his desire, causing his reactions. Her fingers brushed over his smooth skin, memorizing every line, reveling in the velvety feel of it under her fingertips. In response, his firm hand glided along her leg to massage her hip, drawing a panting moan from her.

The persistent knocking grew louder, rattling the door. Chance growled in frustration as he tried to block out the booming sound, but the pounding continued. With a wave of intense anger, he pulled away, breaking their spell of passionate delirium. He stalked across the room and ripped the door open with such force that the hinges groaned.

"I told you to go the fuck away!" The unnaturally deep rumble of his voice made him sound like an angry werewolf in a racy HBO series.

"I gave you your *moment*. We need to talk before the council decides whether we live or die, assuming you still care about the verdict." The white-hot anger infusing Cohen's words made little sense to her. It seemed grossly disproportionate to the current circumstance. Of course, her unsated lust might have skewed her perception.

"The luggage is here. Change clothes and get out here unless you want to follow in Gregor's footsteps."

As soon as the demon uttered her father's name, tension traveled up Chance's back, across his shoulders, and down his arms, ultimately clenching his fists. Although she shared his desire to rip Cohen's throat out for even speaking that name, it was her turn to be the level-headed one. "Chance. Don't."

With those two words, Chance slammed the door in his face with a little too much enthusiasm. Then he stood there, every muscle tensed, staring daggers at the door. The seconds stretched out into minutes, and when he still didn't move, she crossed the room and slid her hand up the stiff muscles of his back. Each one relaxed in the wake of her fingers, and she pressed her cheek to his warm skin. He still smelled like a warm summer day.

"He's right, even if he *is* being a *fucking asshole* about it." She spoke loud enough to ensure Cohen heard the vital words. Juvenile, perhaps, but she didn't care. "You were right before, but to figure this out, we need him. However, I am going to shower and change first. I can't wear this funeral dress for another second."

She didn't mention the fact that blood saturated the material. Yet another garment clinging to her skin, an all-too-familiar sensation, but this time the blood wasn't hers.

Chance turned his head enough to catch her eye. "If it weren't for him, you wouldn't be wearing it now." A mischievous grin curled his lips, warming her right down to her toes. Considering everything that transpired, she felt guilty, but she needed to focus on this ray of happiness, her reason to survive.

With a heavy sigh, Chance turned and slid his hands over her hips. When his eyes met hers, they held a million things he wanted to say and do, but he kept himself in check. "Can you grab our bags? If I go out there, I'll punch that little weasel in the throat. Then, he wouldn't be doing much talking."

"Yeah. I can do that. He may be a weasel, but he's not wrong. We don't have an unlimited amount of time."

Chance gazed down at her with an incredulous expression. "You don't honestly think the only reason he tried to break down the door was an urgent need to take care of business, do you?"

She frowned in confusion, completely lost. "What?"

Chance chuckled and tenderly kissed her forehead. "He's an emotional flypaper demon, Lily. He knew *exactly* what he was interrupting?"

When the realization finally dawned on her, she gaped, horrified. "Oh, god." After clapping a hand over her mouth, she glanced up to find him laughing.

"How can you be so adorably naïve and sexy at the same time?" The roguish grin on his lips made her want to push him onto the bed, regardless of what Cohen sensed.

Get a grip, Lilith. Bigger problems.

During her inner pep talk, he lightly kissed her smile before quickly pulling away. "You get the luggage. I…uh…need a *very* cold shower."

The comment made her cheeks flush a brilliant crimson as she nodded. "You aren't the only one." He crooked an eyebrow with a leering grin, but she finally recovered and patted his shoulder with a chuckle. "*After* you finish yours. I don't care for the idea of Cohen sensing everything we do, like a mental peeping tom."

The off-putting thought wasn't the only reason she shivered. The heat and passion before Cohen interrupted sparked from the same despair as the alley in Tennessee. They suffered so much anger, pain, and fear that they clung to each other, desperate to experience something else.

Then, sudden questions rose to the surface, forcing her to swallow a nervous lump in her throat. *What if that's all we ever have, acting as an emotional crutch to one another? What if these intense emotions we feel don't exist outside of life-and-death situations?*

Chance backed away hesitantly, too lost in his own thoughts to pick up on her sudden doubts. As he wandered toward the bathroom, his hungry gaze traveled over her body. Then he paused, leaning against the door frame, and exhaled deeply. "When this is over, you, me, and my apartment...for a week. No work, no distractions."

His brilliant grin, which instinctively illuminated her face, told her they were more than a simple escape from their torment, much more. "That's a pretty unconventional first date, but..."

Chance shook his head with a radiant smile containing all the charisma and charm that made her knees weak. "That's not a no, which makes it a date." With a sly wink, he disappeared into the bathroom.

She stared at the closed door with a beaming smile plastered on her face until he turned on the shower, and reality crashed down on her like a face full of cold water. To have that week in Chance's apartment, she needed to figure out what Cohen's family wanted and how to use it to their advantage.

The heady lust distracted her out of her grief coma, but the danger still existed. Farren shot her father in the head with no hesitation. The man probably put more thought into choosing his tie. She had no difficulty determining where Cohen learned his cold, calculated detachment. With a deep exhale, she steeled herself for the awkward walk into the living room.

Cohen sat, seething, in the center of the room, staring down at his hands. When she stepped forward, his eyes snapped up with a weird mixture of anger, relief, regret, and frustration, making her immediately self-conscious. The sensation itched under her skin, spreading to cover her cheeks with a bright blush.

"What?" The clipped word rang with defensive pride as she firmly planted her hands on her hips.

She expected a smartass remark or a condescending quip, but Cohen dropped his head as if unable to look her in the eye. Then again, perhaps it merely made it easier to lie. "I am sorry about your father and about what I said. It was out of line."

"You're damn right it was." Lilith swallowed the tears threatening to return, refusing to break down again. Instead, she latched onto Chance's interpretation of events—*I saved my father.* "At least he's at peace. You can't torture him anymore."

"I had nothing to do with that. Perhaps you didn't notice, but I sat on the same side of the table as you." His tone was somewhere between apathy and empathy, as if trying hard to care without knowing how.

Rose of Jericho

"It doesn't matter. Drop it." She no longer possessed the energy to indulge his shifting facades.

"No." Cohen straightened in his chair and stared at her with a stony expression, which made him resemble a younger, more human version of Farren. Not precisely a compliment. "Working together is the *only* chance we have of surviving. We *are* on the same side."

Lilith tilted her head quizzically. "Are we? I don't think a single person knows who you truly are. The one thing I know is that you will protect yourself at all costs. If that lines up with someone else's agenda, awesome, but ultimately, you will put yourself first every time, which makes you dangerous."

Cohen frowned and sank back down, startled by the brutal declaration. "Untrue. If there was any way to help Gregor..."

"No! Don't use *him* to backpedal and make excuses. Save it for someone who gives a fuck. Do not mention his name again. You don't have the right."

Andrew flinched but said nothing else. He merely nodded in agreement and folded in on himself. For some reason, he seemed genuinely hurt by her words. She chalked it up to either an elaborate act or the shock of someone calling him on his shit. Either way, it didn't matter. Without another word, she moved past him and grabbed the luggage.

"After we shower and change, you will be straight with us, or I won't protect you from Chance again. No more of your damn games and manipulations. If you want our cooperation, be a real ally, stop picking fights, and no more secret agendas."

She started to walk away but stopped and turned. "I swear to god, if I ever find out you've engineered any of this crap, I will break every single bone in your body." She didn't wait for a response.

Chapter 5

Lilith stood in the shower, hoping the water crashing over her face would wash away her anguish along with the blood. No matter how hard she tried to clear her mind, the memory of cradling her father's dead body continued to play behind her eyelids.

Then she started scrubbing in a manic desire to feel clean. Her red skin felt raw by the time she dropped the rough washcloth and sank into the tub, sobbing. For a while, she merely lay there, letting the piping-hot water wash away her tears.

When the uncontrollable weeping stopped, the hollowness returned. Without Chance to distract her, she found herself alone with the grief and guilt, continually retracing her steps. What led to her father's death? Was there some pivotal point of no return? Did it matter? Even if she could pinpoint the crucial moment, she couldn't change it. Her father was dead, and she couldn't go back in time.

Eventually, she crawled out of the tub, wrapped herself in a towel, and blankly stared down at her suitcase resting on the oversized sink. All her court clothes lay inside—suit jackets, pencil skirts, and pastel blouses. She couldn't help but wonder what the demons planned for them. Her forensic skills didn't depend on business clothes, but their plan must involve her talents somehow. Otherwise, why bother with her?

Much to her relief, they packed a few hairbands, and she wrangled her shoulder-length auburn curls into a sleek ponytail. She faced the mirror after slipping into a spring-green sleeveless top, charcoal skirt, and matching jacket. The reflection looked like a woman heading to court or an FBI crime scene, not a pow-wow with a demon. *Talk about overdressed for the occasion.*

The red, puffy eyes betrayed her inner sorrow, revealing the gaping wound in her heart. Farren destroyed the center of her world in the blink of an eye. She kept trying to gather the tattered remnants of her life and create something recognizable, but no matter what she did, they refused to take shape. What would her world look like if they survived?

Her eyes slid down to the black funeral dress clutched in her hands, still soaked with blood—her father's blood. She squeezed her eyes shut and jammed the dress into a trash can, fighting to banish the infinite loop in her head. *Come on. Pull it together.*

After camouflaging her heartache with some makeup, she emerged from the bathroom. As soon as she set foot in the bedroom, Chance released a slow wolf whistle, dragging her out of the brooding thoughts lingering in her mind. She glanced up with a genuine smile and blinked as a rush of heat shot up her spine. He stood there, leaning against the wall, freshly showered, and sporting black slacks with a gray button-up shirt complete with a simple black tie.

If the council intended them to impersonate anyone in law enforcement, Chance would stick out like a sore thumb. Outside of television shows, agents and detectives didn't resemble GQ models with a badge in thousand-dollar suits. More often than not, they appeared average and forgettable, with coffee stains on their cheap ties and a rigid set of morals. In her experience, they focused solely on *the job,* and the city severely underpaid them.

"You look rather incredible yourself, handsome." Her mind started to wander, but they had things to do. *Focus, Lilith.* "Now that we're all dressed up, should we deal with Cohen?" In mid-smile, a twinge of pain crept into her head. She rubbed a palm over her neck and winced until the headache receded.

"You, okay?" When she opened her eyes, Chance hovered in front of her. "You look a little pale." He studied every line of her face with concern as his hands rubbed gently at her shoulders.

"Yeah. I'm fine. Merely a small headache." She flashed a brief smile she hoped he found reassuring. "I'll be okay. We shouldn't keep him waiting."

Although he frowned at her quick dismissal, his loose grip slid down her arm to take her hand but stopped at her wrist. While his eyebrows knit together, he raised her hand and turned it palm up. "I should put something on this." His fingers gently brushed the scratches from her fangs.

"It's fine. It'll heal." She sighed in irritation as he ignored her, pulling the hand closer to inspect each red mark.

"They should be healed by now, but they haven't even—" Before he could finish his sentence, she yanked her arm away, somehow embarrassed.

"I said it's fine." The words emerged in a much harsher tone than she intended, which earned her a frustrated sigh. "I'm sorry, but can we focus on the bigger picture? They're only scratches."

"All right, *cher.*" Without another word, he moved past her into the living room, leaving her to trail behind. The white noise of an approaching migraine began sneaking into her brain. She closed her swollen eyes, taking a few deep breaths, before moving into the main room.

Cohen still sat in the same cream linen chair, staring at his hands. When they both entered the room, he leaned back with confidence but didn't meet their eyes. For a moment, she struggled to suppress the smoldering ember of hatred in her stomach. To an outsider, her wrath would appear unjust. Although he didn't pull the trigger, his grandfather did, and the detective sat idly by while labeling her father a mass murderer.

"I need to be real with you." He hesitated, carefully choosing his words.

Real. Somehow, she doubted he could differentiate truth from fiction anymore. Despite her skepticism, they both took a seat on the couch while Cohen's jamming device blinked on the coffee table.

"If they decide not to execute us…If they send us after something…" His sky-gray eyes glanced up, and she flinched. Seeing the color of her father's eyes in his head completely unnerved her, and she quickly averted her gaze. "They *will* kill us once we give them what they want. Cooperating is merely a stay of execution."

"We understand. Doom, gloom, and murder. But what happened in there, and why didn't you fill us in on your family drama?" Chance showed remarkable restraint, much to her surprise.

As Chance took the lead, she tried to shake off the jarring sight of Cohen's eyes. *Is he conscious of the change? Can he control it? If so, why torment me with that color? A misguided attempt to console me, or yet another way to pick a fight?*

"For one, we didn't have time. Besides, I wouldn't describe you two as skilled actors. I've already stuck my neck out far enough as it is."

Jenny Allen

Lilith blinked in complete shock before latching onto a valid reason to express her anger. "Stuck your neck out? How have you done that? According to you, we are in the same boat. So, don't pretend you're swooping down to save the day from the kindness of your non-existent heart."

A deep from creased Cohen's brow.

Her snarled words seemed to have struck a nerve, which she found puzzling. Of course, with Cohen, appearances were always deceiving. After a moment of internal debate, his clenched jaw relaxed, and he changed tactics.

"Let me back up and explain. I wanted my grandfather to see what he's always seen in me—failure." He released a long breath, revealing one absolute truth buried deep. His past with Farren was an old, festered wound that only grew worse with time. "I need him to underestimate me, and I couldn't let you in on my plan because your shock and outrage had to be real. We are emotional lie detectors, and acting isn't your forte."

After a few moments of silence, Cohen leaned forward, resting his elbows on his knees. "I know neither of you thinks I'm trustworthy, and perhaps I have done little to prove otherwise, but I *am* on your side, not just mine. I'm not used to all this..." The frustration appeared genuine, but before she could respond, Chance cut in.

"Not used to what? Being in a tough spot or thinking about anyone other than yourself? Not sure you excel at either of those."

Something about Andrew's crestfallen expression quelled her fury, and she rested a hand on Chance's arm before focusing on the flustered demon.

"You have a dark history with Farren. I understand, but I'm not interested in excuses or explanations, only information. Your war with Farren doesn't involve us." Despite keeping her voice calm to de-escalate the situation, Cohen's eyes narrowed harshly.

"Wrong. If they underestimate me, I will have more room to maneuver so I can help you. Besides, I only had to yell in Farren's face because the two of you screwed up." Her distant anger from earlier came roaring to the surface in vibrant colors.

"I told you not to speak about that again..."

Cohen rolled his eyes in patronizing frustration. "Not *that*. When the two of you clung to each other like frightened rabbits. You did the one thing I told you *not* to do!" His eyes focused fiercely on Chance with open hostility. "You started giving her energy, and Farren sensed something, which is why I got in his face. If he knew you had a single drop of my blood in your veins, we would *all* be dead on the floor, exactly like Gregor. Period! Carrying our blood is immediate death in his eyes, no matter the cost."

"Watch your fucking words, detective." Chance growled as his fists clenched, vibrating with barely restrained rage.

"Fuck your bravado, Chance. You don't want to listen to me, then fine. *Va te faire foutre, trouduc.*" While Cohen's patience ended abruptly, Chance surged to his feet before she even realized he had moved. Whatever Cohen said pushed him over the edge, and she jumped between them just in time.

"Whoa!" She put both hands on his chest while he continued to stare daggers over her shoulder at Cohen.

"*Ferme ta gueule, démon.*" Chance snarled the words with ease, leaving her utterly confused.

"Girls, girls! You're both pretty! Now, knock it off and stick to damn English. Cohen, stop trying to pick fights, and Chance, stop rising to the bait. Damn it!"

"I'm tired of defending myself to your puffed-up bodyguard. He needs to keep his attitude in check." Cohen flipped a hand toward the six-foot-three wall of rage with a petulant expression.

"As if that doesn't apply equally to you! At least I'm not lying to your face constantly!" Chance shouted over her shoulder, and she sighed heavily.

"Are you two serious? I understand conflicting personalities, but this is fucking it. Chance, drop it! Cohen, if you don't want to keep defending yourself, stop creating problems. You know *exactly* what you're doing. This ends now!"

Once Cohen grunted in agreement, she turned her full attention back to Chance. "He's not lying about Farren. I saw surprise on his face, like he had unformed questions, right before Andrew picked the fight with him. I didn't know what it meant, but I remember a tingling glow running up my arm when you took my hand. The story fits."

"Thank you, Lily." Without a single thought, she turned on her heel and slapped Cohen across the face with commanding force. Once the initial shock of the sharp crack wore off, he rubbed his vividly red cheek before meeting her eyes with genuine surprise. "What the…"

Before he finished forming his question, she bent down, grabbing him by the collar. "*You* don't get to call me that! Ever!" Angry tears flooded her eyes, but she ignored them. "Just because I'm willing to work with you out of necessity does not mean you can use the nickname given to me by my *father*, the man your family tortured and shot in front of me while you did nothing."

When the demon sat still, speechless, she released him, stepped back, and looked him square in the eye. "Let me make this *perfectly* clear. We are not friends or partners. We are temporary allies, and if you're playing us, I will hunt you down and shoot you myself. Am I understood?"

Once he nodded meekly, she finally turned away.

"I apologize, Miss Adams. I did not intend to upset you." She ignored him. Until he showed genuine cooperation instead of instigating fights, his words were meaningless.

After a tense few seconds, she regained her calm and took a seat at the far end of the couch. She needed to focus, and more importantly, she needed the two testosterone-poisoned men to focus.

"Now, before we deal with our immediate problems, we need to ensure all the cards are on the table. Is there anything else you haven't told us, Mr. Cohen? If I discover more lies or omissions later, I will never trust you, and neither will Chance." Lilith pinned him in place with an authoritative stare, and the demon dropped his head again.

"In the interest of full disclosure…"

Chance immediately tensed, but Lilith shot him a warning glare.

"Whitmore *did* insist on keeping Chance in lock-up until we verified his story. However—"

She closed her eyes, struggling to contain her anger, knowing what he'd say next.

"I didn't try very hard to dissuade him. Still, I swear upon everything sacred that I never expected Spencer to attack you. I merely thought if you had no other allies, you might confide in me. Unfortunately for us both, you were more scared of me than being on your own."

"*Fils de pute!* You son-of-a-bitch!"

"Chance! Stop." After throwing him an icy scowl, she turned her furious eyes on the demon as his fingers touched above his right eyebrow—a sign of shame.

"I'm sure you understand how insanely reckless that decision was now. Is there anything else?" She forced the overly polite words through clenched teeth. Naturally, she wanted to fly off the handle, crack him in the jaw, scream at him for being a manipulative bastard, but none of those reactions helped their current situation.

Cohen merely shook his head while staring despondently at the floor.

"Great. Now that we've settled everything, can we get to work? This is about a book, correct?"

"Yes, and no. The council is already aware of the book's location. They sent me to approach Duncan about the cipher. They've studied the script from a distance, but it's an enigma. No one has ever cracked it completely."

"If they don't know what it says, why do they want it so bad?" Amazingly, Chance's question held only lingering traces of resentment. Hopefully, that meant she finally got through to him about the gravity of their situation and how aggression merely hurt their cause.

The demon glanced at Chance and finally dropped the last traces of hostility. "Let me start with a brief history. That will help you understand. An unknown author wrote the text in the 1400s, but it passed through many hands before surfacing in recorded history. One of my relatives, Athanasius Kircher, received a sample in 1639 from Georg Baresch, an obscure Czechoslovakian alchemist in Prague. He procured the odd book from Jacobus Horcicky de Tepenec, a chemist and pharmacist for the Holy Roman Emperor Rudolph II.

"My great-uncle, Athanasius, was a Jesuit scholar from the Collegio Romano who was skilled in translating Egyptian hieroglyphics. Baresch thought my relative could translate the mystery, which had eluded everyone at that point."

Lilith settled into her corner of the couch, expecting a lengthy story. If it was relevant, she'd listen. When Cohen paused, waiting for some sort of objection, she gestured for him to continue.

"Athanasius couldn't decipher the entire script, but he discovered enough to deduce that the words didn't involve the crude illustrations of plants or cosmic diagrams. They merely served as a distraction, another layer of encryption to disguise the context. No one knows what he found to warrant his actions, but he sent a letter to the council stating that he believed the piece referenced dangerous things about our kind.

"They instructed him to purchase the book, to retrieve it at any cost. Athanasius tried everything he could, but Baresch refused to sell. The council eventually ordered his execution, and Jan Marek Marci, the rector of Charles University in Prague, got his hands on the book. He then sent it to Athanasius, but it never arrived. The script disappeared until it resurfaced in 1912, bought from a Jesuit college near Rome by..."

"Wilfred Voynich."

Both Cohen and Lilith stared back at Chance, caught entirely off guard when he finished the sentence.

"The Voynich Manuscript," Chance continued. The hushed tone made the words sound ancient and mystical.

"Uh... Yes."

"Wait. Why does that sound familiar?"

"Miriah had a dozen books on the subject in her home office, and Duncan had a few as well. I flipped through them. Two years ago, Gregor and I..." He paused, his eyes watering as he swallowed his grief and forced himself to continue. "We visited the Beinecke Rare Book and Manuscript Library at Yale Museum, and he told me a lot of the backstory, without the demon angle, of course. I always thought he loved the unsolvable enigma it represented."

"That explains Duncan's journals," Lilith added.

Cohen relaxed in his seat, watching the epiphanies like a tennis match.

"In one of them, he repeatedly referenced a book he wrote in a complicated cipher a long time ago. He said the book circulated after someone stole it and ended up in a museum. That must be it, right?"

"Yes. Did his journal say anything else?" Cohen leaned against the arm of the chair with his interest piqued.

"The book is not complete." She racked her brain, dredging up everything she could remember. A lot happened, and she didn't think his ramblings about a mystery book warranted much attention. "He tore some pages out, the dangerous ones, and put them with the cipher somewhere safe."

Then something else occurred to her. In all the history he quoted, the demon never once mentioned a connection to her uncle or Scotland. "How did you know Duncan was the author?" Suspicion and mistrust gnawed at her again.

With no hesitation or calculated stares, Cohen blurted out his answer. "I didn't. The council sent me to Tennessee with orders to question Duncan specifically. They didn't give me a source paper or explain their actions."

Nothing in his face indicated a lie, and considering Farren's disparaging description of his grandson, she could see them dishing out blind orders with no justification. "Okay, so, someone on the council knew. Who gave the orders?"

"The collective council, consisting of the eldest members of the participating families. In theory, they share all data openly to arrive at a plan of action." For the first time, he volunteered more than a direct answer about his species' social structure, elaborating on details without the threat of physical violence. Hopefully, this meant he was finally willing to cooperate.

"Wait. *Participating?*"

"Yes, Mr. Deveraux. Some choose not to take part in our organization. They believe severing ties and hiding on their own is safer. Of course, the council keeps dossiers on them to prevent incidents like Ashcroft's."

Cohen turned his attention back to Lilith, and she breathed a sigh of relief. His eyes returned to a pleasant, innocuous blue. "Ms. Adams, did those journals mention where he hid the pages and the cipher?"

"No, but I think I might have a clue where to find them." In a secret compartment of her uncle's desk, she'd found a tin holding loose papers and a filed-down safe deposit box key. If she was right, the answers to Cohen's quest were hiding under her nose the entire time.

"However, getting to the information will be... problematic." The tin still rested where she left it—cold storage at her family's private lab, Goditha, in Knoxville, Tennessee.

"If we get them without the council finding out, we may discover why they want this book so bad, which might give us leverage."

"How in the hell are we supposed to do that?" Chance wasn't as quick to jump on the hope bandwagon, and she honestly didn't blame him. Ever since they'd boarded the plane to Knoxville over a week ago, nothing had gone according to plan.

"I never claimed to be a religious man, but you might consider praying for a miracle. Stranger things have happened."

Chapter 6

A demon advocating prayer didn't exactly provide a lot of reassurance. Lilith leaned forward on the couch, desperately trying to arrange the scattered facts in her head. She glanced up at Cohen in his posh navy-blue suit, hoping for some help despite her instinctual suspicion. *Why is my head so scrambled?* She could easily chalk it up to life-threatening stress for the past nine days. Perhaps she simply reached the limit of her ability to cope. Understandable when she considered the circumstances.

"Do you have any practical ideas that don't include rosary beads and candles?"

Cohen's crisp blue eyes studied her carefully for the first time since she slapped the attitude out of him. "Perhaps..." He seemed distracted, focusing his laser-like attention on her face without really hearing what she said, making her feel self-conscious. "Are you alright? You... look pale."

When he voiced the same question as Chance, she blinked in surprise. "What is it with you two? I'm fine. I think I'm allowed to be a little rundown and worn-out given the current state of things."

Embarrassment burned across her cheeks while both men frowned in confusion, as if she started speaking in tongues. Their expressions deepened her frustration, which only made the headache worse.

"For fuck's sake. I just witnessed Farren execute my father. Cut me some slack!"

Cohen didn't buy her rhetoric for a second. His calculating eyes never wavered, meticulously observing every movement she made.

"Damn. Can't you go back to being the southern detective who's too polite to stare at me like I'm a lab experiment?"

"No. Something is wrong, and stress isn't the cause."

Thankfully, a knock at the door saved her from any further scrutiny. With one last suspicious glance, Cohen snatched up his jamming device, clicked it off, and tucked it in his pocket. Then he focused on Chance.

"Keep an eye on her, Deveraux. Maybe she'll tell *you* what's wrong."

As soon as he disappeared into the hall, Chance slid across the couch. "Lily, what's going on?"

A sudden spike of pain behind her eye left her rubbing her temples. Maybe they were right. *What if something is wrong?* "I... don't know."

"When was the last time you fed?" Once the words left his mouth, she felt like a colossal idiot.

Of course! Why the hell didn't I think of that?

All the side effects from Cohen's blood affected her treatment schedule, throwing her entirely out of whack. The emotional sensations dwindled to mere wisps since they left Tennessee, but she realized days had passed since she'd drunk a single drop of blood. The ability to draw on energy wasn't strong enough to sustain her anymore, and she ignored the signs of oxygen deprivation, chalking it up to extenuating circumstances.

"I guess it's been a while. Honestly, it never occurred to me. Shit." She drew in a deep breath, vibrating with frustration. *How could I be so stupid?*

"Would mine help? At least for now?" The question held merit. As a half-blood, he naturally circulated more functional hemoglobin. However, the very idea made her queasy.

"This isn't a bizarre fantasy of yours, is it? Some deep-seated desire for me to bite your neck in the throes of passion?" She cracked a sarcastic smile, but he didn't appear amused. "I appreciate the...offer, but the thought grosses me out."

"Uh, am I supposed to say thank you? Because that vaguely resembled an insult." A substantial amount of defensiveness tainted his usual smart-ass humor.

She closed her eyes for a moment, sinking into the couch while she tried to think. "I didn't mean it like that, but this isn't Hollywood. I've never consciously fed from a person before."

He lowered his head, fixing his eyes on her with determination. "I know, but you need blood, and you have those fangs for a biological reason."

"This is not just about the creep factor. Despite what movies tell you, veins and arteries are delicate. Even with my more modest fangs, someone unpracticed can't accomplish that level of precision. It's dangerous. Despite the demon blood running through your veins, you could bleed out in minutes if something went wrong." She wrapped her arms around herself and shook her head. "I can't risk hurting anyone like that, *especially* not you."

"Cohen sliced his wrist and fed you with no problem. I don't see the difference."

"But he's a fucking demon and probably knew exactly what he was doing." She huffed, exasperated. *Why can't he drop the subject and let things be?*

"Lily, you are a crucial part of figuring out this situation. If you snap and attack one of them...I don't think they'll be very forgiving."

"These people abducted three vampires and stopped to pack our luggage. I doubt they are oblivious to our needs. Assuming they want our cooperation, they'll have to take care of us."

Chance still appeared skeptical, staring at the carpet with deep concern and fear.

With an appreciative smile, she lifted his chin. "If they don't help, we'll revisit this idea, okay?"

Before he could respond, Cohen returned, but not alone. A petite woman trailed behind him. Deep black hair gathered into an intricate arrangement of curls and braids cascaded down her slender back like something from Middle-earth.

In stark contrast, the black asymmetrical jacket and vibrant green pencil skirt screamed high fashion. The woman looked as though she would be more at home in proper gypsy attire. This seemed like overcompensating, trying to connect with the modern world through designer labels.

When she peered over at Lilith and Chance, the eerie blue of her eyes shone like the crystal-clear ocean in the Bahamas and held a lot more age than her youthful face.

"Mr. Deveraux, Ms. Adams, this is Luminita Dragomir."

Lilith changed her focus, scanning Cohen as he made the introduction. All his facial cues showed profound relief.

When he looked back at the seemingly delicate woman, he expressed a kinship typically reserved for close family. Reading people became second nature to her, and although he probably only showed what he wanted, she could still glean information from his choices.

"Ah, you must be *Crin*." The unexpectedly deep voice exuded a thick accent reminiscent of the Romanian vampires from Hollywood. After displaying a radiantly warm smile, she settled into the cream-colored chair with all the grace of a royal dignitary.

"I'm sorry?" The heavy accent made most of the woman's words difficult to understand. But the last one wasn't English. Despite pop culture's claims, not all vampires originated in Transylvania, and foreign languages didn't come imprinted in their DNA.

The pale woman blushed apologetically. "*Crin* is Lily in my language. Cohen spoke of you."

Lilith glanced up at him with a quizzical expression that held an edge of hostility. He hovered behind Luminita's chair and simply shrugged before focusing his attention elsewhere.

His guest didn't miss the awkward silence or the seething tension emanating from Chance's general direction. "Did I misspeak?" Her rounded face tilted in curiosity, like an elf wrapped up in futuristic clothing. "English is not my best."

After a frozen moment, Lilith recovered enough to display a small smile. "My name is Lilith Adams. A *select* few call me Lily, so I understand the mix-up. What can we do for you, Ms...? Dragomir, was it?"

When she nodded, her raven-black tresses glittered in the light. "*Da*, I am here for two purposes. Vone of tose is to see vhat *I* can do for *you*." Lilith took a second, sifting through the tones to realize the woman replaced *W*s with *V*s and dropped the *H* from the *TH* sound.

"Luminita sits on the council. She is...a close friend." The weight underlying his description implied the woman might be Cohen's inside contact. "She wanted to meet the two of you and determine how she can help." His relief made perfect sense. Perhaps the situation wasn't hopeless after all.

The woman lifted a graceful hand to silence Cohen, but the motion held none of the anger or contempt Farren displayed with the same gesture. In fact, she found it difficult to imagine a council where the two sat on equal ground.

"First tingk is first, Andrew." Again, Lilith paused, noticing the dropped *H* and the hard *K* sound following the *G* as the woman's blue-green eyes inspected her with concern. Being the center of attention started to wear on her nerves as she squirmed under the unrelenting scrutiny.

"De guard at de door has sometingk she requires. Retrieve it, Andrew." This time, *D*s replaced the *TH* sound as Luminita's quizzical eyes drifted to Chance while Cohen stalked toward the hallway. Somehow, she seemed surprised by what she saw. "You are…different, are you not?"

"I'm afraid I don't know what you mean." He glanced at Lilith, hoping for some insight, but she had a hard enough time deciphering the woman's choppy English, much less delving into more profound meanings. When she merely shrugged with a helpless grimace, he nervously ran his fingers through his chestnut hair, still damp from the shower.

"Cum spui în limba engleză, apology. I am sorry. I did not explain vell. Lilith is vampeere. It is strongk in her blood, but you…"

"I'm a half-blood. I don't suffer from the same needs, but I don't reap the same benefits either." A slight bitterness edged into his voice, catching her attention. She knew precisely which benefit he was referring to—longevity.

Gregor's most significant objection to their relationship, the reason he threatened Chance thirteen years ago, centered on the fact that he'd grow old and die before she looked thirty. Although she argued with Alvarez and her father about it, Chance never voiced concerns before.

"You had only vone vampeere parent?"

"I wasn't aware of it, but yes, my father." Chance shifted uncomfortably, with a gruff edge of defensiveness in his voice. She noticed his reluctance to discuss his family before, but something about Luminita put him at ease enough to talk. Either that, or he figured she'd share if he did the same. *Give a little to get a little.*

"Dey did not tell you?" She leaned forward in the chair with genuine interest, which appeared more academic than personal.

"No." The clipped word held a million unspoken things, weighing on him.

"And your moter, she vas hooman?"

"Yes. They both died in a car crash when I was ten. I didn't know why I was sick until…" When he paused, pain haunted his green-flecked eyes. He glanced down, carefully choosing his words before continuing.

"Gregor found me and gave me a real life. He helped me to be more than the shadow of my parents." Although she knew his folks didn't win any parenting awards, the tension and contempt in his face revealed a much darker past than she imagined. It made her wonder how bad his first ten years truly were.

Lilith reached out, her fingers curling over his knee in a reassuring gesture. A faint smile tugged at the corner of his mouth as he slid his hand over hers. Then, she felt a tiny spark crackle over her skin, like a circuit completing.

"*O Doamne!*" Luminita's ocean eyes widened in shock. "Andrew told me much, but not dis." Her petite hands rubbed together anxiously as Lilith's breath caught in her throat.

How loyal is Cohen's ally? Enough to overlook something that warranted an immediate death sentence?

Cohen stepped back into the room and halted. His eyes wandered from their guest to the two of them and back. A sudden sweat broke across his brow as he swallowed the lump in his throat. For the first time, he genuinely appeared terrified.

"I'm sorry. I should have mentioned…"

The graceful woman turned in her chair and gestured to Cohen, who thankfully understood the odd motion. After handing Lilith a blue thermos, he pulled out his jamming device, switched it on, and placed it on the coffee table again.

With intense curiosity, she twisted the cap on the thermos and sniffed the contents. The warm, fresh blood instantly made her mouth water, which disturbed her on a deep level.

Although she was twenty-seven, she didn't develop the need until fourteen years ago. She never grew accustomed to this aspect of her life. It was merely a necessity, like taking a daily vitamin, a fact of life. She *definitely* didn't identify with Hollywood vampires who drooled over the throbbing external jugular of every exposed neck. The very thought made her cringe.

While she stared dismally into the dark liquid, fighting her sudden revulsion and embarrassment, Chance broke the odd silence. "I don't suppose that guard has a hamburger and fries out there, does he?" When he had everyone's attention, she squeezed his hand in gratitude and lifted the thermos.

The healthy gulp warmed her down to her toes, eased her headache, and allowed her to breathe a little deeper. Until that moment, she hadn't realized how much she needed it. She was a lot closer to snapping than she thought. Once again, Chance was right, a rather annoying habit of his.

"My apologies, Mr....?" Luminita paused, unsure how to pronounce his name.

"Deveraux, it's Cajun-French, but please, call me Chance." He smiled politely and pushed the charcoal sleeves up his forearms. She could tell the stuffy shirt and tie made him uncomfortable, though she appreciated the view.

"Ah, Chance. *Da*, tank you. I'm sorry. Ve have been poor host." A friendly smile graced her lips, but Lilith held no illusions. As warm and helpful as Luminita appeared, she represented a council that considered them nothing more than condemned prisoners. One person might not make a difference.

"Food is on de vay as ve speak." Then, the delicate woman returned her attention to Cohen. "Andrew. Please, sit." She smiled again and gestured to the vacant spot on the couch next to Chance.

With a nervous smile fixed on his face, he apprehensively sat on the edge.

"I understand now vhy you vere so...anxious about Farren. If he saw..."

Cohen hung his head and sighed. "I wanted to tell you, but I couldn't. It wasn't safe. I didn't know giving them my blood would produce these...results." When he glanced up at the delicate woman, his almost handsome face set in an expression of resolve. "Honestly, even if I knew ahead of time... I still would have done it. We *need* her, and the effects are wearing off..."

"Andrew, stop. I know you vould only risk dis for good reason. You do not need to defend yourself or Ms. Adams. I sense dem fadingk in Lilith, but not in Chance. Dese...side effects, if dey are *pentru totdeauna*... vhat is Engleesh vord? Pair-man-nent...dis could be serious problem. If he can feed, even Chance..."

"Luminita. We can cross that bridge when we come to it." Cohen quickly cut her off, leaving Lilith to wonder why.

What is he hiding now? The possibilities itched under her skin, and apparently, she wasn't the only one.

"Shut it, Cohen. What does *'even Chance'* mean? What about me?" He focused directly on Luminita, fixing her with a penetrating stare. However, the intimidation tactic didn't seem to work on her. She merely considered him carefully, allowing the silence to stretch out with no apparent intention of breaking it. Then she finally spoke again.

"Are you sure your moter vas hooman?" The unexpected question left all of them staring at her in bewilderment.

"Uh, yeah. That's what Gregor told me. Why?"

The elven woman paused again, carefully weighing her options.

"Look, I don't want to appear ungrateful, but if there is something we should know, you need to tell us. This isn't Cohen's call. It's ours." Lilith shot a sharp glare at the detective before returning her calm attention to the petite woman with all the power.

"No, it is mine. I'm afraid Andrew is right. Dere is no point gettingk hopes up or putting you in panic. De current situation is too…serious for dat. Ve can talk on dese tings later."

Lilith began to protest again, but the delicate woman raised her hand. "I understand. I do." She leaned forward, crossing her wrists over her knees as a sincere weight flooded her Mediterranean blue eyes.

"I give promise. Vonce matters at hand are done, I vill answer all questions about his…cone-dee-tion. Dis is great favor, and I vant you to tink on it carefully. Dere is not any of my kind dat vould offer dis. Not even Cohen knows tings I know." The more the woman spoke, the more accustomed Lilith became to deciphering her thick accent with its rolling *R*'s, dropped *H*'s, and transposed *D*'s, as well as her choppy English.

However, the true meaning of Luminita's words worried her. *Why is my cooperation so valuable?* Yes, Lilith was a gifted forensic investigator, but she wasn't a paragon in her field by any stretch. Even with her knowledge of the paranormal and her connection to Duncan, why would this woman risk everything now?

"Why make this deal? If Cohen is correct, and Farren would immediately slaughter all three of us for taking his blood, why are you calmly willing to not only overlook it but help?" She never thought to question the woman's motives until then. Perhaps her endearing demeanor or Cohen's introduction as a friend swayed her. Of course, she could be merely losing her edge under the overwhelming circumstances.

Luminita displayed an understanding smile full of trusting warmth. For the first time, Lilith reminded herself that she was dealing with two demons. Perhaps the petite woman merely possessed better acting skills than Cohen.

"Your…mistrust is expected. If I vere in your shoe, I vould question helpingk hand as vell. I vill not lie to you. Cohen is correct. Ve need you. It is simple as dat. I could intimidate you as Farren has, but I find people are more…mo-tee-vated vhen dere is agreement."

Rose of Jericho

Lilith sat back, seriously considering Luminita's offer. Everything from the subtle sensations to her microexpressions indicated Ms. Dragomir merely wanted her help and would do whatever it took to gain her trust. She couldn't see or feel a single reason to doubt the woman's sincerity.

"You said you are here for two reasons…"

"Ah, *da*, yes." A relieved smile tugged at her lips, happy that she satisfied their doubts and could move forward. Lilith kept searching her elven-like face for some sort of devious master plan, but once again, everything bolstered her credibility.

"I convinced council to appoint me as advocate. I am here to give deir instructions." Her delicate hands ran over her edgy black jacket, smoothing the stiff material like a dignitary on official business. In a way, she was.

Every person on the couch breathed a collective sigh of relief. Luminita delivering news from the council brought with it a sense of hope. If the demons decided they weren't worth the trouble, they would have sent an executioner, not a diplomat. At least they didn't need to face the council as a collective. She could go her entire life without seeing Farren again and be perfectly happy. Not to mention, hiding Chance's new abilities and her lingering effects would be next to impossible.

"Dere has been an…" Luminita paused, as if trying to remember an unfamiliar phrase in a very exact manner. "… oon-expected development and ve need somevone of your talent and knowledge, Lilith."

"My talents?"

"*Da*, as a…" Another pause as she concentrated on forming the strange words. "…for-rain-seek examine-air. Dere has been an…ill-timed crime at a Museum in New Haven, Cone-nay-tee-cut. Bodies vere found, vhich local police believe connect to robbery. Dey vere killed in… strange manner." Something in her face gave Lilith the impression that *strange* was one hell of an understatement.

"Dey must have been hired since de object vas not found. Ve need vhat dey stole."

"New Haven? The Yale Museum?" Chance displaying a mind for details shouldn't have surprised her, but it continually did, for some reason.

The notion of *Chance the Intellectual* felt alien, which said volumes about her tendency to stereotype him. Although it wasn't entirely her fault. They never shared an intelligent debate with any substance, only witty banter about their personal lives. From an early age, his role as bodyguard labeled him a classic jock in her eyes. When forced to view him as a sophisticated, complete person, she found the experience pleasantly surprising and a little jarring.

"Someone stole the book?" Either Cohen suddenly became a consummate actor, or he wasn't faking his surprise.

"*Da.*" Luminita nodded, her raven tresses cascading over her shoulder.

Perfect. Now their mission extended from merely tracking down the cipher and missing pages to include solving a robbery at a prominent university. Not to mention, they still needed leverage to keep them alive *after* accomplishing the growing list of tasks.

"Wait. The museum extensively photographed every page. The books in Miriah's apartment featured a full HD pictorial. Why do you need the original?" Although Chance had a valid point, she already knew the answer.

As if on cue, Luminita gazed at him with a sympathetic yet patronizing expression.

"Not all pages vere photographed, and… Al-chem-easts have secret vays. Dey hid tings dat ve cannot see from photograph."

Luminita turned her attention back to Lilith, settling on her as the leader. Perhaps she recognized a need to keep the alpha males in check, a way to dilute the testosterone poisoning.

"I vill be your contact for dis. Tankfully, de council is too conflicted over de book to let anyvone else take lead. If you find book and cipher, I may speak on your behalf. I am only sorry dat I could not do same for your fater."

Her eyes misted at Luminita's words, which were full of genuine sorrow and anger. Lilith took a deep gulp of warm blood, taking a moment to keep the flood of tears at bay. After a steadying breath, she smiled weakly at their guest. "Thank you for the sentiment."

"It is not mere sain-tee-ment, Ms. Adams. I opposed verdict of execution. I alone knew Ashcroft's crimes from speakingk to Andrew. Vhen your fater's crimes came to light, I shared vhat I knew, but dey… refuse to listen. Sir Orrick vas a *scârbă*, an uh…a-bomb-ee-nation, and his son vas a…mon-stair. Mr. Adams could have been strongk ally. I am only vone, and most council members are…blood tirsty." The frustration and outrage in her heavily accented voice became palpable, hanging in the air like a dense fog. "Short-sighted *proşti.*"

Rose of Jericho

At least there was one person who saw Ashcroft and his family for what they were—evil. Perhaps the others didn't consider Clyde's feeding habits of raping and killing young girls unusual. The thought alone sent chills down her spine. Then something else occurred to her, snapping her mind into clear focus.

"How did his crimes come to light?"

"Farren brought charges, and Helton shared information as vell, but dere vere several on council dat did not seem...shocked. Sources vere not named."

"Helton?" Cohen finally spoke up as his almost-handsome face wrinkled in confusion and dread. "What did he share?"

Luminita rubbed her hands together, hesitating, as her focus turned to Andrew. "Facts about Ashcroft, his..." She wore the same frustrated expression as before when trying to think of an English word. "... biology? How he vas different from us. He knew notingk of Mr. Adams. Dat came from Farren alone."

"But how? How could he know? How could either of them?" Lilith stammered through the questions, completely bewildered.

Luminita exhaled slowly, her ocean blue eyes brimming with empathy. "I do not know. Farren and Helton...neider like to share. Perhaps you vill learn more in your...studies, no, your...investigation." She let the silence fill the room, giving them all time to sift through her accent and absorb the answers before she moved on.

"I have plane tickets in your names. Your flight leaves at ten a.m., vhich gives you few hours to eat and rest before escort to airport..."

"What about the jet?"

"Andrew," she glanced over at him with a mixture of impatience for needing to state the obvious and sympathy for his frustration. "Law officials do not take private jet to crime scene."

Lilith had to agree. If local law enforcement checked them out, flying in on a private jet would represent a glaring red flag.

"A rental car vill be vaitingk. Inside, you find credit card for expenses, phone to contact me, as vell as standard police-issue revolvers for Cohen and Lilith. You receive no more resources. Your personal phones and computers are not in your tingks. It vould be...unvise to get dem. I'm sure dat you can get equipment you need from local police. Dey vill be avaitingk you at morgue." After mentally replacing Luminita's *V*s with *W*s, Lilith turned to a more familiar subject, which gave her a concrete problem to resolve.

"How did you explain a detective from Tennessee, a forensic examiner from New York City, and a civilian? You realize they are not obligated to let us examine the bodies, right? We have absolutely no jurisdiction."

The Romanian beamed at her questions like a proud teacher. "Yes, but New Haven is not big enough for major crime dee-vision. As far as dey know, you tree vere handpicked by FBI. Since dis case vill most likely cross state lines and involve much violence, dey need specialist. Also, de robbery of priceless artifact needs specialist as vell. Dere vill be much pressure from community for fast...recovery of book, so locals vere happy to hand... consequences of failingk to somevone else."

"Make no mistake." Her blue-green eyes held a firm warning as she continued. "If you run, dey find you, killingk anyvone in deir vay. Your best chance is for you and me to vork togeter. If you find vhat council needs, I vill do my best to get you home. Dis is best I can do."

Lilith let the gravity of her words sink in, knowing they were true. After five seconds with Farren, she realized running would only get more people killed.

For a moment, the thought of a classic bad-cop-good-cop scheme occurred to her. First, Farren scares the crap out of them, and then a friendly face puts them at ease. A small part of her latched onto any reason not to trust the delicate woman, but she needed the modicum of hope Luminita provided.

Beyond that, she never gave Lilith a single reason to doubt her sincerity. All her micro-expressions echoed her distaste for Gregor's treatment, her disapproval of Farren, and her deep desire to help them.

The woman's genuine affection for Cohen became quite clear throughout their conversation, and he appeared to feel the same way. From what she'd seen so far, Cohen trusted no one, ever—except Luminita. A fact which spoke volumes about a long personal history that neither was likely to share.

"How do I figure into all this?" Chance brought up an excellent question. Having a license to carry a gun in all fifty states and most countries didn't make him a cop.

"You are here because you vere involved in de...incident in Tennessee. You may travel because Cohen made it clear dat you keep Lilith safe. Also, dat her...cooperation vould not happen if you vere harmed. After meetingk you, I can see his information vas...true."

An amused smile crossed her petite lips as she glanced between Chance and Lilith and their clasped hands. "Farren agreed because you are…pressure point to use if she becomes…oon-cooperative. You do not vant dat to happen. From Cohen's stories, I suggested dat ve name you as…" She paused again, trying to pull exact words out of the air.

This time, she came up empty and motioned Cohen toward her with a questioning frown. He quickly rose from the couch, whispered something, and returned to a more comfortable position, standing behind her chair. "Ah, yes…in-day-pen-dent security expert. He informed me you have much experience in field, no?"

Chance glanced over at Cohen with a shocked expression plastered on his face. "Seriously?" He never expected to hear Cohen stand up for him and appeared pleasantly surprised. In stark contrast, Lilith instantly realized the glowing recommendation made Chance a bigger target, but no one else focused on that angle.

The detective bristled and raked a hand through his blonde hair. "Yeah, well, I wasn't wrong. You're the muscle. This isn't the start of a bromance—it's business. We need Lilith's expertise, and, like it or not, you're *apparently* a package deal." By the scowl on the demon's face, he clearly fell into the category of not liking the *package deal.* Considering how much they both seemed to hate each other, she didn't find it surprising.

Thankfully, Chance focused on the task at hand and finally answered Luminita's question. "Yes. I have plenty of experience. I ran security for Gregor and his companies. I am also familiar with advanced alarm systems and security measures, including military-grade."

Lilith frowned at him with genuine confusion. "Gregor used state-of-the-art systems for investment banking?"

He nervously licked his lips before reluctantly meeting her eyes. "Not all of them belonged to him, but the short answer is yes."

Her eyebrows skyrocketed as she fixed him in place with a steely glare. "And the long answer?"

He exhaled slowly, eyes flickering to the two demons. He obviously didn't want to talk about it but knew she wouldn't drop the subject. With a reluctant sigh, he finally continued. "I led the team that created the security upgrades for all the labs."

Lilith blinked in shock until her mind zeroed in on one moment at Goditha. "Wait. Then, why don't you have clearance? Not to mention, you seemed genuinely surprised that I had a universal code." She carefully avoided using specific names, not that it mattered. Cohen's people seemed to know an awful lot about them already.

Chance raised one eyebrow in an expression that was part James Bond, part Cheshire cat, all to hide his guilt. "The project was a highly classified secret. Gregor realized radical groups would target the labs if we ever went public. He also didn't want them vulnerable to industrial espionage. No one on the re-fit team gained clearance because he didn't want anyone who knew all the protocols to hold any access. I recommended the safety measure to prevent someone from manipulating us to bring down the system. Once we completed the re-fit, they locked us out. So, I don't know who has access or what kind they have."

Although he tried to hide his sadness, the grief shone through. Bringing up Gregor stung every time, causing him to fixate on his murder. At least she wasn't the only one suffering from the infinite loop plaguing her mind.

"*Mon cherie*, keeping secrets comes with the job, which occasionally requires a little acting."

"So, I noticed." For a moment, she frowned in thought, unsettled by his polished acting skills. After all, he hid his feelings about her for over a decade. *What else is he hiding?*

Then she noticed his ominous silence and remorseful expression. Now wasn't the time to focus on her personal hang-ups or lash out at him for doing his job.

"Who knew you were so handy and secretive?" Lilith cracked a smile, which eased the brooding tension, and he wasted no time latching onto her olive branch of playful sarcasm.

"Are you disappointed I'm not all brawn?" If the implication offended him, he hid it well. He merely flashed a mischievous grin containing a volume of things Luminita and Cohen didn't need to understand. Despite her concerns, he successfully raised a blush to her cheeks.

Thankfully, the demons ignored them, and Luminita rose from her chair with the same fluidity she noticed in Farren and Cohen. "Good. It is settled. It has been a pleasure to meet you, but I must go. I vish you safe journeys and good luck on your task." Her smiling eyes passed over them before resting on Cohen.

"Do not forget to limit use of device. Too much time and somevone vill notice. Dat vould be…oon-fortunate."

He nodded absently, deep in thought. "Thank you, Luminita."

Rose of Jericho

Her lips curled into an expression of friendship. Lilith never expected to meet a nice, reasonable demon, but stranger things happened —granted, not many, but still.

Luminita Dragomir strolled toward the hall in her ultra-high fashion outfit, leaving the room in uncomfortable silence, which none of them seemed eager to break. Cohen snatched up the jammer, turned it off, and stuffed it back in his pocket before breakfast arrived.

The room-service cart held a variety of foods, from fresh fruits to miniature burgers. The three of them had been running on fumes and adrenaline for so long that the smell alone made them all ravenous. Once they devoured every scrap, Cohen grabbed his suitcase to paw through it while Chance and Lilith repacked their luggage.

Afterward, none of them could sleep. So, they waited in silence with a million thoughts, making the air heavy. No one dared voice them since unintentionally blurting out the wrong information might cost their lives.

Lilith curled against Chance as his arm draped around her in a natural familiarity while she focused on their mission. Soon, they'd be flying to Connecticut and more dead bodies. Honestly, she didn't care where they went if she escaped Farren's building and the one body she couldn't forget.

Chapter 7

Lilith would never describe New Haven as a metropolis, despite being the second-largest city in Connecticut. Growing up in Manhattan skewed her opinion. After all, this place only contained one hundred and twenty-five thousand people, the equivalent of about five square miles back home.

The city featured a mixture of colonial architecture, gleaming modern buildings, opulent homes, shady docks, and dilapidated slums. In this booming college town, the well-off flaunted extravagant wealth while the poor suffered in desperation, and the middle class appeared non-existent. The gaping disparity between the classes explained why New Haven sported one of the highest crime rates in New England—the perfect place for an Ivy League University.

To her dismay, the city morgue was located inside the Yale Medical Center, which meant picking their way through hordes of graduate students. At least it got her away from Farren. She didn't want to spend another second in the zip code as the monster who slaughtered her father.

After making their way through squeaky-clean hallways featuring monstrous walls of glass, they finally reached the basement. Despite the fluorescent lights brightly illuminating the corridor, the lack of windows provided a darker, more comfortable atmosphere, at least to Lilith.

Bodies made sense. They presented straightforward puzzles with right and wrong answers. She preferred cold, hard science to the political Russian Roulette of dealing with Cohen's family. Besides, a dead body couldn't kill anyone, threaten her life, or hurl insults.

Inside the Medical Examiner's office, they were greeted by a plain-clothes detective and two uniformed officers. All of them appeared eager to escape, and with Luminita's ominous yet vague description of the bodies, Lilith didn't blame them. Most cops never experienced gruesome crimes or the corpses they left behind. They typically dealt with bullet wounds, rapes, and stabbings, not whatever happened to the men in the next room.

The detective, who stepped forward and introduced himself as Blaire, appeared to be in his mid-forties, not handsome, not hideous, but ordinary. He kept his medium-brown hair short, framing his round face, while his muddy-brown eyes hid behind wire-rimmed glasses.

The officers behind him didn't follow his lead, preferring to watch in silence with assessing glares—a skill every cop developed in the academy.

"The examiner is waiting for you. His schedule is tight, so you might want to get in there." Although his words sounded brusque, an expression of relief filled his face. Perhaps he didn't possess the social skills for polite conversation. A scary prospect if the awkward man interrogated suspects. That talent required expertise, finesse, and confidence, all of which he seemed to lack.

"Thank you. Perhaps you can fill in Detective Cohen and Mr. Deveraux on the case while I'm busy. We appreciate your cooperation." Lilith pulled on a well-practiced smile, which exuded professional courtesy, and immediately made Detective Blaire nervous. *Huh.* Maybe his social awkwardness merely extended to tall, curvy redheads.

"We'll be right here." Chance's smooth voice dragged a genuine expression of gratitude to her lips. He didn't need to say anything at all. She knew where he'd be, but the implied bodyguard jargon said, "one scream, and I'll come running". The gesture somehow made her feel more comfortable.

After nodding, she pushed her way through the double doors into the exam room. In front of her lay two covered bodies with laboratory lights hovering brightly above them, giving the white sheets an unearthly glow.

"Ms. Adams, I presume? I'm Dr. John Winslow." A thick man in a lab coat shuffled toward her, offering his hand, and she quickly stepped forward to shake it. She placed his age at mid-to-late fifties, judging by his vastly receding hairline and remaining gray stubble.

The rosacea reddening his snubbed nose and plump cheeks, combined with the network of broken capillaries, revealed more than a slight affection for the bottle. Alcoholism wasn't uncommon in his line of work. Coroners spent too many years examining the corpses of rape victims and abused children to escape the emotional toll unscathed. Eventually, they needed a crutch, and alcohol was more socially acceptable than the alternatives.

"Yes. A pleasure to meet you."

Dr. Winslow nodded gruffly and turned toward the workstation behind him. "You might not be so quick to thank me after seeing our two John Does here." He grabbed some gloves and tossed a pair to Lilith.

"There's a lab coat and an autopsy apron in the corner. Wouldn't want you getting your clothes dirty or contaminating our bodies." The tug at his lips showed contempt—a sure sign he didn't share the detective's enthusiasm about her arrival.

She honestly didn't blame him. Nothing rubbed a medical examiner the wrong way more than requesting a second opinion. They typically acted as the final expert on a person's life. Bringing in an outsider, especially a young woman, was bound to rattle someone.

She knew from first-hand experience. Frank, the ME she occasionally worked with back home, hated it when she walked into his morgue. The grudge boiled down to a professional difference of opinion during a court case a few years ago, and Frank had no intention of dropping the issue.

"Of course. Thank you for letting me borrow a few things. They didn't give me much notice." She saw no need to poke the grumpy bear. At least, not until she had what she wanted. Once she donned the proper attire and snapped on her gloves, she made her way around the first table.

The doctor gazed down at the covered body and glanced up at her. "You aren't squeamish, are you?"

She struggled not to laugh at the question. Five years working with Major Crimes and everything she'd seen in the past two weeks eliminated any chance of a sensitive stomach.

"No, I can handle it." He huffed skeptically, upholding her theory of bias, whether because of her gender, age, or both.

With a dramatic flourish, Dr. Winslow yanked the sheet back, exposing the head, torso, thighs, and knees as her eyes widened. After a steadying exhale, she moved to the head while he studied her, placing mental bets on when she'd puke. "Do you have a disposable recorder I can take with me?"

He raised a thick, graying eyebrow but didn't comment on her lack of resources. He merely grabbed one from a drawer and pressed the button.

"Thank you." After flashing a grateful smile, she grabbed a probe off the exam tray. Unlike the bodies she usually examined, someone had already cleaned this one, leaving the wounds and marks clearly visible. The lack of blood made her job a lot easier.

"Lilith Adams at the New Haven city morgue, examining John Doe 389 on October 28th. The victim appears to be in his late twenties to early thirties, judging by skin condition and facial lines. Caucasian. Ear-length, light-brown hair. Left ear pierced and gauged..." She gingerly tilted the head toward her. "... and the right ear matches."

She raised his eyelid with one gloved thumb. The glazed, milky surface revealed a faint iris. "Eyes were likely dark brown. A contusion runs under the left eye, along the infraorbital margin and lateral orbital wall of the zygomatic bone, most likely due to a concussive blow."

Lilith rotated the face away with a light touch and used the probe to move through his thick hair, closely inspecting the scalp. She frequently saw trauma to the back of the skull when bruises and wounds consistent with a solid punch were present.

"Abrasions above and below the external occipital protuberance, possibly from a fall." She glanced up at the Doctor, whose sour expression appeared less skeptical. "Did you retrieve any trace from these?"

He nodded solemnly, unwilling to hand over more information until he finished evaluating her.

While shrugging off his defensive silence, her deft fingers moved along the massive bruising covering his neck. "The larynx, trachea...and cricoid cartilage are...crushed is the only description I can come up with." She paused as her mind worked through the puzzle. "Do you have the X-rays for this area?"

"On the lightbox behind you."

The light blinked to life with a whir and pop, revealing a tight shot from below the mandible to the clavicles. "The C5, C6, and C7 vertebrae show severe stress fractures, and the hyoid bone is obliterated."

She stood still for a minute, gaping at the impossible x-ray. "The extensive damage to the spine indicates a tremendous amount of force...one only a mechanical source could produce, but the skin doesn't support that theory. Externally, the deep contusions show irregular patterns, usually seen in manual strangulations."

Lilith flicked off the lightbox and turned her back on the bewildering film. *I must have missed something.* While closely re-examining the throat's surface for impressions or tool marks, she noticed an odd angle to the jawline.

Initially, she assumed the bruising around the mouth was linked to the same fight that produced the massive black eye, but from her current vantage point, her initial assessment seemed...wrong somehow. As her fingers ran over the zygomatic processes on both sides, she closed her eyes, recreating the structure in her mind as she palpated each joint. Her eyes snapped open when she hit ridges that shouldn't exist.

"The mandible is dislocated, the bones intact but separated."

A slight huff of approval escaped Dr. Winslow's throat, but she ignored him. After picking up a small penlight, she pried the mouth open and used the probe to push back the bruised lips. Beyond the inflamed gums, she found little bits of tissue caught between his teeth.

"I assume you ran trace on this as well?"

The Doctor nodded stoically, and she tried not to sigh. The tight-lipped way he studied her was more reminiscent of taking a final exam in med school than collaborating on forensic evidence. Although reading the report might have been sufficient, if she caught something he missed, the awkward experience wouldn't be a waste of time.

Lilith shook off the unhelpful thoughts and moved on to the extremities. "Several dark areas of ecchymosis on the victim's upper arms bilaterally...and the same on the thighs. The victim was held down...but they are too deep to be caused by hands, not enough weight, or pressure. However, the marks are too inconsistent to be from restraints." She took a step back, eying the patterns from a wider angle.

"If several attackers used their knees...that scenario would also explain the abrasions on the head." Most likely, the trace he recovered was dirt or gravel.

When she moved down to the hands, she stopped again. "Visible bruising and abrasions on the knuckles, most likely originating from the altercation that produced the black eye."

She drew in a deep breath and glanced up at Dr. Winslow before broaching the main event. Although the cause of death was a crushed airway, the most extensive damage occurred after the victim died. The doctor's eyes shone brighter, and his lips curved into a grin with blatant curiosity. He wanted to see how she'd interpret the massive chest trauma, expecting the same steaming pile of nothing he came up with during his initial examination.

"There are extensive lacerations to the thoracic region, which occurred postmortem, centering on the pericardial cavity." She leaned in close, using her probe to push and pull at the tattered edges of the gaping hole.

"Streaks of light to heavy abrasions in varying widths appear inferior and superior to the major tissue damage. They could result from a tapered object or…perhaps, fingernails." As puzzling as the marks were, the wound presented a more significant challenge.

"I don't see any discernible tool marks *in* the trauma. The flesh is shredded as if something repeatedly punctured the victim's thoracic region and ripped the tissue away. The perp removed the sternum along with most of the costal cartilage." Lilith clicked on the penlight again and peered down into the open chest.

"The edges of the true ribs are fractured and splintered, not cut, indicating the use of a torqued, wrenching motion to remove the sternum." Once again, she stood there, baffled. Nothing with enough power and force to produce the injuries could do so without leaving mechanical marks. The corpse didn't make any sense.

With a frown of determined resolve, she pushed forward. "The perpetrator forcibly extracted the heart, causing tremendous damage to the aorta and vena cava. I believe the killer manually tore it out of the victim's ribcage."

With a frustrated sigh, she placed the instruments back on the tray while her brain buzzed with a million ideas, none of which fit the evidence.

"Are the wounds the same on the second body?" A throbbing headache began pulsating behind her right eye, but this time she couldn't blame a lack of blood. It resulted from good-ole-fashioned aggravation. So much for the theory of bodies having only right and wrong answers.

Dr. Winslow crossed thick arms over his barrel chest. "Almost identical. Similar chest wounds, contusions on the extremities, facial bruising, and fight wounds on the knuckles. Judging by the placement, I'd say these two got in a brawl before they met their grizzly end. The only difference is the mandible."

She glanced up sharply at his last statement. "It wasn't dislocated?"

"No. The perps removed it with no tool marks, just like the thoracic trauma. All I can figure is someone took enough steroids to rip off the damn thing."

She fought to keep the shock off her face as a sense of doom settled over her shoulders again, threatening to send her mind spinning out of control. *No. Stop and focus. Gather the facts and try to make sense of them later.*

"I assume you ran fingerprints on the victims?"

The aging doctor pulled the sheet back over the human-shaped puzzle and grunted. "Yes, but you can ask the Detective for more information. All I do is retrieve the prints. I can tell you our friend here had one glove on his hand when he came in, which the cops found important. Beyond that, no IDs, wallets, or personal effects. The corpses were covered in mud and blood when they arrived. I also found foreign tissue and trace on the ribs in both chest traumas, and the areas you spotted. I'll have a full report for you in the morning."

The tight-lipped medical examiner became a fountain of information once she had proved her worth. After seeing the cadaver, she understood. None of it made sense to him. When the police had requested a second opinion, he'd become defensive, fearing he might be too old to perform his duties properly. A young hotshot leaving with no new insights reassured him.

"Since I'm here, I should examine both bodies."

"Of course." The man's gruff attitude melted into warm camaraderie, which lightened the mood and made her job more manageable.

The coroner was correct about the second body. Everything appeared identical except that something had removed the bottom half of his face.

While inspecting the zygomatic processes, she spotted tiny greenish-brown flecks in the victim's ear canal. Using tweezers with a steady hand, she plucked out a few fragments and laid them on a sterile tray. "Did you send some of these to trace?"

The man's brow furrowed as he shifted his weight, giving her the answer—no. "Let me see." His deep voice took on an assertive tone.

After transferring the sample onto a slide, he popped it under a microscope. "It's plant material of some sort. I'll send it up to the Botany professor right away."

"Thank you." She stood back, considering the entire body. Something tore the flesh off the face, but not directly. The skin split along naturally weak areas as the perp ripped the jaw away. She had to be missing something. Then a thought dawned on her. Perhaps what she *wasn't* seeing held more importance.

"Did they recover anything else biological at the scene? The mandible, sternum, bone, heart?"

He appeared genuinely surprised by her question, as if the notion had never occurred to him. "Nothing. The perps must have taken them. Perhaps they wanted a souvenir or something to sell them on the black market."

"None of the organs or tissue would be suitable for transplants after being ripped out."

The doctor frowned in disapproval, his thick eyebrows knitting close together. "*Not* what I meant. Plenty of sick, twisted people pay top dollar for crime memorabilia and crap for their idiotic rituals. Besides, I stopped asking questions like *why* a long time ago. I never liked the answers." His meaty arms crossed his chest again, signaling an end to his cooperation.

"I'll wash up and get out of your hair." After pulling off the gloves, she scrubbed down while her mind continued to work the puzzle in silence. She didn't see any point in prolonging her visit. The doctor shut down, and she gleaned everything possible from the bodies. She wouldn't find the answers she needed here.

Considering the conflicting evidence, only one plausible explanation jumped to mind—Ashcroft. He had possessed the strength to inflict the wounds without the help of machinery, but he was dead.

Even when alive, he hadn't harbored any interest in punishing cat burglars. Besides, none of this fit him in a stylistic sense. These men had died quickly. All the horrific trauma had occurred postmortem. Ashcroft had purposefully prolonged suffering until he could no longer delay the inevitable. He'd inflicted the antemortem wounds with compulsive precision while these men had fallen victim to sheer brute force.

No, the perpetrator's mission didn't extend to torture, but it exceeded simple assassination. They had taken parts for a purpose, but she couldn't discern a reason without context.

Dr. Winslow began to prep the bodies for cold storage, ignoring her presence as she slowly pulled off the thick apron, still plagued by questions. Was the mutilation a way to *destroy* them? Remove the human aspects? Were the extra bits payment, proof, or trophies?

No. A signature killing involved an emotional statement, a cerebral interpretation of their desires carved into flesh. If that existed in those cadavers, she hadn't seen it. Sure, removing the hearts could be a message of some sort, but the way the killer had removed them didn't show any cognizance.

With one incision below the ribcage, they could have reached up through the cavity to pull out the heart and *viola*—a practical solution requiring very little thought. The ragged holes and broken ribs displayed a mindless approach too powerful to be futile and an absence of critical thinking.

In stark contrast, crushing the throats showed an intelligent plan to disable their enemies quickly and quietly. Two completely unique minds at work, perhaps? The bruises on the arms and legs meant more than one attacker.

The mandibles, however, held an important clue. Why rip off one and not the other? They dislocated the jaw, but what had stopped them from finishing the job? Had someone interrupted them, or did they choose to leave it? Better yet, why the hell take them in the first place? It hadn't been part of the initial attack. The killer had ripped off the jaw postmortem.

Behind her, the coroner cleared his throat, obviously unable to ignore her presence any longer. Lilith quickly shimmied out of the lab coat and turned around with a professional smile fixed in place.

"Thank you for your cooperation, Dr. Winslow."

The frustrated expression on his reddened face clearly stated he intended to have a few drinks over this case tonight. The bewildered man grunted a goodbye and turned back to his work.

After slipping the digital recorder into her pocket, she passed through the double doors and stepped back into the office. The detective and his officers had disappeared, leaving Chance and Cohen alone to flip through magazines in synchronicity. She was reasonably sure neither of them harbored a secret interest in Science Weekly, but that's what bored men did in waiting rooms before cellphones. They blankly scanned through the closest magazine, wishing they were anywhere else.

Chance glanced up as her heels clicked against the linoleum. An immediate smile crossed his lips and reached his hazel eyes with a glimmer of desire. For a few seconds, she let the barrage of questions fall away, relaxing in the momentary reprieve.

His deep well of affection still seemed surreal. Less than two weeks ago, he had only existed as the man who guarded her father's back. Now he routinely held her together while the world fell apart around them.

It didn't take long for her thoughts to spiral to a darker place. Chance would never again stand behind Gregor while they ate at their favorite Italian place. Her father was dead, and she couldn't even give him a proper burial. Thankfully, Cohen's voice snapped her out of the trance before her tears fell.

"The detective had to split. He got a call about some graveyard on the other side of town. We got the info we needed from him, though."

Lilith steeled her focus and turned to face Cohen as his words sank in. "Another murder?"

"I asked, but it's not related. Just some kids causing trouble, and one of them is his son." Cohen shrugged and tossed his magazine on the table. "He arranged for us to meet the director of security at the Yale library and visit the homicide scene. The detective also mentioned a glove and a few prints they found, which matched one victim. No hits locally, but the results from out of state should be back by morning."

"So, what happened to them?" Although Chance's question sounded simple, the potent undercurrent of concern made it seem more significant, as if asking how bad her resulting nightmares would be tonight. She should have found the sentiment sweet and endearing, but somehow, she didn't.

The tone reminded her too much of her father's every time she tried to tell him about her day. Perhaps she had more in common with Dr. Winslow than she thought. A sudden defensiveness swelled in her chest, offended by his assumption that she couldn't do her job without breaking down. *Stop. Concentrate on the real problem.*

She pushed aside her stubborn nature and exhaled deeply before speaking. "Honestly? None of it makes sense. I saw no evidence of tool marks, but the force required exceeds anything human..." Her mind wandered as she talked through the puzzle in her head. "The killer crushed their throats with so much pressure they shattered the vertebrae..."

"Well, you're holding up pretty well." Hesitant concern flooded his voice again, catching her off guard. She frowned and rubbed at her neck in frustration, too distracted by her thoughts to filter her reaction this time.

"Of course I am! Hell, I deal with dead bodies every day. I'm not related to these men, and at least one of them still had a face." Her sharp tone even drew a surprised expression from Cohen. She hadn't intended to bite Chance's head off, especially not for worrying about her mental health. *Dammit, Lilith. Get a grip.*

If she didn't stabilize her emotional rollercoaster, she'd keep flying off the rails. Everything felt off-kilter *before* Farren put a bullet in her father's head. Now, she had no balance at all, stumbling through the dark while spinning plates. If she didn't fix things, one of them would inevitably fall and shatter.

With a self-conscious smile, she quickly changed tactics. "Besides, Medical Examiners have it made. The techs clean the bodies, which makes them easier to handle. Do you think my new partner would clean the bodies before I get to the scene?" Humor—the deflection device of champions.

Cohen snorted a laugh while Chance sat still, jaw clenched, far from amused. Apparently, her deflection device needed work.

Lilith avoided the six-foot-three brooding man and focused on Andrew. Snapping at Chance was unfair, but it would keep happening if he continued to ask if she was okay every ten minutes. She was *not* okay. She might never be again. But he didn't need to handle her like a China doll, either.

They needed to set ground rules before either of them snapped again. Chance wasn't psychic, and despite being around most of her life, he didn't know her very well. Holding her when she broke down in tears under moments of extreme stress slanted his perception. He never witnessed her daily life and didn't hear much about her work, since Gregor never discussed it.

Although she rarely conducted investigations under threat of death, it was still a familiar, logical process that would reveal concrete, definitive answers—the one thing she *could* handle. She desperately needed the distraction to keep her mind busy and stave off the endless horror looping in her brain.

With a forced smile, she shook off her rambling thoughts and refocused on the demon. "Could you bring the car around? I have one more thing I want to do before we leave."

Cohen's blue eyes glanced between them, and although he saw through her relatively transparent ruse, she hoped he'd let it go without acting like an ass. "I'll meet you out front in ten minutes."

Without another word, he stood, straightened his tie, smoothed his suit, and strolled out of the room with dignity.

Chance folded his magazine with precise motions and placed it on the table before looking up at her. "I'm guessing you got rid of Cohen because you wanted to talk?" He didn't seem entirely pissed at her. Concern still lingered in his face. Of course, her interpretation of his expression could be wishful thinking.

She wandered over to the empty chair across from him while collecting her thoughts and settled into the seat. "I'm sorry. I didn't mean…" She sighed and leaned forward, rubbing her temples. All her internal arguments about ground rules evaporated, leaving nothing but the gnawing anxiousness of having no idea what to do.

"I've only seen you around a few dead bodies, and they all traumatized you. I tend to forget you do this for a living. I keep remembering Miriah's body…and how devastated it left you."

"But Chance…" She grabbed his hand and waited until his eyes met hers again, begging him to understand. "I'm trying to focus on this case, so I *don't* think about Miriah and all the rest. I can *deal* with these bodies, but when you infer the opposite by acting like I'm going to fall apart at any second…" A sudden rush of guilt for sounding selfish and ungrateful made her eyes fall to the floor.

"I flashback to Miriah's office and Farren's courtroom. All I see is her unrecognizable body on that desk and Gregor's lifeless face. Thinking about them won't help me solve our current problem." Her heart started pounding in her chest, terrified that saying all this out loud would only end in disaster. But would repressing it and biting her tongue make anything better? No.

"Please, Chance…I can't express how thankful I am. I couldn't survive all this without you, but I have to keep my focus on work, for all our sakes. I can, and probably will, break down later, and then you can coddle me to your heart's content, I promise."

With a heavy sigh, she hesitantly glanced up at him, expecting to see anger. To her surprise, he looked more lost than upset. He leaned forward with his eyes focused on some distant spot while rubbing his stubbled jaw.

"I don't know how to do any of this, *mon cherie*. As often as I dreamed about you and me, I've never actually been in a relationship, and these aren't exactly normal circumstances. I've spent my entire life walling off emotions, and now…with you…" He paused, frowning at the floor as he swallowed hard.

"I feel things I never thought possible, which is terrifying. Then, with this demon blood, I'm suddenly feeling everyone else's emotional crap, too. It's a lot to handle, and it doesn't help that every time we have a moment to ourselves, someone dies or threatens to kill us."

Chance surged to his feet with adrenaline pumping through his system. Every lean muscle in his body tensed, ready to attack, as he paced the office, trying not to punch something. His searing frustration emanated from an inability to fight back or control the things throwing him off-kilter—a perfect mirror image of how she felt.

Then he stopped, his intense hazel eyes boring into her. "I worry about you, and I haven't worried about anyone that way in…well, ever. I will *not* apologize for that."

All her anxiety melted when she realized he felt as lost and unsure as she did. Under his unrelenting stare, she stood and crossed the room to stand in front of him. Even in heels, she stood a few inches shorter.

"Hey, we are in this together, all of it, from Farren to the emotional fly-paper stuff. You and me."

His expression softened with each word, which lightened the weight on her heart again.

"Be patient with me, and I'll do the same. Okay? We will find a way out of this."

He nodded and released a slow breath as he brushed a stray curl from her face. "You and me." Traces of distant sadness lingered in his voice, hinting at things he still wanted to say, but for some reason, couldn't. If only she had the power to banish that melancholy forever, or at least for the moment.

When she leaned up and tenderly kissed his lips, a sense of calm settled over them both. She could no longer tell if the serenity came from Cohen's blood or the way they affected each other but finding out terrified her. The thought of their connection being anything less than real left a sour taste in her mouth.

"In the meantime, let's see what we can find at the library and crime scene. Then we can get some rest at the hotel, hopefully. The trace and fingerprint results won't come back until morning."

He stood there holding her tight as if afraid to let go, drinking in the comfortable silence. After a few minutes, he finally cleared his throat and spoke up.

"Okay. Let's get moving. I'll stay professional as long as you don't smile at me too much. It's distracting." A roguish grin curved his lips as he pulled back. Their witty banter didn't come from demon blood. It was familiar, honest, something that had always belonged to them.

"Oh, no. That is entirely your fault. I am not taking the fall." She quirked a playful eyebrow and started for the door.

"Wait. What? How the hell is *that* my fault?" Chance jogged up beside her, still confused.

She abruptly stopped to gaze at him in his charcoal dress shirt and black slacks—a leanly muscled, six-foot-three package of sarcastic wit and compassion she found irresistible. With a wry grin, Lilith patted his shoulder.

"Yes, my smile is *completely* your fault. Why don't you think about it on the way to the car? You can thank me later." She winked and heard his deep chuckle rumble behind her as they picked their way through the gleaming hallways to the front door.

Chapter 8

Lilith stood in the expansive courtyard, shielding her eyes from the midday sun, and stared at the strangest building she'd ever seen. As a native New Yorker, that said a lot.

The Beinecke Rare Book and Manuscript Library, the *precious jewel box* of Yale University, was a vast modern-art rectangle standing amid classical and neo-gothic architecture. Geometric grids littered every side like massive acoustic tiles. Instead of windows, they used translucent marble to construct the walls. Although she understood using the material to filter out damaging UV rays, the marble gave the structure an eerie biomechanical quality.

The odd building hovered over four seemingly delicate supports, with the doors hidden by the building's oppressive shadow. Stepping foot beneath the ominous monstrosity was an intimidating experience. Lilith stared upward, expecting the building to collapse on them at any second, as Cohen led the way toward the revolving doors.

A blast of cool air scented by old leather flooded her senses as soon as she set foot inside, instantly transporting her to another universe. Then she stared up in shock at the five-story bookcase on steroids surrounded by soft lighting and warm wood. She visited plenty of impressive libraries in Manhattan, but nothing like this. A climate-controlled cocoon of sparkling glass encased the center, protecting everything from the elements and any other source of harm, people included.

How in the hell did the thieves steal one specific book from this massive place? How would they even know where to look? She didn't see any flashing neon signs pointing out ancient cryptic texts.

Jenny Allen

While she continued to gape at the towering bookshelves before them, Chance bumped her shoulder. "I think security is heading our way. The police probably phoned ahead. Close your mouth and look like a professional." He leaned in and winked with a sarcastic grin as she resisted a sudden desire to smack him. She settled for flicking him off discreetly before directing her attention to the man who marched toward them.

Although he wore the typical Ivy League uniform, the stiff navy-blue jacket, red and blue striped tie, and khaki slacks fit nothing else about him. Sure, he sported a close-clipped haircut and a freshly shaven jaw, but his pot-marked face and the disciplined intelligence in his deep-set eyes betrayed his story.

The man's background most likely contained military or police training. While his tan faded from too much time indoors, the weather damage to his skin remained obvious. He moved with an awkward gait because his stocky five-foot-ten frame stretched the stuffy uniform to its unforgiving limits. She doubted tailoring ranked anywhere on his list of priorities, especially with a robbery to solve.

When he came to a stop, his dark blue eyes scanned each one of them, stalling on both Cohen and Lilith. *Odd.* Chance easily held the title as most intimidating by comparison, but this man didn't seem to agree.

"You must be the team Detective Blaire phoned about."

The demon nodded and stepped forward, extending his hand. "I'm Detective Andrew Cohen, and these are my colleagues, Forensic Investigator Lilith Adams and Security Specialist Chance Deveraux."

The man took his hand in a firm shake but kept his eyes on the entire group. With this guy in charge, the theft seemed even more impossible. So far, the facts didn't support a high intelligence level for either man in the morgue. Of course, since the cops never recovered the book, a third person had to be involved, the brains of the operation. The daunting task of stealing one specific item from this overwhelming place could even suggest an inside job.

"I'm Terry Eckhart, Director of Security. I'll need to see your badges if you intend to carry your firearms." Well, that explained the extended evaluation. Chance was the only one without a weapon, which indicated a silent metal detector at the entranceway.

Cohen had his suits tailored to hide the gun bulge, and she stashed hers in the forensics case she carried. Whoever packed her suitcase decided not to toss in her holster, and since women's business attire didn't come with pockets, she had no other choice. The movie solution of wedging a pistol into the waistband of her clothes wouldn't work since the pencil skirt clung to her body like a second skin.

Both Lilith and Cohen fished out their badges, while Eckhart considered Chance with a calculated stare. She could practically taste the testosterone as they faced each other in a silent alpha-male show of dominance. *Men.*

Lilith cleared her throat, breaking the odd stand-off, and passed over their badges. Once he examined them thoroughly and appeared satisfied with their credentials, he wasted no time leading them toward a side door. They fell in line behind him, and once the door closed behind them, he broke into the debriefing while they walked.

"The incident occurred two nights ago…around 22:00 hours—"

Definitely ex-military.

"—right at shift change. All the researchers and support staff had already vacated the premises, and, with recent budget cuts, we can only afford two armed guards at night for the *entire* building. Thankfully, neither of them sustained injuries during the robbery."

An enormous amount of resentment saturated his words, squarely placing blame on the executives responsible for his budget crisis. However, he didn't know the people involved or their capacity for violence, not only Farren but whoever butchered the two thieves in the morgue. If more guards had been present, it would have merely resulted in more corpses. She held no illusions about that.

"We don't have much to go on since the perps wiped the security feeds." Eckhart swung another door open with purpose, signaling everyone inside. His deep-set eyes scanned the trio again as they passed, thin lips pressed into a natural scowl.

His direct, brusque mannerisms lacked the niceties of a social filter, which probably indicated more than a simple military background. The man lived for his job, the only thing that mattered in his life. The absence of a wedding band didn't surprise her. His intense dedication to the mission wouldn't leave room for romantic entanglements. So, assuming her assessment was correct, why would an ex-special forces soldier take a job at a library?

"How long have you worked here, Director Eckhart?" She kept her voice casual as he led them down another utility corridor.

"Eleven months, one week, and five days. I acted as Director of campus security for ten years before accepting this post."

Unsurprisingly, the answer contained all the pertinent facts with no personal investment in the conversation.

"I'm guessing you're ex-military. So, how did you fall into this line of work? Guarding a library seems like a step down from running the entire campus."

A ripple of tension across the man's back preceded his gruff tone. "Navy Seal, and this is *not just* a library. The Beinecke is the largest assembly of original works in the country, containing some of the world's rarest books and manuscripts. This is an extremely coveted position. The guy I replaced served as a Green Beret in Desert Storm."

"Point taken." Although his response wasn't exactly what she expected, it should have been. No puffed-up ex-military man enjoyed someone implying their job was a waste of physical and mental prowess.

Chance shook his head and shot her a frown full of patronizing humor with a smidge of disapproval. "Smooth." He whispered the word just loud enough for her to hear. This time, she didn't worry about an audience seeing her middle finger.

Eckhart swung open his office door with a little too much enthusiasm and rushed inside while they trailed behind him. An all too familiar military mindset dominated the small room. The cream-colored walls stood bare except for a corner displaying various awards and diplomas. He kept the desk spotless with everything in a very particular order—stapler on the left, cup of pens on the right, polished name plaque in the center.

Lilith and Cohen claimed the two chairs while Eckhart pulled open the top drawer of his olive-green filing cabinet, deftly flicking through files. In a matter of seconds, he slapped a manila folder on the desk and took a seat while adjusting his stapler. The scowl on his face deepened, less thrilled with their presence than he'd been in the lobby.

Granted, poking at his career choice didn't help, but he seemed overqualified for the position, as did his Green Beret predecessor. Despite the priceless, irreplaceable nature of the building's contents, retired special forces felt like overkill. How many security threats could they really have?

"That contains everything we have on the incident." His eyes went straight to Chance, who hovered beside his organized desk. With a nod, Chance grabbed the folder and began scanning its contents. "As you can see, these guys came prepared. They knew our security protocols and how to bypass them."

"Which means they either had inside information or they cased the place." Chance rattled off the automatic answer while flipping through the papers. "What about the former head of security?"

Eckhart frowned, torn between defending a fellow service member and appreciation for the valid question. "Patterson retired to Florida with his wife of thirty years. Besides, when I took this post, I revised the protocols, a standard practice when changing management. If it was an inside job, Patterson was *not* involved."

Chance nodded as if he expected the guarded response and ran his fingers down a page. "I assume someone properly vetted all your guys?"

"Of course. Full background checks, security clearance, and credit reports. Standard procedure. Nothing out of the ordinary." Eckhart sat a little straighter in his chair, puffing out his chest, which, along with the minuscule pursing of his lips, betrayed him. Although it didn't mean an outright lie, he was overcompensating. The man didn't feel one hundred percent confident in his assessment. Finally, something she could contribute.

"So, you *personally* vetted each person on your security team?" When she spoke up, Terry Eckhart's firm blue eyes fell on her with an expression of open dislike mixed with an undercurrent of concern.

"No. A few men started several years back when Patterson was in charge, but he ran a tight ship."

Chance shot her a stern glare, clearly asking her to pipe down and let him handle things. Then his focus shifted back to their host. "What about disgruntled workers? Has anyone been laid off recently or not shown up for a shift?"

"No. No one in security."

Well, that said volumes.

Chance jumped on the bait eagerly. "Anyone who works on the premises would know at least some of your protocols. The report says they stole the item from a secure workroom?"

Eckhart nodded with his square jaw set in a firm line. "Yes, a key-coded room on the far side of the building. We store certain items there in a locked case of reinforced glass. And to answer the previous question, a restoration technician has been out on sick leave since the theft, but I doubt he was involved."

"Why is that?" Despite Chance's warning, she blurted out the obvious question. The immense weight of Eckhart's hostile gaze fell on her, causing an instinctual desire to squirm, but she refused to give him the satisfaction.

"Because, Ms. Adams, the man has stage four pancreatic cancer and started chemotherapy treatments last week. Everyone expected him to take sick days."

Chance closed the file and tossed it on the desk while a frown furrowed his brow. "All right, Terry. Walk me through this."

When Eckhart tore his unfriendly stare away from Lilith, his expression transformed into one of cooperative kinship. Clearly, he disliked her insinuations and respected Chance's ability to assess the situation without bias.

The man leaned forward, resting his arms on the desktop in an unconscious sign of disclosure. Despite his questionable choice of careers, the guy seemed dedicated to his job, which made his involvement unlikely.

"At 21:58, the perpetrators used a keycard scanner to gain access to the building."

"Not to state the obvious, but you're certain they didn't use an employee's key card?" Chance's question earned him a curt but friendly nod.

"The employee ID number was the lowest in the active codes, which belongs to the Dean. As I'm sure you know, a scanner starts from zero and works upward until it finds the first approved sequence. It's not a coincidence, and the dean went out of town a week ago."

"What about the workroom? You said it's key coded as well?"

"Yes, and they used the same code for that door."

"And the reinforced glass case?"

"It takes a physical key, but they picked it. Judging by the tool marks, they used a pin-by-pin method."

When Chance nodded, agreeing with his assessment, the burly man continued.

"We've begun combing through older security footage, starting with last week. The perps wiped the vids clean from the night in question, but hopefully, we'll catch them casing the place. The coroner sent a picture of one perp, so we have a place to start."

Then Eckhart turned his steely gaze on Lilith. "The police stated the other body wouldn't help us. Was his face messed up or something?"

"Or something." Both Chance and Eckhart scowled with zero appreciation for her smart-ass humor. "The bottom half of his face was…removed, which makes facial recognition a little difficult."

Eckhart's brow furrowed in a thoughtful frown as he stared at her. "The cops did say they were in awful shape, but...how was it removed?"

Lilith shrugged and flashed a sympathetic smile. "I'm afraid I can't reveal further details about an active police investigation, but I work on a lot of weird cases. I've seen stranger." Okay, the last sentence qualified as an outright lie. Even with Ashcroft, all the wounds made logical sense.

The two cadavers in the New Haven city morgue defied any reasoning she could wrap her head around. Still, advertising her bewilderment to the ex-military guy with a chip on his shoulder didn't seem like a prudent plan.

"Okay, so no usable video surveillance, a scanner-created code, and a gifted lock pick. The medical examiner mentioned a glove?" Lilith prompted the stoic man, eager to move his attention back to the business at hand.

Lilith's interactions with Dr. Winslow and Security Director Eckhart so far had illustrated her lack of diplomatic skills. Something she should probably work on if they made it home.

Chance spoke up before Ekhart, intercepting the question. "Yeah. It's here in the report. The forensic team recovered it from the workroom along with prints on a glass case and a door handle, which match one of our John Does. They also found blood drops on the floor."

Eckhart gave a curt nod. "Correct. From the evidence, I figure the men had a disagreement, threw a few punches, and one of them lost a glove during the struggle. Their work before the altercation was meticulous, so something drastic must have happened."

Chance peered down at her with a professional gaze, signaling for her input.

"I agree. Both men had antemortem bruising around the eyes, cheeks, and knuckles—all classic signs of a fistfight. The extent of damage displays a high probability that they traded punches. I agree with Eckhart on the glove issue as well. Leaving it behind meant asking to be caught. They either ran from or after something. Perhaps the third crew member double-crossed them. There truly is no honor among thieves."

"Wait. We need to back up." Cohen finally joined the conversation instead of merely observing the exchange. "Why did they pull the book from the shelves, and how would these guys know where it was? That wouldn't be public knowledge, would it?"

Eckhart paused for a moment, giving the question thought. "We circulate books from the main case for public display based on the discretion of our curator. When he marks a text for an upcoming show, it's pulled and sent to a workroom for restoration and cleaning. Then it's stored until the reveal."

His weather-worn face frowned as he pulled open the top desk drawer and pulled out a calendar. He flipped through the pages before coming to an abrupt halt.

"The press release for the Voynich Manuscript is set for two weeks from now. Even if they discovered the text was slated for display, they couldn't know the precise timing of our process. They hit at the most vulnerable point."

"How so?" Chance asked as he leaned against the wall.

"Well, during restoration work, we actively surveil the rooms via cameras and a 24-hour watch due to the high risk of employee theft. Footage of the storage cases is only recorded. Our thieves hit hours after techs completed restoration and stowed the book."

"Well, the timing seems suspicious—" Cohen started, but she quickly intercepted him, finding her diplomatic footing.

"That doesn't necessarily mean an inside man." She leaned back, crossing her arms as she glared at the demon before smiling at Eckhart. "I'm sure people log the manuscript's location electronically. This crew hired a tech capable of wiping digital camera feeds and overriding key-coded locks. Hacking the inventory system isn't much of a stretch."

All three men nodded without comment, leaving her to ruminate on the facts. A third guy escaped with the prize, and all the physical evidence pointed to the two dead men. They needed to ID the victims and figure out what killed them, neither of which they'd accomplish here.

"May we take a copy of the report?" Lilith rose to her feet, signaling their imminent departure, much to Chance and Cohen's surprise.

Eckhart studied her for a second before finally nodding. "That's a copy. You can keep it."

She grabbed the folder and extended her hand toward the burly man. "Thank you, Director Eckhart. You've been a great help. We'll call if we have any further questions."

He stood and straightened to his full five-foot-ten height before giving her hand a firm shake. "Of course."

After nodding politely, she turned on her heel and stalked through the door without waiting for her chaperones. Frustration burned down every nerve. So far, nothing they'd uncovered had provided any answers. Figuring out how the perps pulled off the heist wasn't necessary. They needed to ID the third person, figure out who hired them, and locate the book.

Farren wouldn't care about a step-by-step analysis of the theft if they couldn't give him what he wanted. Without the book and the cipher, he'd kill them all without mercy.

While she waited in the hall, Farren's callous execution of her father kept replaying in her mind. Most children thought their parents were invincible. However, after learning how Gregor endured centuries of torment and survived Ashcroft's bloody crusade for vengeance, she had truly believed it.

A tiny piece of metal bringing everything to an end still seemed unfathomable. Her father, the world she knew, her sense of self, had all evaporated in that moment. Her chest tightened with the spiraling thoughts until a panic attack loomed on the horizon. *Breathe, just breathe. Come on. Don't do this now.*

Finally, the door swung open, and Andrew emerged with Chance close behind. They both came to a halt, displaying concern as she took slow, deep breaths. Thankfully, neither of them commented. Perhaps chivalry wasn't dead after all.

"Well, that was useless." Cohen sighed and dug the car keys out of his pocket. Whether his words stemmed from genuine frustration or polite sympathy, it didn't matter. He was right.

"I want to stop at the murder scene. I don't expect to find any fresh evidence, but I'd still like to see it. After that, all we can do is wait for the cops to ID our vics and deliver the lab results." Creating a plan eased the panic enough for her to breathe.

"All right. We'll stop there. Then, I want to swing by Wal-Mart before we settle in at the hotel." Cohen's to-do list earned him skeptical frowns from both Lilith and Chance.

"What?" Cohen scowled defensively. "You have something against Wal-Mart?" Asking that question with an aristocratic accent seemed horribly wrong.

"No. You just don't strike me as a *People of Wal-Mart* guy." Chance grinned like a Cheshire cat, pulling a laugh out of Lilith.

"How cute." Cohen did not appear amused in the least. "It's the only store that lets you pull out over forty dollars on each purchase, and we need cash. Finding the book and this mystery killer is great, but if we don't get to the cipher and those missing pages without the council knowing, we'll still die."

"Won't they wonder why you spent a grand at a big-box store?" Lilith raised one eyebrow and stared him down. Although she considered it a valid point, he didn't seem to agree.

"Let them wonder. Perhaps we all bought new wardrobes or stocked up on shotguns to go raccoon hunting. I don't care what they think. Cash is untraceable, and they have bigger things to worry about than my shopping habits at Wally World."

"Well, all right. Crime scene, Wal-Mart, hotel, and dinner. Sounds like an awful prom date."

Both men chuckled as they made their way to the rental car.

Twenty minutes later, Lilith stood in a rain-drenched alley reminiscent of New York City's seedier sections. The recent downpour cut the probability of finding new evidence to Hail-Mary odds but visualizing the scene first-hand and understanding the surroundings helped.

All the windows facing the secluded alley were boarded up, painted over, or sported heavy blackout curtains. In this type of neighborhood, people ignored the outside world. Getting involved meant risking the delicate homeostasis that allowed them to survive. Even if they avoided retaliation for squealing to the cops, being dragged into court meant missing work when every dime counted. It didn't surprise her that the police canvas came up empty.

Lilith strolled into the center of two intersecting alleys, precisely where the corpses were found. If her theory about multiple assailants proved correct, this presented an ideal spot. The vacant lanes contained nothing to hide behind or use for protection.

Although fire escapes lined the surrounding buildings, none of the ladders reached street level without being lowered from above. Further up, clusters of trash bags, bikes, dumpsters, and other obstacles littered the alleys in all directions. The stark contrast made her consider whether the killers cleared the space in advance.

"They planned this. Whoever killed these men knew their escape route and had lain in wait, but how could they be certain? Especially if things didn't go according to plan?" Lilith frowned as her mind worked the problem.

"Well, I'm not a *forensic expert* or a *security consultant,* but a third person worked the job, the brains of the operation. What if they ran off with the book and lured them into an ambush to tie up loose ends?" Cohen sounded resentful and bored, rattling off his explanation without a second thought. The theory held merit, but something nagged at her.

"Why go through the trouble? Tearing off jaws, ripping out hearts? It's a messy way to clean up loose ends." She stared at the muddy pavement, begging the inanimate concrete to reveal its secrets.

"Maybe that's the point."

When Chance chimed in, she shot him a quizzical frown. "What?"

"What if they used the horrific bodies to confuse the police? To keep them from piecing things together?"

She nodded thoughtfully as her eyes drifted back to the scene, recreating events in her mind. "Possibly." Once again, frustration burned up her spine, and she stretched her neck while exhaling slowly. Chance made a brilliant point, but something still didn't feel right. The wounds still defied scientific explanation, and nothing in the alley helped her make sense of them.

"Hopefully, the IDs and trace results will give us a better idea of what happened. We should get moving. It's getting late, and this isn't the kind of neighborhood that helps strangers."

"Yeah, let's move." Chance's voice sounded anxious as he scanned the rooftops, windows, and doorways with a calculated stare. An ideal ambush spot made him less than comfortable. Of course, if he had seen the cadavers, he never would have let her out of the car.

Chapter 9

Two hours later, Lilith stared at a blurry dolphin tattoo emerging from the painted-on jeans of the next woman in line. The *people of Wal-Mart* existed in New Haven, Connecticut. Apparently, no place escaped the stereotype.

Although the fashion disaster wasn't unexpected, the trip still seemed surreal. Two vampires and an emotion-sucking demon standing in line at Wal-Mart on a Thursday night felt darkly amusing. *Nothing to see here, folks. Just buying supplies so we can hunt down a killer who's ripping people apart.* When she added the threat of execution from a clandestine council, the pit stop resembled some ridiculous moment in a Mel Brooks movie.

Of course, even supernatural creatures required body wash and razors. The prepaid phones, pistols, extra ammo, snacks, and casual clothes would come in handy too. Chance refused to walk around unarmed, no matter what Luminita said. After all, he held a national concealed-carry permit because of his job. Her mind stuttered, unable to accept the fact that he was now unemployed because doing so meant admitting why.

Both Cohen and Chance stressed the importance of a backup weapon, but she'd never used an ankle holster. A *concealed* gun would be pointless if it caused her to limp around. So, she settled for picking up a shoulder holster to carry her pistol within easy reach.

The squealing demands of a three-year-old ripped through the air, piercing her ears. Lilith rubbed at her temples as she turned toward Chance and Cohen, hoping to minimize the high-pitched screams for candy. In all the chaos, she forgot Halloween was on Sunday, three short days away. Hyperactive kids running rampant and fighting over costumes was a painful reminder.

"Does this line ever end?" She muttered the question through clenched teeth as the toddler's shrieks reached super-sonic levels.

Cohen peered up with a good-ole-boy smile as his elbows rested on the cart. "Relax, sugar." Oddly enough, he seemed comfortable using his charming-southerner persona to blend into the blue-collar atmosphere. Only the suit and tie set him apart.

After narrowing her eyes in a *fuck you* expression, she glanced over at Chance, who didn't seem to hear Cohen's flippant comment. To her surprise, he eyed the crowd without a flicker of impatience. He didn't seem aware of his casual vigilance, an ingrained habit from years of working security, most likely.

While he excelled in identifying physical threats, he was oblivious to the women gazing, starry-eyed, at his six-foot-three, leanly muscled frame. He peered over their disappointed faces with no acknowledgment, but Lilith noticed them. Their hostile sighs weren't precisely subtle when his fingers brushed the curve of her back.

Then Chance leaned in close to whisper, successfully pulling her attention away from the nosy women. "After we get to the hotel, you and Cohen grab takeout while I secure the rooms. Then I'll use a burner to touch base with Timothy. The last thing we need is the cavalry riding to our rescue."

He continued to scan the crowded lines while he spoke, avoiding her gaze. That's when she saw the slight twitch of his lips and the skin tighten around his roving eyes.

Odd. If she didn't know better...no. *Why would he lie?*

Timothy's involvement could get them tossed in jail for pursuing a case under false pretenses. Still, she couldn't unsee the clear signs of deceit. What was he trying to hide from her?

She quickly shifted her focus to a kid in a vampire costume holding out his cape as he ran in circles. She couldn't meet Chance's eyes, not yet. The deception took her by surprise, and she kept hoping her over-analytical brain was merely jumping at decade-old shadows.

"Yeah. You should contact Timothy before he calls it in." She hesitated as the words caught in her throat. He didn't seem to notice her reaction as he continued to study the crowd with a casual smile.

Come on, Lilith. Stop jumping to conclusions.

After a deep breath, she steadied her voice. "That reminds me. The precinct assigned me a new partner today. I should call, so they don't raise any red flags. Being *rescued* might be inconvenient at this point."

As he stooped down to comment, the squat cashier coughed, drawing their attention. Cohen pushed the cart forward with a warm smile and apologized, but the woman's deep frown lines made her resemble an irritable bulldog. She seemed unimpressed by his set of pearly whites.

Cohen divided things into separate transactions and navigated the credit screen, repeatedly requesting cash back. Each time he stopped the cashier, her frown deepened, and Lilith swore the woman growled as her age-spotted hands jabbed the screen. By the end, the woman was practically foaming at the mouth while the people in line released overt groans of impatience.

Cohen grinned at Lilith and Chance, oblivious to the angry horde, and handed them each fifty dollars for emergencies before stuffing another four hundred into his wallet. "So, are we all set?"

She nodded half-heartedly, still stewing over Chance's cryptic behavior. He wasn't brooding over their conversation from the morgue. In fact, he appeared downright chipper, so why did he suddenly want to send her away with Cohen? Something didn't fit.

Chance settled his arm across her shoulders, and she jumped in surprise. While they walked toward the door, he leaned close to whisper. "What's wrong, Lily? You look as pale as that anorexic, sparkly vamp from the movies."

She couldn't help but crack a grin as the noise in her brain ebbed away. "Is that an admittance of guilt? Did you *actually* watch that nonsense? Willingly, or was it torture? Please tell me the perp at least tied you up or restrained you somehow. Being a Twi-hard is a deal-breaker."

He straightened, scanning the parking lot as they crossed the street. "Well, there was a time I *dated* humans, and most of them didn't have great taste. I wasn't tied up at the time, but later…" His deep chuckle rumbled over her like a warm blanket, but the words made her stomach churn.

"Ugh, I don't want to hear about your past sexcapades." She frowned in disgust and shoved him away. Although her actions appeared playful, she had zero desire to hear details about his previous sex habits.

"Aww, Lily, *mon petite cherie…*" Fingers tickled across her hip before his arm slipped around her waist. Then he tugged her close with a roguish grin.

"Gee, let me guess. This is the part where you say you finally wised up and discovered what you were missing?" She quirked an eyebrow and glared up at him. "Before you say anything, I should warn you. I have an excessively low tolerance for mushy crap." Her nose scrunched at the thought. "I don't wanna hear any of the insincere nonsense that qualifies as romance in Hollywood."

"I'll remember that and make the cheesy moments worth incurring your wrath." Chance's smile broadened as he kissed her temple. His lips lingered there, the warm breath rushing over her skin as he whispered. "Besides, I always knew what I was missing."

Despite her aversion to mushy sentiments, a blush blazed across her cheeks. His raw honesty seared into her heart, making her eyes water for a moment. That was the problem. With Chance, the cheesy moments didn't feel insincere and hollow.

How could she not trust him when he consistently proved that she could? If he held something back, he had a reason. She needed to let it go and trust him. Unfortunately, she never excelled at either of those things.

After loading the car, they drove to the Clarion, a modest single-story building painted yellow and terracotta with blocky pillars. The hotel fit Gregor's rules: not too fancy, not too low rent, both of which drew unwanted attention. It seemed Cohen shared his opinion, opting instead for mediocrity.

The lobby embodied a half-hearted attempt to update a late-seventies hotel with a few tricks from HGTV. Behind the faux cherry-wood counter, an uneven stone backsplash covered the wall, matching the resurfaced fireplace. However, they left the odd wood trim covering every edge and the orange paisley carpet. Like most hotels in the below-average price range, they used prefab furniture designed to appear opulent.

In front of the fireplace sat a pair of uncomfortable wing-back chairs upholstered in powder blue. She strongly doubted anyone used the seating area. The place didn't appear busy for a line, much less an overflow of guests seeking to rest their weary bones while they waited. Except for her, of course.

With a deflated sigh, she sank into a high-backed chair, which felt as stiff and uncomfortable as it looked, while Cohen paid for their rooms. Chance hovered over his shoulder, prodding the demon to ask for non-adjoining rooms with easy access to the main road. She couldn't help but smile at his desire for privacy, coupled with an easy escape route.

While she waited, her thoughts drifted back to the puzzling cadavers. The wounds still defied logical sense. The lack of tool marks, the direct and challenging approach for removing the hearts, the missing and dislocated jaws... All the actions appeared animalistic, instinctual, but held purpose, and the location proved the crime hadn't been random.

No. The instrument used had been feral, but an intelligent person with a mission had orchestrated the attack. Perhaps Chance was right about the carnage. What if the killer used excessive violence to confuse the motive? Still, what possessed the strength to produce extensive damage without mechanical assistance?

A hand touched her shoulder, shaking her from the circling thoughts. "The rooms are all set." Chance passed her a keycard as she climbed out of the stiff chair. "We're in 105, and Cohen is in 109 on the front side of the hotel."

Lilith nodded as she tucked the keycard into her pocket, with questions still buzzing in her brain. When she glanced up, he stared at her expectantly. *Did he ask a question?* "What? Did I miss something?"

"No. You just seem a million miles away."

"I'm sorry. It's the bodies from the alley. I can't figure out what happened to them." With a steady exhale, she pulled on a brave face. "We can talk about it over dinner." After waving a dismissive hand, she started for the door.

"Or..." He jogged to catch up, but his grimace didn't stem from a lack of physical conditioning. "... And I'm only throwing out ideas here, but we could enjoy a nice dinner first and save the gory details for after I digest my food."

She peered up at him while muffling a laugh.

"Hey! Not everyone stares at blood and guts every night. I'm merely suggesting we relax and eat before digging into gruesome evidence. I mean, if it's rattling you this much, the bodies must have been horrific."

With a sympathetic frown, she patted his shoulder and swung the door open. "Aww. Okay, I'll save the scary talk for later. If I do, will you have nightmares, though? I'd rather have my bodyguard deal with a sensitive tummy than sleep deprivation." She turned around as she walked and tapped his stomach with a smirk. "Maybe we should wait until morning. I hear sunlight keeps away the monsters."

Chance came to an abrupt halt with a playful scowl, but she could tell he resented her remarks. "Smartass." He muttered the word under his breath as he continued toward the car.

"Well, that's the last bag." Lilith set her forensic case on a small table by the window. "You're sure you want me and Cohen to pick up takeout? Why don't all three of us go out to dinner? There's a restaurant right outside, and I don't like the idea of being alone with him."

"Aww, *mon cher*. Are you saying you'd miss me too much?" Chance flashed his Cheshire cat grin, which typically sparked an instinctual desire to slap him or kiss him, sometimes both.

"Seriously? That's your response?" Her nose scrunched in distaste.

"Come on. You hate breaking up our arguments. Besides, I need to talk with Tim, and I'd rather not call him in front of Cohen. The less he knows about our lives, the better."

She sighed heavily, disappointed in his sudden lack of protective chivalry.

Chance chuckled at her pained expression and rubbed her shoulders. "Unless, of course, you want to call Timothy while I pick up dinner with Cohen."

Lilith shook his hands off with a somewhat playful glare. "Yeah, right. You'd only kill each other and leave me to solve this by myself. Still..." She dropped the sarcastic humor and stared up at him with genuine confusion. "I never thought I'd see the day that you encouraged me to go somewhere, alone, with *him*."

The implied question hung in the air like an oppressive weight. He didn't trust the demon, and she knew it. So why the sudden change? Why entrust him with her life now?

"I know what you're thinking." His hand slid around her waist, lips hovering inches above hers as his breath tickled over her skin, sending tingles down her spine.

"And you're right. I don't trust him, but he needs you alive, not me. I have complete faith in his instinctual need to protect himself, something he can't do without you. He'll do whatever it takes to keep you safe until he gets what he wants." His lips barely brushed hers, a mere whisper of a kiss, taking her breath away and evaporating her apprehension.

"I'm sorry. You were saying something?" She blinked several times before flashing a cheeky smile, which earned her a deep chuckle. "Right, Cohen." Her nose wrinkled with a lopsided frown, and she reluctantly pulled away from the enigmatic man.

"Okay, okay. Make your phone call." Her deflated sigh and slumped shoulders only made him laugh harder.

"Ah, *amour de ma vie*." He reached for her, but she danced out of range.

"Nope. You call Timothy. I'll grab dinner. Someday, you'll have to teach me French. Leaving me clueless while you say whatever you want is unfair. It's like hiding in plain sight, something you're quite good at, by the way."

He lunged forward as she turned to leave, captured her hand, and tugged her toward him. His hazel eyes held both intimacy and skepticism, as if she'd disappear if he glanced away for even a moment.

"I'm not hiding anymore, Lily. Speaking French is…habit, but all you have to do is ask." His hand caressed her cheek before sinking into her auburn curls, leaving shivers in their wake. "*Amour de ma vie* means *love of my life*, what you have always been." Her skin blazed crimson as his lips crashed against hers in a tender kiss that made her head swim. Then he pulled away, taking all the heat with him.

"You should go, or we won't be eating dinner." His sly grin didn't inspire a desire to leave, but she knew he was right.

"Okay, okay. I'm going." She rubbed her red cheeks and slipped out of the hotel room before she could change her mind. His magical ability to distract her from all the dark things cluttering her life still amazed her.

Once the door closed, she peered across the parking lot and spotted her ride. Cohen leaned against the hood, arms folded over his chest, and sandy hair glinting in the setting sunlight.

For a moment, he resembled the friendly southern police detective she'd first met. Unfortunately, she now knew his shifting facades camouflaged equally indiscernible motives, but he needed her alive, at least for now.

Lilith strolled past Cohen with a frown. "Chinese takeout? I saw a place down the road." Without waiting for a response, she climbed into the passenger seat. Awkward tension crossed his back before he stalked to his door. *Oh yeah. This should be fun.*

Jenny Allen

After a car ride filled with hostile silence, they passed a gated self-storage place and arrived at a nondescript strip mall with a packed parking lot. *China Wok* sat between *H&R Block* and *Rainbow*, a women's clothing store, neither of which seemed very busy.

Inside, the place resembled a million other generic takeout joints, complete with cheap wallpapered tables and metal chairs covered in pink and teal vinyl. Lilith perused the paper menu while waiting in a long line, which explained all the cars out front. Although she already knew what to order, browsing kept her busy and, as a bonus, encouraged Cohen to stay quiet. Or so she thought...

She became painfully aware of the demon as he inched closer, hovering over her shoulder. With an exasperated sigh, she glared at him for invading her personal space. "The menus are on the counter if you don't know what you want."

"Look, I just wanted to say..." Cohen's nervous whisper dripped with a sincerity she still couldn't believe. "I apologize for everything. When I helped you in Tennessee, I only wanted assistance locating the cipher. I didn't know any of this would happen. I'm sorry for dragging you into this."

She turned on her heel to face him with a less-than-cheerful expression. In response, he took a step backward, genuinely confused by her anger. "You want to discuss this now? In public?"

The corner of his lip lifted as his fingers raked through his hair. "Approaching a volatile topic with you in public is a matter of personal safety. I figure you're less likely to slug me and more likely to listen."

She tilted her head, eyes narrowing as she stepped closer.

"Andrew, you always hide your motives, and because of that, I can't accept your words at face value. I have to sift through every sentence, every microexpression, trying to decipher all the possible reasons for saying anything. That's why I can't trust you. I don't want an apology because it seems more like a negotiation tactic than an acknowledgment of culpability. Please, save the heart-to-heart and pick your dinner. We're up next."

In a split second, Cohen's shocked expression transformed into an impassive mask. Even if she wanted to believe the demon had a soul, his constant acting made it impossible. She couldn't understand why he bothered. Why keep trying to befriend her? Did he want her trust so she wouldn't see the double-cross coming, or...was it a misguided attempt to connect with someone?

Thankfully, Cohen didn't broach the subject again. He merely ordered pepper chicken and fried rice while her mind struggled with demon ethics. Of course, everything changed when they left the restaurant.

"Lilith, I know you don't trust me, and I understand why. However, there are no ulterior motives behind my apology. I'm sorry for involving you in my family drama and putting you on Farren's radar. If you choose not to accept my apology, fine."

Cohen slid into the car and slammed his door. If she considered the drive over awkward, the ride back would be worse if she didn't settle the issue. Why did it fall on her to coddle everyone's fragile ego? Cohen reminded her of an anorexic beauty queen, complete with erratic mood swings and a constant need for reassurance. The ordeal was draining her remaining energy.

She exhaled a weary sigh before opening the door, sliding into the seat, and buckling her seatbelt. The stifling tension went beyond uncomfortable, like a thousand needles pricking her skin.

"Look, Andrew. For the moment, we need each other, but why try to mend fences? You don't need my friendship. You need my cooperation. So, I don't understand your motivation. Stop trying to manipulate me and be straight."

"I am…"

"Stop!" she interrupted him with a frustrated growl. "I'm tired of having the same conversation. You're always a different person. Nothing about you is straightforward. Hell, even your eyes change color. How do you do that?"

The man frowned with a wounded sense of pride. "I'm *not* my family. Yes, I did some acting here and there, but always to benefit the greater good. I'm not as selfish as you think I am."

She leaned back, crossing her arms over her chest. "I don't want to argue anymore. You want my trust? Fine. It starts here. Either answer my question or stop trying to recruit me."

His jaw set in a firm line while his hands flexed around the steering wheel. "You're asking me to reveal secrets that endanger your life. You realize that? Every bit of info I tell you is one more reason for Farren to put a bullet in your head."

"Don't take the moral high ground now. You know damn well your grandfather plans to kill us once he has what he wants."

"Point taken. You know worse things anyway, so what the hell." He drew in a deep breath, and beneath the irritation lurked something else. It took her a minute to identify because she never thought to associate the word with Cohen—embarrassment.

"We are all born with unique gifts. The *chanteur d'âme*, or *siren*, as you like to call her, is an extreme example. Most talents are more subtle and, in cases such as mine, useless."

"So, Peisinoe can control minds by singing, and your super-power is changing your eye color at will?" She struggled to contain her amused chuckle. The embarrassment made sense when put into context. "What's Farren's super-secret ability?"

Cohen stared straight ahead as resentment poured off him in waves. "The ability to continue living without a soul." He took a steadying breath while she wondered if he was serious or being sarcastic. "Farren doesn't share. Honestly, I have no idea."

"And it's not at will, by the way." Cohen continued once he had a handle on his deep loathing. "My eyes change based on the other person's desire. It's an instinctual reaction, not a conscious manipulation. In theory, the change makes feeding easier by showing people what they want."

She studied him with skepticism. "So, you have no control over it?"

"None, and it's more of an annoyance than an advantage."

"I understand why it's not useful, but how is it an annoyance?"

"Well, first, there are the questions." He cast her a pointed glance. "However, most people don't enjoy confronting their desires."

"What do you mean? How can the color—"

After stopping at a red light, he interrupted her with a stern frown. "Whose eye color did you see before Luminita arrived? It freaked you out, so I'm assuming…Gregor's? Am I right?"

She swallowed hard on the fresh lump of anger in her throat. Although the memory made her blood boil, he wasn't wrong.

"I'm not trying to poke at wounds, Lilith. Honestly, I would never deliberately choose to show you that. It's cruel. But at that moment, you wanted to see his eyes more than anything else. There are plenty of reasons to be angry at me, but that isn't one. I know all too well what it's like to lose loved ones."

Nothing but genuine sorrow filled his voice, and for once, she couldn't bring herself to doubt his sincerity. A million unsaid things hung in the air, making her realize one simple thing—she knew nothing about Cohen and his real life.

Rose of Jericho

The moment stretched out in odd silence while she searched for something to say. The light turned green, and the car rolled into the intersection as she finally opened her mouth.

"I understand, Andrew, and I believe you. We need to work together to escape this mess. None of this is easy...but for now, I accept your ap—"

Before she finished her sentence, the night exploded in screeching metal and shattering glass. The car lurched sideways violently, tires squealing. Screams filled the air as Lilith's stomach twisted in fear. Then her head slammed into the window frame, and everything went black.

Chapter 10

The shriek of a blaring horn rattled in Lilith's throbbing head like a bull kicking her skull while she opened her eyes. Her shaky fingers reached up, tentatively touching the right side of her head until she winced. After pulling her hand back, she stared at the blood covering her fingers while her mind scrambled to make sense of what had happened.

The pungent odor of Chinese food flooded her nose as she peered at the random chicken, noodles, and rice plastered across the car. Then her eyes drifted to the driver's seat. Cohen sat slumped over the steering wheel, which explained the unrelenting horn, and blood trickled from his swollen nose.

A sudden stabbing pain in her right arm made her glance back with a confused frown. The entire passenger door crumpled in against her. Then her gaze moved to the shattered window, and she spotted the black SUV that T-boned them in the intersection.

Of course. What else would bad guys drive? Recent events made a simple accident highly unlikely. *What next? More SWAT-style henchmen with guns?*

Lilith blinked, trying to clear her blurry vision as the SUV doors swung open. Four men, dressed in black, complete with ski masks, stumbled out carrying assault rifles. She immediately thought the sight was a concussion-induced hallucination. It couldn't be real. Nothing like that happened outside of Hollywood.

She shook her head, trying to clear the delusion, a huge mistake. The dizzying pain made her gasp as she fought to stay conscious.

When she opened her eyes again, the men began their approach, circling the car toward the driver's side, one of them limping. At least they didn't all escape the accident unscathed.

The realization brought a sudden sense of reality as everything clicked into place and sent her heart racing. In a panic, she reached for her gun but found nothing inside her jacket. *Shit.* Not only did she forget to put on her holster, but the gun was in her forensics kit, which still sat on the hotel room table. From now on, she wasn't going anywhere without a weapon, not even to the stupid vending machine.

Lilith threw off her seatbelt and shook Cohen, while panic burned in her lungs. "Wake up! Shit!" He flopped against the door, which stopped the blaring horn, but didn't wake him.

Her eyes darted up, peering through the cracked windshield to see three men. While they formed a semi-circle about 5 yards out and came to a halt, the fourth assailant hung back with a phone to his ear as if waiting for orders. *Why aren't they attacking? Why wait?*

With a growl of anger, she slapped and shoved the demon, but he didn't even blink. She needed to do something *now*. Time was running out while the mercs milled around. She had to handle this herself. *Focus.*

Lilith grabbed Cohen's collar and pulled him closer, ignoring the bone-deep pain in her arm. She dug into his jacket, fishing around until she found his 9 mm. Once she felt its weight in her hand, the frantic energy humming along her frayed nerves began to dissipate.

"Okay. You have a weapon. Now, assess the situation before you do something stupid," she whispered to herself. She was outnumbered and outgunned. One wrong move and they'd turn her into Swiss cheese.

Thankfully, the crash turned the windshield and her window into panels of spiderweb-cracked glass. The henchmen couldn't see her clearly from their vantage points. Also, the colossal SUV embedded in the passenger side prevented them from grabbing her from behind and provided cover if she stayed low.

Two small car lots stood on either side of the intersection, both closed for the evening. However, she spotted peeping eyes from a yellow house on the left and people lingering by a tree line behind her.

Hopefully, a bystander called the cops, but she couldn't depend on the helpfulness of strangers, especially if the mercenaries opened fire— time to take things into her own hands.

With careful movements, she crept on top of Cohen's unconscious body to peek through the window. Her rapid pulse made the throbbing in her head almost unbearable as she calculated her dismal odds—four trained killers versus one forensic investigator who could hardly lift her right arm.

The mind-numbing stabs would make squeezing the trigger an accomplishment, much less hitting a target. Of course, shooting at them might escalate things, but what choice did she have?

She propped her wrist on Cohen's shoulder, using it to steady her shaking hand. As she drew in a deep breath, two men came into view. Her focus narrowed in on them, waiting until they moved closer to each other, which would lessen the time required to re-aim after the first shot.

"I'm flattered..." Cohen's groggy voice nearly startled her into firing. "...but I think your bodyguard would remove my spine if we made out."

While trying to tame her erratic heartbeat, she shut her eyes and cursed. "Shit. You scared the hell out of me."

"Sorry, but why are you on top of me?"

Lilith held up a finger, requesting a moment to catch her breath. Eventually, the pounding in her head decreased as her pulse returned to a normal rhythm.

When she glared at him, she faced hazel eyes flecked with green— Chance's eyes. After Cohen's confession, the sight caught her off guard but didn't surprise her. Even if she dismissed the life-threatening circumstances, she wanted Chance with her, not the motive-shifting demon.

"Four men armed with assault rifles are circling outside, dressed in black with ski masks. Friends of yours?"

Although defensive anger tightened his eyes, he borrowed a move out of her playbook and deflected the question with humor. "You know I don't have friends."

"Well, you better grab your backup weapon, then. I borrowed the other one."

Without skipping a beat, he nodded and bent to slide the pistol from his ankle holster. "Since I can't move, can you tell me where they are?"

"You can't move?" She frowned in confusion and scanned him for injuries. The man reached for his gun without a problem, and the SUV plowed into *her* side of the vehicle. He couldn't be *that* hurt.

Cohen rolled his eyes and grinned, a somewhat disquieting expression of playfulness that didn't suit her image of him. "I can't move because you're on top of me, not that I'm complaining." He flashed a smile full of the same southern charm from when they'd first met.

She wrinkled her nose in disgust but ultimately chose not to comment, since their lives were in imminent danger. Assuming they survived, she could throw a right hook at him later.

"I can see two of them from here, but I don't know where the others went."

"Can you take them both down?" Cohen adopted a calm, business-like tone that surprisingly soothed her rattled nerves. She nodded briefly. "Good. Don't worry about the others. If we can't see them, they can't see us. Once you have them lined up, take the shots."

After a steadying breath, she squeezed the trigger, hitting the first man in the chest—a collapsed lung, enough to keep him down. She ignored the burning pain in her arm and readjusted, taking aim at the second target.

The man raised his assault rifle. Before he popped off a shot, she squeezed the trigger again. The bullet ripped through his throat, sending him to his knees as he gagged on the blood.

Then, the rear window exploded in a hail of bullets, quickly drowning out her shocked screams. She sank lower and buried her face in Cohen's chest, covering her ears as bullets whizzed by. Cohen raised his arm, squeezing off a shot before shouting instructions over the deafening noise.

"Stay low and scoot over to your seat."

Obediently, she inched back as bullets continued to tear through the car like a tornado of shrapnel and glass. Fluffs of shredded upholstery went flying as she crawled into the floor space and curled up, shaking with fear.

Then, somewhere beyond the overwhelming roar of assault rifles, she heard sirens. *Thank god for good Samaritans.* They only needed to hang on a little longer.

Cohen creaked his door open and rolled to the ground before shimmying under the vehicle—a reasonably intelligent plan. A few seconds later, the endless blaze of bullets came to an abrupt halt as a shriek ripped through the air. Another shot fired, and then the sudden silence rang painfully in her ears as she tried to slow her racing pulse. At least she still had one.

With a sigh of relief, she climbed off the floor to collapse against the crumpled door, closing her eyes. It was all over. Apparently, they didn't need latex suits and badass ninja skills to survive a movie-style assassination attempt.

"Lilith!" Cohen yelled her name seconds before a hand grabbed her hair. She screamed as someone tried to pull her through the window. Without another thought, she raised the gun and blindly shot behind her. Blood splattered everywhere, and the man's hand fell away, followed by a thud on the SUV's hood.

After that, the only sound she heard was the wild beating of her heart. She slumped into the seat, fighting for air past the terrified lump lodged in her throat. Her nerves couldn't take much more of this crap.

Then, Cohen suddenly appeared at the opposite window, panting as his hands slapped the roof. "Are you okay?!"

She jumped, instinctively balling her hands into fists. "Damn it! Enough jump scares! Yes, yes, I'm fine! I thought they were all down."

He leaned in, offering to help, but she slapped his hand away with a scowl. "I said I'm fine." However, as soon as she put weight on her right arm, it crumpled, sending her face-first into the armrest with a muffled scream.

After opening the door, he watched in amusement as she stubbornly re-adjusted to use her uninjured arm. Once she scooted across the car, she finally stumbled out onto the pavement. He automatically moved to steady her, but she shoved him back.

"Damn it! I'm fine. Can the white knight shit. It doesn't fit your personality." The words emerged far more venomous than she had intended. "Sorry. You didn't do anything wrong. You're just…a convenient target." The past two days turned her into an enormous ball of continuously displaced anger.

Despite her brusque apology, his face returned to the familiar impassive mask while he stared down the street. "The police will be here any second. There's no avoiding it." He turned to scan the area. "We have an audience…there at the yellow house…and over by the Thai place."

"Yeah, I spotted a few people earlier. One of them must have called 9-1-1."

His brow furrowed, as if something only now occurred to him. "They had to know someone would call when they slammed into us. So, if they knew they had limited time, why hesitate?"

Lilith leaned against the wrecked car, rubbing at her arm as blinding pain ran down to her fingertips. "The guy in charge spoke to someone on the phone while the others maintained a holding pattern.

They didn't make a move until I fired the first shot." Her thought progression ground to a halt as her jumbled brain throbbed again.

"The guy who crawled on the hood could have shot you before I saw him. Instead, he tried to drag you through the window. Why?" While talking things out, he paced beside the destroyed rental, occasionally glancing over at her, expecting input.

"Perhaps for leverage to lure Chance? Perhaps they hesitated because he wasn't with us."

"But they had to know that. Unless they followed us from the hotel, they wouldn't have known where to strike."

"The hotel...Chance!" A sudden sinking sensation crashed over her as panic tingled up her spine. She frantically fished out her burner cell and dialed the number for the Clarion. "Room 105." She waited impatiently, every second stretching into an excruciating eternity, each ring making her heart sink deeper.

"There's no answer!" She slammed both hands on the bullet-riddled roof—not the most brilliant move. Sharp, searing pain raced up her arm, forcing a strangled scream from her lips.

"Hey! Calm down!" Cohen moved to grab her but stopped at the last second. He was learning not to invade her personal space... finally. "Don't panic. He could be in the bathroom or at the vending machine. Pull it together. The cops are going to ask questions."

She huffed impatiently as the pain receded. "What are we going to tell them? Anonymous henchmen are a normal job hazard for us? That they can't arrest us for murder because a group of clandestine demons needs us to find a magic book that my uncle wrote six hundred years ago?"

Cohen glared at her as he wiped the blood from his nose. "Very cute, and please stop calling us demons—*Durand* is the official term."

"Durand?" she muttered while rolling her eyes. "Another French word, I assume? Both you and Chance are driving me crazy with this crap."

"Plenty of people speak French, Lilith, and it's not like we're a public species. They aren't making heartthrob films about us in Hollywood. *Le Durand, Il Duraturo, Durandus, Durándi, or The Enduring* in English...they are all traditional names among our kind. But the French translation has been the preferred term since the first century. Or you could just call me Andrew, but I'm not a fucking demon."

"The Enduring? That's a little arrogant, isn't it?"

Rose of Jericho

After a piercing glare, he dropped the subject. "As for the cops, we know nothing. We have no idea why anyone would want to attack us. We are fellow law-enforcement personnel, and we have at least one witness. They won't charge us. It's clear self-defense. They'll have our injuries checked out and ask us for a statement."

"I need to get back to the hotel now! I can't sit here playing twenty questions. If they got to Chance…"

"Stop. I know you're worried, but he's a tough guy. We took down four heavily armed guys after they slammed an SUV into our car. I think…"

While he rattled out a line of reasoning, she recounted the events in her head. She took down two. Cohen shot toward the passenger side before dropping another behind the car. Then, she killed the man who grabbed her through the window. "Wait. Didn't you take down two? That would make five…"

"Uh, no. When I rolled under the car, I shot the guy spraying bullets in the ankle. Once he hit the ground, I shot him in the head."

"So, I took down three to your one?" She couldn't help but revel in a temporary sense of smug satisfaction.

"Yeah, yeah. You're a badass, Kate Beckinsale. My point is, I'm reasonably sure Chance can handle whatever these guys throw at him. The police will insist on a statement, so you have no choice. If you play ball, perhaps we can get an officer to drive you to the hotel. I can wrap things up here and pick up dinner since our Chinese food exploded. I'll meet up with you two afterward."

Forming a concrete plan eased her panic a little. Once she made it through the gauntlet of questions, she could haul ass back to the room. Besides, Cohen had a valid point. Chance possessed the skills and training to handle a death squad, but it didn't stop her heart from flip-flopping in a nauseating fashion.

Cohen stepped back, inspecting the rental vehicle, its frame twisted around the front of the black Escalade, riddled with more holes than Swiss cheese. "I should have opted for the insurance."

The random statement existed so far down their priority list that she couldn't help but laugh. "To hell with it. It's on the council's dime. Next time, upgrade to a sporty number. Actually, considering how many people want to kill us, rent a damn armored truck."

They both broke into semi-hysterical laughter as five police cruisers and two ambulances pulled up to the scene, bringing their time for mental breakdowns to an end. They had parts to play, although the role of the clueless victim required little acting.

Calamity quickly descended upon them, with forensic photographers, lab techs, and investigators milling around the area. The cops circled with caution tape, securing the perimeter from the growing crowd. Apparently, their car crash and the ensuing gun fight were the neighborhood's chaotic entertainment for the night.

Soon, hundreds of yellow tags littered the asphalt, a startlingly unfamiliar sight. Although her job consisted of investigating crime scenes, she worked alone and always vanished before the buzzing onslaught of activity. She stood to the side, allowing everyone space to work, and waited for someone to take her statement.

Anxiety burned over her skin as she glared down at her phone, which refused to ring. Finally, a vaguely familiar cop escorted her to an ambulance. She peered at him as they walked, trying to place him, but it took her jumbled brain a few minutes to remember him from the morgue.

While the EMT cleaned her head wound, the officer flipped open his pad and began taking notes. She stuck to the facts, emphasizing that she had no idea who the men were or why they would attack them. She repeated the shooting sequence several times before he appeared satisfied.

The entire time, she gripped the burner cell, praying for it to ring. Why wasn't he calling her back? What if he was hurt? The sight of him bleeding to death in Phipps Bend flashed through her mind, momentarily distracting her. *Damn it. Focus.*

When she tried to block out the spiraling thoughts and concentrate on the cop's questions, the intrusive rambling slithered back under her skin, tightening her chest with every passing second. She had to leave… soon.

Once the cop moved on to Cohen, Lilith let the EMT finish wrapping her right arm while she tapped her foot impatiently. When he pulled out an arm sling, she tried to bolt, but he made her sign an AMA form stating she refused recommended treatment before he allowed her to leave.

By the time she escaped, Detective Blaire arrived. She released a weary sigh as he pushed his wire-rimmed glasses up his nose and surveyed the scene with his hands on his hips. Their lack of rapport wasn't the only reason his presence irritated her. More questions meant more time until they let her leave.

Rose of Jericho

Blair compared notes with the officer, who took their statements while Lilith studied them. The detective's hand hung loosely at his side while they talked but clenched into a fist when he glanced at the SUV and bodies. The tension in his arm disappeared as his gaze drifted to the ambulances. He didn't suspect them of anything, reserving his judgment for the hitmen.

Once she felt confident of the situation, Lilith strolled toward Blaire as she redialed the hotel number. The desk clerk put the call through to their room, but it only rang with no answer. *Dammit. Where the hell is he?* She swallowed hard on the rising bubble of panic threatening to send her into a tailspin. *Come on, Lilith. Get it together.*

Cohen was right. Dozens of mundane reasons existed not to answer a phone. Still, she couldn't help but jump to worst-case scenarios. What if another team went after him? What if they had already killed him or started torturing him? Her lungs burned with a desperate need to leave. *Now.*

The detective spotted her approach and ambled forward to meet her. The man's prominent wrinkles seemed deeper than earlier. Of course, a professional assassination attempt on consulting investigators tended to increase one's stress levels.

"Miss Adams. I'm very relieved you and Detective Cohen are alright." His voice sounded softer and more pleasant than earlier. Perhaps she dismissed him too hastily at the morgue.

"Thank you, Detective." Cohen flashed a smile as he stepped up beside her. "We took advantage of their momentary disorganization. I only wish we knew more."

Blaire shoved his glasses up the bridge of his nose again and nodded. "We'll figure out who arranged this." Although he attempted to appear resolute, the minuscule shrug of one shoulder and the twitches around his mouth as he took a step back betrayed his lack of confidence.

It didn't matter if Blaire was an exceptional sleuth. He would never crack this case. After pulling on a reassuring smile, she lied through her teeth. "I'm sure you will." *Okay. Time to change the subject.*

"Could I ask you a favor? Our security expert, Mr. Deveraux, stayed behind at the hotel while we picked up dinner. He hasn't answered his phone, and I'm worried that someone sent others to...deal with him."

"Yes, could a uniformed officer drive Miss Adams to the hotel? I will stay behind and help in any way I can." Cohen took over, most likely because he sensed her struggle to control the panic rising in her chest. For once, she truly appreciated his help.

"Of course." Blaire immediately turned to call over the policeman who took her statement. "Tramble, escort Miss. Adams to her hotel and back her up if there's any trouble."

"Thank you, Detective Blaire." Before she took off, she glanced back at Cohen, hesitating.

"Go. I've got this."

She mouthed *thank you* before jogging after Tramble.

Seconds later, they sped off in the officer's cruiser, heading toward the Clarion hotel with sirens and lights blazing. The closer they got, the more anxious she became, until her heart pounded in her throat.

Officer Tramble killed the sirens a block away so he wouldn't alert the enemy. Then he pulled into the lot, parked two doors down from her room, and handed her his service revolver.

"In case you need it. I'll back you up." He nodded and exited the vehicle while she did the same. As he pulled out a shotgun and gingerly closed the trunk, she spotted flickering lights through the sheer curtains—fire.

Terror stole her breath as all sense of logic evaporated. Images of the Marriott inferno rushed through her mind—shrieks of soot-covered people in search of family members, emergency personnel barking orders, twelve stories of raging flames, explosions of glass.

Dammit. No! She couldn't lose another person in her life.

While she rushed forward, the cop put his back to the wall and nodded to her, bringing some semblance of order back to her rattled brain. With a steadying breath, she took her position on the opposite side and clicked off the gun's safety. Her right arm blazed with agony as her fingers tightened around the grip, but she ignored the sharp throbbing.

The man held a finger to his lips and leaned in to listen. She hovered with her ear near the hollow door but couldn't hear anyone inside.

When he finally gave the go-ahead signal, she exhaled slowly, turned, and kicked the door. They rushed inside, guns drawn, scanning every inch. Lilith's mouth dropped as the gun quickly fell to her side. Of all the scenarios she imagined, *this* one never occurred to her.

Chapter 11

Chance jumped to his feet in shock with a lighter in his hand as they burst in, guns drawn. The guilt of being caught red-handed made his cheeks immediately blush bright red. Tea lights littered every flat surface in the room like a scene from the sappy movies that made Lilith dry heave. Her face turned crimson in absolute embarrassment as she became painfully aware of the policeman behind her. With her jaw clenched tight, she turned to Officer Tramble and shoved the gun into his hand.

"I am so sorry I wasted your time. Thank you for your assistance, but *apparently*, Mr. Deveraux is fine…for now." Her glare swung to Chance with an intense fury that burned hotter than the tea lights. "He just doesn't know how to *answer his phone.*"

Tramble nodded while he holstered his weapon and tucked the shotgun under his arm. To his credit, the man maintained a straight face out of professional courtesy. However, the amusement in his eyes left no doubt that this scene would be the talk of the station for the next five years.

"Well, if you are both safe, I'll return to the scene." He nodded again, flashed a humorous grin at Chance that clearly said *good luck*, and strolled through the open door.

"The scene?" Chance moved forward, but she held up a hand, stopping him short. His bewilderment quickly transformed into concern as the bruising, ripped clothes, bandages, and blood finally registered.

"Thank you, Officer Tramble." Lilith turned to ensure he safely reached his cruiser, taking her time. As the vehicle pulled out of the hotel parking lot, she reluctantly walked into the room and locked the door. Then she rested her aching forehead against it, trying to organize her conflicting emotions. Although a small part of her found the romantic gesture moving, despite the strong resemblance to a Nicholas Sparks novel, the rest of her writhed in overwhelming fury.

Not only was she mad at him for not answering the phone or calling back, but some irrational piece of her was furious that while she fought for her life with *Cohen* as backup, Chance was playing Romeo with a hundred candles.

She realized her outrage wasn't entirely fair. He couldn't have predicted the assassination attempt. The man wasn't psychic. Still, despite the logical rhetoric, her anger burned like the hot embers of a threatening forest fire, ready to consume them both.

"I'm sorry I didn't see your call. I ran down to the corner store. What happened?" Chance's voice shook with uncertainty and barely contained anxiety. "Are you alright?" She felt him behind her, his warmth soaking into her skin, which caused a sudden desire to lean back into him, regardless of her seething fury. *Damn him for having this effect on me.*

Of course, her father called her stubborn for a reason. No, her father *used* to call her stubborn. Forcing herself to change the tense only inflamed her anger, overpowering her desire to touch him.

She turned on her heel and stared him down. The door was at her back, and the handsome man hovered inches from her, but she shoved the hormones away. At the moment, her arousal was as welcome as a Mormon at Mardi gras.

"What the hell is all this, Chance?" He shrank back a step or two as his cheeks flushed. Confusion and frustration pinched his face, and he raked a hand through his hair, struggling to find the right words.

Something inside her snapped.

"I am not Sonja, or Michelle, or Becca, or Lila…" His eyes jumped to her sharply as she began ticking off the names on last month's dance card. "Dammit, Chance. I'm not some insecure bimbo who relies on showy romantic shit to bolster my self-worth. Is this what you think I care about, fucking candles?"

"Lilith, that is not…" He stepped forward, jaw clenched, as his hazel eyes burned with defensive pride.

"Then, what is it? Do you honestly think you have anything left to prove? After all the shit we've endured? If you truly want a shot with me, covering the place in a thousand tea lights in some insincere fucking gesture is *not* the way to go."

"That's not what this is. Fuck. I know who you are...who we are to each other...or at least I thought I did. After everything that's happened ...Alvarez, Gregor...I wanted to do something and give you a relaxing night. That's all!" He huffed at the slightly shocked and repentant expression on her face. "Guess I missed the mark by a fucking mile."

The words hit her like a face full of ice water, and she sank back against the door, feeling about an inch tall. She didn't know what to think, much less say. Her mind was a jumbled mess of stress and panic. Once upon a time, the world made sense to her. *What the hell happened? How do I do any of this?*

When she finally glanced up, he stood in the center of the room with his arms crossed, waiting for her to say something. "Shit." After a slow exhale, she wrangled her chaotic thoughts into a response. "I'm sorry for biting your head off. It's...beautiful, really." *That's the best I can come up with? No wonder I've been single for so long. God dammit.*

He snorted an indignant laugh while his fingers raked through his shaggy chestnut hair again. "Forget it. It was a stupid idea."

"No." The pain in his expression cut her to the core, and all she wanted to do was wipe it away. "Honestly, I'm sorry, Chance."

He nodded, acknowledging her apology as a vacant mask covered his disappointment. "Just tell me what happened."

She sighed softly, wishing she could undo the last five minutes. "An Escalade full of men with assault rifles T-boned the car and tried to turn us into Swiss cheese." She couldn't handle seeing his reaction, so she strolled past him to the table and blew out the tea lights on top of her kit. After popping open the case, she dug out her handgun. After the evening's fun-filled firefight, she wasn't willing to go unarmed anymore.

"Holy shit. Farren's men?" At first blush, the question seemed valid, considering the man's penchant for hiring anonymous henchmen to do his dirty work.

"I'm not sure. They weren't as organized as his usual flunkies, and their gear wasn't the same." Lilith slid the pistol into her shoulder holster and placed it on the nightstand while she considered all the implications. *Could Farren be behind the hit, altering his M.O. to throw off suspicion? No.*

"Killing us is counterproductive, considering he wants us to find this book."

"Are you okay?"

Lilith shrugged as she wandered across the room. "I have a killer headache and a hell of a bruise on my right arm, but I'll live."

"What about Cohen? Is he..." A faint trace of hopefulness lingered in his tone, which wasn't surprising.

"He's fine. He's still at the scene answering questions."

She froze as his hands slid over her shoulders, and relief rippled in their wake. When his lips brushed her neck, the noise in her head dulled to a soft roar. She had zero desire to fight with him anymore, especially over her stupid insecurities and irrational outbursts.

She couldn't explain why the candles prompted sudden suspicion or made things between them feel less sincere. Perhaps the thoughtfulness scared her into acting out of fear. In her limited experience, grand gestures always echoed an apology for dark deeds. *Chance is not David*, she reminded herself for the hundredth time.

She hated that the man was somehow still her measuring stick, a fucked up and twisted one, but still. After nearly a decade, she continued to compare every relationship to that dark train wreck, waiting for the shoe to drop.

"Jesus, Lily. I'm sorry. I should have been there. I didn't think..." His voice startled her out of her introspective thoughts.

"How could you know? Food poisoning is an expected risk with Chinese takeout, not a death squad. To be honest, I think you saved our lives by staying behind." She turned to see a bewildered expression furrowing his brow. "The men hesitated, waiting for orders. I think it's because you weren't in the car." Then she leaned her forehead against his chest with a heavy sigh as all her anger evaporated, leaving her exhausted. "I swear, Chance. Two car accidents in as many weeks."

"I'm sorry, *mon cherie*." He brushed a blood-crusted strand of hair from her face as a shadow flickered behind his eyes. Before she could wrap her mind around it, he shut down. "Let me grab the first aid kit, and you can break it all down..."

He pulled away, but she reached out and lightly grabbed his arm. "I'm fine. The EMS already patched me up, and all I really want is a long, hot shower." With a reassuring smile, her fingers fell away, and she stepped toward the bathroom.

"You are not fine, Lily."

She stopped halfway to her destination as a weak smile tugged at her lips. "No, but I will be."

His eyebrow lifted as his arms crossed his chest, clearly unconvinced. "There's something else bothering you, and it's not about the candles."

She drew in a shaky breath and exhaled slowly as her mind rattled to a stop on one thing. "I thought they sent someone here. If they knew where we were staying... Then, when I called, and you didn't answer..." She swallowed her lingering anger, and the fear returned, filling her eyes with tears. "I'm just glad you're okay, Chance."

Disbelief broke through his business-like facade. Her genuine concern for his safety confounded him. It wasn't logical confusion, more like an ingrained, instinctual surprise that someone cared about his well-being because no one ever had. Then it vanished, swallowed down into the dark depths of his scarred psyche.

"I'm sorry, *mon petite cherie.*"

"I was so damned worried that I nearly rattled out of my skin. When I saw the flickering light through the curtain..." She kept her voice from breaking but couldn't finish the sentence as tears trickled down her cheeks. The adrenaline was gone, leaving her raw and off-balance, struggling to find a foothold like a rock climber in a mudslide. "I can't lose you. You're literally all I have left." Her voice shook as her gaze fell to the carpet, overcome with fear and hopelessness.

Silently, Chance stalked up to her. His powerful hands sank into her hair, and he angled her face up toward him. Then, his lips crashed against hers with a bittersweet hunger, stealing her breath. After a moment of shocked paralysis, her arms slid around him, clinging to the intoxicating rush that made her head spin, and let the sudden heat burn away her doubts.

His lips brushed against hers in a feather-light caress, and the sudden wildfire dimmed to smoldering embers while his hands moved down her neck to her shoulders. *Well, that knocked all the conflicting stuff right out of my head and reduced it to ash.*

Reluctantly, she stepped back, her eyes lingering on his chiseled jaw and inviting lips. "You..." She released a slow, steadying breath as her mind reeled from the steamy kiss. "I need a shower." The unexpected words escaped in a disappointed sigh.

As much as she wished to forget the world and hide in bed with him, she needed to wash away the evening more. Blood and tissue coated her hair in a crusty texture, and sticky splatters adhered to her skin once again. *I should be used to it by now. Ridiculously sad but true.*

When she turned around, heading for the bathroom, he lightly gripped her left arm. She tried not to frown, but her head pounded with irritation. A weary sigh escaped. "Chance, please…I'm covered in blood."

Before she said anything else, he scooped her up as if she weighed no more than a China doll and carried her into the bathroom. Once he carefully set her on the counter, he wandered toward the shower and started the water. Despite the exhaustion weighing her down, she smiled as he tested the temperature.

Then he stepped away, padding across the tile floor until he stood in front of her again. To her surprise, his eyes never met hers. Instead, he focused all his attention on removing the butterfly bandage on her temple. She merely watched him, hypnotized by the methodical movements.

He still avoided her gaze when his hands slid over her shoulders, carefully pushing off her suit jacket and letting it fall onto the countertop.

"Chance, this is incredibly sweet, but…" He pressed a finger against her lips, cutting her off, and his eyes finally rose to hers. The quiet seriousness in them was a far cry from the lusty urgency in the kiss they'd shared.

Suddenly, the moment terrified her. Sure, he had claimed to hold a decade-old torch, but all too often, fantasies didn't live up to reality. *An incredibly hot moment in an alley is one thing, but this?*

The way his eyes lit up made her feel ridiculous for bringing up his checkered past. He didn't consider her a fling. This all meant more to him than she could fully comprehend, and *that* was what scared her.

Then he broke eye contact to focus on his fingers, moving nimbly from one button of her blouse to the next. He took his time peeling off the satin blouse and winced when he revealed the black and purple bruise dominating most of her upper right arm.

"It's okay. Just bruised," she reassured him.

After a silent nod, he continued, and by the time he slid her shirt off and tossed it over his shoulder, the unfamiliar intimacy made her entire body blush.

His breath rushed over her neck as he leaned in to unclasp her bra. She sat perfectly still, all too aware of how close he was. His calm movements directly opposed the alley in Tennessee. This wasn't a mad rush of hormones compelling them to tear off each other's clothes. His hands moved purposefully, tenderly, the fingertips caressing her skin as if she were composed of the finest porcelain.

When he unfastened the last hook and gently pulled the straps down her arms, the intense weight of his gaze made her avert her eyes. She fought the impulse to cover her breasts as fear and insecurity buzzed under her skin. Instead, she gripped the counter, kept her eyes focused on his black t-shirt, and struggled to breathe.

"*Mon petite cherie…*" His finger curled under her chin, slowly lifting her face until their eyes met. "You are beautiful as you are." His warm breath washed over her cheek before his lips gingerly touched the flushed skin. Then he stood back and held out his hand.

When Lilith took it, she let her shoes fall and slid off the counter, watching his tranquil face the entire time. A slight uptake in his breathing betrayed a strong desire, but his restraint meant more than the abrupt lust from the alley. Every moment displayed one clear purpose—to express how badly he wanted to take care of her.

His warm fingertips traveled over her stomach, leaving a trail of shivers before the whir of the skirt's zipper echoed off the tiled walls. Her heart pounded with nervous tension when his palms caressed her hips. Then he crouched down and ever so slowly pushed the fabric down until it pooled around her ankles.

For a moment, she forgot to breathe, the cool air tickling her bare skin as she stood there, exposed, naked, and vulnerable with Chance kneeling in front of her. For a fraction of a second, an irrational fear of rejection roared through her brain.

Chance gazed up at her, his eyes shining with deep adoration. All her skepticism seemed utterly ridiculous now.

His palms glided up her legs in a slow, luxurious caress. The man's calm composure briefly broke, and a smile curled his lips. When his hands reached her hips, he placed a delicate kiss on her stomach before rising to his feet.

Lilith stared up at him in absolute wonder, mesmerized by his gentleness. Part of her felt unworthy of such attention, but the fierce conviction in his hazel eyes refused to let the doubt take hold.

And I thought I'd lost him… All the panic and sorrow from earlier gripped her chest as she realized how much she loved him and how lost she'd be without him.

Fingertips brushed over her neck as he pulled her against his chest and wrapped his arms around her as if he knew her thoughts. "Shh, *cherie*. I'm right here." The tenderness broke the dam holding everything at bay, and she wept against his chest as the room filled with steam.

When the last tear rolled down her cheek, he wiped it away with a reassuring smile. "It's okay, *amour de ma vie*. We'll figure this all out. I love you and I won't stop fighting for that."

A warm smile spread across her lips as she witnessed the truth of his words reflected in his features. *He absolutely believes that. How could I have doubted him?*

Then, without warning, he picked her up again and carried her into the steamy shower, still dressed in his t-shirt and jeans.

"Chance! What are you doing?" She chuckled and grinned as he set her back on her feet with the hot water splashing against her back.

"You obviously aren't a candle kind of gal. You wanted a shower." A wide grin cracked his sober demeanor as he gently tilted her head back into the water.

Before she responded, he grabbed the shampoo and massaged it through her hair. The exhilarating sensation of his strong fingers instantly melted her stress, and her eyes fluttered closed as each movement lulled her into nirvana.

Once he rinsed the last of the shampoo from her auburn curls, she grabbed the front of his soaked t-shirt, ignoring the bone-deep pain in her arm, and pulled him closer. Their lips met in an excruciatingly tender kiss, filling her with a glow that reached deeper than she thought possible.

His palms cradled her face as his tongue caressed hers in dizzying circles that coaxed the embers of passion out of hiding. The need to touch his skin overwhelmed her, and she snatched the wet fabric, breaking the kiss to tug his shirt over his head. Then his lips crashed against hers as he moved forward, putting her back against the tile.

It wasn't an escape from grief that motivated them or a desperate need to feel alive. The moan that whispered against his lips when his hands slid down her slick body didn't stem from animalistic lust. Their genuine connection stemmed from something much deeper and utterly unknown to her.

His touch followed the water down her stomach and between her thighs as she leaned her head back against the tile, breathless. The teasing circles he drew made her hands tighten around his shoulders and sent a heady rush up her spine.

A mounting heat spread through her body, addictive and delicious, and she arched toward his fingers as his mouth found hers again. The pressure built as each wave of pleasure threatened to send her over the edge.

She broke the kiss with a panting moan, letting the water wash over her face as his teasing fingers drove her bliss to dizzying heights.

"Chance…" His name escaped in a mewling moan drenched in desire seconds before his lips grazed her nipple. Then his mouth claimed the sensitive flesh with a thunderous groan, and the world burst into vivid color. She dug her nails into his skin and clung to him as wave after wave crashed over her until a delirious scream tore from her throat.

When the last pulsating surge subsided, he hauled her up off her shaky legs and wrapped them around his waist. As she panted for breath with an intoxicated grin, she leaned her forehead against his.

"You definitely like showers more than candles." The low rumble of his voice sent a decadent shiver down her spine, but the words made her giggle as she opened her eyes.

She studied his face, memorizing every curve before placing a lingering kiss on his lips with a little growl of her own. When she leaned back against the tile, she grinned. "Candles have their place—"

He darted forward, interrupting her with a heated kiss that brought the heady rush right back. The sudden motion made her arms and legs tighten around him, holding on as his body moved against hers.

While he fought with his soaked jeans, the water suddenly turned icy cold. Her giggling scream echoed off the tile as they both scrambled out of the shower, laughing and shivering.

"I think the shower is trying to tell us something." She chuckled as Chance wrapped a towel around her shoulders and rubbed her arms with a luminous grin.

"That they need a larger water heater?"

"Actually, I think," Lilith started as she turned and walked toward the door. Then she peered over her shoulder at his confused expression and flashed a wicked grin. "…you should take off those pants before you become hypothermic."

His confusion evaporated as his lips tugged into a roguish smile. "Whatever you say, *mon petite cherie*."

Chapter 12

A knock echoed through the hotel room as Lilith tugged on some jeans and a *Dunder Mifflin* t-shirt. Chance peeked out from the bathroom, one hand loosely grasping a towel around his hips. When she glimpsed the lily tattoo below his navel, it brought a distracted smile to her lips.

For a second, she forgot about Farren, the puzzling bodies, Cohen, and even her father. Unfortunately, the persistent knocking woke her from the dream-like state.

"It's probably Cohen with dinner." A sudden ravenous hunger overcame her...for food this time. "I'll grab the door, but you may want to...put on some pants." She winked and sauntered off toward the door.

"Yes, Ma'am." Chance chuckled warmly, making her grin widen. "If that's what you *really* want."

She glanced over her shoulder and playfully narrowed her eyes, but warmth flushed her cheeks. "Necessity, smartass."

After swinging the door open, she ushered Cohen inside, but as soon as he entered the room, he came to an abrupt halt.

"Well, I guess Chance wasn't in mortal peril after all." A dark sarcasm saturated his voice, making the words sound hostile. "Thank you for the phone call, by the way. I also see he found a *practical* use for the emergency cash I gave him." He glared around the room at all the burned-out tea lights littering every surface, as if each one offended him.

Embarrassment burned across her face, making her defenses bristle. He had a right to be mad at her for not calling and at Chance for wasting money. But his bitter outrage felt disproportionate, and she had zero desire to discuss her romantic life with him.

"Please, by all means, come on in and make yourself comfy." After the muttered remark, she stopped herself and remembered how he had saved her life and helped her escape the circus to check on Chance. "Sorry. I should have called."

He stared her down, tight-lipped, with an expression as cold as Farren's. "That's the first thing you should have done. Instead, you found other ways to occupy your time." For a brief second, his nose scrunched as his top lip raised—a microexpression of disgust. The realization hit her like a slap in the face, more so than his clipped words.

Without a response, she turned on her heel and stalked away, fuming, as Cohen closed the door. After sinking into a chair at the table, she cut right to the chase.

"The gun-happy foot soldiers found our location some other way. If they followed us from the hotel, they would have known Chance stayed behind."

While she cleared away the tea light husks, the way he reacted kept nagging at her. Cohen was an exceptional liar who rarely showed emotions unless they served a purpose or ran deep, like his hatred of Farren. With his brief expression of disgust, neither of those reasons seemed to apply. It felt out of place...

Before she followed her thoughts down the rabbit hole, Cohen dropped the takeout bag on the table and collapsed into a seat with none of his usual grace.

"Unless they didn't give a shit about him." Cold hostility rang in his voice, making his words less of a statement and more of a personal attack. "If this is connected to the case, you and I are the only ones worth their time."

Men and their damn posturing. His disgusted sneer earlier probably revolved around Chance. She couldn't care less about Cohen's issue with him. It didn't involve her. Frankly, she thought Cohen was far too accustomed to getting his way.

Even if he didn't control his shifting eye color, he pulled on new personas and engineered situations to get *precisely* what he wanted. His confession about the holding cell made that point quite clear. Perhaps Chance's ability to see through his parade of crap merely ruffled his pompous feathers.

Before she could respond, Chance strolled out of the bathroom in a dry pair of jeans and a fresh t-shirt with all the grace of a satisfied jungle cat.

"*Or* they pinged the GPS built into the rental car. From what Lilith said, the hit sounded professional. Using the GPS makes more sense than tailing us. I doubt they'd risk being spotted." His eyes bored into Cohen's back as he struggled to contain his hostility and stay professional.

"While you two stopped to play house, I called Luminita." The demon continued as if no one had spoken. "Obviously, she wasn't thrilled about the attack. She thinks someone on the council wants to keep us from finding the book." The whole vibe in the room soured, becoming painfully awkward as she began unpacking dinner.

"You know, Chance made a valid point. If they tracked our GPS, it would explain why they hesitated."

Cohen only snorted in response with his jaw clenched on a tirade of angry words. As long as he remained in a stubborn state of rage, he wouldn't be any logical help. It clouded his vision, rendering him useless. Worse. His animosity would infect them all, and they'd accomplish nothing but pissing each other off.

With calm resolve, Lilith bagged his meal and handed it to him. "I need to make some calls. You should eat in your room." She fixed him with a steely stare that left no room for arguments. Of course, that didn't stop Cohen.

He glared at the suddenly offensive bag before raising his pale blue eyes to hers with anger churning in their depths. "Excuse me?"

She dropped the takeout in front of him and stood. "Your attitude is not constructive. Go cool down and eat your food. Maybe you'll be capable of a rational discussion in the morning. Currently, I'd like to focus on solving our problems, not finding out what bug crawled up your ass."

"Not constructive?" His eyebrows flew up in genuine surprise, waiting for a punchline that never came. "You're serious?"

When she nodded, he moved his sharp eyes to Chance as the muscles around his nose twitched in disgust. "You know what's *not constructive*? A billion tea lights in a fucking hotel room!" Then he turned back to her in bewilderment. "You can't tell me you aren't the slightest bit upset. While we fought for our lives, he was here trying to recreate some damn Harlequin book, for god's sake?! Doesn't that bother you?!"

"He isn't psychic. He couldn't have predicted…"

"Because the past week has been so uneventful?" Cohen rubbed his face with an exasperated huff. "*Pour l'amour de Dieu*, wake the fuck up! We are in the middle of an investigation that could condemn or free us. Now is *not* the time to indulge your fucking hormones."

"I am not having this discussion with you…" Lilith bristled until his icy stare targeted her with all the warmth and compassion of Farren's soulless eyes.

"Why do I bother wasting my time? You're a vortex of death. I should cut and run before you get me killed like everyone else around you."

The sense of camaraderie he had earned earlier vanished, undone by a vicious proclamation he could never unsay. Although his words cut to the bone, echoing her self-disparaging thoughts after Gregor's death, they somehow brought a calm stillness infused with strength.

"Walk away, Andrew."

He defiantly stared at her until the rage leaked from his eyes, as if realizing he had gone too far. The man made no attempt to apologize, however.

"Right." His aristocratic voice emerged flat and emotionless as he pushed away from the table. His eyes flicked over to Chance, who stood still in the center of the room. For once, the demon didn't add a smartass comment, trying to goad him into a fight. He'd already said plenty.

"Good night. Enjoy your dinner." Once again, he reminded her of Farren, his stoic voice sending a chill down her spine. Cohen straightened his tie, composing himself before he slipped out of the room and slammed the door behind him.

"I hate to admit it, but he was right about the candles." She turned on her heel, surprised by Chance's sudden confession. "This isn't the time for romantic gestures, but we finally had a few minutes to ourselves, and so much awfulness has plagued us recently. I wanted to…forget, even if we only had an hour." His fingers raked through his hair as he released a heavy sigh. "I got carried away trying to show there is more than death and mayhem connecting us."

She merely nodded, too conflicted with Cohen's words rattling around in her head.

"But he's not right about you. He'd either be an abomination or a corpse if you hadn't taken on Ashcroft."

When she still didn't speak up, he attempted to lighten the mood. "At least tell me I don't need to thank him for saving your life. I'm not sure I'm up to that."

She reclaimed a sliver of her old self and grinned at him in smug satisfaction. "Not really. I took down three of them myself."

Genuine surprise sent his eyebrows sky-high, which she found vaguely offensive. "Seriously?"

When she nodded, the disbelief transformed into a proud smile, easing her wounded pride.

"Well, look at you. Next thing you know, you'll be wearing a latex bodysuit." He flashed a leering smile, brimming with hope, as he took Cohen's empty seat at the table. "I wholeheartedly support the decision, for the record."

"Ha, ha. You wouldn't be so quick to suggest that if you'd ever taken one off." After settling back into her chair, she slid his food across the table and opened her peanut chicken to take a bite. *Delicious.* Most restaurants either made it too savory or too sweet, but the strip-mall place made it just right, which probably explained the long line.

"Wait. You've *actually* worn one?" All the humor drained from his face, and he paused with a crab rangoon halfway to his mouth.

She grinned like a bobcat and took another bite of her peanut chicken. "So, how's your food?"

"You didn't answer my question." She couldn't help but laugh at the expectant look on his face.

"You're right. I didn't." The sassy smile only made his petulant frown deepen as he dug into his General Tso's.

"The food's great. Now answer the question."

After playfully rolling her eyes, she set her fork down. "My freshman year at UCLA, I got roped into a themed Halloween party—Heroes and Villains. It was the first and last time I dressed up as Catwoman."

Chance nearly choked on his food as his eyes lit up with genuine amusement. "Michelle Pfeiffer or Halle Berry?"

Lilith arched an eyebrow and jabbed at her chicken. "Michelle Pfeiffer is the only one that counts." A soft smile curved her lips as a happy memory emerged from her chaotic mind. "Dad took me to see that film at the Westbury Drive-in over on Long Island before it closed."

"You know, I've never been to a Drive-in. I always wanted to, but they were pretty far away, and…" He stopped short, taking a quick bite of food to fill the ensuing silence.

"And what?"

"Well…" He scarfed down another rangoon, clearly buying time. When he finally spoke, his eyes stayed locked on his food while he pushed the fork around aimlessly. "No one goes to those places alone. The long drive followed by sitting in a car for two to four hours seemed too much like an actual date. All that pressure to get to know someone… It was just too intimate."

"Wait. So, you never took anyone on a serious date like a small road trip, a friend's wedding, a cooking class, none of that stuff?"

Chance bit his lip while a faint blush crept over his cheeks and shook his head.

"Wow. I mean, I always joked about you being a dog, but…"

He glanced up with a deepening frown, which held none of his usual humor. "I didn't see the point. There was only one person I wanted to do those things with, and I'm not fond of misleading people."

This time, her cheeks burned as she stole a spring roll from the center of the table. "Can I ask you a question?" Her eyes remained locked on the table as she picked at the roll's flaky exterior.

"Of course."

"Why me?" The words hung in the air until she finally met his eyes. "I mean over a decade… I just…how did I earn that?"

Chance stared across the table, dumbfounded. "You say that like you aren't special."

"I'm not, not really. I have the same problems as anyone…scratch that. My problems are ten times worse than most people's." Lilith moved her fork through the rice as her gaze fell to the plate.

"Things are awful right now, but I don't see you giving up. You could have left us to die in Phipps Bend to save yourself, but never once considered it. You don't give yourself enough credit."

"Okay…but why spend over ten years refusing to move on from the person you couldn't have? All the girls you *dated*, and you never gave any of them a serious chance?"

He set down his fork, gathered his thoughts, and finally met her inquisitive stare. "Do you remember my nineteenth birthday?"

Lilith frowned in thought. "No…" Then she realized she didn't know the month, much less a particular date. A rather embarrassing thing to admit about someone she loved.

A soft chuckle emerged as Chance smiled. "It's okay. I wouldn't expect you to remember. Your folks invited me over for dinner that night. When I got there, Rosaline was in the kitchen, cooking shepherd's pie while listening to the radio."

Lilith's eyes misted with tears at the mention of her late mother. It seemed like forever since anyone had talked about her.

"She said Gregor wanted to speak to me in his office, but when I grabbed the doorknob, I heard voices. You and Gregor were arguing about UCLA. It's funny. Your father always scared me, but there you were calmly cutting him down for being a *small-minded, over-protective asshole.*"

"Because I yelled at my dad?" Lilith raised an eyebrow in disbelief.

"It wasn't the whiny screams of a teenager throwing a tantrum because they didn't get their way. You were intelligent, brilliant, and fierce. I always loved that about you."

"And that's why?"

"No." A blush rushed over his cheeks as he stared at the table again. "A song came on the radio…The Police…*Every Little Thing She Does Is Magic.* The door to Gregor's office swung open as you stormed out, but then you caught sight of me standing just outside the door. All your anger disappeared in an instant, and when you smiled at me. It reached your eyes, made them glow. You walked up, hugged me, and said *Happy birthday, creeper. Stop eavesdropping.* Then you winked and went to help your mom in the kitchen."

His eyes lifted to hers as she sat there mystified. "That's when I knew I didn't want to settle for anything less, *mon cherie.*"

She had no idea what to say, but thankfully, he didn't appear to expect a response. They merely finished their dinner in a comfortable silence that settled around them like a worn-in blanket.

Once they finished eating, Lilith perched on the bed to check her voicemails while Chance stretched out his six-foot-three frame beside her and clicked through the local channels.

The first two voicemails featured Timothy's frantic voice asking the same litany of questions—"*Have you heard from Gregor? Where the hell are you? Is Chance with you? Why aren't you answering your phone? What is going on?"*

"Chance, while you were lighting candles, you did stop to call Timothy, right?"

When he didn't answer, she craned her neck to see him staring slack-jawed at the TV. She peered over at the screen and immediately understood why it held his rapt attention. He'd landed on a news report about the attempted assassination.

"Violent gang activity on the once safe streets of New Haven. A car crash and ensuing gunfight at the intersection of Dixwell Avenue and Treadwell Street rocked our quiet neighborhood tonight, leaving four dead. Let's go to Julia Palmer, who is on the scene with a News 8 WYNH exclusive."

"Thank you, Christopher. A few hours ago, a group of unidentified males T-boned the car of two out-of-state investigators and opened fire with automatic assault rifles, according to homicide detective Anthony Blaire. He confirmed that both investigators, who are currently assisting in an active police investigation on the Yale campus, escaped with minor injuries but were not available for comment. All four assailants were pronounced dead on the scene."

"Local resident, Yvonne Griffin, who lives in the house behind me, had this to say."

A woman in sky-blue scrubs with a smooth mocha complexion came on the screen, nervously smoothing her red-tipped hair. The shell-shocked expression on the poor woman's face spoke volumes.

"I have never seen anything so terrifying. I had my key in the door when I heard screeching tires. I turned around and saw that SUV slam into the car, so I immediately called 9-1-1. Then the men opened fire, and I dropped to the ground, yelling into the phone while bullets went flying. A few shots shattered my window! I thought I was a goner, but the gunshots ended before the police arrived. Those brave people from the car saved my life!"

"Thank you, Yvonne. As you can see, the assailant's vehicle collided with the victim's car at high speed, crushing the right side. Then, the men riddled the vehicle with hundreds, if not thousands, of rounds. One EMS stated it was a miracle the two victims survived at all."

Her eyes widened as the camera zoomed in on the damage. The reporter was right. The collision had thoroughly demolished the passenger side, and the stark images appeared far worse than she remembered. Hell, the crash alone should have killed her. Not much of the roof or trunk remained after the shootout. Even the sturdy metal frame sagged, decimated by the countless bullet holes.

After all the excitement, her urgent desire to leave and check on Chance had distracted her from focusing on the aftermath.

She quickly turned her back on the TV to face Chance as he stared at the screen in disbelief. The news segment shook her, but she saw no sense in rehashing things. Her arm still ached, but it would heal, and the gash in her scalp was already closed. She survived. She was fine.

"Hey."

Finally, his glazed eyes snapped over to her. "What's up?" The attempt to make his voice smooth and casual failed, revealing all his nervous energy.

"Did you call Timothy?"

"Uh, yeah, briefly." He closed his eyes for a moment, most likely trying to erase the annihilated rental car from his mind. "I told him we had things under control, that you and Gregor are fine, and I'd contact him soon. Then, I hung up."

She frowned, her head tilting to one side. He didn't need her to voice the question.

"There's no sense telling him Gregor is…well, anyway, he is more likely to keep his trap shut and stay put if he thinks everything is fine."

Keeping Tim in the dark felt fundamentally wrong, but Chance's logic made sense. They didn't need him running to their rescue or calling in the cavalry.

Chance returned to gawking at the TV as she moved on to the next message. An unfamiliar female voice with a distinct New York-Italian accent rumbled over the cheap speaker.

"This is Detective Nicci DeLuca. The captain pulled me from the 5th precinct and assigned me as your new liaison. The guys at the station filled me in on your current situation, and I wanted to send my condolences. I met Alvarez a few times. Good man. I grabbed all the files on his last case, so I'll go over them until I hear from you. Talk 'atcha later."

Although the woman sounded sincere, Lilith heard the understandable anxiety in her voice. Leaving a message on a grieving stranger's voicemail was tough enough. Replacing their recently deceased partner was even worse. Cops took the bond seriously, and if the woman spoke with Boyd, Detective DeLuca knew Lilith and Felipe were closer than most.

She skipped through two panicked messages from Timothy before listening to a monotonous voice rattle off a well-practiced script, one she'd heard a hundred times.

"Good afternoon. This is Barry from the 19th precinct forensics department. We came across some rather unusual samples involving case #529-821456 and sent them over to Solasta for further analysis. I forwarded the file to you and your new partner, Detective DeLuca."

Solasta, the lab Lilith worked for, featured an ultra-high-tech lab, and the NYPD frequently took advantage of their equipment, even when it wasn't vampire-related.

For a moment, Lilith racked her brain but didn't recognize the case number. It had to be something Alvarez worked on before he flew to Tennessee with Gregor. Whatever it was, it could wait.

After pressing the delete button, the robotic voice announced a saved message. She frowned in confusion, unable to recall saving a voicemail. It wasn't a habit of hers.

The moment her father's warm voice rattled through the speaker, tears sprang to her eyes, and her chest tightened.

"Lily, I'm heading to the airport, and I'll be back in New York in a few hours. I know you're hurt and angry, but please know that I love you, and that has never changed. From the moment you were born, you became the redeeming light of my life, my purpose for existing."

"I hope one day we can overcome the specter of my past and become closer. I realize I didn't react well to your new... relationship with Chance on top of everything else. He's an exceptional person, and lord knows he's carried such a bright torch for you all these years."

"Perhaps I never handled it well, as fathers are prone to do. However, the thought of you watching him wither away and die before your eyes broke my heart." A heavy sigh crackled over the line before he continued.

"Like any other father, I only want what's best for you. If he makes you happy, I will be here for you when the time comes. You were right. As much as it hurts to lose people, I wouldn't trade my time with Margareet or your mother for anything. I love you, my sweet Lily, and I want us to have dinner when I get back in town. Please, call me."

Lilith opened her mouth to respond until she remembered it was only a voicemail. For a moment, she forgot her father was dead, and her finger instinctively hovered over the call-back button.

Tears burned down her cheeks as the delusion evaporated and the harsh reality settled back in. She must have started the message last night before the funeral and pressed the save button when she heard his voice, unable to expend the emotional energy.

Then, the scene flashed in her mind—Gregor crumpled on the floor, blood trickling from the hole in his head, lifeless gray eyes staring out. The image overwhelmed her, making each breath a struggle until a wave of nausea sent her sprinting to the bathroom.

"Lily? What's wrong?" Chance grabbed at her wrist, but she dodged his grasp and rocketed into the bathroom, locking the door behind her. After ripping up the toilet lid, she hit the tile hard. Her stomach twisted into knots while Gregor's grotesque death looped in her head with vivid realism.

Distantly, her brain registered a soft tap on the door. "Lily? Are you okay?"

The unrelenting vision of Farren's bullet tearing through Gregor's head plagued her until she vomited, providing Chance a straightforward answer. By the time she purged everything from her system, her muscles ached from the effort.

Finally, the scene faded, and she curled up on the tile floor, letting the chilly surface soothe her burning skin. Hearing her father's voice hit her like a blow to the gut. But what had sent her over the edge was his desperation to fix things between them.

He wasn't blind to her feelings of betrayal, but he didn't want to lose his daughter to the ghosts of his past. Now, she could never reassure him, apologize, or tell him how much she loved him, and the guilt became overwhelming. Why did she have to be so stubborn? If she had answered the phone that night... he would still be dead.

Chance had been right about a lot of things. There was no perfect scenario where she could have saved him. Perhaps knowing she was powerless only made things worse. What if it happened again? What if she found herself in another impossible situation that cost Chance his life? What if the merciless world she found herself in took *everything* away?

Her mind dissolved into an endless torrent of worst-case scenarios, and Peisione's threat played a significant role in most of them. The onslaught of dark thoughts spiraled out of control, swirling around her like a wicked tornado of masochistic agony until her sobbing tears dripped onto the cold tile.

Something scraped softly over the door before Chance's voice rumbled from down low, snapping her out of the horrific delirium. She drew in deep breaths and slowly exhaled as she pictured him sitting on the floor with his back propped against the door.

"I miss him, too. Not being able to save him tears me apart. It's not only because I failed in my sworn duty, but because he was a great man. The work he did to promote our species, the way he loved you...

Knowing him made me a better man. He didn't only save me from that hospital in Louisiana. He taught me to rise above my past and overcome my demons. I never realized how personal those lessons were until that night in Tennessee."

She pressed her cheek into the cold tile, letting his tranquil voice lull her into a relaxed state. His choice of topic wasn't a coincidence. He probably listened to the voicemail, but his words transcended a hollow attempt to comfort her. He merely voiced his thoughts and feelings in a moment of shared grief.

"You know, my childhood was completely messed up. My parents were strung out on drugs most of my life. Even the rare moments they were sober weren't happy. They fought all the time, and my welfare never really occurred to them."

"After they died, I didn't fare much better in foster homes. The people who didn't want a punching bag were only interested in an easy payday. When I got sick, they dumped me in Our Lady of Lourdes in Lafayette. The staff was friendly at first, but the doctors struggled with a diagnosis, and they couldn't find any other facility willing to take a ward of the state with complex needs. When Gregor showed up, the whole place breathed a collective sigh of relief."

"Despite our occasional disagreements, your father was the opposite of everything I knew. He held you up on this pedestal and talked about you with such glowing pride. For years, that was my connection to you—his stories. If giving my life would have saved him, I would have gladly made the sacrifice, but I knew, perhaps better than anyone, that Gregor's only wish was to protect you at all costs. That's why he shot me down years ago. I will honor him by doing everything in my power to keep you safe. I loved him, too, *mon cherie*."

For a while, they stayed that way, Lilith lying on the bathroom floor while Chance sat outside. She couldn't see him, but she knew he was there. He never pushed her to open the door or prompted her to speak. He merely stayed close by in case she needed him.

Chapter 13

Somewhere in the dark, a phone rang.

Lilith threw out her hand, blindly feeling around for her cell. Answering calls in the middle of the night had become second nature after six years of working graveyard shifts. But when her fingers brushed against something wet and sticky on the nightstand, her sleepy brain struggled to understand why.

Did I spill something?

The tips bumped into a solid object, something warm and moist. Panic flared down her nerves with an instinctual recognition she couldn't comprehend. She frantically grasped for the lamp but couldn't find it. The once comforting darkness transformed into an oppressive weight as her hand fumbled over the slick surface.

From across the room, a weak, flickering light penetrated the suffocating blackness—flames. Her pulse quickened, and she glanced over apprehensively to see an office desk next to the bed.

What the hell? Where am I?

As the illumination grew, it revealed a vague shape on the table, causing Lilith to glance down at her trembling hand for some sort of clue. A horrible sense of dread blossomed in her chest as she realized the substance coating her fingers was thick, sticky blood. Terror vibrated down her spine when the pieces finally clicked into place. Her eyes shot back up to the desk as her brain finally made sense of the shape.

No!

Long blonde hair cascaded over the side, a horrifically familiar sight that sent her pulse racing. She sat there, frozen, knowing what she'd find if she stood up—her cousin's body mutilated by Ashcroft's vindictive hands.

Lilith tucked her knees under her chin and clamped her hands over her ears, attempting to block out the burgeoning nightmare. "Come on. Wake up! We buried Miriah in New York City. You attended her funeral! This isn't real!"

When nothing changed, she squeezed her eyes shut and screamed. After a few silent moments, she opened her eyes again, hoping to see the cheap hotel room, but still found herself in Miriah's office. Desperation clawed at her insides as tears flooded her eyes. Why did her brain continue to torment her? Hadn't she endured enough in the waking world?

While angrily wiping her cheeks, she noticed the shimmering blonde hair move. It was only a slight twitch at first. Her blood ran cold, paralyzed with fear, unable to look away. When the strands began to dance across the mahogany, receding over the edge, Lilith shook her head, vehemently refusing to take part in another night of mental torture.

"No! This is NOT real!"

No matter how hard she tried, she couldn't make it stop. The mangled cadaver continued to move, intent on serving its purpose.

"Please! Stop!" Lilith screeched the words, but the abomination slowly twisted to face her as sickening cracks and pops of tearing tendons and stretched ligaments punctuated each tiny movement.

Miriah's dissected face loomed closer, bringing with it the pungent stench of decomposing flesh. The lidless eyes rolled loosely in their sockets, the milky blue irises finally focusing on their target. Then, the shredded lips opened as the corpse attempted to speak, but only a ghastly rattle of bile-scented breath emerged, instantly souring Lilith's stomach.

The corpse's hand, a mass of flesh and shattered bones, reached toward her, the swollen skin splitting as dark brown drops of old blood soaked into the white comforter. She tried to move, back away, run, but couldn't. She sat there frozen as the weeping limb hovered closer and closer.

Then something hot scratched Lilith's shoulder, leaving a trail of burning welts in its wake. She shot off the bed, scrambling to escape another attack, but her bare feet slid on the wet floor. She thudded to the ground, knocking her head on the unforgiving concrete.

Rose of Jericho

For a moment, the world spun on its axis. Then, her eyes snapped into focus on Alvarez's lifeless face hovering above her, cloudy eyes staring intently. She gaped in horror as he loomed closer, the deep slash across his neck dripping hot splotches of blood onto her chest. His mouth opened and closed, trying to speak, until a gush of blood emerged, splashing over her face. Lilith screamed in horror as a surge of nausea crawled up her throat. She quickly scrambled backward, desperate to get away, and collided with something solid.

When Lilith whirled around, she saw the charred corpse of a man shackled to the concrete floor—Duncan. She was back in the Phipps Bend basement.

"You…left…me." The stench of burnt tissue accompanied the eerie croak of each word. The burnt remnants of his nostrils flared in disgust, cracking the surrounding skin to reveal the bloody muscle below.

"I had to…" The whispered words betrayed her gut-wrenching guilt. Her father had been right about rescuing Duncan from a life full of eternal anguish, but the man had deserved a merciful death. Instead, he'd burned beside the monster that took everything away from him.

"You didn't even *try* to save me! Selfish!"

His burnt hand reached for her with a crinkling sound as the charred, inflexible skin broke. She screamed with every ounce of remaining strength in a vain attempt to purge the blackness from her soul.

Why am I torturing myself? Why can't I wake—

Before the thought fully formed, someone hit her like a pile of bricks, knocking her back to the floor. Spencer's contorted face grinned at her with bloody teeth. He pinned her down, red-rimmed eyes manic with hate, as he slashed and punched. She screeched and tried to protect herself from the sudden barrage while warm droplets splattered her face. For a moment, she didn't realize where the blood came from, but then she spotted the fresh bullet wound in his head.

The scene from Goditha unfolded in her mind with one recurring image surging to the forefront—Chance standing over Spencer, the callous expression making his face almost unrecognizable as he pulled the trigger.

That picture left her with the same conflicting emotions she had experienced when her cousin died. If Chance suffered the same losses as her father had, would he fall victim to the same dark demons? Would he burn the world to avenge their deaths?

Spencer's corpse took advantage of her distracting thoughts and cracked her in the jaw. Throbbing pain spread across the entire side of her face like wildfire as spots danced across her field of vision.

Before she recovered, his fangs clicked into place, and he darted toward her, aiming for her exposed throat. Lilith squeezed her eyes shut, shrieking in panic, but nothing happened. The stabbing agony she expected never came.

When she opened her eyes, Spencer was gone, leaving her alone on the blood-soaked floor with only the flickering light for company.

"Wake up! Dammit! Just wake the fuck up!!!" Tears slid down her cheeks as she slapped them until her face stung, but nothing changed.

"Get up and stop sniveling." She instantly recognized the cold, contemptuous voice, which instilled a chilling sense of futility.

Farren's vicious face hovered inches away, with his calculating eyes piercing through her, exposing the agonizing guilt in her chest. A hideous smirk slanted his lips. Bony fingers dug into her arm, drawing a whimper of pain before he yanked Lilith to her unsteady feet.

"I will end you like I ended your father." Farren spoke the words with calm, emotionless precision while gripping her jaw. When he wrenched her face to the side, forcing her to stare down at Gregor's corpse, her eyes flooded with tears.

Overwhelming grief suffocated her as she stared at the oozing bullet wound in his head. This wasn't how she wanted to remember him, broken and lifeless. She endured enough torment without her screwed-up mind showing her all the things she never wanted to see again.

"No!" Lilith shrieked as she violently struggled against the nightmare's grip, but to no avail. "Come on! Wake up!" As hard as she fought, she couldn't break the dream's hold over her any more than she could escape the demon clutching her arm.

Farren snatched her face again, the nails digging into her cheeks, forcing her to watch as her father's corpse slid up the wall. Her stomach twisted in hateful knots as she tried to close her eyes, but her lids refused to obey.

She stood there, utterly powerless, hypnotized by the cadaver stumbling to its feet. The cloudy gray eyes opened, and a raspy, guttural tone rattled from its mouth. "Liiillllly."

"No! This isn't real!" She repeated the words in ear-piercing screams until her throat felt raw. When nothing changed, she slammed her elbow into the demon's solar plexus, and his iron-clad grip vanished.

She didn't stop to think twice. With a mighty shove to Farren's stocky body, she turned and sprinted toward the flickering light with hopeless desperation.

Between the tears burning her eyes and the growing brightness, her vision blurred and spun until she hit something warm and solid. The abrupt halt jarred her, like running headfirst into a brick wall. She tried to push away, but strong arms quickly clamped around her, escalating her blind panic.

Lilith wailed in mental exhaustion, writhing and scratching while her legs kicked. She couldn't take any more. Why wouldn't these demons leave her alone?

"Lily. Stop." Chance's voice flowed over her like a soothing balm for her tormented soul. She immediately collapsed into his arms, overcome by wracking sobs of relief. She finally woke up to her safe harbor, the one place she wanted to be, and the only person she knew would never hurt her.

The flickering light was gone, and the room appeared blissfully normal again—no moving corpses, no Farren, no stench of rot and charred flesh. The nightmare was truly over, and she clutched him tighter with tears of joy.

"Are you okay?" Chance softly wiped her cheeks before tilting her sore chin until she met his hazel eyes.

When the lump of tears in her throat blocked the words, she merely shook her head as his hand smoothed through her hair.

A faint headache blossomed along the back of her skull. Still, she ignored the pain and kissed him with a desperate need to experience something beautiful after so much ugliness.

A faint whisper of music eased into the room, and the sound inexplicably sent a slight chill down her spine. Before the apprehension took hold, Chance caressed her hair, fingers traveling over her ear and along her neck, easing her worries as she melted into his touch. Nothing could hurt her while in his protective arms.

One hand snaked around her waist, drawing her body tight against his as the dizzying heat trickled down her nerves. The swell of passion surging through her as their kiss deepened became more urgent, and when his palm brushed over her throat in a tender caress, her heart skipped a beat.

Somewhere in the back of her traumatized mind, alarm bells sounded as the caress turned into a grip, but she ignored the unwanted memories of her past relationship. This was Chance, not David, and the tender touch felt more like a thrilling display of possession, which only fueled her fire. She let the heat of their kiss burn her hesitation to ash as she leaned into his touch and wrapped her arms around him.

Chance pulled back, breaking off the hypnotic kiss. When her eyes fluttered open in confusion, what she witnessed sent her pulse racing in soul-crushing fear. The enigmatic eyes that had contained adoration seconds ago stared off vacantly. The horrifying sight cut through her like a knife. Her ears began to ring, the distant music swelling to a more audible level.

"Chance?" She raised her hand to touch his cheek, but he caught her wrist and clamped it behind her back. Panic and dread swelled in her chest, paralyzing her as she fought to breathe around the sudden lump of fear. "What are you doing?"

He continued to gaze sightlessly through her as his grip tightened. She gasped and tried to push away, but he held her firmly against his body. "Chance, stop! You're hurting me."

"Go ahead and fight. It makes things so much more amusing!" The familiar lilting voice sent a chilling sense of dread rocketing down her spine.

No! Why would Farren send her now? We didn't break any rules.

Peisinoe's face hovered above Chance's shoulder. Manicured nails curled over his arm, glinting crimson. The malicious grin she wore reminded Lilith of a hungry cat staring at a mouse.

Once the siren firmly held her attention, she brushed her blood-red lips up Chance's neck to his ear, but kept her blue eyes locked on Lilith, reveling in every ounce of terror and fury.

"Squeeze." Her voice rose and fell melodically as his grip tightened. Lilith gasped for air, lungs burning, while tears ran down her cheeks. She ignored the siren and stared hopelessly at the vacant expression on his handsome face.

"Chance…please. It's me…Lily." Her voice emerged as a raspy whisper, a desperate plea for some spark of recognition. If only she could wake him up, prove their connection exceeded the banshee's control. But did it?

She watched in horror, waiting for a flicker of hesitation that never came. He didn't know her. The siren severed all his cognizant ties to her, made him her puppet, a blind slave unable to resist her whims.

Rose of Jericho

Peisinoe's bubbly laughter dominated the room, stabbing into Lilith's head like white-hot pokers. "Oh, he's in there. He's aware of what he's doing."

The siren rested her chin on his shoulder, examining him with a reverence reserved for unique specimens. Then she caressed his cheek before tickling her fingers through his hair. "He merely has no physical control. I own him, and when I release him from my thrall, he will be irrevocably broken, a hollow shell of self-hatred for murdering the woman he loves."

The Marilyn impersonator released an over-dramatic sigh as her bright-blue eyes roamed over his handsome face. "Such a pity. Perhaps I'll play with him a while longer. Shame to ruin such a striking man so early."

With demented glee, Peisinoe cast her malevolent gaze on Lilith, watching the blood drain from her face. The smug satisfaction lingered for a few seconds until it transformed into boredom. "Oh, the suspense is just killing me." Her lilting voice dripped with sarcasm as Lilith fought for every wisp of air she could drag into her lungs.

"Enough games. End it, now!" Peisinoe sang the words with vindictive delight before her teeth tugged at his earlobe. Then she settled in to drink Lilith's blossoming horror.

Without any hesitation, his hand clenched forcefully around her throat, making her vision blur. She clawed desperately at his iron-clad grip, her teary eyes wide with fear. When she drew blood, his face didn't change. He still wore the same impassive mask as he captured her wrist, wrenched it behind her, and leaned forward, pinning both arms behind her.

Her legs thrashed as he stared with the same blank expression he would give a stranger. No. Worse than that. She was nothing to him, not even a person.

A pop and crunch echoed through the room while pain blazed through her chest as if she were drowning in molten lava. With a crushing wave of hopeless panic, the world went dark.

"Lily!!!" The scream sounded like it originated at the end of a long tunnel, somewhere in the weightless dark. Lilith became distantly aware of someone shaking her, but she didn't feel connected to her heavy limbs. She floated in the inky black, disoriented like a diver struggling to find the surface.

"Dammit! Lily! Wake up!" The voice sounded louder, with hints of a Cajun accent. *Chance? Am I dead? In a coma? Why can't I move? Why can't I open my eyes?*

A thunderous force suddenly crushed her chest, bringing with it a torrent of pain. It scorched her body, lighting up every frayed nerve. For an instant, she recoiled from the torment. She had endured enough, but a deep-seated need clawed at her insides. She couldn't give up. Not now.

As the sensation faded, she latched on to the agony, drawing it in, wrapping it around her, and followed it back through the dark to a glimpse of light.

Slowly, Lilith's eyes fluttered open, and the ambient brightness pierced her brain like a brilliant spotlight. She gasped as the pain spread quickly. When she tried to inhale, a coughing fit racked her body, and she curled into a fetal position, desperately trying to drag air into her burning lungs. A warm hand caressed her back in soothing circles as the blurry world swirled around her.

Then, reality snapped into clear focus as the memories crashed through her mind—Peisinoe, Chance's blank face, his iron-clad grip, the snapping cartilage in her throat.

Lilith instinctively scrambled off the floor and into the closest corner. Her eyes flashed around the semi-dark hotel room, frantically searching for the blonde bombshell from hell.

"Lilith, *cherie*..." Chance was the only person in the room, kneeling on the floor in his black t-shirt and matching boxer briefs. Hours ago, he would have been a welcome sight, but now the view terrified her to her very core. She kept seeing the vacant expression he'd worn when his hand crushed the life from her as if she meant nothing.

"Where is she?!" She didn't recognize her own voice as the shrieked question escaped her raw throat. The torrent of memories kept flashing before her eyes. She squeezed them shut, trying to block everything out as she crawled to her feet and wedged herself firmly into the corner.

"Where is who?" He appeared genuinely confused.

"Dammit. Tell me where she is, Chance?!" Her whole body shook as her eyes nervously bounced around the room.

"There is no one here, *cherie*. You had a nightmare..."

"No!" That couldn't be true. Her throat throbbed, her lungs burned, her chest ached. She'd never felt anything like it before.

However, if it was real, why was she still alive, and where was the banshee? Was she toying with her? Did she wipe his memory?

"You kept screaming, but I couldn't wake you up." He slowly stood and started toward her, but she held up a hand while shrinking against the wall.

"No! Stop!" Her heart pounded faster with each movement he made. Could it have truly been a dream? *No. He is wrong. He has to be.*

The entire scene played through her head again as her fists clenched her hair, and she screeched for it to stop.

"Lily, what's wrong? It was a dream…"

"Stop saying that!" But what if he was right? Could the banshee alter memories? Why would she leave before accomplishing her mission? *Shit. Is it all in my head?*

"Lily, *cherie*." His wounded voice broke her heart as he stepped forward with his hands outstretched in a sign of peace. "I'm not going to hurt you. Please, you had a horrible dream, and then you… stopped breathing. I had to drag you to the floor and give you CPR." Tears filled his hazel eyes as his voice wavered. She wanted to believe him, more than anything, but couldn't wipe away the memory of his hand clutching her throat.

Lilith covered her face and wept, unable to separate dreams from reality. Was she losing her mind? She had suffered night terrors since college, but this one…it had felt so damn real. And no matter how awful her previous nightly torments were, none of them required CPR.

Could Peisinoe implant a latent command and turn him into a sleeper agent? The ridiculous thought made her sound like a paranoid nut job in a shiny new straitjacket, but she couldn't dismiss the possibility.

A hand caressed her shoulder, shocking her out of the chaotic thoughts. On instinct, she screamed, ducked out of the corner, and scrambled away on shaky legs. "Please don't. I…I can't…"

She still felt his hand clamped around her neck, and she gulped down as much air as she could draw in. A wave of dizziness hit her as the panic attack froze her lungs. She scrambled to latch onto the dresser, but her sweaty palms slid along the top, and she crashed to the ground.

She gasped and wheezed, trying to force her body to comply as her hands reached for her throat, but found nothing. There was no steely grip restricting her airway, no noose strangling her neck. Despite the realization, her vision turned splotchy, blurring as she hunched over, uselessly gasping like a fish out of water.

"God, Lilith. Please! You need to calm down. Let me help you!" As his voice grew closer, it became harder to pull the wisps of oxygen into her lungs. She clawed across the cheap carpet toward the door, but the pain became too overwhelming. The room spun. Lilith collapsed on the floor with one last ragged inhale and lost consciousness.

Muffled voices argued somewhere in the background. Lilith moaned and shifted position as the grogginess melted away. Hesitantly, she cracked one eye open. The sunlight streaming through the sheer curtains blinded her, stabbing into her brain. With a harsh groan, she squeezed her eyes shut again and inhaled deeply. Although her chest ached and her throat felt raw, she was breathing okay.

After a few moments, she braved the light and glanced at the clock. Ten-thirty? *Crap.* The cops promised her lab results. She reached the edge of the bed and wiped at her tired eyes as the voices outside grew louder, making them recognizable. Cohen and Chance were arguing. She stood and crept toward the door with a burning sense of curiosity, leaning close to listen.

"I don't know what the fuck happened! She wouldn't tell me. She was terrified. She kept screaming *where is she* and then had a damn panic attack when I tried to help her up." Anger dominated Chance's booming voice, but underneath, he was heartbroken and lost. The subtle undercurrent brought tears to her eyes as she rested her forehead against the hollow aluminum.

Now that she could think clearly, she felt confident that none of it had happened, but it had felt so real. Even now, the attack lingered clearly in her mind, indistinguishable from true memories. If Chance was right and it never happened, how could she fear someone who never hurt her? How could she be angry at him for something he didn't do?

"Well, we don't have time for her to visit a padded cell, so let me talk to her. The information from the local cops will let her focus on something else. Take this and get some breakfast...and don't stop for flowers or candy or some other romantic nonsense on the way, Romeo."

"Let it fucking go. You want me to grab you some tampons while I'm out?" His smart-ass comeback made her smile.

"Go!"

Lilith waited until Chance stalked away to open the door. Cohen was reaching for the knob. It only took a split second for his shock to melt into his indifferent facade.

"Great. You're awake. We need to chat." Without so much as a sideways glance, he strode past her and took a seat at the table.

"Good morning to you, too." Then she closed the door and locked it, before sitting on the bed.

While ignoring her sarcastic greeting, he shuffled a few papers and spread them over the table. When she reached for one, he smacked her hand, turned his chair so he could face her, and rested his elbows on his knees. For a moment, he merely stared at her while she frowned in confusion.

"First, tell me what happened last night."

She shifted under his intense gaze, wrapping her arms around herself in embarrassment. "I'd rather not talk about it."

His eyes tightened in harsh scrutiny. "I'm sorry. Did that sound like a half-hearted request? You couldn't breathe, and your heart stopped. Chance had to give you CPR. So, suck it up and tell me what happened." His unrelenting tone left zero wiggle room.

Although she didn't want to expose her messed-up psyche to Cohen, she needed answers only he could give. With a heavy sigh, she relented and shared her side of events. As she spoke, he studied her but displayed no signs of surprise, disgust, or any other emotion. He simply absorbed the whole story in nerve-wracking silence.

"Peisinoe's threat from the airport?"

Lilith swallowed the lump in her throat and nodded.

He huffed and leaned back in his chair. "Perfect. This is the last thing we need." When she didn't interrupt with an angry retort, he peered over in surprise. "What?"

Her body trembled, unsure if she could force herself to ask the question, because the answer terrified her. Either Chance tried to kill her, or she was losing her mind. Neither possibility seemed comforting. "Could it have been real?"

His calculating eyes studied her, giving the question genuine consideration. "No. I can assure you, Peisinoe was not here. She's only allowed to go where Farren directs her."

"But what if he…"

"No. She is always guarded by a specially trained unit. They wouldn't allow her into your room alone. He must have massive leverage because she's never contemplated talking back to him, much less going rogue. Also, she cannot alter memories, nor can she implant latent commands. It seems you had the mother-of-all nightmares."

Although his brusque reaction put her on edge, the information helped, and he gave it willingly, without a fight. He had also made no attempt to psychoanalyze her insecurities, allowing her to process things rationally without becoming defensive.

"Thanks." She muttered the word, feeling suddenly uncomfortable. "Can we talk about lab results now?" Anything to pull the spotlight off her masochistic brain.

"Of course." Cohen nodded and swiveled back to the papers. "Take a look. I don't understand most of it."

With renewed purpose, she slid over to the second chair, more than happy to bury herself in scientific facts and figures.

"Okay. So, some of this stuff is fairly straightforward. The trace found on the back of the head is here." He pushed a sheet toward her, which revealed nothing surprising. "Asphalt, gravel, and mud from the alley."

"What about the trace from the teeth? Anything biological? Any salvageable DNA?" She leaned forward, eager to see the report. If she couldn't resolve the chaos in her head, perhaps she could shed light on the puzzling bodies.

"That's where it gets weird."

Or maybe not.

Cohen shoved two pages toward her with a bewildered expression. "The report doesn't make any sense to me."

She scanned through the mass spec results, eventually echoing his confusion. "The specimens from the teeth are human tissue. *Dead* human tissue."

"Well, of course. It's no longer attached. How is that a revelation?"

She couldn't help but chuckle at his oversimplified explanation. "This tissue shows considerable decomposition, which means it's been dead for quite a while."

He leaned on his elbows as he frowned in thought. "So...what are the options? They shoved something dead in his mouth, or a dead man tore him apart?"

"Unless you know something about zombies, it has to be option one." She started the statement in a joking tone, but it ended up sounding more like a genuine question.

"Uh, no. Well, except for the guy in Florida high on bath salts who ate someone's face."

"His tox results came back clean. Interesting case, but the man was bat-shit crazy and very much alive when he attacked that poor guy. Perhaps someone planted the tissue. Did they find a DNA match?"

"Nope."

"Okay, back-burner then. What else do we have?"

"Well, they found lots of dirt in the wounds. The analysis is there." Cohen pointed at a graph further down the second page.

"Hmm, very high carbon monoxide and ammonium with the presence of lipids. Someone went through a lot of trouble."

"How so?"

"Well, I'm not familiar with the chemical composition of soil around here, but this suggests it's from a grave. Of course, the missing hearts could be ritualistic. Perhaps these grave elements are part of that ritual. All I know for sure is that this isn't a garden-variety assassin."

"Maybe it's a scare tactic? Psychological warfare? I'm sure our third burglar is running scared. Speaking of which, we have IDs on our two John Does. Jimmy Tome and Denny Hickson. I think their home addresses will look familiar."

Lilith grabbed the last papers and glanced at them. "They're both from New York City? What are the odds?"

He merely shrugged. "It's close by and contains plenty of people desperate for money with loose morals. Plus, the major crime syndicates have trained thugs for hire. Doesn't seem too unusual. No mastermind would use locals for a robbery of this caliber, and they wouldn't risk exposure with airlines by contracting anyone far away."

"Well, if our vics are from New York City, it's reasonable to assume their partner is also from there. Assembling a crew and heading here together makes the most sense. Guess we're heading to the Big Apple. If we search their homes, maybe we can find a connection to the third guy and whoever hired them."

"Alright. After we eat breakfast, I'll get a new rental car, and we can head out. I strongly suggest we don't go anywhere familiar. That means your apartment, Chance's place, Gregor's, and the precinct are all off-limits. The council gave explicit instructions."

"I can work around their rules. I can't directly access my police connections, but there is an alternative. They assigned me a new partner. I got a voicemail, but we've never met. It's doubtful the Council will know anything about her. Perhaps she can help us with research and lab requests."

"Well, that's convenient." Cohen cracked a smile that didn't reach his eyes as he leaned back.

Something else weighed on his mind, but he chose not to voice it, or maybe he didn't know how to. Either way, Lilith was content to stay blissfully ignorant. She had zero interest in deviating from the comfort of black-and-white facts.

Before she had time to enjoy the silence, a knock at the door rattled her frayed nerves. She kept herself busy by studying the reports, leaving Cohen to answer the door. Then, her eyes caught on a result Cohen failed to mention. "*Selaginella lepidophylla?*"

Andrew frowned at her as he moved back to his chair. "I'm sorry, what?"

"The bits of plant I found on the victim. The common name is Rose of Jericho. I've never heard of it, you?"

"The resurrection fern." Chance's Cajun-flecked voice rumbled from the doorway where he stood with a McDonald's bag and two cup carriers full of drinks.

His signature black T-shirt clung to his leanly muscled frame, loosely covered by a new hoodie. Yesterday, the sight would have made her pulse race with desire, but today it quickened with instinctual fear.

Lilith glanced at the frustrated expression he wore, and her face flushed with shame and embarrassment. *No. Concentrate.* Her eyes darted back to the papers in her hand. "That doesn't sound very common."

When Chance leaned in to place the food and drinks on the table, she automatically scooted her chair back a fraction. Suddenly, it all flashed through her mind again—his crushing strength, the vacant expression, his eyes devoid of any recognition. The attack had never happened. She knew that now, but the images lingered, freshly seared into her brain. Real or not, they refused to go away.

Chance swallowed hard as his jaw clenched, unable to ignore her subtle retreat. He pulled out a breakfast sandwich and claimed an orange juice before stepping back. "It's not found in these parts. It's a desert fern."

He retreated to the bed with his head hung low but made no other comments. Her immediate sense of relief didn't help to reassure him either.

He knew he frightened her, but he didn't realize why—not that it would help. How could he make up for something he didn't do? And how could she erase the memory of something that seemed so real it had stopped her heart?

"You are the strangest dictionary of odd knowledge." Cohen made no attempt to hide his surprise.

"People use it a lot in Cajun country."

A tickle of excitement infiltrated her brooding thoughts as she began to connect the dots. "Do they use it for rituals?"

He nodded with a mouthful of McMuffin. "For death rituals, yes. Most commonly when speaking with the dead."

Her face lit up as the puzzle pieces clicked together into a partial theory, no matter how unlikely or outlandish it sounded. "The evidence could suggest using voodoo rituals to keep the dead men silent. The crushed throats, the removed mandibles…the killer destroyed the parts necessary for speech. If I'm right, this is the most bizarre assassin I can imagine."

Chapter 14

The ensuing silence had become painfully awkward once the revelations about the case ended. Chance had glanced up at Lilith several times with a wounded expression full of concern while she'd pretended not to notice. Now, she concentrated on picking apart her hash brown, praying for a new distraction.

Thanks to Cohen's blood, Chance sensed every volatile emotion pinging around her brain, but he would never understand them without context. Still, she couldn't find the words without opening an emotional floodgate that would overwhelm him, just like on the plane.

For a while, Cohen had seemed content to observe them with an obnoxiously amused smile, but eventually, he grew bored with the silent brooding.

"I can't take this anymore. The anticipation is killing me." When Cohen unwittingly echoed Peisinoe's words, the stab of panic left her short of breath. If he noticed her reaction, he ignored it.

Cohen crumpled up a wrapper and turned his attention to Chance. She wanted to protest, but hesitated, considering whether to let him explain. Oh, who the hell was she kidding? The demon took far too much pleasure in needling Chance, but before she could interrupt, Cohen barreled ahead.

"Stop looking like a kicked dog. She had a vivid nightmare that Peisinoe seduced you into strangling her. The ordeal was so realistic and traumatic that she stopped breathing. She had a panic attack when you tried to help because she didn't *know* it was a dream. There. I ripped off the band-aid." Cohen settled back into his seat and stirred his coffee.

Chance swung his gaze to Lilith as the explanation sank in. "Jesus, Lily. That's what she threatened you with at the airport. *Mon petit cherie,*

I would never hurt you, and I'd never let that bitch—"

"Stop!" Cohen held up a hand as his expression hardened. "I may not like you much, Chance, but you are a man of principle. Do not make promises you have no prayer of keeping. Yes. Lilith had a bad dream, *but* if Peisinoe wanted you to crush Lilith's throat with a smile on your face, nothing you could do would stop it. You can't resist her wiles through sheer willpower. If she wants control, she takes over completely. Period."

"Cohen." Her quiet voice held just enough volume to catch his attention. "I appreciate the honesty, but…"

"But what?" His gaze grew colder as he waited for her response. When she couldn't find the words, he chuckled, slapped the lid on his cup, and pushed away from the table. "I'm going to pick up a new rental car. If you want to tell each other fake promises and hollow truths, be my guest. I suggest you pack your stuff while you're pretending everything is hunky-dory."

Then he slipped out the door, leaving nothing but a vacuum of silence behind him. As much as she hated to admit it, sugar-coating things wouldn't help. Only two things would—truth and time.

"Don't apologize, and please don't make promises. Cohen is right. You did nothing wrong. It's my problem, my stupid brain torturing me. I simply need some time to shake off the after-effects."

He nodded sullenly and continued to pick at his breakfast sandwich. She didn't blame him for being at a loss. If the roles were reversed, she wouldn't know what the hell to say or do either.

"We still need to discuss getting leverage over Farren and his flunkies. Even if we find the book, we still need the box from Goditha." He made a great point, but the gloomy tone in his voice tugged at her guilty conscience. Despite that, she gratefully accepted his willingness to ignore the six-hundred-pound elephant in the room.

"But how do we get to it without *anyone* knowing, including Luminita and Cohen? Even if they honestly want to help us, it's still dangerous information."

After rubbing his jaw, Chance ran his fingers through his hair—body language she recognized. He had a plan, but he didn't like it.

"Agreed. So, here's what I suggest…" He leaned forward, resting his elbows on his knees, and hesitated. When his jaw clenched tight and his brow furrowed in a determined scowl, she knew she wouldn't like his plan either.

"I'll tell Timothy to meet us in New York. I'll take his car, which they won't be tracking, and haul ass to Knoxville. Tim can stay with you and Cohen to fill the third spot. He's roughly my height and almost a brunette, so anyone with a basic description will mistake him for me."

"No!" He glanced up in surprise at her adamant answer as fear, sadness, guilt, and shame all clawed at her insides in unison. The warring torrent of emotions became too much, and she settled for deflective logic.

"You can't go there by yourself. Besides, what am I supposed to tell Cohen? You went on a road trip? No. I don't like it." She frowned deeply, arms crossing over her chest. "Plus, you can't get into the building. You don't have an access code, remember?"

He scooted closer but stopped when she tensed. "Lily, I can take care of myself, and if no one knows where I'm going, I'll be safer than the rest of you. The tin is our only leverage to avoid execution, and Cohen will realize that. I'll just use your access code."

"What? You can't—"

Chance held up a hand to cut her off. "If you call ahead, they'll let me in."

"Wait. Then why didn't we do that before? Why did you wait at the desk?"

"Once you initiate the emergency protocol, they flag your code and render it useless. They will only assign you a new one *in person* at your home facility. I knew you'd need it again, so I made a judgment call. Besides, it allowed me to assess Coffee, and if anything happened, it'd come up on the monitors."

As much as her gut rebelled against the idea, she couldn't come up with one valid, non-emotional reason his plan wouldn't work. A heavy sigh escaped her lips as her melancholy deepened. First, her brain drove a wedge between them, and now he wanted to leave. She understood the reasoning, but it took her a moment to rein in the chaotic feelings and work through the logic.

"I still don't like it, but I don't see any other way. Timothy doesn't know what we're looking for, and I wouldn't trust Cohen inside one of our facilities in a million years. If they let him in, he'd use the cipher to save his own skin. I need to be in New York, working the case…"

"That leaves me." Chance nodded and flashed a confident smile that faltered quickly. "Besides, you need…space to shake off this nightmare."

"Not half the damn country."

Jenny Allen

He glanced up from beneath a deeply furrowed brow, his lips tightening as if he had something else to say but wasn't sure he should.

"What is it?" A different sort of dread clutched her heart as he stared at her with flickers of fear and remorse.

"Is it *just* the nightmare?" When she blinked, completely lost, he continued. "I mean, is there another reason you're scared of me?"

"Of course not. What are you talking about?"

While gathering his thoughts, he rubbed at his hands—a self-soothing gesture she hadn't seen him use before. "Last night, you were angry about the candles, and..."

"I almost died, and I rushed in here thinking you were—"

"Yeah, but it's more than that. You started rattling off names, and..." He hesitated again as she struggled to follow his logic. "When we got back to New York, I didn't see or hear from you until Alvarez's funeral..." Then, his hazel eyes met hers with a deep need for truth. "Are you scared of me, of us?"

His logic came so far from left field that her brain had trouble processing it. She paused, thinking over his question. Before she could open her mouth, he closed his eyes with a weary sigh, resigned to accept her silence as a yes.

"Chance, wait. This is not the conversation I expected to have." Fresh panic crawled up her spine as she fought to assemble an answer. *No. Just speak the truth, all of it.* "Yes. I'm terrified, but that doesn't mean I want you to leave!"

The fear in his eyes eased slightly, and he nodded.

"God, I'm not good at this." A wave of desperate panic froze her thoughts. *No. Stop freaking out. Just breathe and be honest.*

"Chance...For you, this is...something you have imagined for a long time. For me, this is all new and surreal. I've had no time to process the idea of *us* with all the insane shit going on."

"I wasn't trying to push."

"You aren't. That's not what I meant." Her eyes welled with tears as her deep desire to curl up in his arms warred with her PTSD. "I'm scared *because* I want *us*. I didn't call when we got back because I'm not used to letting people in or sharing my burdens. They have only ever belonged to me." She exhaled slowly, lowering her head as her arms wrapped around herself.

"I'm sorry for bringing this up. We don't—"

"Stop." Her eyes lifted to his with fierce determination. "You wanted the truth, so let me finish, please. Being open and vulnerable has never been easy, but I want that with you. I just...I've said the words *I love you* before, but I don't think I knew what they truly meant...not until you."

Tears flooded his eyes as she spoke, a fine tremor running through his arms. "Lily..."

"Let me finish." Lilith heaved a sigh and forced out the words. "The nightmare emphasized fears I already harbored. I watched your essence and personality drain from your face until you looked like a stranger. You didn't recognize me, didn't care what happened to me." She paused, swallowing the lump in her throat as the images flashed through her mind.

"Yes, you scare me. In less than two weeks, you somehow evaded all my defenses and set up shop. You became my haven, the one place I feel safe. I'm petrified of relying on you, terrified you'll change your mind and walk away. What happens when the rush wears off and we return to our normal lives? What happens when I don't need you to save me from the monsters?" Her eyes drifted to the floor, afraid of what she might see.

"The rush?"

The incredulous tone drew her gaze back up to his tear-filled eyes.

"Lily, *amour de ma vie*, I had walls, too. You have existed as an impossibility for more than a decade. Simply having this discussion with *you* feels like an insane dream, and I'm scared of waking up. Don't you think I'm terrified of the same things? You aren't a fantasy or a notch, and I'll always be there to save you, monsters or not. I'm not going anywhere."

"Except Tennessee..."

"*Cherie*, I don't want to go, but..."

"I know the logic." She stood and started to cross the space between them, intent on showing him she could conquer her fear. After all, a stupid night terror paled in comparison to her waking life at the moment.

The crippling anxiety blossomed in her chest, more potent with every step until her muscles froze and her fists clenched in exasperation.

When her legs refused to move, she turned to the dresser and pulled open a drawer. Sure. That's what she planned to do. A glance back at Chance told her he didn't buy it either.

"I'm sorry. We should start packing. It won't take Cohen long to pick up a new car."

"Thank you for trying." His voice shook as he slid off the bed and strode toward the bathroom.

Lilith threw her stuff on the bed, silently cursing her damaged psyche. Her unconscious mind seemed determined to get rid of the only thing Ashcroft and Farren hadn't taken away. How could she expect Chance to believe her soul-baring words when she couldn't muster the strength to touch him? Was her brain hard-wired to sabotage her only remnants of happiness?

The trip from New Haven to New York City felt as comfortable as sunbathing on a porcupine. Lilith curled up in the back seat and reread the lab results, ignoring the complex silence dominating the stuffy rental car. Chance stared mutely through the window the entire drive while Cohen focused on navigating through heavy traffic.

She sighed in relief when they finally arrived at a random hotel in downtown Manhattan around two in the afternoon. All the chain hotels looked the same to her. Marriott, Doubletree, Hilton, Sheraton, the list went on and on.

Cohen pulled up to the lobby doors and hopped out of the car without a word, leaving them alone.

"I should call Tim while he's getting the rooms."

"I'll start pulling out our luggage." Although she didn't enjoy one-sided conversations, that wasn't why she decided to play bellhop. She needed a few minutes alone to breathe. Since leaving for Tennessee, she'd been white knuckling an emotional rollercoaster that made the world spin in dizzying circles.

Once she opened the trunk, her focus drifted to the aluminum forensic case, and she popped open the lid. The chaotic city sounds swirled around her, but brushing her fingers over the swabs, probes, containers of dust, and the fluffy brush brought a sense of calm.

This was familiar, the one constant in her life since she had returned home from college. People had come and gone in her life, but she'd always had her work, no matter how pointless it seemed some nights.

A dart of panic accompanied the realization that Gregor's death meant more than merely losing her father. He held majority ownership of all the US labs, including Solasta, her employer. With him and Duncan gone, who would oversee them?

What about his other businesses? Hell, she didn't understand what they were, much less how to manage them. What about the elder's plan to take their race public? Could she spearhead such a delicate endeavor? The vacuum left by her father's demise suddenly felt stifling. It was no longer a matter of her survival, but their entire race. No pressure.

Lilith snapped the lid closed on her kit, overwhelmed by a litany of unanswerable questions. *No.* She couldn't spiral out and drown in a sea of theoretical problems. She needed to focus with laser precision on the case at hand. Figuring out who should take over her father's mantle wouldn't matter if they all died.

The passenger door opened and closed as she piled their bags onto a luggage cart. While grabbing the last suitcase, she peered around the car. Chance stood by his door with a stiff posture, keeping his distance. Although part of her appreciated the space, the rest of her felt miserable about the whole thing.

"So, Timothy is freaking out, but I didn't fill him in on anything yet. I told him I need his car with a full tank of gas and his credit card. He agreed to meet us at the Brooklyn Diner on 43rd at six o'clock on one condition—we explain everything. He didn't sound thrilled about me borrowing his precious Honda, but he knows if *I'm* asking, it's important."

Lilith's nose wrinkled in distaste as she closed the trunk. "The Brooklyn Diner? Why? It's in the middle of tourist town."

Chance leaned back against the car while shrugging his shoulders, reclaiming a fraction of his typically relaxed posture. "The man has a sweet tooth. He loves that Noodle Kugel crap."

She chuckled as her eyes drifted to the lobby doors, but a flicker of motion in her peripheral vision set off alarms. She glanced over to see Chance's arm draped over the roof, his hand dangling close, and an irrational dart of panic ripped through her.

Flashes from her dream erupted again—that same hand tightening around her neck, squeezing, snapping the cartilage. She closed her eyes, furiously fighting the impulse to take a step backward. Not that it mattered. Chance could sense everything she felt.

When the images passed, she opened her eyes and fell back against the car. "This is so fucking stupid. It was only a damn dream!"

Although he tried to keep the sadness off his face, it still lingered in the quick shrug of his lips when he pulled his arm back.

"Hey! I got the rooms." Cohen's voice shattered the awkward moment as he jogged toward them.

Lilith rubbed her face as if it would abolish the nightmare, tugged on a hollow smile, and walked toward Cohen, leaving Chance behind. At that point, the guilt hurt worse than the tormented dreams, and she already carried enough to drown a catholic parish.

"Before you start bitching, they don't have rooms on the ground floor." Cohen flashed a friendly smile at Chance, which only made things more surreal. "Guess you'll have to jump through the 14th-floor window in an emergency."

He waited for a smartass comeback, but none came. Chance merely grunted, too lost in his thoughts. For a moment, Cohen frowned, perplexed by not getting a rise out of him. Then, his sky-blue eyes swung to Lilith, and he shook his head.

"Seriously?" Cohen slapped a keycard into her hand with a stern grimace. "You can't let Peisinoe rattle you. She's under guard in another state, and I need your head in the game. Our lives are on the line. What I *don't* need is a pair of vampires more useless than the sparkling emo vamps in Hollywood. Do what it takes to snap out of it."

Without a word, she nodded and headed straight for the lobby doors, leaving the guys to navigate the luggage cart. Cohen was one hundred percent correct. She had allowed the siren's threat to control her—precisely what the bitch wanted.

As she grabbed the door handle, she heard whispered words behind her, but ignored them. Knowing Cohen was right and acting on his advice were two separate things. No magic wand existed that would erase the pseudo-memories and return everything to normal. Her only option was to block it out, concentrate on the case, and hope the after-effects faded into nothingness.

Thirty minutes later, Cohen, Chance, and Lilith emerged from the rental car on a busy street in Queens, which resembled something straight out of *Coming to America*. The only thing the dilapidated area lacked was a barbershop with old men arguing over the legitimacy of fighters from their youth.

Unfortunately, street parking meant they had to leave the car several blocks shy of their destination and walk the rest of the way— joy of joys.

As they crawled out of the car, Cohen straightened his tie and smoothed his suit while eyeing the run-down surroundings—a behavior she had noticed before. Usually, it preceded him pulling on another mask in moments that would make most people anxious. Perhaps he wasn't an unsolvable mystery if she paid closer attention.

In any case, she found his subtle apprehension amusing. Sure, graffiti covered most of the brickwork, trash littered the sidewalks, and the porches consisted of rotten wood and cracked paint. Still, the borough's broken-down facade was a far cry from the actual ghettos of New York, where people didn't venture outside in broad daylight, much less at night.

"Classy area, huh?" She grabbed her kit and fearlessly started down the sidewalk.

Two weeks ago, she would have waited for nightfall and snuck inside while jumping at every sound. But after meeting the real boogeymen, a bunch of thugs didn't inspire the same level of fear. Hell, her nightmares scared her more than the mean streets. Besides, she had a bodyguard watching her back and a demon co-conspirator.

A sudden, random thought occurred to her. *I wonder how old Cohen is?* With his regenerative gifts, he might be older than her father.

A cluster of men on a nearby stoop fell silent and eyeballed them with open hostility as they crossed the street. They reminded her of a territorial pack of dogs, eager to defend their turf. Although Cohen led the way, the assessing glares quickly dismissed him as a threat and moved on.

When their eyes lingered on Lilith, a different instinctual drive took over. She could tell by the upturned twitch of their mouths and puffed chests. Although the indicators of dominance and carnal desire made her skin crawl, she strode forward with confidence. Any sign of intimidation would be the equivalent of wearing a flashing sign that read, "*Please, sexually assault me.*"

When their stares landed on Chance and his six-foot-three, muscled frame, a few of them stood, fists clenched, brows drawn down and together, upper lids lifted with tightness beneath their eyes—all indications of violent intentions. Thankfully for everyone involved, the alpha held out an arm, holding back his ravenous pack, keeping their bravado in check.

As the trio crossed an alley, Chance broke the silence. "Huh? Guess they have all kinds in Queens."

She turned, following his line of sight to a petite woman in dark skirts with a black shawl wrapped around her shoulders. The woman turned and shuffled down the alley, heading north, which gave them a profile view. Her long hair, twisted into dreads, swung back and forth, revealing glimpses of odd necklaces swaying as she walked.

"Yeah, not the typical club-girl style." Lilith shrugged and stepped onto the sidewalk.

"I bet she owns a shop, tells people their fortune, and makes voodoo dolls for angry women to torment their baby-daddies."

She burst out laughing and grinned back at him. "That's a little stereotypical, isn't it?"

He quirked an eyebrow and fell in step beside her, still keeping his distance. "All stereotypes begin with a grain of truth, *cherie*. Things are what they are. Do I think all people in Queens are like that? No, but a lot of them are. I know from experience. The same way I know the gang back there planned to jump us until the guy in charge spotted Cohen's badge on his belt, and the lady with the shopping cart up ahead will ask Cohen for change, but not us."

She stopped to watch the demon as he walked up to the door. While double-checking the address, the woman, buried in layers of ratty clothing, sidled up to him. She spoke too softly to hear, but the pleading expression on her face told Lilith everything she needed to know.

"Okay, but what makes you think she won't ask us?"

"People assume panhandlers play a numbers game, asking every Tom, Dick, and Harry that comes along, but they are more strategic than people give them credit. Cohen sticks out like a sore thumb here with his slick suit, but we blend."

The grin on his face warmed her heart. Not enough to abolish the nightmare, but it helped. "I know the streets. I spent a long time watching them for…" He paused, faltering as the moment ended abruptly. "Well," Chance cleared his throat, glanced down at Lilith, and pulled on a hollow smile. "We better get to work."

"Chance." Her voice softened as she reached for his arm. When he turned back around, her hand fell to her side, and words failed her again.

"Let's get this done, Lily. We'll figure everything else out later." He moved past her, then stopped and glanced back. "Give me a head start so I can clear the scene. I won't touch anything, promise."

This time, it wasn't only her PTSD that kept her from grabbing his arm. His sudden change to business mode brought a startling revelation. With her father dead, Chance no longer had a job. What would he do for work? Would he stay? Would her Uncle Aaron scoop him up and take him out to L.A.? Lilith stood there, contemplating the future, as Chance disappeared through the door.

"It's not the end of the world, dearie." The raspy voice jolted Lilith out of her spiraling thoughts. She whirled around and found herself face-to-face with the homeless woman who had asked Cohen for change. This close, the smell of her unwashed body became almost palpable. The woman's broad smile revealed yellowing teeth and a mass of wrinkles from years in the sun, but the rosacea covering her nose and cheeks came from the bottle.

Yep, most stereotypes contain some truth.

"I'm sorry, but I need to catch up with my partners." Lilith ducked toward the door, but the woman's thin hand snatched her wrist. While biting back the edge of panic, Lilith turned toward her. "I don't have any cash. I'm sorry."

The woman frowned, deepening the network of creases across her weathered face. "No, dearie. I don't want your money. I can see you have a heavy heart." Her gnarled finger tapped at Lilith's chest. "Don't look so sad. Things can always be worse."

Lilith couldn't keep the skeptical expression off her face. The last thing she had expected was a pep talk from someone living out of a shopping cart.

The older woman released her arm and laughed. "You think being me is the worst thing? Well, I'm not dead yet, and neither are you. It sounds like we are both doing better than some. So, chin up, honey."

Lilith chuckled at the woman's simple logic. "True enough. Thank you." After sharing a conspiratorial grin, Lilith hurried into the building, feeling a tad less gloomy.

Chapter 15

Lilith mulled over the menu at the Brooklyn Diner, trying to ignore the frustration gnawing at her insides. After combing through the dead guy's apartments, their only promising clues were more fragments of green fern and a pair of check stubs for identical amounts. She discovered one under a magnetic bottle-opener on Tome's fridge and the other in Hickson's bathroom trashcan.

The plant fragments told her the assassin had beaten them to both sites, cleaning up loose ends. Considering the bad guys had had a head start and the victim's wallets, being late to the party didn't surprise her.

The company name on the check stubs was nothing but meaningless initials with a P.O. box address in Florida, both of which were probably fake. Without someone who could filter through dummy corporations to find a trail, the clues were useless.

Glancing over their rap sheets revealed a combined and rather lengthy history of petty thefts and felonies, so the checks could be from anything, not necessarily the library heist. Unfortunately, their criminal record didn't mention any other professional co-conspirators. Lilith was back to square one.

While she brooded, Cohen slid into the seat beside her and gazed across the empty table. "Where's Chance?"

"He's outside, waiting for Timothy," she replied while studying the menu. The longer she could postpone the inevitable litany of questions, the better.

When they'd sprung the meeting on him, Cohen had made it clear he didn't like bringing in another person, but let it go. Now that they were alone, she fully expected an interrogation.

Cohen glanced out over the packed restaurant without a hint of righteous indignation. "This place is insanely busy for a simple diner." The nonchalant timbre of voice both surprised her and made her suspicious. When she turned on him with a skeptical frown, he merely smiled.

"Yeah, well, it's Friday night in New York City. Plus, it's what, two days until Halloween?"

"Ah." He nodded and began perusing the lengthy list of food. "So, what's good here?"

"Are you serious?" When he appeared genuinely confused, she slapped down her menu with a growl of frustration. "Chance isn't here, and instead of grilling me for information, you want to chit-chat about the food?" She arched an eyebrow at his feigned expression of shock.

"Okay." He released a soft sigh and turned to face her. "Bringing someone else in is a risky move, but you asked me to play nice and trust you, so I am. If you prefer to sit in uncomfortable silence until Chance comes back with an extra helping of depressive guilt, then I'll shut my mouth. It makes no difference to me." The quick downward tug of his mouth told her the last sentence was a lie, or he wanted her to believe it was.

"I used to come here all the time with my parents when I was younger. They had the best breakfast in town." His puzzled frown made her chuckle.

"Yeah, I know. It seems so mundane for a vampire family. Of course, it was more like dinner for my dad. My mother, Rosaline, loved their sky-high lemon meringue pie, but the recipe changed, and it's not the same anymore."

"So, your mother wasn't old enough to be affected by the sun?"

"No. My mom was only sixty-nine years old when she died, and not all of our kind develop the allergy. My Uncle Aaron is a prime example." Lilith cleared her throat, trying to push back the memories of that night. To her relief and surprise, Cohen moved right over the touchy subject and the glimmer of information to something else.

"Did you and your mother stay on his schedule?" His head tilted in genuine curiosity.

"No. My mother took naps while I was at school. Then, she put me to bed early and woke me up around four in the morning to spend a few hours with Dad before school. Why do you ask?"

He shrugged his shoulders as his eyes returned to the menu. "I'm curious. It's not every day I share dinner with a vampire. I'll ask questions as they occur to me. By the way, you never answered my original question."

She stiffened, replaying the conversation in her head. When she remained silent, he peeked sideways at her with an expectant smile.

"What's good here?"

She studied every line of his face but found no signs of deception. Of course, she still had trouble gauging his acting skills. She couldn't tell if the glimpses were genuine or part of his act. Not knowing made her very uneasy.

"It *used* to be great, but they changed the recipes, and I haven't eaten here in years. You can ask Timothy. He's the Noodle Kugel authority."

He chuckled with a slight cringe of disgust. "What the hell is that?" He glanced down at the plastic-coated page and frowned. "There's no description."

"It's noodles cooked with sugar, cream, vanilla, and cinnamon, then formed into a square. Kinda like bread pudding."

The demon's blond eyebrow arched in disbelief. "Seriously? Hmm. Guess people will eat anything."

"It's not bad. Kugel is a New York City staple, especially for tourists. I'll warn you, though. The single-serving size could feed a high-school football team."

The casual conversation took her mind off the frustrating case burning in her brain, but speaking with Cohen about everyday things felt incredibly odd.

A bell chimed when the front door opened, and Lilith glanced over her shoulder as Chance strolled inside. His eyes caught hers with nervous apprehension, but as her lips stretched into a smile that reached her eyes, he visibly relaxed.

The man who trailed behind him wasn't his twin but looked similar enough to match a general description. Timothy stood a couple of inches shorter than Chance and resembled a linebacker with broad shoulders and more bulk in his upper torso.

Timothy's hair was lighter, more of a dark blond with a bit of curl. His eyes were a darker brown than Chance's hazel ones, and the slight bump on his nose told her he'd broken it more than once. Despite the differences, the two of them could easily pass for brothers.

When they reached the booth, Chance hesitated and stepped back, waving Timothy in first. Apparently, he thought sitting across from Lilith might be too close for her comfort.

"Who's the suit?" Timothy raised his square chin at Cohen with a wary expression that bordered on contempt.

Hmm. Guess Chance isn't the only one who dislikes the demon on sight.

"This is Detective Andrew Cohen. He's helping us on the case." Timothy took her introduction at face value and centered his focus on Lilith.

"Can you fill me in now? I don't see how I'm supposed to do my job when I don't know where my boss is?" The man stopped abruptly and glanced around. The sun hadn't fully set, but it was dark enough for her father to venture outside. "Wait. You're both here, so where is Gregor?"

Lilith immediately glanced at Chance, unprepared to say the words out loud. Timothy caught the exchange and turned to face Chance with a stern frown.

"Spit it out! Where the hell is Gregor?" He kept his firm voice low, mindful of the people dining around them. The restaurant boomed with loud conversations, but they didn't want to attract eavesdroppers.

Chance held her gaze with a deep well of sadness, ignoring the man staring him down. This time, the melancholy didn't involve her nightmare. It had everything to do with losing the closest thing he had to a father.

"He's dead." Chance threw the words out like a land mine, his eyes never leaving hers. The stark declaration stabbed at her heart, and judging by the expression on Timothy's face, she wasn't the only one.

"What?!" His question boomed through the crowded diner, bringing the restaurant's thunderous roar to a faint buzz. People were listening now, intrigued by the glimpse of drama and hungry for more.

Chance leaned in close to Tim and whispered in a firm tone. "The last thing we need is a building full of humans overhearing our conversation or worse, posting videos on YouTube."

"To hell with them." Although his words seemed rebellious, he obediently lowered his voice. "Gregor doesn't show up at the airport. Then you two disappear together. Now you tell me Gregor's dead? What the hell is going on?" The man's tanned face turned rosy with his barely contained anger.

"It was beyond our control. Let's focus on the things we *can* do." The commanding tone in Chance's voice shut him down, definitively proving why he outranked Tim.

"Shit." He nodded with a solemn grimace and pushed the menu away. A gloomy silence hung over the table while they waited for the onlookers to get bored.

Then, as if it suddenly occurred to him, Timothy peered up. "I'm so sorry, Lilith. Damn. First your mom, then Miriah, Malachi, Spencer, Duncan, Alvarez...and now this."

Every death flashed behind her eyes as he ticked off the names. With a tight smile, she shook the thoughts away and steeled herself, refusing to go down the rabbit hole. A lump of tears lodged in her throat, and since she couldn't trust her voice, she settled for a nod of acknowledgment. Besides, what could she say? Thanks for the lovely stroll down memory lane?

As Timothy nervously fidgeted with his menu, she realized her father was the lynchpin that held them all together. Without him...they all felt disoriented and directionless.

The somber moment passed once the noise picked up again, and they started filling him in on the case, omitting specific details, of course. They steered clear of Cohen's family, his species, and dodged the subject of Chance leaving town. The less Cohen knew, the better.

Lilith had never considered Timothy a deep thinker, but she admittedly didn't know much about him. Chance had typically accompanied her father whenever she had spent time with him.

To her surprise, Tim calmly absorbed everything while digging into his Kugel and raised some valid points. Unfortunately, he didn't come up with anything new.

"Once we finish eating, I'll call my new partner. Perhaps she can research the check stubs." Lilith knew reaching out to someone in the department was a gamble, but what choice did they have?

"What about Aaron?" She glanced up at Tim, caught off guard by his random question.

"I don't think this is the time. I want to keep Gregor's...death between us until we solve this case."

"That's not what I meant. Finding out more about Duncan's book could help, and Aaron might know something. He is his brother, after all."

Lilith rubbed at her face while she considered his words but came up with the same reaction. "No. Aaron left them long before Scotland, and I wouldn't say they've grown any closer over the years. Hell, I only remember meeting Aaron and his son once at the family reunion before I left for UCLA. I lived in Los Angeles, less than fifteen miles away from him, for four years and never saw him. He's made it quite clear that I'm not family, and I seriously doubt he knows anything about that book."

"I realize they weren't close, but Gregor talked to him on the phone every month." Timothy shrugged and shoveled another bite of Kugel into his mouth. "Usually, they went over new projects, but the last few years, they often discussed their concerns about Duncan's mental state. Maybe Gregor mentioned something about the book. It couldn't hurt to try."

"It could if he asks questions!" The snapped response held a sharper tone than she had intended. The entire table stared at her, shocked by her overreaction. "Sorry, Tim. I'll consider it," she muttered diplomatically.

To be honest, she didn't want to call Aaron for any reason. The man gave her the creeps, and her father rarely mentioned him. He only existed in her world as one of thirteen vampire elders she barely knew. Not someone she would call family.

They spent the rest of the meal discussing random information about the robbery. Of course, the guys steered her away from the gruesome autopsy details, which they didn't consider proper dinner conversation.

Lilith devoured half of an enormous cheeseburger and a few fries before Chance snagged her leftovers. Timothy peered at her when she didn't protest before moving his stare to Chance with an unspoken question. Oddly, he didn't seem surprised, though.

"Wipe that look off your face, Tim. You aren't writing a damn gossip column." Chance growled between mouthfuls with a teasing grin she sorely missed.

Like a good soldier, Tim shrugged his broad shoulders and polished off his plate in silence. Wise man.

"I'll pay the check." Cohen wiped his mouth with a napkin and slid out of the booth in one fluid motion. "Afterward, I'll head outside and call Luminita. Take your time while I fill her in on the massive amount of evidence we've gathered."

The scathing sarcasm reminded Lilith of how much she disliked him at times. She felt frustrated enough without him twisting the knife. Still, they needed a Cohen-free moment to send Chance off in Timothy's car, so she ignored his condescending comment. Besides, lecturing him on the art of teamwork seemed like a pointless endeavor.

If he genuinely wanted their trust, he'd include them instead of sneaking off to make the call.

As soon as Cohen left the restaurant, the three of them picked their way through the crowd. Lilith peered outside and spotted the demon with his back to them about thirty yards away, phone to his ear. The trio crept through the door and around the building before jogging down to the corner.

"I'm parked in a garage two blocks down." Timothy dug out his keys and tossed them to Chance. "I wish you luck on your super-secret mission, brother." Then he slapped Chance's shoulder with a smirk. "And don't worry. I'll keep her safe." His conspiratorial wink said it all. Who knew the man was so skilled at figuring out people?

"Thanks, Tim. Hey, can you give us a second?" Chance nodded back toward the diner, and Timothy strolled off to play lookout.

Lilith fought the nervous energy clawing at her brain and willed herself to let the siren crap go. "I still don't like this." She rubbed at her arms and stared at the concrete. The slight nip in the night air had nothing to do with her sudden chills. "You shouldn't be going by yourself."

"Lily, *cherie*, we went over this. I need you to make the call."

After a slow inhale, she nodded and dialed the number.

"Yes, this is Lilith Adams, security code A09178. I am initiating the emergency protocol and allocating my security code to Chance Allen Deveraux... Yes, I understand." She hung up and stared down at her phone as if she'd somehow signed his death warrant.

Chance slowly slid his hand over hers, and its warmth seeped into her skin. She smiled down at the simple gesture with tears in her eyes because she didn't feel the need to pull away. When her eyes raised to meet his, panic lingered in her chest, but not as strong.

"You did great." The reassuring smile on his lips gave her the strength she needed to stand still and ignore the flickering images from her dream. She refused to give in and back away. She owed him that much, but the effort required a considerable amount of willpower.

The charade didn't fool him, of course. He sensed every emotion warring within her, but he still smiled in appreciation. "I wish I could help it go away. I'm so sorry, Lily." Silence filled the air, but it wasn't awkward, just quiet as his thumb caressed the back of her hand.

"Then, don't go." Irrational dread sat heavy in the pit of her stomach, but she couldn't discern if it stemmed from a selfish desire to keep him from leaving or something more ominous.

"I'll be careful, get what we need, and be back as fast as possible. You may not like me going solo, but I hate leaving you with Cohen more. I still don't trust him, *cher*. Watch your back and stick close to Timothy."

With a centering breath, she pushed past the fear and caressed his stubbled cheek. "I will, and you better get your ass back here. Nightmares or not, I can't survive this crap without you." Burgeoning tears welled in his eyes as he subtly leaned into her touch.

Her phone rang, shattering the moment, and Chance stepped back with a frown. "Who's calling you on a burner phone?"

She glanced down at the local number but didn't recognize it. "I cloned my number to the burner since they are probably tracing our physical devices, not the accounts. I can't risk missing another call that might help, and I don't want to raise suspicion by calling from an unknown number."

Chance's warm chuckle filled the crisp night air. "That's damn smart. I think you'd do fine without me, *cherie*."

Without any hesitation, she gazed up at him and spoke from the heart. "Perhaps, but I never want to find out."

"*Je t'aime tellement*, Lily." As he leaned closer, her heart began racing with a disturbing mixture of desire and throat-crushing fear. Chance simply placed a soft kiss on her cheek and quickly stepped back.

"That's cheating. You know I don't speak—"

He darted in to brush his lips against hers in a swift kiss that stole her breath for a multitude of reasons. "I love you so much, Lily."

She rubbed at her crimson cheeks as he stepped back again. "I love you, too."

For a moment, he stood there, beaming, before he glanced back at the corner with a sigh. "I'd better take off before Cohen comes looking for us. Once I get close to Tennessee, I'll stop for a few hours of sleep before heading to the lab." His hazel eyes filled with trepidation when his gaze returned to her. "Please, be careful."

She wanted to stop him, jump into his arms, kiss him with feverish passion, anything to keep him from leaving, but she merely nodded. They needed the tin from Goditha, and he was the only one who could accomplish the mission.

"Good luck, handsome."

"I don't need luck. I have all the inspiration I need." He winked with a roguish grin, dug his hands in his pockets, and started down the street.

With a heavy heart, Lilith watched him walk away before the darkness engulfed him. She caught glimpses of him as he passed under the sporadic lights, and then disappeared.

Someone cleared their throat, and she turned to see Timothy standing behind her, staring down the street. "He's the toughest guy I know. Wherever he's heading, he'll be fine." A soft and friendly smile stretched his lips, something she'd never seen him do. "Also, Cohen is wrapping up his call. He'll be joining us any minute now, so you might want to wipe away those tears."

Lilith swiped at her cheeks with a mock scowl and lightly punched Timothy's shoulder. "No need to be a smartass."

His surprised laugh resembled more of a booming wheeze than a chuckle, and the sound caught her so off guard that she joined in.

As Cohen rounded the corner, Lilith's phone rang again. She sent a silent thank you to the higher powers before sliding her finger over the screen and hurriedly put it up to her ear. "Hello?"

"Oh, hi. I'm glad I finally got hold of you." After a second, she recalled the energetic female voice from her voicemail.

"Nicci DeLuca?"

"Yep. That's me. I left a message the other day. I didn't want to bug you while you're on bereavement, but I came across something. Do you have a sec?"

She glanced down the sidewalk as Cohen scanned the area with a confused frown. "Perfect timing. I was about to call you."

"Oh yeah? Do you need something?" Either she failed at hiding her excitement or wasn't trying. Not everyone felt the need to bury their emotions in a political persona.

"I'm working on a private case and need some *discreet* help, off the books. Can we meet up?"

"Oh, sure. You're welcome to come by my place."

Lilith watched while Timothy moved forward to intercept Cohen, keeping him at a distance. "Do you mind if I bring a couple of people with me? I'm not working this alone, and they won't let me sneak off without them."

The hyper woman responded without hesitation. "Yeah, sure. No problem. I'll text you the address. See ya soon." Well, she seemed like a big-ole ball of sunshine, not an attribute Lilith typically sought in a partner, but it could have been a lot worse. Then again, maybe the woman was just nervous.

The phone buzzed with a new text before Lilith even hung up—remarkably efficient.

As Cohen stormed around Timothy, heading directly toward her, she drew in a deep breath. No more delays. Time to face the music.

"What the fuck is going on?" The angry demon stalked up to her, wearing a deep scowl. "Where is Chance?" His sky-blue eyes bored into her, pinning her in place, daring her to lie.

Lilith held up her hands in surrender and kept a calm and even tone. "He's chasing a lead."

His eyebrows raised in disbelief as he stepped closer, hovering inches from her face. "Chasing a lead? Are you kidding me? Did you not understand Luminita? He is part of the team. If the council gets wind of this, it won't matter if Chance finds Jimmy Hoffa sitting on the Ark of the Covenant, chugging beer out of the Holy Grail. We will all be dead!"

To her surprise, Lilith kept her cool. She calmly laid her hand on Cohen's arm and held his stormy gaze. "*If* is the keyword, Andrew. Timothy is a close match for a generic description, and they won't track his car or credit cards. The council will only find out if *you* tell them."

Cohen released a frustrated grunt and raked a hand through his sandy blond hair. Then, he turned his assessing glare on Timothy, who merely shrugged with a weak smile. The detective groaned and scanned the street as if waiting for Chance to pop out as a joke. After a few tense moments, he turned back to Lilith, scrutinizing her with slitted eyes.

"What the hell is so important?"

"I'm not prepared to share that yet." Her arms crossed over her chest while he blinked in surprise.

"I'm sorry, what?" He took another step closer, head tilting to the side, as Timothy tensed behind him. When she didn't respond, his face hardened in stone-cold anger.

"If this is about your fucked up nightmare… You can't put all our lives in danger because you had a scary dream about your boyfriend."

Not only did his outburst successfully piss her off, but now Timothy would ask a million questions, all of which she had hoped to avoid. Sure, Tim suspected, but Cohen had just concretely confirmed their relationship. Somehow, she stood still, refusing to flinch as his rage reached a fevered pitch.

"God dammit, Lilith! This isn't a fucking high-school drama. If you want to be a jumpy, nervous wreck around Chance, fine, but you don't swap out partners because you're fucking uncomfortable!"

When he stopped screaming, she took a step closer, and her voice dropped to a chillingly calm tone as she met his blue-gray eyes.

"Thank you for finally expressing your honest opinion of me. I hate to disappoint you, but this has nothing to do with my nightmare PTSD, you self-righteous son-of-a-bitch. Have I *ever* once shown myself to be untrustworthy?"

Then, Cohen's eyes sparked as if something occurred to him, which she felt certain had nothing to do with her question. "He's trying to find the cipher, isn't he?"

Yep. He completely ignored ninety-five percent of what I said.

When Lilith remained silent, seething with rage but refusing to budge, he released a heavy sigh. "Fine. I'll give you the benefit of the doubt... *for now.* I do *not* like this. It's an enormous gamble, so it better pay off!"

He maintained eye contact for a moment, probably waiting for her to concede or show gratitude, neither of which happened.

The man grunted in exasperation. "This is fucking nuts. *You* are fucking nuts."

Cohen turned on his heel and found himself face-to-face with Timothy, who weighed at least sixty pounds more than the demon—all muscle. "I don't think Gregor would appreciate you speaking to his daughter that way."

"I don't think he gives a shit because he's fucking *dead.*"

Tim's jaw clenched tight a second before his fist did the same.

Lilith suppressed a similar reaction. She recognized the demon's attempt to start a fight this time and refused to give in. Before Tim could throw a punch, she jumped between them and stared up at her new bodyguard. "Don't. He's just lashing out. It's not worth it."

Tim swallowed his anger, nodded, and took a step back. After a steadying breath to drown her own fury, she turned back to the demon, who appeared utterly unaffected.

"All right, Lilith, Chance-substitute, can we head to the car before we end up on YouTube?" Cohen gestured up the street, where several faces peeked around the corner. "I need a long hot bath and a valium cocktail."

"We need to stop somewhere first. The address is on the way to the hotel, and it won't take long."

"Another secret, or are you going to share this time?" The scathing sarcasm in Cohen's voice didn't surprise her, and once again, she refused to rise to the bait.

"My new partner's place. I'm hoping she can help us get some useful information from the check stubs."

"That would be a welcome change of pace." Cohen started walking, every muscle singing with tension. He didn't bother checking to see if they followed.

"What's his deal?" Timothy fell in step beside her as they trailed behind the fuming demon, keeping their distance.

She shrugged her shoulders, uncertain how to answer that question. "I've been trying to figure that out since I met him. I've had more luck trying to smell the color nine."

Timothy's booming laugh filled the air, causing Cohen to glance back, and Lilith swore she saw a vein in his temple throb like a water balloon ready to burst. So much for the friendly moment they'd shared in the diner. As odd as it seemed, she felt more comfortable when Cohen acted like his usual prickly self anyway. At least, she thought that was his normal. Who could really tell?

Chapter 16

Half an hour later, they were knocking on a door in a modest apartment building in Little Italy. Like Lilith's place, the lobby contained a reception desk and a generic row of mailboxes, but security wasn't a priority. At least, not to the guy on duty. The guard stared down at his phone as they passed through, too busy scrolling through his Facebook newsfeed to bother asking their names. Fortunately, they weren't scary monsters there to reap the residents' souls—just two vampires and a demon needing assistance.

When the door swung open, a petite brunette with an athletic build stood in the doorway dressed in yoga pants and a sports bra. Her deep brown eyes scanned Timothy and Cohen with what a casual observer would consider mild curiosity. The slight pull to her cupid bow's mouth and the tightness around her eyes betrayed an intelligence Lilith appreciated. The overly friendly demeanor appeared to be a cover, encouraging people to underestimate her.

People naturally assumed that beauty and IQ shared an inverse correlation. Expecting a supermodel to have a ten-year-old's intellect, for example. Lilith had experienced the stereotype first-hand, and it seemed Nicci had, too. Despite her slight overbite and prominent Italian nose, Nicci resembled a tiny movie more than a cop, and judging by the goofy grin on Tim's face, he wholeheartedly agreed.

"Hey, guys. Come on in." Nicci waved a hand before striding down the entry hall. Her long ponytail swished from side to side with each purposeful step while they trailed behind her.

Their perky hostess stopped in the living room and turned her brilliant smile on them again, focusing on Lilith. "Nice to meet you, finally. The guys at the station had great things to say."

The statement surprised Lilith, considering the dramatic scene at Alvarez's funeral. "Honestly?"

Nicci nodded with emphatic enthusiasm, which was a relief. Although the funeral fallout wasn't an immediate concern, it was one of many reasons she had delayed calling Detective DeLuca. She didn't want to hear the office gossip after her partner's widow slapped her at the graveside.

"Well, I'm sorry I took so long to call. I've been tied up." *Literally*.

"Can we skip the small talk?" Cohen's well-practiced boredom didn't fool Lilith. Unconsciously tapping his fist against his thigh betrayed his frustration.

"Yes, sorry. Detective Nicci DeLuca, this is Detective Andrew Cohen..." Nicci's smile strained when she shook Cohen's hand. Yet another person who didn't plan to become his best friend. What a surprise.

"... and security specialist Timothy Bardow."

"Bardow? From Mr. Adams' security firm?"

Timothy surged forward to eagerly shake her hand while a smile stretched his thin lips. "Yes. A pleasure to meet you, detective."

Lilith bit her lip. His formal greeting sounded awkward and unfamiliar but held an odd bravado. She couldn't tell if the petite detective made him nervous or if it was the small talk. Most of Gregor's bodyguards didn't talk much. Chance was the exception, not the rule.

"Have you lived in the city long?"

Nicci flashed Tim a tight smile, bordering on a grimace. "All my life but let me stop you before you hit me with another cheesy pickup line." She lowered her voice to a whisper and stepped closer while Tim's eyes widened.

"I'm in a committed relationship, and you don't have the right equipment." While Tim gaped like a wide-mouthed bass, she straightened and winked unapologetically. "But if you want someone to train with at the gym, I'm game."

Timothy blinked a few times, letting everything sink in, while Cohen choked on a laugh. "Oh, I like this one." Once he regained his composure, he gave Nicci a nod of appreciation and patted Tim's shoulder. "It's all right, big fella. You can't win 'em all."

"What? I wasn't...I was only being friendly." Timothy frowned at the demon's gloating grin.

"Hey, no offense, but I'm smart enough to realize a guy only asks you something personal for one reason, and it isn't the obligation to appear polite." Nicci shrugged her slender shoulders as she backed up toward Lilith. "I like to be upfront and avoid mixed signals. Plus, I'm always looking for a decent sparring partner. Too many guys take it easy on a five-foot-nothing girl."

"As amusing as this is…" Cohen strolled past everyone and perched on the arm of an overstuffed chair before continuing. "…perhaps we should skip ahead to the reason for our visit?"

"Uh, that chair has a seat." The scolding glare on Nicci's face made Lilith's day. Cohen locked eyes with her in defiance, but then slid like silk into the seat. Oh, yeah. If she had to replace Alvarez, this woman seemed to be a great substitute.

While Nicci claimed a chair identical to Cohen's, Lilith and Timothy sat gingerly on the sofa. Once they were all settled in, Lilith finally spoke up.

"A private party who wishes to remain anonymous enlisted our help to recover a stolen artifact, a rare book from the…"

"Beinecke Library at Yale? The Voynich manuscript?"

Lilith paused, startled by Nicci's sudden leap in logic.

"Sorry. The heist is all over the news. I mean, how many rare books go missing these days? Anyway, continue."

"Yeah. Well, the burglary went south. Someone tore two of the perps apart, and the third is missing. We have IDs on the corpses but are coming up empty on the guy who escaped with the book. All I've managed to—"

"Wait. Back up. *Torn apart?*"

Lilith gave her a quick rundown of the autopsy report, while Cohen and Timothy turned various shades of green. Unsurprisingly, Nicci didn't appear bothered by the gruesome details—homicide detectives tended to have strong stomachs.

"Do you think the killers planted the trace elements in the wounds to throw you off? It'd be an effective way to send a forensic investigator of your caliber on a wild goose chase."

"No, I don't see how they could plant it in such natural patterns."

"Any other evidence?"

"Only these." Lilith pulled the stubs from her pocket and slid them across the coffee table. "I found them in the apartments of our dead perps. Do the company initials mean anything to you?"

She shook her head after studying the slips of paper. "No. Sorry, but I can research them. I'll access some databases and the logo registry, try to track down the company. I'll warn you, though. If they wrote these for illegal services, I guarantee the initials represent some fictitious shell company. It may take hours or days to track down anything recognizable."

"Whatever you find is more than we have now."

Nicci nodded while her mind wandered elsewhere. "Before you take off, I wanted to update you on a case. Can we talk alone in my office?"

Lilith glanced at Cohen, who merely shrugged his shoulders without a hint of concern, content to stare out the window and brood.

"Yeah, sure." Lilith followed her into a small bedroom that the woman had converted into an office. A simple desk wrapped around two walls with three monitors, while the left wall held a collection of pictures, photographic evidence of Nicci's accomplishments. The frames displayed images of her rock climbing, flying a plane, skydiving, snorkeling, riding a camel, walking along the Great Wall of China, and on and on.

"Wow. You have a lot of hobbies."

Nicci glanced up from the computer chair and beamed. "I wouldn't call them hobbies. I want to leave no stone unturned. Those are both proof and inspiration." They shared a friendly smile before Nicci turned back to the screen.

"First, I want to say this in private. If we are going to be partners, we need to trust each other." When she turned in her chair again, the warm smile transformed into a steel mask of resolution. "You're hiding things about your case. I understand. You don't know me, but I want you to trust me, and it goes both ways. So, for now, I only want to say that I have faith in your judgment. If you told me everything, perhaps I could help more, but if you aren't sharing, I'm sure you have reasons."

The blunt honesty was refreshing after enduring Cohen's shifting demeanor. "Thank you. I do, and it's nothing against you. There are things…I simply can't tell you for *your* safety."

A bright smile crossed Nicci's lips, and she nodded. "Alright. Since that's settled, I want to ask you a few questions about your last case with Detective Alvarez."

Panic tightened her throat as she contemplated the million things she couldn't tell Nicci about the insanity in Tennessee.

"Case number 529-821456, Malachi Sanders?"

A flood of relief washed over her, and she slid into the other chair as Nicci opened the file. The number nagged at her until she remembered the voicemail from the forensic lab.

"I got all the results back today. Malachi was a pureblood, correct?"

"Yeah. I think his father comes from an old line in Austria, and his mother is a pureblood from Syria. Why?"

Nicci squinted at the screen and shook her head. "I thought so. The results don't make any damn sense." She swiveled back to Lilith with an expression of utter confusion. "Malachi was sick."

"What?" Lilith sat there, shell-shocked by the sheer impossibility of her statement. One of the few benefits of being a vampire was a kick-ass immune system. They never contracted a common cold, much less a chronic illness. "The abnormality must be a mistake. Perhaps they mixed up the samples. It happens."

Nicci rotated back to the screen, clicked away at the keyboard, and pulled up the M.E.'s report. "Yeah, I thought the same thing until I found a note on the autopsy. So, I called and spoke to the coroner, who confirmed his findings."

"What did Frank say?"

"Malachi had an unknown viral infection, so he sent samples to Solasta for further testing."

Lilith's brain raced around in circles until she landed on a seemingly distant memory—*Ida*. Mariah and Malachi's neighbor had mentioned he was sick, but she had dismissed the comment, assuming the elderly woman read too much into things or had seen him when he'd gone too long between feedings.

But how could it be true? Did Spencer and Ashcroft leave them a special surprise? *No.* Their only focus was revenge with immediate gratification, and Spencer seized every opportunity to gloat. If they had engineered a virus to infect a vampire, her cousin would have bragged nonstop. So, who was playing viral Frankenstein, and how could she ensure the threat was real?

Then, she recalled Miriah and Malachi's recent problems conceiving, something not uncommon within their species. Duncan always described their fertility issues as nature's price for their long lives, a way to keep them from overpopulating.

If Miriah and her husband had been dead set on having a child, they would have gone to Goditha for a complete workup. If so, Chance could grab their samples along with the tin. Solasta needed every resource to investigate this unknown viral infection, and fast.

"I may have a way to get more information for the lab." A heavy sigh escaped her lips as she stared at the impossible words on the screen. "I already have my hands full with this...situation, and now we have a theoretical virus in the mix?"

"When it rains, it pours." Nicci shrugged sympathetically.

"At this point, it's more like the apocalyptic, water-based punishment of a higher power."

Nicci snickered and patted Lilith on the shoulder. "Sorry to be the bearer of bad news. Why don't you and your pals leave the check stubs with me and head home for the night? I'll call you first thing in the morning with anything I find."

"There's one more thing I need." Lilith paused, uncertain how to ask without raising a slew of questions she couldn't answer. "I can't go to Solasta. I don't want to give the people who hired us any more information about us than I have to, and..."

Nicci flashed an understanding smile. "You need some supplies? I have a bag and some pills in the fridge. That should hold you over for now. I can pick up some more blood tomorrow if you need it."

"Thank you, and I'm sorry about Cohen and Timothy. *Men.*"

Nicci chuckled merrily, her entire face lighting up. "Oh, don't apologize. I've been a cop long enough to understand them. You can't let 'em get a rise out of you."

"Easier said than done, especially with Cohen. He possesses a natural talent for finding buttons you didn't realize you had and hitting them with a nuclear warhead."

"Fun times, but I'm guessing you launched a few missiles of your own?" Her lips stretched into a sly grin as she nudged Lilith's arm.

When Lilith flashed a Cheshire-cat grin, Nicci burst out laughing.

"I've dealt my fair share."

The one drawback to keeping Cohen in the dark about Chance's departure was the hotel room. Lilith and Timothy stood in the doorway, staring at the queen-sized bed.

"Well, at least there's a couch. Beats sleeping on the floor." He rubbed at his clean-shaven chin and tossed his duffle on the khaki sofa against the far wall. Although the couch was a somewhat stylish addition, she doubted the thing had more padding than a park bench.

Under different circumstances, she would have done the courteous thing and offered him the bed. However, after the catastrophic night terror, she needed every bit of comfort possible, even if it only consisted of a ten-year-old hotel mattress.

"Sorry, Tim. I couldn't tell Cohen, and…" She hesitated, uncertain what to say.

"And he assumed you and Chance only needed one bed?" He finished the sentence for her in a matter-of-fact tone. "I thought you were smarter than this."

Timothy turned back toward her as she stood there, puzzled and offended. He released a long sigh and rubbed at his square jaw again. "Sorry. This isn't my business and not why I'm here."

"If we are gonna be bunkmates and work together, I'd rather you say your piece now instead of letting it loom over us like a two-ton elephant."

Of course, she knew what he wanted to say. After all, Chance had a colorful history of changing girls as frequently as he did boxers, but Tim didn't realize the playboy image was a facade. Fortunately, she didn't need to convince him of the truth. She merely wanted him to purge his negative opinions so they could move forward.

As Tim bit his lip indecisively, he plopped on the sofa, staring at his hands. "Dammit. I shouldn't…"

"I've already suffered through lectures from my dad and Alvarez about why I should steer clear of Chance, so nothing you're about to say is a surprise, Tim. Spit it out."

His brown eyes snapped up at her with an odd hostility. "*You* aren't the one I'm worried about." When she merely blinked in surprise, he continued. "Chance spent more time with Gregor than any of us, which frequently involved you. Most people view him as a player with a different girl each week, but I knew better. He used them as a distraction because he loved someone he couldn't have."

His train of thought caught her off guard, and she sat on the bed with a newfound curiosity.

"The man has *never* been in a relationship, and you are a fantasy he has built up over the last decade. Shit. No one can live up to that, and what happens when this case ends? How are you going to feel when you don't *need* him, and you face the normal day-to-day?"

Tim's insightful logic cut right to her core, verbalizing all her deepest fears, which brought out her typical defense mechanism—sarcasm. "Sweet Jesus, Tim. Are you spending your mornings watching Steve Harvey or Oprah?"

"Hey, you told me to spit it out, and the man is my best friend. I don't want to see him hurt." He shrugged his broad shoulders, refusing to rise to the bait. "Chance doesn't let many people close enough to realize he's a great guy. He told me…about Tennessee…just before Alvarez's funeral. His head was all twisted up."

The humor drained from her face as she read the indicators on Timothy's, all of which suggested a straightforward instinct to protect his friend. "What do you mean *twisted up?*"

Tim rubbed at his jaw, clearly uncomfortable. "All that stuff went down, and then you ghosted him when you got back to New York."

A frown furrowed her brow. "I did *not* ghost him. He didn't reach out to me either, and I was burying my partner and best friend. You *know* that."

The man nodded thoughtfully again. "Yeah, I get that. I even explained that to him, but I just don't think you understand Chance."

"I know who he is. He told me everything, and as impossible as this may seem to you, I truly care about him."

Tim snorted a mocking laugh. "How can you? *You don't know him,* not really. You never talk to any of us. We're just part of the background."

"That's not fair. You never tried to talk to me either. And you don't know what we went through in Tennessee."

"One week in a pressure cooker doesn't mean you understand a person. If he's just a rebellious fling or a temporary knight-in-shining-armor…if you—"

"What? Break your best friend's heart?"

"Well, yeah," he grunted with defensive pride.

"Tim…" When they'd started the conversation, she hadn't felt the need to prove anything. That suddenly changed. She locked eyes with him, willing him to believe. "He almost died in Phipps Bend. Someone shot him in the chest, and he was bleeding out fast. I did impossible things to save him because…I love him. I can't explain how or why, but I knew the truth in my bones seconds *before* that shot. We don't know what the future holds with Gregor gone, but I don't want to lose him, ever."

His eyes narrowed in suspicion. "Then why did you both look miserable?"

Lilith stretched her neck, aggravated by the constant need to repeat the story. "I had a bad night terror that I'm finding difficult to shake.

I'm not pushing him away, and I'm not giving up. And before you ask, yes, he knows how I feel."

Tim nodded thoughtfully, apparently finding common ground in her answer. "I was a Green Beret before joining Gregor's team. Did you know that?"

Lilith nodded but remained silent, curious where he was going with this.

"I served in the 1ˢᵗ Armored Division during the Battle of Najaf in Iraq. They deployed us to relieve the 3ʳᵈ Infantry Division out of Georgia. The city sat between two highways we used for supply lines to Karbala and Baghdad, so seizing control would be an incredible asset." A haunted shadow of grief and regret settled over his face as he continued to talk, never quite meeting her eyes.

"Although we eventually captured the town with the help of the 101ˢᵗ Airborne and the 70ᵗʰ Armored Regiment, it came at a price. I watched them shoot down Apache helicopters and take the survivors prisoner. Hell, even the civilians carried rifles, and if they didn't shoot you on sight, they'd turn you over to the Iraqi Republican Guard."

"Then, on March 29ᵗʰ, 2003, a man wandered into our camp on the edge of the city. He was a regular supplier but didn't have any goods that day. The man held up his hands in surrender, babbling wildly in Arabic. I was up in a sniper blind with one of my men. I saw everything.

"No one knew what he was saying, and the rest of my team drew their weapons, yelling for him to get on the ground. Gibson and I covered them from the blind while they moved in to secure him. The suicide bomber took out four of my squad mates, splattered them against the crumbling walls like raw hamburger, a scene that regularly replays in my dreams."

Slowly, Tim tore his attention away from the ghosts of his past to meet her eyes. "I understand how powerful survivor's guilt can be, but you can't let the darkness prevent you from honoring the sacrifice of others and enjoying your life. They didn't give up their lives for you to hide in a corner, cut off from everything that makes life worth living."

Tears welled in her eyes as she stared across the room at the surprisingly wise man sitting on her couch. "I need to apologize. I *really* underestimated you, and I'm sorry I never took the time to get to know you, Tim."

"Yeah, well, most people underestimate me, and I'm fine with that. Makes my job easier." He shrugged his broad shoulders and stood up, signaling an end to their deep conversation. "I'm gonna head to the lobby for a bit if you'll be all right here. I need to make a call."

Judging by the flickers of emotions on his face, he wanted to call a girl. Not a romantic interest, but someone he loved, someone he worried about, perhaps a mother or a sister?

"Of course. I'll be fine, and thank you, Tim."

They shared a hesitant yet friendly smile before he walked through the door, closing it softly behind him.

While the conversation replayed through her head, Lilith wandered into the bathroom, filled the sink, and slid the bag of blood from Nicci's into the hot water. The slight headache gnawing at the base of her skull told her she was overdue.

As soon as the blood warmed to an acceptable temperature, she drained the bag without the civility of a cup and immediately felt a warm sense of relief disperse through her body.

Almost on cue, her burner phone rang. After a few seconds, she wrestled it out of her pocket, slid her finger across the screen, and answered.

"Lily?" The Cajun-flecked voice warmed her down to her toes more effectively than the blood.

"Were your ears burning?" She couldn't help but laugh at the coincidental timing.

"Talking about me, huh?" He hesitated, uncertain if the news was good or bad.

"Well, we just got back to the hotel, and Timothy...*questioned my intentions.*"

"He did what?" His rich, velvety laughter wrapped around her like a plush blanket, even over the crackly speaker of a cheap phone.

"He came awfully close to threatening me. I didn't realize you two were best friends."

"Tim took me under his wing when I signed onto Gregor's detail. He's been through a lot, but he's a great guy when you get to know him. Hell, he threw me a party when your dad promoted me over him despite seniority."

"I can tell by the way he stood up for you. I also didn't realize you *told* him about Tennessee."

"What did he say?" The nervous tension in his tone came through loud and clear.

Lilith wasn't to ask about the conversation, about what Tim had meant by *twisted up*, but now wasn't the time. "Basically...not to break your heart."

"And what did you say?" She could almost hear the smile in his voice.

"The same thing I told you before you left, but I'm guessing that's not why you called."

"No. I wanted to make sure you're okay. How did Cohen take things?"

"Oh, he went ballistic, but nothing I can't handle. He's fuming and pouting in his room right now. By the way, I was about to call you."

"Oh? Miss me already?" The hopeful grin in his voice was contagious.

"Perhaps..." The playful yet seductive tease brought back a sense of normalcy. Bit by bit, she was reclaiming the pieces of herself that shattered when Peisinoe appeared in Chance's apartment, but she still had a long way to go.

"Oh, you know you do." His slight growl sent delicious shivers skittering along her spine. She could listen to him all night, but she didn't have much time. Tim would be back soon. "But we can settle that debate later. So, what's up?"

"I met with Nicci, my new partner, who agreed to work on the checks for us. While we were there, she asked to speak with me alone about a case—Malachi's homicide. An impossible abnormality popped up on the autopsy report that I should check out. Miriah and Malachi should have blood samples at Goditha. Can you request them for me while you're there? Hopefully, the results are a mistake, because if not..." Lilith slowly exhaled as she tried to keep her mind from unraveling with all the dire implications.

"What's wrong, *cherie?*"

"The medical examiner reported an unknown viral infection."

"That can't be right, Lily. It's impossible."

"That's what I said, but the report from the lab said the same thing. I don't know. Hell, two weeks ago, I thought turned vampires were impossible, too."

"Ashcroft was never human, *cher*. This must be a mix-up. I'll grab the samples for you, don't worry." After a moment of silence, he continued, but his voice didn't hold the same confidence. "So, are you really okay?"

She paused for a second, uncertain how to answer. "Honestly? No. I'm terrified of falling asleep, and I miss you. I haven't made things easy, and I'm sorry for—"

"Lily, you don't need to apologize."

"I know, but...just please be safe and get your ass back here."

"I will. I'm coming up to a toll booth, but call me when you catch a break, okay? Love you, *cherie*." He hung up before she had an opportunity to respond, and Lilith beamed as his words resonated through her mind.

A crack of thunder shook the room, startling Lilith from a blissfully deep sleep. She lay there, sightless in the inky blackness, trying to slow her racing heart.

As the blood pounding in her ears subsided, she heard muffled voices outside the room. The thought of Timothy and Cohen hanging out was laughable, so who was out there? Perhaps a few drunks stumbling to their room after a late night of partying in the big city?

"Tim?" No one answered, and she heard no indications of movement, only the incomprehensible voices whispering on the other side of the wall.

An all-too-familiar panic blossomed in her chest as she squinted, trying to garner every stray bit of light, but absolute darkness still enveloped her. Even with the blackout curtains drawn, she should be able to see something. Why was the room so dark?

Lilith moved to swing her feet off the bed but couldn't find the edge. In fact, the scratchy material beneath her palms didn't feel like the comforter.

Did I fall off the damn bed? She crawled to all fours and moved forward until one hand landed on a thin carpet. The other slapped down on cold tile.

Wait. The hotel room isn't tiled. Where am I? Okay. Get a grip. After a deep, calming breath, she forced her body forward again, reaching out with her hands until they bumped into the legs of chairs—three of them—sitting behind some sort of table.

Bone-chilling dread replaced the panic when she suddenly realized where she was—Farren's courtroom.

A flurry of questions immediately darted through her mind, one after the other. *Why am I here? Did we run out of time? How did I get here?*

Rose of Jericho

Did they drug me? Where is everyone else? Is Tim okay? Did they find out about Chance? Is he still alive? Where is Cohen? Why am I alone?

"Timothy? Cohen? Chance?" She called out nervously, uncertain if she honestly wanted a response or not. Only the whispering voices broke the deathly silence. Nothing else.

With determination, she inched toward the hushed tones, feeling around until she found the wall. Then, her heart raced with the sudden memory of her father's blood and brains splattering against that same surface. *Focus. You can't panic—not yet.*

Her eyes closed against the oppressive darkness as she slowly stood, every muscle trembling. *Come on. Keep it together.*

Lilith pressed her forehead against the wall, inhaling and exhaling in a slow rhythm. Once she managed to move her limbs again, she felt along the smooth surface, heading toward the door she remembered Farren using.

Each tenuous step became a brutal battle as terror strummed through every cell. She kept expecting her fingers to touch the dried blood she knew existed—her father's blood. *Breathe. Just breathe.*

The murmuring voices grew louder, but the garbled tones didn't seem familiar, and she still couldn't make out actual words. *Come on. Keep moving.* Her fingers glided, smooth as silk, over the drywall as she took another step.

Suddenly, her fingertips brushed over something rough, and she froze with tears flooding her eyes. Her entire body shook as she carefully pulled her hand away. The prickly sensation from the dried blood's texture lingered on her skin, causing the bile to rise. *Don't lose it! Think about the others. Think about Chance. They need you.*

Lilith released a ragged breath past trembling lips and summoned the memory of Chance holding her, comforting her, wiping away her tears. The flickers were faint at first but grew in intensity with each image until she absorbed their warmth into her bones.

Then, the whispering voices fell silent, followed by a metallic click echoing through the cavernous room. Up ahead, a sliver of light penetrated the inky blackness. The door was open and only a few steps away. A mixture of hope and dread stole her breath as she stared, transfixed, waiting for any sign of movement.

As a shadow briefly flickered across the threshold, an icy hand snatched her ankle and yanked viciously. Lilith screamed in surprise when she hit the ground with brutal force, her cheek colliding with the tile. The blinding pain left her dazed for a few crucial seconds.

When the world finally snapped into focus, she kicked toward her assailant as sharp nails raked over her bare skin, leaving bloody furrows in their wake. With a screech of anger, she kicked again. This time, she connected. A guttural, inhuman howl followed the sickening crack of crunching bone.

As soon as her attacker relaxed their grip, she took off like a rocket, slipping and skidding on shaky legs. But she didn't move fast enough. The clammy hand locked around her ankle again, holding her back. She stretched out in despair, fingertips brushing uselessly over the doorknob, before she collapsed to the ground.

The unknown assailant clawed their way up her body while she squirmed and desperately reached for the door. Finally, her fingers curled around the edge, and she pulled, widening the sliver of light. That minuscule amount of hope allowed her to breathe a little easier, even if it didn't make logical sense.

The light flickered for an instant, drawing her attention, and then someone ripped the door away from her, slamming it closed. Once again, she found herself submerged in absolute darkness.

"No! Let me out!" She screamed through her trembling sobs.

The attacker continued to climb up her body, bringing with them the putrid stench of decay.

"Please, let this be a dream! Let me see Miriah, or Duncan, or Alvarez. They can blame me for letting them die, but please, don't let this be real!"

An acrid puff of breath washed over her face as a sickening gurgled sound vibrated through the air, sending tremors of terror through every muscle. "You aren't real." The whimpered words held no confidence, only a desperate plea.

An overhead light suddenly drowned the room in painful brightness, scorching her retinas even through her closed lids. She tried to shield her eyes, but the monster's knees pinned her arms to the tile with bruising pressure.

Hesitantly, she blinked against the light, unable to see anything but vague blobs of color at first. Nails scratched at the center of her chest, tearing at her skin. She screamed and violently tried to buck the body off her.

As her eyes adjusted to the overwhelming illumination, the amorphous shape took form. Someone hovered over her, tearing brutally at her chest like an animal digging for a bone while her endless screams echoed off the walls.

Then, horror clenched her entire body as the monster's face suddenly became crystal clear from inches away. A hungry snarl distorted the familiar features.

No...

Lilith stared into her father's face, pale and jaundiced from decomp. Crusted blood surrounded the bullet wound above his left eye. A wave of nausea more intense than the pain from his vicious attack made her cough and gag as tears flooded her cheeks. *No. This isn't real. This can't be real.*

The monster's fingers clamped victoriously around the edges of her sternum, and a blood-curdling scream erupted from her throat.

A hand slapped Lilith's cheek hard, leaving a sharp burn behind. Her eyes snapped open to see Timothy straddling her waist, knees pinning her wrists to the mattress. He said something, but she couldn't hear him past the blood thundering in her ears. Her olive eyes searched wildly for Gregor's corpse but found no one lurking in the faintly lit hotel room.

"Lilith Marie Adams!" Timothy shook her shoulders with an expression of panicked worry while he screamed her full name. "You are having a nightmare. You are in New York City...in the Hilton Hotel, Room 1408. You are safe."

Slowly, she became aware of her body, slick with clammy sweat, as her heart continued to beat furiously. She quickly glanced down at her chest—no wounds or scratches. "It wasn't real?" Desperate hope stained her raspy voice, and Tim shook his head but didn't release her.

With an uneven exhale, she relaxed into the mattress, letting the whirlwind in her mind calm to a dull roar. When he decided she was no longer a threat, he lifted his knees and moved off the bed.

"That must have been one hell of a nightmare! I think your screams woke the entire hotel." Then he turned his arms to inspect them and winced. "Shit. Do you have any bandages?"

After shaking off her drowsy shock, she peered at the deep scratches, welling with blood. "Oh my god, Tim. I'm so sorry!" Her face flushed with embarrassed heat, and she scrambled off the bed.

Although nightmares had plagued her since college, none of them had compared to the hyper-realistic night terrors of the past week. These torturous dreams had real consequences—CPR, PTSD, and now she had physically assaulted Tim.

Lilith glanced up in the mirror as she wet two towels with hot water and barely recognized herself. Her features appeared the same, but the haunted shadows in her eyes tainted everything. What if she never recovered? If she escaped the council's clutches, did she possess the strength to survive the scars she had accumulated since leaving New York?

With a fierce scowl, she shook off her melancholy thoughts and walked back to Tim. She couldn't afford to wallow in self-doubt, not now.

"Are you okay?" He winced as she meticulously wrapped his forearms, unable to meet his inquisitive frown.

"With everything that's happened…my nightmares have gotten worse, much worse."

"Something like this happened with Chance?"

Her hands froze as her gaze slowly lifted to meet his big brown eyes. "Worse."

"You hurt him?" Tim tensed protectively.

"No," she huffed and refocused on cleaning his scratches. "I dreamt that someone forced Chance to strangle me, and…"

The immediate burst of wheezing laughter caught her off guard. "That's ridiculous! The man would slit his own throat first, not just because he's a bodyguard, but because the man has been crazy in love with you since he was seventeen."

"Are you done?" When he frowned in confusion at her angry scowl, she continued. "There are things you don't understand, and I can't explain. However, the dream felt so real that I…stopped breathing. Chance had to perform CPR."

"Shit. Like dying in the Matrix, huh?" He exhaled deeply when she shrugged.

"When you woke me up, using my full name and telling me where I was…it helped a lot. How did you know to do that?"

Tim shrugged with a faint blush to his cheeks. "A lot of us didn't make it out of the war without emotional scars. Let's just say I've had a lot of experience with PTSD, and I know what helps. So, what was your dream about this time?"

She hesitated, uncertain if talking about the new mental trauma would help or make things worse. "Dad, mostly." She paced across the room, popped open her kit, and retrieved the antibiotic ointment, a roll of gauze, and some tape.

Lilith focused intently on cleaning his wounds, trying not to think about Chance and how much she already missed him. The dream permeated her bones with a dreadful chill she couldn't shake.

Rose of Jericho

She kept picturing her father's rotting face hovering over her, nails digging through her skin, fingers clutching her sternum. It seemed so real, precisely like the nightmare about Peisinoe and Chance, more like a memory than a dream.

"How did he die?" The vulnerable softness in Timothy's voice dragged her back to the present moment. "Did he suffer?" He swallowed hard, staring at his calloused hands.

"It was fast." She wanted to leave it at that, but he had worked for her father five days a week for the past eighteen years. The man deserved every grain of truth she could share without bringing up Cohen's family.

"They tortured and beat him for hours before bringing him out." Tears trickled down her cheeks as she thought back to her father's battered and bruised face. "I begged them to release him...but they shot him in the head in front of us—a warning to cooperate and a reminder of what awaits us if we don't." The guilt still weighed heavily on her shoulders, but no longer suffocated her.

"Chance taking off violates the rules, doesn't it? That's why Cohen is pissed?" She merely nodded while bandaging his arm. "Well, I'm sure it's worth it. Chance would never take the risk otherwise."

Once she taped up the last bit of gauze, she sat back with a heavy heart, unable to meet his eyes again. Chance only left because *she* felt the risk was worth it. What if she was wrong?

The pages in the box could be blank paper or part of some other project. She based their usefulness on a hunch, a presumptive guess about her uncle's organizational skills. She found them inside a tin with Ashcroft's blood sample and tiny portraits of Gregor and Duncan's family from that time—all things connected to the Voynich manuscript but were circumstantial evidence at best.

"Who the hell are these people?"

"I can't tell you." He tried to object, but she cut him off with a stern warning. "You can't win this argument. The info we've already told you is dangerous enough, and trust me, knowing who they are won't help. You should know as little as possible for your safety."

"So, in other words, they are badass evil motherfuckers?"

"That about sums it up." Lilith released a slight chuckle, amused by his colorful interpretation. At least he knew when to stop asking questions, which was a talent she had never perfected...or learned, for that matter. Her insatiable curiosity and inability to let go always got her in trouble. Of course, it had also kept her alive...so far.

Chapter 17

Timothy, Cohen, and Lilith sat in the hotel restaurant, staring bleary-eyed at more plastic-coated menus. They owed their early wake-up call to Nicci and the thrill of a lead, which was the only reason Lilith crawled out of bed after a few hours of restless sleep.

Although the two stiffs in New Haven provided some odd insights, all the evidence from the heist and murders had led to dead ends. They needed something concrete, or last night's dream would become a reality, and the council members weren't the only ones after them. Someone had tried to stop their investigation using an assassination squad complete with assault rifles.

An uncomfortable silence surrounded the table, each of them lost in thought and unwilling to break the verbal stand-off. The dining room was nearly vacant, odd for a Saturday morning in Manhattan.

Of course, when Halloween fell on a Sunday, like it did this year, most people partied on Saturday night—tonight. Some claimed religious reasons for moving the festivities, but she suspected it was more about avoiding a Monday-morning hangover. Either way, people tended to sleep in, resting for a fun-filled evening. What she wouldn't give to be one of those blissfully unaware humans, oblivious to the darkness infiltrating her life.

"Morning, guys." Nicci confidently strode toward the table, her ponytail swinging wildly with each step, and slid into the seat beside Lilith. The petite brunette had traded in last night's athletic wear for more professional attire, sporting pinstripe slacks, a vibrant orange blouse, and a sleek leather jacket while her badge flashed from her belt.

Lilith felt horribly underdressed by comparison, but at least the blazer over her T-shirt and jeans lent her some level of respectability. Of course, professionalism wasn't the reason she wore a jacket. Not only would it protect her from the chilly fall air, but it also hid her shoulder holster.

The pencil skirts the demons had packed for her lacked any useful purpose. Sure, they looked great, but she could barely move in them, much less chase down leads and investigate scenes. The same went for the stilettos.

"Did you order yet? I'm starving!" If Nicci had noticed the uncomfortable silence, she'd chosen to ignore it.

"Nope. We waited for you. So, what did you find?" Anxious energy itched under Lilith's skin with the gnawing desire to do something, anything that would end all this. She wanted her every day, boring life back, one that didn't include demons.

"Let's at least order first." Nicci waved down a waiter and gave him her order. Judging by her choices, Nicci owed her athletic frame to a high metabolism and intense workouts, not diet control. Cohen and Tim unsuccessfully tried not to stare as she ordered three scrambled eggs, sausage, bacon, biscuits, French toast, and a large side of hash browns, extra crispy.

Nicci frowned at their shocked faces with distinct disappointment. "I'm not an anorexic beauty queen. I'm Italian. Food is love, and I eat whatever the hell I want, so you can stop gawking." Lilith appreciated her slight defensive growl as the men averted their eyes and placed their orders.

Once the waiter trotted off, Nicci finally scanned the table. Her stare landed on Lilith's sleep-deprived face before moving to the gauze peeking from Timothy's sleeves. "Did I miss all the fun last night? You two look a little rough." Her heart-shaped face tilted with a quizzical expression.

Lilith chewed her lip, trying to come up with a plausible explanation without delving into her night terrors. She'd never liked discussing them, and the recent ones seemed impossible to convey without sounding like a nutcase. "Nothing dramatic. I had a bad dream. Tim tried to wake me, and I wasn't immediately grateful."

"Oh, hell. Another one?" Cohen frowned with a heavy sigh, but Lilith's stern scowl sparked Cohen's sudden interest in his water glass.

"Understandable. Hell, your life hasn't been a bed of roses as of late." The petite woman seemed to sense her apprehension and quickly changed the subject. "So, Detective Cohen, what precinct are you from?"

"Knoxville isn't big enough for precincts. The violent crimes division operates out of the main building on Howard Baker Avenue." Cohen rattled off his former workplace information without thinking. When he glanced up to witness the surprise and suspicion on Nicci's face, he realized his mistake. Odd. The man typically covered his bases three times over. Perhaps he didn't sleep well either.

"Knoxville?" Her slitted eyes swung to Lilith as if hot on the trail of something. "This has something to do with Phipps Bend and your uncle's family, doesn't it? I mean, why else would he follow you up here from Tennessee?"

Well, she saw no use in denying things now. Besides, the admitted connection didn't qualify as dangerous information unless she kept digging. "In a way, yes. Detective Cohen *helped...*" Lilith nearly choked on the word. "...in Tennessee and has a vested interest in this case."

"Wait." Nicci frowned and rubbed her right temple. "I read a name in the report, the guy from Gregor's security team who flew down with you. I'm positive it wasn't Timothy. He had an odd name. Chester... Chandler..."

"You read the report?" Lilith quirked an eyebrow in suspicion, which made Nicci squirm slightly and her cheeks flush. Apparently, office gossip wasn't her only source of information.

"Uh. Yeah. I wanted to be prepared, so I skimmed the statements from you and the other guy...damn. What was his name?"

"Chance Deveraux."

"That's it! So, why isn't he here? I mean, if your case is connected to those events..." Nicci frowned at the tense look exchanged between Lilith and Cohen as her words trailed off. "What am I missing?"

"Why don't *you* explain?" Cohen leaned back, folding his arms over his chest with a smug grin, which held more than a hint of anger.

Lilith rolled her eyes at his overdramatic response. "Stop posing like a pissed-off peacock."

Cohen merely huffed at her chastising words, choosing to remain silent.

With a frustrated sigh, Lilith turned her attention back to Nicci. "Sorry. The detective is angry we didn't consult him before Chance left town. He's still involved with the case, but he's chasing leads elsewhere." The explanation was simplistic but accurate, which bolstered her credibility. Thankfully, her new partner appeared satisfied and didn't pry any further.

Cohen opened his mouth to say something, but the waiter arrived with their plates, and he let it go. He seemed more than happy to dig into his breakfast while Nicci began sharing information between bites.

"So, I tried to trace the company that wrote those checks, but they don't want anyone to find them. I tracked them through three different shell corporations before the trail became exponentially complicated. I can keep digging, but it will take a lot more time, probably more than you can spare."

Lilith sighed heavily, crestfallen. "Another dead end?"

"Not quite." A proud smile stretched her lips. "I *was* able to hack into the bank account. I located copies of three cashier checks for identical amounts dated two weeks before the robbery. Two of the numbers match those stubs, so I bet the third belongs to your mystery man."

"Why wouldn't they cover their tracks if they went through the trouble of a convoluted company shuffle?"

"I guess they decided the records of a dummy corporation weren't a high-security priority, especially since the entire company could disappear into the ether. Plus, they only implicate the three men, not the people who hired them."

Nicci shoveled a big bite of ketchup-smothered hash browns into her mouth as Lilith and Cohen waited in anticipation, desperate for a genuine lead.

"The bank wrote all three cashier checks to specific individuals. At first, I found it suspiciously convenient for illegal activity, but if the guy pulling strings wanted to implicate these men in the crime, it makes sense…"

After another quick bite, Nicci shifted a few papers around and slapped their arrest records down one by one. "Jimmy Tome…Denny Hickson…and Stephen Haverty." When she revealed the last file, Lilith immediately scooped it up.

"As you can see, he has a lengthy rap sheet, which covers his teens and early twenties—B&E, hacking, identity theft, tampering with an ATM, theft by deception, forgery, criminal mischief, petty theft, etc. Then…nothing for the past sixteen years."

"He cleaned up his act?" Timothy inquired skeptically.

"No." Lilith jumped into the conversation. "This guy is a lifelong criminal. He learned from his mistakes, took precautions, like at the museum. He put two patsies in places, ready to take the fall, leaving him free to run off with the prize. Nicci, did you find a last-known address?"

"Yes. He renewed his driver's license three weeks ago, so this should be the real deal."

A tingle of excitement raced around the table. They finally had a valid lead.

"I'll bring the car around front." Without another word, Cohen slid out of the booth, tossed a few twenties on the table, and strode toward the elevators with renewed purpose. The sooner they solved the case, the sooner their awkward partnership ended, and Cohen seemed eager to return to his solitary lifestyle.

Nicci watched him leave with a question lingering on her face. When the elevator doors closed, she turned to Lilith with a frown. "He's not one of us, is he?" Lilith shook her head with a sigh. "So, he's human, but he knows about us? And we're ok with this?"

"No. All I can tell you is he's not human either."

Nicci mulled over her statement as her mind worked the angles. Then she shrugged. "Eh, doesn't matter. He's still an asshole no matter what species he is."

Lilith called Chance on the way to Haverty's apartment, but it went to voicemail. Although he had planned to grab a few hours of sleep, she still felt uneasy when he didn't pick up.

"Hey, Nicci found us a lead—Stephen Haverty. We're heading to his place now..." She hesitated while self-consciously glancing around the car and whispered into the phone. "I miss you. Be careful."

Cohen quirked an eyebrow at her through the rearview mirror, and Lilith flashed her middle finger in response.

When the vehicle came to a stop, it became immediately apparent that Stephen Haverty enjoyed a much more lucrative career than his cohorts. He lived on the middle floor of a moderately priced high-rise in Midtown Manhattan, quite a leap from the rundown flophouses of Queens. Hell, he probably paid twice as much as Lilith did in rent, if not more.

Although Nicci's badge granted them access to the building, the guard refused to tell them if their mark was home. Considering Haverty had avoided police suspicion for nearly two decades, he probably paid security to tip him off when they came calling. Nicci seemed to think along the same lines.

"We should split up in case he runs. Lilith, you and Cohen take the stairs. I'll take this elevator, and Timothy, you take the other. Everyone's armed?" The entire group nodded in unison. The woman displayed sharp intelligence and didn't shy away from taking charge.

Of course, Lilith preferred not to team up with Cohen, but she understood the reasoning. Nicci didn't trust him, and it made sense for the person who knew the demon best to play chaperone.

After pulling her gun from the shoulder-holster, she held it loosely at her side and followed Cohen to the stairwell. At least she had the forethought to choose comfortable footwear and leave her forensic kit in the car. She couldn't imagine climbing to the eleventh floor in a pencil skirt and heels while lugging a twenty-pound aluminum case.

Hopefully, they'd catch their target, and she wouldn't need her kit. If he was home, they might finally get some answers, and if he wasn't, she could always go back for her case once they cleared the scene.

They made it up four flights in blissful silence before Cohen seized his opportunity. "You left something in Tennessee, didn't you? Something you kept hidden from the FBI investigation? You know where the cipher is."

Lilith released a frustrated sigh. She had expected an interrogation, but when he hadn't needled her with questions at the Brooklyn Diner or made some excuse to corner her alone, she had begun to think he might trust her.

"We are not having this conversation. All I'm willing to say is that it *may* help us. I can't make any guarantees, but we don't have a lot of options. We need to explore every possibility, and that's what Chance is doing."

"*We* as in *you* and *Chance*, or am *I* included?" The question caught Lilith off guard. She had never stopped to think about things in those terms. When she didn't respond, he barreled ahead.

"Yes, my family put you in this position, but I don't have any advantages, quite the opposite. You saw for yourself how Farren feels about me, and that's only the tip of the iceberg."

"I saw what you *wanted* me to see, which is all you show anyone. If the rest of your family is as manipulative as you, how do I know your grandfather angst isn't an elaborate show?" As the words passed her lips, she became increasingly less confident in them. Deep in her bones, she believed the hatred between them was genuine, cultivated over decades of trauma.

Cohen came to an abrupt halt, and Lilith nearly ran into him. He turned on his heel to glare down at her. A muscle in his cheek twitched, and his fists clenched. "He is the damn devil. Do *not* infer that I would *ever*..." When she took an instinctual step back, shocked by his sudden display of emotion, he stopped.

Cohen swallowed his rage and pulled on his familiar mask of indifference. "Farren is my enemy, and he has *never* been anything else." He searched her face but didn't find what he'd hoped to see. "You still refuse to trust me?"

"Yes." She didn't hesitate. "How can I when you change to suit every situation? A second ago, you showed me something honest— genuine fury—but you immediately pulled back. If you can't be real with me for more than a split second, how can you ask me to trust you? I don't know your agenda or motives. You are demanding blind faith! I won't turn on you or condemn you to hell, but..."

"But when push comes to shove, you'll sacrifice me to save Chance and yourself."

His blatant accusation bothered her. To be honest, she had never thought Cohen might need saving, but her answer boiled down to a simple concept.

"You seemed ready to sacrifice me in the Phipps Bend basement, scalpel in hand. I have the scar to prove it."

"Lilith, I told you that was—"

"A diversion, yeah, so you said. What if the plan never came together? Were you willing to hack pieces off me until you could escape?"

When Cohen blanched and opened his mouth to protest, she cut him off because she didn't want to hear his response. "To answer your question, you're asking if I'd risk myself and the man I love to save someone I don't know, a person who nearly got me killed multiple times, cut me to appease a monster, and clearly doesn't trust me. No."

His apologetic expression quickly hardened into something darker. "Yeah. *I'm* the one who's selfish and untrustworthy." Without another word, he spun around and started up the stairs with renewed vigor.

Apparently, they were in a stalemate, both unwilling to trust the other without a show of faith.

They climbed the remaining floors in hostile silence as she waged an internal debate. Would she throw Cohen to the wolves if it meant saving her life? Perhaps. Would she sacrifice him to save Chance? Absolutely. So, why did that decision feel immoral, and could she live with herself if she had to make that choice?

As they approached the 11th-floor landing, Cohen readied his gun and waited until she signaled to open the door. He peered right while she peeked left. Nicci and Tim stood by the elevators, impatiently waiting, but the rest of the hall was vacant. Finally, after a nod from Nicci, Lilith slid through the door and hurried to join them.

"Okay, let's see if our bad guy is home, shall we?" The petite detective strode down the beige hall with purpose, her ponytail swaying like a pendulum. When they reached Haverty's door, Nicci gestured Tim into position on the right, with Cohen behind him. Then she took the left side, and Lilith fell in line behind her.

With everyone in place, guns ready, Detective DeLuca firmly knocked on the door. Lilith heard shuffling feet, the creak of a floorboard, and rustling fabric. Although she didn't possess the same superhuman hearing as movie vamps, it was still above average. Someone was inside, someone in a hurry.

Nicci knocked louder this time. "Stephen Haverty. NYPD. Open the door!" Her commanding voice boomed down the hall, and a few doors creaked open, but not the one they wanted.

With a determined grimace, Nicci raised her weapon, stepped back, and nodded to Timothy. Lilith knew the five-foot-nothing woman could easily kick down the door, but why bother when they had a linebacker eager to play hero?

Tim squared off with the door, staring it down, and landed a massive blow right near the handle—the proper technique. The door slammed against the wall with a thunderous crack that spooked their suspect. Time froze for a moment while the man turned and stared in horror at the four armed people standing in his doorway.

The slight twitch of his left eye told Lilith precisely what he intended to do. "He's gonna run!" As soon as she shouted, he broke left, sprinting toward the back room.

Nicci took off like a shot and jumped on the man's back, slamming him face-first into the hardwood. Before Cohen and Timothy got five steps inside, she had Haverty pinned to the floor, knees to his spine, and wrists cuffed behind his back. Apparently, her comments about sparring weren't only for comic relief. At five feet tall and perhaps a hundred pounds, she made every bit count.

"Nice try, Steve, but I'm faster." The man struggled and bucked until she ground her knee into his back while grabbing his sling-style backpack. "Got a bag here!" She tossed it toward the door, and Cohen snatched it from the air.

"You got anything else on you? Weapons?"

"No! Get off me!" the man squealed while she frisked him.

"He's clean."

"I'll guard the hall." Timothy nodded to Lilith and closed the battered door behind him. Not a bad idea. His presence would discourage the curious neighbors from investigating.

"Clothes, toothbrush, cash, passport, razors. It's not here!" Cohen angrily tossed the bag on the ground.

"You skipping town, Steve?" Nicci hopped off his back and hauled him up by his handcuffs. Watching her effortlessly shove around a guy who stood six inches taller and weighed at least twice as much was both impressive and amusing. In fact, the sleek, waist-length ponytail whipping about as she moved made her resemble an Italian *Sailor Moon* character.

"My name isn't fucking Steve. It's Stephen!"

"Well, look at that. It speaks!" Nicci flashed a triumphant grin. "Why don't we sit and chat, *Steve*?"

Lilith wandered toward the back room while listening to the conversation. Haverty had made a break in that direction as if his life depended on it, and she wanted to know why.

"Please! They're coming! I'm dead if I don't leave now, and so are you!" Lilith watched Stephen pull against the cuffs, to no avail. Hardly surprising. He fit the bill of a stereotypical jewel thief with his moderately expensive clothes, manicured nails, and flecks of gray in his black hair—a trendy metrosexual. However, his bloodshot eyes reminded her more of his mug shot, desperate and panicked.

Nicci ushered him over to an Ikea sofa and shoved him down before taking an authoritative stance over him. Despite her attempt at intimidation, the thief kept his eyes on Lilith when she moved closer to the backroom. His breaths grew shallow, more so with each step. He had something in there he didn't want anyone to see.

When her foot touched the threshold, his quick release of air confirmed her suspicion—exhale marks the spot. Lilith stepped inside with a victorious smile.

Calling the place a home office was about as accurate as stating a cruise liner was simply a boat. A dozen monitors comprised the massive computer display above the expansive desk, which was littered with device components, a soldering station, and a row of 3D printers. Haverty had converted the opposite wall into a corkboard mural of electronic schematics, blueprints, sketches, and photographs focused on one common theme—the Voynich Manuscript.

"You don't understand!" Stephen's shrill voice strained with desperation. "I *have* to leave. Now!"

"Who is coming?" Cohen demanded an answer as his heavy footsteps moved across the floor.

Lilith studied the blueprints and extensive notes, mapping out each stage of the heist. The robbery occurred precisely as Chance described and confirmed a few of her theories as well. Haverty engineered the fistfight between Tome and Hickson. The evidence they left behind would make them perfect patsies. However, his plan contained one significant flaw, which would be glaringly obvious even to a novice— the book. If the police didn't recover the stolen property from the two corpses left behind, they'd continue to chase every lead.

Then Lilith came across a note and detailed sketches that bridged the gap. He had planned to drop a replica he'd consigned, a classic bait-and-switch. So, what went wrong? The cops didn't find the forgery, so where was it?

"I don't *know* who they are!" The condescending derision in Haverty's tone clearly stated he thought Cohen was stupid for even asking the question.

"Who hired you?" Cohen spoke louder, accentuating each word as if dumbing it down for the man. A moment of silence descended until a scream of pain split the air. Applying *incentive* seemed like an uncharacteristic departure from his usual interrogation techniques. Of course, she doubted his change in tactics would pan out.

The only names displayed on his mastermind wall were those of his two co-conspirators, which meant the man most likely didn't know who hired him—standard practice in the criminal world.

"We know you stole the Voynich manuscript with Jimmy Tome and Denny Hickson. We also know you double-crossed them and escaped with the book. So, tell us where it is and who hired you, and you'll be free to go. I give you my word." Nicci had smoothly slipped into the role of *good cop*, playing off Cohen's newfound aggression to win Haverty's confidence.

"Are you deaf? I told you! I don't *know!*" The man shouted with complete conviction.

"Bullshit!" The sound of shattering glass immediately followed Cohen's outburst.

"Okay, let's back up. How did you get the job?" Nicci kept her tone soft and soothing to counteract the demon's rage. To Lilith's surprise, they balanced each other well, making an excellent interrogation team, but it wouldn't help if the suspect didn't know anything.

"Fuck. You don't understand! I need to leave right now!"

"Stephen, help us out, and we can protect you."

As Lilith continued to investigate the room, something under the window caught her eye—an industrial-strength eyehook with a spool of thick climbing rope. That explained why Haverty ran for this room and didn't push his way through the front door.

The thick layer of dust covering the equipment and the even coat of paint on the wall implied it wasn't a recent addition. He'd probably installed it the day he moved in. Paranoia often became a lifestyle for people in his line of work.

After examining the obvious evidence, Lilith rejoined the party while Haverty explained.

"I received an envelope in my post office box with all the details and three cashier's checks made out to us. They didn't include a contact number, a name, or anything else. I investigated the company on the checks—nothing but a dummy-corp shifted through over a dozen hands. The information promised a bigger check once they had the book. Can we go now?"

"If you had no way of contacting them, how were you supposed to deliver the book?" He never outlined the handoff in his plans, which made sense to Lilith. Maintaining anonymity and distance were crucial elements.

Stephen clenched his jaw angrily before speaking up. "They already knew who I was, who I worked with, and where my rather secretive post office box was located. They never specified a drop. Now, I've told you *everything!* Let me go!" His voice reached a fevered pitch, and his panicked paranoia became infectious.

Something felt wrong. Lilith couldn't explain what, but chills traveled up her spine when she witnessed the sheer desperation in his eyes.

"If you've never met this mystery client, why are you panicking like a blonde in a horror movie?" Nicci rocked back on her heels with an inquisitive expression. Although she posed an excellent question, Lilith already knew the answer.

"Paranoid Personality Disorder. He installed an escape route in the other room, which also contains blueprints, itineraries, schematics, every tiny detail required to plan the heist." Lilith paced around Nicci and crouched down, meeting Stephen at eye level.

"The fight between Jimmy and Denny in the library. You orchestrated it, didn't you?" Haverty blinked hard before the skin around his eyes tightened, eyebrows lifted, cheeks raised, and the corners of his mouth depressed—Surprise and guilt.

"You pushed them into an argument, knowing they'd resort to physical violence, which would not only leave evidence to implicate them but also provide a diversion so you could run off with the goods. How am I doing so far?"

The man silently chewed his lip but kept his eyes glued to her with a mixture of fear and attraction. He didn't want to spill his secrets, but her figuring them out made her a kindred spirit.

"So, why go through all that trouble if you knew the cops were going to find them dead?"

"What?! No! I had *nothing* to do with that!" His eyes widened in pure panic, and his breath quickened. "They shouldn't have chased me." Stephen squeezed his eyes closed in emotional torment. She doubted his tears stemmed from grief over two men he had no problem sending to jail for a long time, which only meant one thing.

"You saw what happened, didn't you?" She whispered the question, surprised by the sudden realization. But unfortunately, Cohen didn't hear her.

"This is fascinating, but I don't care how he stole the fucking thing. I just want to know where the fuck it is!" Cohen stormed over and grabbed the man's chin, yanking his face upward to meet his steely stare. "Where is the book?"

An unnatural calm settled over Haverty's features. "It's here."

"The book is here?" Lilith blinked in shock, unable to believe they could be so lucky. "Or do you mean the forgery you planned to leave at the library? Of course, you never got the opportunity, did you?"

Stephen glanced over at her in confusion, as if disoriented. "No. When I started for the door, Jimmy and Denny stopped fighting. They tried to jump me before I could drop the fake."

"So, you still have the replica?"

"No. I dropped it to distract them when they started gaining on me in the alley. I figured they'd think it was the real deal and give up the chase. Well, it worked." The color drained from his face as he stared off into space, reliving those haunted moments.

The cops hadn't found it with the bodies, which meant the mysterious assassin had it. However, the pieces of resurrection fern in his cohort's homes meant they were still hunting Stephen, so they most likely knew it was fake.

"I don't give a shit about the forgery." Impatience burned through the last remnants of Cohen's calm civility. The man stood there, snarling with rage. Somehow, she got the sense that he wasn't acting.

"Please! They are coming, and I don't want to end up like Jimmy and Denny." When the fuming demon continued to stare him down, he sighed heavily. "Fine. I stashed it in my mailbox downstairs. I planned to leave directions and a key with the front desk on my way out. Now, please, can I fucking leave?"

"Take us to the book first." Cohen snatched the man's arm, yanked him to his feet, and shoved him toward the door.

"Wait! I need the key. It's on the kitchen counter." He turned back, but Cohen blocked his path.

"Lilith, grab the key." He kept his eyes locked on Stephen like a wolf eyeing its prey.

As she wandered toward the kitchen, Timothy pushed the door open and leaned into the room. "Are you about done? I don't think we should stay much longer. The natives are getting restless, and it won't be long until the cops show up. This neighborhood comes with a quick response time."

"Yeah. We're leaving now." Lilith called out as her fingers closed around the key—their salvation. She jogged back to the door with a smile. "All set."

"Cool. There's a place we can take him if you have more questi—" A thud interrupted his words, and suddenly, Timothy fell to the floor like a redwood tree.

"Tim!" She bent down to check his pulse, but footsteps grabbed her attention, and she glanced up to stare into the barrel of a semi-automatic rifle. For a moment, she forgot how to breathe.

Chapter 18

In a split second, Cohen threw Stephen at Lilith, kicked the door closed, and dove to the side. He landed on his back, gun trained, as she fell clumsily to the ground with the stunned thief.

The automatic reflex to grab Stephen left her unable to control the fall, and her head cracked against the hardwood, leaving her dazed. Before she could recover, a burst of shots showered them in splinters while the world slowed to a crawl, lit by muzzle flare.

"Lilith! Get up!" The screeching voice dragged her back to the present as elbows and knees dug into her, followed by the sound of pounding feet. A sense of urgency gnawed at her, but she still couldn't focus her swirling vision.

"Move, Lilith! He's getting away!" Cohen prompted her again.

Once she rolled onto her knees, she saw Haverty dash toward the backroom. Her cloudy brain struggled to comprehend why until everything clicked into place—the emergency line.

Lilith skidded and stumbled, trying to stand, but the entire room spun, and she collapsed awkwardly against the wall.

"God damn it!" Cohen growled as he rocketed past her.

"He's heading for the window. We still need him!" Lilith pulled her gun from the holster and tried again to stand until fingers dug into her hair.

The hand yanked her backward, sending searing sparks across her scalp as she screamed. A moment of déjà vu from the wrecked rental car overwhelmed her. She raised her gun and squeezed the trigger. Hot blood splattered against her skin while the hand in her hair jerked and fell away.

Lilith twisted around and scrambled backward as the uniformed man grabbed his throat, widened eyes meeting hers in shock. She kept her gun trained on him as he gurgled and choked before collapsing. With a frustrated grunt, she hopped to her feet and kicked the body away from her. Why did anonymous men in tactical gear keep grabbing her by the hair? Was she stuck in a damn Steven Seagal movie?

"Get down!" Nicci peeked around the sofa as she fired at the door. Then she ducked out of sight before a spray of bullets sent splinters and couch stuffing flying. Lilith plastered herself against the wall, too terrified to move, heart thumping wildly in her chest. *Come on. Get it together. I should be used to this shit by now.*

As soon as the gunfire stopped, Nicci appeared again. "Lilith!" The woman's brown eyes caught hers with an expression of urgent concern. "I'll draw their fire while you run to the back room. You have to move."

In her bones, she knew Nicci was right. If she didn't find cover now, she might as well tie the toe tag on herself.

Nicci popped up, pistol blazing. "Now!"

Lilith swallowed her fear and bolted just before the front doorway exploded. Boots stormed into the apartment, but she didn't waste time glancing back. Instead, she sprinted desperately forward with her blood pounding like thunder and a prayer on her lips. Although Lilith never described herself as religious, if it helped, she'd pray to whoever or whatever listened.

"Get down!"

Lilith slid to the floor at Nicci's command while bullets ripped through the air above her. Once she scrambled into the backroom and sat against the wall, Lilith fought to control her shaking nerves and relearn how to breathe.

In between the sporadic gunfire, she heard a scuffle followed by something big hitting the ground.

Lilith's sweaty hands trembled around the 9 mm. *Dammit. Pull yourself together. Nicci and Timothy still need you.* If she didn't focus, she'd lose another partner and Chance's best friend.

After a deep exhale, she peeked around the corner. Tim was still lying over the threshold with most of his body in the hall. Everything had happened so fast. She didn't know if they had knocked him out or shot him.

Lilith's gaze traveled to two guys in tactical gear, dead on the ground. Then she caught sight of a third man pinning Nicci to the floor behind the couch. *Shit.*

Lilith exhaled through pursed lips, leaned out, and fired. The first shot went wide, but as he reared back to punch Nicci, the second shot hit him in the hip. When the man howled and fell to the side, Nicci took full advantage. After kicking him in the jaw with her heel, she rushed behind the couch.

Lilith shrank back against the wall and finally took a moment to scan the room she was in. Haverty lay sprawled out, face down, with Cohen crouched beside him, eyes locked on the climber's rope under the window.

"Cohen! Nicci and Timothy are still out there. I need your help." Lilith crawled over and checked Haverty for a pulse. Although he'd given them the book's location, she still wanted to know what he saw that night. A sigh of relief escaped her lips when his artery thumped under her fingertips.

The man groaned as he started to wake up, and Lilith moved quickly to pin him down. "Andrew."

When Cohen still didn't answer, she glanced up. The demon hadn't moved. He still stared at the rope with laser focus, oblivious to anything else.

Gunshots tore through the door frame, sending splinters flying, and Stephen panicked. He flailed and kicked, catching Lilith with an elbow that sent her reeling back with the taste of her own blood. *Dammit! Why does everyone keep hitting me in the head? What happened to a good-ole-fashioned gut punch?*

Lilith leapt on Haverty's back, slamming him down with a forearm pressed firmly against the back of his neck. Then she leaned down, speaking in an ironclad tone. "Stop, or you'll get yourself killed." Sadly, he didn't listen, bucking and fighting with the strength of genuine terror, high on adrenaline.

"*Andrew!* I need a hand!" Her heart pounded with trepidation as she stared at his tense back. He had the book's location. He could climb down to the street, break into the mailbox, and escape.

Of course, that meant leaving the rest of them to die, but she wasn't sure he'd view that as a downside. Perhaps his family would welcome him back if he accomplished his mission and tied up loose ends.

The memory of his emotionless eyes in Phipps Bend flashed through her brain. Cohen had stood there, ready to mutilate her to save himself, with a smile on his face. The man even bartered with Ashcroft to keep her alive, maimed but still usable.

Was it really an act? If the plan hadn't worked, if they'd never caught Ashcroft off guard, would he have followed through on his promises? Would he have carved her up enough to satiate the abomination and then use her as a guinea pig?

Finally, Cohen turned around, pulled her out of the way, and yanked Haverty to his feet. After shoving him into the wall, he met Lilith's eyes with a significant weight. "Take the escape line."

"What?" She blinked in absolute shock as he uttered the last words she had ever expected to hear from him.

"You know the locations of the book and cipher. Take the escape line and get out of here. I'll…buy you some time." His defeated tone inferred that he considered his part a suicide mission. Her brain balked at his orders, unable to accept the words. After all, self-sacrifice didn't fit his image, at least not the one she'd constructed in her mind.

When she merely stared, he grabbed her shoulder in exasperation, his almost handsome face looming before her. "Take it! If you die, I'm dead anyway. Go!"

Her eyes flickered to the window, a portal to life, freedom, Chance… Then, the question she had asked herself while staring into the bathroom mirror jumped to the forefront. Did she have the strength to survive the scars she'd accumulated? Could she honestly deal with more?

Lilith gritted her teeth and pulled away from his grip. By pushing her to take the easy way out, Cohen had reignited the fire in her belly, hardening her resolve. Maybe that had been his true goal. "No! I'm not leaving *anyone* behind. Not this time."

For a moment, he appeared speechless, but the spell quickly broke. "Damn it! This is not the time to play hero! Go! Now!"

Defiantly, she stepped closer. "No! I can't live with any more blood on my hands, not even yours. We all get out together, or not at all." She ignored his furious scowl and rushed back to the doorway to assess the situation.

Bullets tore through the sofa as Nicci curled into a ball, arms hugging her head to her knees. When they stopped, she caught sight of Lilith and mouthed that she was out of ammo with a helpless expression.

Then, movement registered in Lilith's field of vision as five men piled into the door, one of them dragging Timothy into the apartment. His chest still rose and fell rhythmically, which flooded Lilith with relief.

Rose of Jericho

If they wanted any chance of skipping a trip to the morgue, she needed to drop the henchmen. Lilith fired a few times, aiming at the man closest to Nicci, but her shaking hands sent the shots wide. Apparently, her newfound bravado didn't extend to fine motor control. After releasing a growl of frustration, she finally scored a hit to his shoulder. The man spun around and cried out as his gun erratically fired before clattering to the ground.

Nicci moved with lightning-fast reflexes, reaching for his weapon, but bullets erupted, tearing up the floor inches from her fingers. She quickly retracted her hand just in time and lunged behind the couch as she flexed her fingers. One split second of hesitation, and she would have lost them.

Then, a hailstorm of lead tore through the door frame millimeters from Lilith's head, sending her scrambling backward in surprise, but not fast enough.

A bullet struck her left shoulder, and she pushed past the blinding pain to shove herself into the corner. Lilith clenched and relaxed her fist several times to relieve the spreading numbness, breathing in through her nose and out through her mouth until the wound settled into a bone-jarring ache. *You're okay. Keep it together.*

Of course, she knew better. Even a shot that avoided the bone could cause nerve damage or sever a major artery, but she couldn't dwell on the outcomes. She had to act.

While the front room fell silent, Lilith popped the clip from her 9 mm and counted the bullets—One, plus one in the chamber. *Shit.* "Cohen, I need your gun. I'm almost out."

The detective struggled to keep Haverty pinned as the man fought in a blind panic. Judging by the exasperated expression on Cohen's face, he wanted to let the idiot go, no matter the consequences. "I lost it in the living room when I tore after this fucking coward." He snarled the words through clenched teeth as he shoved the thief backward, watching his head bounce off the wall with a smug grin of satisfaction.

Dread coiled tighter around Lilith's lungs as she fought to maintain her focus. "What about your backup?"

"I don't have it." Regret and disappointment littered his face as he refused to meet her eyes.

"Now!" an authoritative voice boomed from the main room.

Lilith edged closer to the door to peek. The four remaining assailants stood around the front door, digging in their pockets. Suddenly, she pictured the attack in New Haven and realized they didn't need to take out their enemies. The neighbors surely called the police by now, and, as Tim stated earlier, this neighborhood came with a quick response time. If they could hold their position a little longer…

Before she could finish her thought, she noticed the men shoving something in their ears. The sudden realization hit just before the shriek ripped through the air like a sonic boom, turning Lilith's blood ice-cold. *No. Anything but that.*

She fought to breathe around the lump in her throat, eyes glued to the doorway, praying the ear-splitting screech was only the product of her damaged psyche.

When a second high-pitched shriek doubled her over, she glimpsed Nicci curling into a ball and covering her ears in a silent scream. *God, no. She's really here.* Panic seared through every nerve until it felt like napalm coursed through her veins.

Hesitantly, she turned to peek over her shoulder, both terrified and certain of what she'd see. The matching expressions of lost adoration on Cohen and Haverty felt like a knife to an already festering wound until another scream sliced through her brain like razor wire.

Lilith collapsed, wheezing as she attempted to drag in some wisps of oxygen. She clawed at the hardwood in futility while Cohen and Haverty stumbled over her into the living room. As her eyes followed them, the personification of her nightmares breezed through the door, wrapped in a skin-tight, baby blue dress.

For a moment, her heart seemed to stop, terrified as her night terror flashed through her mind. Then, pure ole-fashioned hate roared through her veins. She clicked the clip back into her Beretta. The noise emerging from the *chanteur d'âme*'s mouth burned like fire, and the agony made her vision blur as she leaned against the wall for support.

With slow, steady breaths, she pushed back the mind-numbing pain. *Come on. You can do this. You still have two bullets. A clean shot between the eyes, and you'll never have to worry about her again. You and Chance will be free from her threats forever.*

As she peered into the living room, her shaking hand wrapped so tight around the gun that her knuckles turned stark white. Nicci was knocked out on the floor, or at least Lilith hoped she was only unconscious. Blood trickled from her ears, but her chest moved with shallow breaths.

The sight pushed her over the edge. *I will not lose another partner!* With a feral grimace, Lilith bit her lip to ease the mounting pressure in her skull and aimed the gun, intent on ending the banshee's life.

Rose of Jericho

Unfortunately, as her finger squeezed the trigger, Peisinoe's ocean-blue eyes swung to meet Lilith's, and she froze. The sadistic smile immediately conjured the twisted images of her nightmare, inducing a paralytic fear. Then the siren opened her pouty lips and released a screech that hit her like a shotgun blast.

The torment seared so intensely through Lilith's body that she collapsed, unable to hear anything but a high-pitched echo. Hands grabbed her, but the desperate need for relief engulfed her in darkness.

"That's enough," A familiar voice barked.

Lilith sprang out of her semi-conscious state to a horrific sight, the only thing worse than Peisinoe, her master.

The misleadingly mild face of the man who shot her father loomed into view. The cold cruelty in his ancient eyes bored into her, instilling an overwhelming desire to put a bullet between them.

At Farren's command, the shrieks abruptly ended, leaving a heavy, ringing echo like the after-effects of a bomb blast. While Lilith attempted to block out the sound, she gazed around the room, assessing the damage. Cohen and Haverty blinked in confusion as their blissful obedience disappeared. Timothy missed the entire show, still unconscious but breathing, and Nicci groaned behind the couch. For the moment, they were all alive.

Before Lilith could mentally celebrate the small win, someone wrenched her arms behind her back, binding them tighter than necessary, and yanked her up on her knees. Then, he did the same to Nicci and Timothy while the other two guards held them at gunpoint.

Cohen knelt beside Tim, head hung low, resigned to his fate, but Farren quickly intercepted when the man approached him.

"No." The demon grinned with malicious intent. "Leave him unbound."

Farren wanted the added insult. He didn't need to restrain his grandson to control him.

"Grandfather?" Cohen gazed up in confusion, as if the man represented a great mystery beyond his comprehension. Lilith wondered how much stemmed from the pathetic persona Cohen wore for his grandfather and how much was genuine surprise.

"Sir, our man checked in. He informed the local authorities of the FBI raid on the terrorist cell. They are pulling back." Farren nodded at his hired help before returning his attention to Cohen.

Meanwhile, Lilith's heart sank into the depths of despair. The police weren't coming. This monster and his men could hold them as long as they wanted, and no one would ever come to their rescue.

"What is going on, grandfather? Why are you here?"

Farren's arctic eyes narrowed with disdain. "*You* do not question *me*, Andrew. Where is it?" His thin lips curled into a snarl as he spat the words. The exchange solidified her suspicion that they had never shared happy, fluffy memories of Christmas. If Lilith had her way, Farren wouldn't live to see another one.

"The book?" Cohen still appeared lost, unable to connect the dots.

Lilith didn't share his confusion. The narrative seemed perfectly obvious. Farren wanted the Voynich manuscript for himself. As soon as he'd caught wind of the cipher's discovery, he had hired a crew to steal the book and a death squad to ensure Lilith and Cohen didn't find it. The car crash and resulting gunfight didn't convey a sense of subtlety, which fit his style.

How could her uncle's book contain anything important enough to circumvent the council? The rest of the demons who comprised their leadership had to be as cutthroat and ruthless as Farren, or he'd have taken control sooner. So, what did he want from a six-hundred-year-old diary?

Of course, her theory didn't explain the puzzling condition of the patsies. She understood killing them to tie up loose ends, but why mutilate the bodies? Did he do it to ensure the council sought her specific talents? And why attempt to kill her before he had the cipher? Missing pieces of the puzzle still prevented her from seeing the entire picture.

A loud crack knocked Lilith out of her thoughts, and she glanced at Cohen, who was reeling from a hard smack that left his face burning red. Farren loomed over him, staring daggers at his grandson.

It only fueled the hatred threatening to consume Lilith.

"What else would I want, you insolent child? Do *not* play stupid with me." The demon reached out with surprising speed, snatching Cohen by the throat, and pulled him closer. "Where is it?"

To his credit, Cohen remained calm, giving Lilith the impression that loathing and violence were nothing new. "I don't know." Before he finished, Farren slammed his forearm into Andrew's face with brutal force, which sent him sprawling to the floor as blood welled from a fresh cut.

Rose of Jericho

Cohen pushed himself up, wiping at his cheek. He stared at the crimson smear across his palm, and defiance burned brightly in his olive eyes. When they slowly rose to meet Farren's, they contained a lifetime's worth of retribution. "I don't know where your god-damn book is! Ask your hired help!"

A sickening smile split the cruel man's lips. "So, there is some fight left in you, after all." He leaned down close as his eyes slitted with pure malevolence. "Let's see if we can kill it, shall we?"

The ominous words hung in the air, and Lilith's dread sprang back to life, coiling around her guts like a serpent. Meanwhile, Cohen's eyes widened, and his breaths became rapid and shallow, proving that her concern wasn't unwarranted. He had overplayed his hand, and he knew the consequences of that mistake. It wasn't the first time.

Farren stood tall and strolled down the line of hostages, keeping his eyes locked on Andrew. Each step brought him closer to Lilith, and when Cohen's eyes darted over to her with an expression of trepidation, she knew he would stop in front of her.

"Sir, I can compel him to tell us whatever you want." The vicious confidence in the siren's voice matched the shark-like grin stretching her pouty lips.

Farren came to an abrupt halt, his body rigid. Somehow, Lilith got the impression he didn't appreciate unsolicited suggestions, no matter how practical. Of course, that benefited them. Peisinoe possessed the ability to sway any man into obedience, and Cohen held more information than his grandfather suspected.

Lilith held her breath, praying that he wouldn't accept her offer, because the thought of all those secrets spilling out terrified her more than the threat of violence.

"I do *not* need to be reminded of your talents, Peisinoe. Hold your tongue, or I'll reevaluate your usefulness." Farren hissed the menacing words through gritted teeth while the siren's smug grin faltered.

"Of course, Sir." Her ocean-blue eyes fell to the floor and stayed there. The creature recognized her place and didn't dare incur the wrath of her master by arguing. Some part of Lilith enjoyed the sight of the brash siren wilting under the man's threat.

"Now, where was I? Oh, yes. My grandson discovered something he cares about." The immense weight of his ancient eyes landed on Lilith before they narrowed with the sharp precision of a sniper.

"He thinks he's grown a spine." A dark expression passed over the smooth lines of Farren's face, which chilled her to the bone. "I intend to rip it out." With a looming sense of dread, she realized he had more in mind than smacking her around a bit.

"No!" Cohen started to stand, but a flunky twisted his arm, forcing him back to his knees. The strong reaction indicated something similar had happened before—Cohen knew what was coming. "The book is downstairs in his mailbox! She has the key. Take it and go!"

A toothy smile slithered across Farren's lips, reminding her so much of Ashcroft that her stomach lurched. For the moment, the ancient demon no longer cared about his prize. He only desired to inflict emotional torment by harming the one person in the room Cohen knew best. It only made sense that he would focus on her.

Farren pulled his gun from the holster and slowly crouched, his arctic-blue eyes studying her as if she were nothing more than an interesting insect. "And where is your little bodyguard?"

Lilith swallowed hard, unable to take her eyes off the gun, which was strikingly similar to the one he had used to end Gregor's life.

Farren lifted her chin with the barrel, forcing her to meet his eyes as her pulse quickened. "He's chasing a lead." Her voice remained calm and even, despite the fine tremors quivering through her body.

He was right in front of her, the monster who shot her father as casually as he'd brush a bug off his sleeve. The infernal demon hovered so close that she felt the heat of his breath, heard his heartbeat, smelled his overly expensive cologne. Hate churned inside, gradually eating away the paralyzing fear.

"Not a very productive lead if I am here, and he is not." His head tilted to the side quizzically, but the act didn't fool her. He didn't care about their investigation skills. He merely wanted to play with her like a cat toying with a mouse before biting off its head.

"Peisinoe. Retrieve the key and find the book. Call Kruger when you have it in your hands and return here immediately." The man's malicious eyes never left Lilith's, daring her to glance away, but she refused to give him the satisfaction. Instead, she poured every ounce of venomous hatred into her eyes while she slapped the key into Peisinoe's outstretched hand.

After five minutes, the gut-wrenching staring contest ended as a generic ringtone broke the silence. The man behind Cohen dug out his phone and answered—Kruger getting his call from Peisinoe. He nodded at Farren and promptly hung up.

A satisfied sigh escaped Farren's lips, but he remained crouched in front of Lilith. "Berman, we no longer require Mr. Haverty. Please thank him for his services."

The guard by the door grabbed Stephen by his handcuffs and wrenched him to his feet. "Wait! Where's my check? I did everything you asked!"

Although Lilith had witnessed firsthand how Farren reacted to demands, silently accepting his fate wouldn't change the outcome either. The demon had no intention of leaving a loose end alive, especially not a human thief.

The desperate man screamed and struggled as Berman dragged him inside the back room and closed the door. Since Farren didn't suffer from a weak stomach and didn't care about upsetting his prisoners, she saw only one reason for killing him in another room—setting the stage.

Considering their cover story with the cops, they most likely intended to set Haverty up as a domestic terrorist. All they needed to do was add a few bomb schematics and architectural blueprints to his command center, and *voila*, instant terrorist. After all, why move a body when leaving it bolstered the credibility of their narrative?

Sounds of a struggle briefly emerged from the backroom until the fatal gunshot made Lilith flinch. Minutes later, Berman rejoined them, carrying a satchel full of papers—everything connecting Haverty to the robbery, no doubt. The man dropped the bag by the front door and took his place behind Nicci, who appeared shaken, but too smart to open her mouth.

Being a vampire didn't automatically translate to a life of violence, no matter what Hollywood said. With Duncan's advances in cloned blood, extending the viability of donor blood, and the new capsule supplements, he'd made their condition very manageable.

Before taking Cohen's blood—which she had been mostly unconscious for—Lilith had never fed from a person before, and she was not in the minority. Attacks on humans raised awareness and drew unwanted attention. Plus, it was a horribly inefficient way to get what they needed.

Being a homicide detective didn't mean Nicci dealt with active violence. It's one thing to study the aftermath of evil. It's an entirely different thing to witness it happening. Hell, Lilith had endured a non-stop whirlwind of terror and mayhem the last two weeks, and she still wasn't immune to the gravity of their situation.

"I found it right where Andy said it would be." Peisinoe breezed into the room, clutching an odd leather-bound notebook worn with age.

The book Duncan wrote in Scotland during his time with Gregor appeared innocuous and ordinary, but she knew better. Those pages contained the story of Mary, Ashcroft, and his son, Clyde. They detailed every atrocity Gregor committed in the name of his murdered loved ones, which had ultimately signed his death warrant.

Lilith stared at Duncan's masterpiece, conflicted by the complex emotions it elicited. Then the cold metal of Farren's gun lifted her chin again. With a jolt of paralyzing fear, she gazed into his ice-blue eyes, lost in their cruel and ancient depths.

"It seems I no longer require your services, Miss Adams." Tears welled in her eyes as he pressed the barrel into the tender flesh beneath her jaw. It didn't matter if Chance found the cipher. Farren had what he wanted—game over.

"Wait! Don't!" Cohen violently shoved himself forward, breaking the guard's hold, and landed face-first on the hardwood.

The vicious demon's head tilted as he studied Lilith with genuine curiosity. "I believe my grandson wishes to spare you." A cruel smile split his lips. He had no intention of complying. She could easily picture him as the kind of man who bought his grandson a puppy, let the kid hold it, and then snapped its neck.

Lilith's heart hammered in her chest as she struggled to draw in slow breaths. After all the hellish crap she had survived, her life came down to Farren's deep-rooted desire to hurt Cohen.

The monster slowly stood, keeping the gun wedged beneath her jaw, which forced Lilith to her feet. The metal pinched her skin, drawing a whimper. The man inhaled deeply, reveling in her fear, drinking it in. Cohen's grandfather and Ashcroft were two sides of the same coin. Both demons craved agony, but Farren's tastes leaned toward emotional torment over physical pain.

The click of the gun's hammer echoed in her ears with finality. She wanted to say something to stop him, but her words would either fuel his fire or endanger others. There was nothing she could do.

"Stop!" The raw desperation in Cohen's voice made it nearly unrecognizable. Farren glanced at his grandson with genuine interest as Cohen scooted closer on his knees with red-rimmed eyes. "That's not what you want. Take me instead."

Rose of Jericho

Before Farren could process his request, Cohen grabbed the barrel of his gun and pressed it against his own forehead. "Come on, you fucking coward! You always wanted a clean excuse to kill me. Here it is! Come on!"

A snarl of anger distorted the ancient demon's features as he wrenched the gun away from Cohen's grip. "Why would I wish to kill my only heir? Foolish boy. Once again, you've missed the lesson." After shaking his head in disgust, he returned his malicious focus to Lilith, shoving the barrel under her chin once more.

"No! Farren!" Cohen panted with desperation, his mind flying through every option. "She knows where the cipher is!"

Lilith squeezed her eyes closed, sending a tear trailing down her cheek as Cohen's words hung in the air. He'd played the only card she had refused to use. Sure, the declaration *might* save her life, but at what cost? The one thing she couldn't live with was Chance's death on her hands.

"Is that true?" A grim determination seared through his sadistic glee as he jammed the weapon into her skin, prodding her to answer.

With a slow breath, she steeled her nerves, opened her eyes, and lied. "No. I thought I found it, but I was wrong."

The demon's lip curled as his patience ended abruptly. Before any movement registered in her brain, the left side of her face exploded in bone-crushing pain as the pistol struck her cheek. Lilith reeled and nearly crumpled to the ground, but the guard held her up as the room spun. While she struggled to focus, Farren thrust the gun under her chin so hard it made her gag.

"Lilith! He's not playing. You *need* to tell him the truth. It's the *only* way." Cohen's voice bordered on hysterical as he stared up at her with tears in his hazel eyes.

"I am. I was wrong." Lilith drew in a steadying breath, bracing herself as she locked eyes with Farren. No matter what she confessed, he would never let her live. She knew about his secret mission to bypass the council. All she could do now was keep the cipher and Chance out of his evil clutches.

"You might as well kill me. I don't know anything, you soulless piece of shit!" Her face snarled in disgust as she spat in his face.

"Enough games." Farren took a half step back and wiped his cheek, finger hovering over the trigger.

Lilith closed her eyes and tried to force her body to stop shaking while her mind flashed through all the things she had left unfinished.

She should have called Gloria back and told the girls how much she missed them. She should have informed Scott at Solasta about the mysterious virus. Above all else, she prayed for Chance to survive, to know how much she loved him, and not to blame himself.

The gun pulled away seconds before a blood-curdling scream filled the room. Her eyes flew open with a sudden sense of dread. Nicci, Timothy, and Andrew were all alive, but their shocked eyes remained locked on the doorway. With growing trepidation, Lilith slowly followed their line of sight, and at first, her brain couldn't understand the information relayed by her eyes. It wasn't possible. It *had* to be a trick

Chapter 19

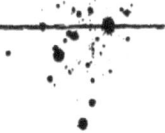

One of Farren's soldiers stumbled into the doorway with his entire lower jaw missing. Tatters of skin and muscle flopped with a hideous gurgling sound as blood gushed down his uniform. Lilith gaped in paralyzed horror while the man collapsed with a loud thud, blood pouring over the hardwood.

Then, shuffling footsteps emanated from the hall, capturing everyone's attention, even Farren's. The same expression of panicked terror distorted his typically calm face, revealing one crucial fact—Farren wasn't responsible for the bodies in the morgue, which meant there was another deadly player in the game.

Every person in the room froze, staring at the ominous door with a mixture of horror and sickening curiosity. Whatever monstrosity lurked outside didn't want to cuddle. They should race for every exit, but no one took their eyes off the empty door frame, much less moved.

Suddenly, the entrance filled with people pushing their way inside like a rabid crowd, uncoordinated, bumping and jostling each other. The guards finally leapt into action, jumping in front of Farren with their guns blazing.

Lilith blinked hard, trying to understand the scene before her. None of the people swarming the doorway fell, no matter how many shots pummeled their bodies. They merely staggered and stumbled from the kinetic force while the barrage of bullets sent bits of bone and tissue flying. Not a single one cried out in pain, screamed in rage, or even flinched as they moved with a singular, unstoppable purpose.

Then Lilith noticed the other wounds—a slashed throat gaping open but not bleeding, sliced wrists, track marks, a half-caved-in head.

Her heart sped up as she realized the gruesome, impossible truth—they were already dead.

Raw fear shot up her spine as she remembered the lab results—dead human tissue, grave dirt, and bits of resurrection fern. It couldn't be true. It had to be some obscene illusion. Even Cohen had laughed at the ridiculous possibility of the walking dead being real. There *had* to be an explanation that didn't defy every law of nature known to man.

The semi-automatic rifles wouldn't save them from the undead mob, which trampled over the few that fell. A horrific scream filled the air as one of them grabbed a guard's gun hand and ripped it off. As blood sprayed from the stump like some sick anime come to life, genuine panic set in.

Peisinoe screamed—thankfully a normal one—and shrank back into the kitchen, crouching behind the island. Farren traded his pistol for a discarded rifle and fired, not caring who he shot. In a matter of seconds, the doorway became a writhing mass of blood, body parts, and bullets.

Then, the smell finally hit Lilith like a brick wall. As the putrid stench of death doubled her over, someone snatched her bound wrists. "No!" she screeched and tried to pull away.

"Hold still!" Cohen yelled over the chaotic noise as he pulled off her restraints. "Run for the back room."

"What about the book? Peisinoe has it!" Cohen wrapped his arms around her waist when she started toward the siren.

"Do you have a death wish? None of it will matter if we're dead!" Andrew shoved her in the opposite direction. "Go!"

A young woman with track marks scarring her emaciated arms broke through the mob and raced toward them. Lilith jumped to the side while Cohen kicked her spindly legs, and the woman crumpled to the floor. The creature's nails scratched gouges into the hardwood as she kept reaching for Andrew. Although the sound sent chills up Lilith's spine, she found the contorted expression of emptiness in her cloudy eyes even more disturbing.

Lilith kicked the undead woman with all her might, as every one of her nightmares flickered through her mind. With a sickening crack, the corpse's head flopped to the side at an unnatural angle while the hands continued to claw and scratch, but with far less coordination.

"What the fuck are these things?" Nicci panted, bouncing on her heels, unable to take her wild eyes off the carnage while Cohen cut her restraints.

"I don't intend to stick around to find out. You two take the emergency line now. I'll grab Chance's stunt double."

Cohen turned just in time to dodge Farren's executioner, Berman, who reached out with one hand, the other reduced to ragged bits of flesh hanging from his shoulder joint.

Cohen backed away, dancing out of reach, and Berman lost his balance as three animated corpses jumped on top of him. Gut-wrenching shrieks filled the air, and Lilith could only watch in horror as the man's blood and intestines spilled over the hardwood.

The rest of the vicious mob forced their way into the room as the terrified screams grew louder. Lilith lost sight of Farren and Peisinoe behind the wall of cadavers and flying body parts, but she hoped, with every fiber of her being, that the monsters tore them into unrecognizable pieces.

As Lilith realized the creatures were about to run out of henchmen to tear apart, two animated corpses broke from the group. They focused on Lilith and Nicci, who promptly turned and hauled ass toward the back room with the sound of pounding feet gaining on them.

Something grabbed Lilith's blazer and violently yanked at the material. While struggling to stay on her feet, she screamed and wiggled desperately out of the jacket. As soon as she slipped free, she shot forward and tripped over a body, which sent her tumbling to the ground.

Before she could catch her breath, a man riddled with holes stood over her, milky eyes staring down at her, emotionless, robotic. Somewhere, a puppet-master pulled his strings because this wasn't a person brought back from the dead. He was nothing more than a rotting shell used for his inhuman strength and expendability. The startling realization made her insides quiver.

Lilith tried to scramble backward, but the bullet wound in her shoulder slowed her down, and the man's hand clamped around her leg like an iron manacle. Her heart pounded against her ribs like a caged animal as she kicked at him, but the grip never loosened. Panic seized her lungs while her eyes filled with hot tears. At any moment, the creature could yank her leg right out of the socket. *I can't die like this!*

Suddenly, Tim body-slammed the corpse, breaking his grip on her ankle. After quickly jumping out of reach, she started for the back room, but hesitated. Tim couldn't pin the dead man to the floor for long. He needed help.

When she turned back, his eyes found hers with fierce determination. "Go! Hurry!" The snarling creature beneath him whipped its head forward and sank its rotten teeth into his forearm. With a ferocious scream that sounded more like a battle cry, Tim slammed his fist into the dead man's face with bone-crushing force and kept hitting him until nothing recognizable remained.

Lilith stared at Timothy's arm as Nicci hauled her up to her feet. Blood gushed from the deep wound that claimed a chunk of muscle. The ragged mess would leave one hell of a scar, assuming they lived long enough to escape.

"Lilith!" Her partner tugged hard, snapping her back to the present as more creatures rushed forward, hiding Tim from view.

Lilith and Nicci skidded around the corner and slammed the door closed after Cohen sprinted into the room. Hands immediately clawed and pounded on the wood, but thankfully, Haverty hadn't settled for hollow interior doors. He had taken drastic measures to protect his equipment, which included installing a fire door on his office—not that he'd care about it now.

Stephen Haverty sat slumped over his desk with a bullet hole in his left temple and a gun dangling from his left hand. Lilith swallowed hard. The sight conjured images of her father, but she quickly shoved the unwelcome thoughts away. Assuming they lived, she'd have plenty of time to mourn her father later. First, they needed to find a way out.

With sudden clarity, she turned to Nicci. "Take the emergency line. We'll follow you once you're clear."

With a nod, Nicci sprinted for the window, threw it open, grabbed the rope, and tossed it down. After one last glance at Lilith and Cohen, she pulled a carabiner off her keys and skillfully worked it onto the line, which didn't surprise Lilith. After all, half the photos in Nicci's office had featured her on various rock-climbing trips. Only a true adventurer would carry a *real* carabiner on her keychain. The cheap imitations sold at gas stations wouldn't hold a toddler, much less a full-fledged adult.

"See you at the bottom." The tone of her voice made the statement sound more like an order. Then, Nicci jumped off the windowsill with the fearlessness of an experienced climber who desperately wanted out of crazy town.

Suddenly, the door lurched forward, almost knocking Lilith to the floor, and Cohen rushed up, using his momentum and body weight to keep it closed. "Go! As soon as Nicci touches the ground, get your ass on that line! I mean it!"

"Timothy…"

With a snort of anger, he grabbed Lilith's shoulder and forced her to meet his eyes. "He's gone! We can't save him, and I will *not* have Chance hunting me down because I let you get ripped apart by fucking zombies! Now move your ass!"

The depth of his concern cut through the panicked haze, which stemmed not only from the insanity outside or confronting her father's murderer. She'd also slammed her head into the hardwood floor before Farren pistol-whipped her. If things didn't change, she'd wind up with permanent brain damage, assuming it hadn't happened already.

Reluctantly, Lilith nodded and ran toward the window, searching the general vicinity for some sort of tool. During an emergency, Haverty wouldn't have wasted time climbing down eleven stories. He had to have something to rappel down the rope quickly. *Thank god for obsessive paranoids.*

She found a clamp in the top desk drawer, which would regulate the speed of descent, but of course, he only had one. Haverty embodied the definition of a solitary dissociative personality who wouldn't lose sleep over leaving someone behind.

Her eyes flashed to Cohen as he shoved his entire body weight against the door, wedging himself into the frame. The pounding and scratching reached a deafening roar, but beneath it all, Lilith heard something else—the faintest whisper of a melody. It wasn't Peisinoe's painful screech, so perhaps the neighbors turned up the music to block out the noise.

After shutting the drawer, she turned toward Cohen, but a hand clamped onto her arm with a steel grip. She whirled around as a gurgling sigh escaped Haverty's open mouth. For a moment, Lilith stared at the bullet hole in his temple caked with blood. Her brain refused to accept reality.

Could I be dreaming? The reanimated corpses in her nightmares kept getting worse, becoming more vivid. *What if I just wake up? Does it really matter?* Whether a dream or reality, she needed to escape.

Lilith tried to pull away, but his grip tightened, nearly breaking the bone. Panic set in as she desperately searched for something to help her break free but found nothing useful. One tug and he could rip off her arm. *Shit!*

When the undead body stood, he appeared unsteady and disorientated, so she kicked at his legs while pulling back her arm. The dead man's nails raked deep, leaving bloody furrows in her skin, but she bit down on the scream in her throat and kept tugging. Finally, his fingers slid on the blood and fell away, sending her stumbling backward.

Haverty moved slower than the others but didn't lack their strength. This wasn't the time to figure out why. She only wanted out of the nightmarish condo.

"Stop playing around and move your ass, Adams!" Cohen struggled with the door, sweat beading across his forehead, muscles trembling with fatigue. A moment of indecision halted her steps while recalling their conversation in the stairwell.

Was she willing to condemn him to a fate worse than death to save herself? Could she live with his blood on her hands despite all the reasons she had to distrust him?

When given the same opportunity, Cohen abandoned his ingrained sense of self-preservation. Even now, he urged her to leave him behind. After witnessing the expression of horror and desperation on his face when Farren threatened to kill her, the answer became crystal clear. Hopefully, the anchor would hold them both.

With a new sense of resolve, she scooped up her gun, which only held two bullets, holstered it, and rushed forward, shoving the door as it bounced in the frame.

"I only found one clamp. We have to go together. There's no way you can climb down before they cut the rope or pull you up." For a moment, Cohen froze in genuine surprise.

Then, the door splintered, and a bloody hand shoved through, grasping around blindly. "Shit. Time to go!"

Cohen snatched the clamp from Lilith's hand and bolted, leaving her with a sudden rush of regret. Lingering doubts surged to the surface. Was it all an act? After everything, was he going to abandon her now?

Halfway to the window, Cohen whipped around to face her with a frown of disappointment. "Come the fuck on! That door won't hold much longer!"

When she didn't immediately fly into action, he grabbed her left arm, jarring the bullet wound in her shoulder, and tugged her toward freedom.

Andrew slapped the clamp onto the rope. Lilith whirled as the door flew open, and an onslaught of corpses burst into the room like a scene from a horror movie.

An arm wrapped around her waist, quickly followed by a falling sensation, her stomach leaping into her throat as the floors flew by.

Screams filled her ears, and Lilith wondered why they didn't fade until she realized they belonged to her.

"Don't look down!" She kept repeating the mantra and stared up at the window to avoid the temptation. Hands grabbed the line, pulling and tugging, which caused the rope to swing. Then, Cohen engaged the brake, and their bodies jerked to a painful halt, knocking all the air from her lungs. Funny enough, the zombies probably saved their lives by preventing the anchor from ripping out of the wall. Although they didn't appear interested in rescuing them, she was still grateful for the assist.

The rope jerked again, and Lilith glanced up as the dead hands worked together to reel them in, bringing them closer—definitely a bad thing.

When she twisted to peer down, her stomach lurched again. They dangled four floors above the concrete. If the undead mob kept dragging them upward, they wouldn't have enough length to reach the ground, and they couldn't survive a forty-foot drop. Without some sort of plan, they were nothing more than morsels suspended in the air, waiting for their inevitable demise.

"Grab on tight!" With fear strumming every nerve, she wrapped herself around Cohen, squeezed her eyes shut, and sent a silent prayer into the universe. Even if they didn't make it, she'd take instant death over being ripped apart.

Cohen released the clamp, sending them zooming downward, and her stomach leapt into her throat as the sidewalk raced toward them. Right before they reached the end of the line, he engaged the brake again, and the whiplash nearly made Lilith lose her grip. She hung on for dear life, nails digging into his skin, judging by the hiss in her ear.

When she mustered the bravery to open her eyes again, they dangled one floor above the pavement—still a ten-foot drop onto hard concrete.

"Hold on to me." Cohen's eyes met Lilith's for a brief second, displaying unexpected desperation as Farren's words echoed in her head. *My grandson has found something he cares about.* Either the expression stemmed from the man's flair for the dramatic, or Cohen didn't have many friends.

With the memory of Cohen pleading for her life, Lilith tucked her head into his shoulder and held her breath as he let go. Seconds later, they tumbled onto the sidewalk.

Cohen hit first, absorbing most of the impact while she rolled free. The deep gouges on her arm stung as they slapped against the pavement, and then her shoulder hit the unforgiving ground. The bullet hole sent razor-sharp spikes of pain down to her fingertips.

"About damn time! Can we please get the hell out of here!" Nicci paced the area, shaking with nervous energy as her eyes darted between the door and the window.

"Nicci's right. We need to move." After scrambling to her feet, Lilith extended a hand to Cohen, which he surprisingly accepted. However, when he tried to stand, he quickly crumpled back to the ground with a hiss.

"Shit. I fucked up my ankle." Lifting his pant leg revealed a mass of purple bruises already forming.

"Yeah. Badly sprained if not broken. Give me a hand, Nicci." The two flanked Cohen and supported his weight, but Lilith stood nearly a foot taller than the petite woman, putting most of the weight on Nicci's shoulders. To compensate, Cohen leaned toward Lilith, and they let Nicci set the pace as they hustled down the sidewalk.

"We need a cab. If those things chase us, we won't be able to outrun them."

"Why not circle back to the car?" Cohen grunted the question while grimacing with each step. "No sane cabbie will stop for three terrified people covered in blood."

"Oh, hell no! I am *not* going anywhere near that fucking building!" Nicci pushed them all forward with intense determination, picking up the pace. "What the hell are those things, and why are they so strong?"

Lilith struggled to keep up while trying to assemble a plausible explanation. "Something or someone is controlling the bodies. I'm certain of it."

"Still doesn't explain why they're so strong."

"Actually, it does." Both Cohen and Nicci glanced sideways at her with confused expressions. "Living, breathing, rational people never use all their muscle mass. Even extreme athletes only harness about eighty percent of their theoretical strength because the body protects itself."

After taking a deep breath and steering Cohen around a rather shocked vendor, she continued. "The corpses respond to simple commands with no regard for their safety, which implies they don't possess survival instincts of any kind. They use every ounce of power, regardless of the resulting tissue, ligament, and even bone damage it causes. That's the only logical reason."

"Logical, my ass! We are talking about dead bodies running around, tearing people to pieces! How is any of this logical?" Nicci stared at the two of them, astounded by their lack of freaked-out panic. Lilith read the next question by her expression—*What the hell haven't you told me?*—but Cohen cut her off before she opened her mouth.

"Interesting science lesson, but I'm more concerned about the person who discovered how to use them like disgusting marionettes."

A sudden wave of dizziness overcame Lilith, and she struggled to keep her balance. With the adrenaline wearing off, her injuries were catching up to her. "I need to stop. Let's cut down this alley."

"Stop? Are you crazy? I'm not stopping until we're miles away from this hellhole. If we go up a few more blocks, we can hail a cab!" Nicci's voice bordered on hysterical, which wasn't surprising given recent events.

"I get it, but Cohen can't walk, and I'm losing blood. We need a second to regroup." Her words cut through the panicked haze, and Nicci steered them toward an opening with a defeated sigh.

The awkward trio ventured down a narrow path shielded from the afternoon sun by the giant brick buildings on either side. The alley ended with a sharp left turn, which came to a dead end. At least it provided some protection, even if it reduced their escape options to one.

They eased Cohen onto an old milk crate before Lilith crouched against the wall, putting her head between her knees as the furious pounding worsened. Between hitting her head on the floor, Farren pistol-whipping her, and Peisinoe's screeching brain knives, avoiding a damn coma surprised her. The blood loss hadn't helped either.

"Wait. Where's Timothy?" Nicci's strained and tenuous voice broke. She already knew the answer, but desperately wanted them to prove her wrong.

"He didn't make it." Lilith's heart sank, weighed down by all the death surrounding her. How was she supposed to tell Chance that she got his best friend killed? *Chance.*

"Crap!" Lilith quickly dug out her phone, hoping the fall hadn't destroyed it. Cohen and Nicci watched in bewilderment while she tapped a number on her call log and nervously held the phone to her ear.

If the zombie puppet master knew anything about Tennessee, Chance could be in real danger. Every unanswered ring sped up her pulse until it raced in her chest. The generic voicemail greeting chimed over the speaker, and Lilith barely remained calm enough to speak.

"Chance! You need to call me. Where are you? Why aren't you answering?" Some darkly cynical part of her brain found it amusing that she still left messages the way she had for answering machines. No one could pick up mid-message, but she still acted as if they could.

"Farren orchestrated the robbery, but there's another player on the board that can reanimate bodies." After a heavy sigh, desperation infused her voice. "Please, be careful. Please be okay. I need you to be okay."

She reluctantly jammed the *End Call* button and stared blankly at the screen. An awkward silence settled over the alley until Nicci ended it.

"Look, I know you want to keep your secrets, but I think you better share right fucking now. Weird ass chicks who scream like a supersonic bad guy from a comic book movie, super-strong zombies, this guy's happy-fluffy grandpa… I can't help you if I don't know what the fuck is going on."

"Lilith, you're still bleeding. You should patch those up." Cohen scanned her injuries with concern from his perch on the milk crate. "The shoulder, too." Then he calmly turned his attention to Nicci. "You've earned some measure of truth."

While Cohen turned to face her partner, Lilith glanced from the bullet wound still trickling blood to gaze down at her right arm. The deep gouges ran from elbow to wrist, constantly welling with blood, which resulted in thick drops trailing down the alley and a small puddle at her feet. No wonder she felt awful.

While Lilith tore off the bottom of her T-shirt, Andrew begrudgingly supplied Nicci with the annotated version of events, only skipping details about his race. He explained Peisinoe's capabilities, the catastrophe at Phipps Bend, the kidnapping, Gregor's death, and the deal they had struck with the ominous council.

By the end, Nicci leaned against the brick wall and slid to the ground, her long ponytail spilling over her shoulder. Sharp eyes narrowed on an invisible spot as her mind worked the puzzle. It was a lot to take in. Hell, even Lilith had trouble wrapping her head around things, and she had experienced them all first-hand.

"I understand if you want to back out. No one knows who you are, and you have already helped enough. Grab a cab and go home. This isn't your fight."

Nicci glared up at her, offended by her offer to bail. "And what the hell are you two gonna do? This whacked-out council won't let you walk away! They control an endless supply of undead cannon fodder capable of tearing you apart in the blink of an eye."

"She's right. Farren might be dead, but he wasn't the only council member after the book."

"Obviously." Someone other than Farren was pulling the strings of the deadly puppets in Haverty's apartment. Now that their mystery villain possessed the real Voynich Manuscript, they only lacked the last piece of the puzzle—the cipher.

Sheer dread twisted her stomach into knots at the prospect of those monsters going after Chance. "They attacked right after you mentioned the cipher."

"Yeah…" He frowned in confusion, unable to follow her train of thought.

"Assuming they want the cipher, and they know Chance isn't with us…"

"They will correctly assume he went after it." He nodded in agreement, finally catching on. "But no one else is aware he's heading to Goditha."

Lilith frowned and tilted her head suspiciously. "I didn't tell you where he was going."

Cohen arched an eyebrow and released a cynical howl of laughter. "Wow. You really think I'm stupid, don't you? Let's see. He has to retrieve something from out of town. Based on your lack of concern earlier when he didn't answer the phone, I figured he had a lengthy drive, which is why I guessed Tennessee. Now, where would you keep something of value in Knoxville? A highly secured, private lab, of course! It doesn't take a genius to connect the dots."

"Does anyone else on the council know about Goditha?"

"I never mentioned the place by name, but I did state that Duncan most likely hid the cipher somewhere in Tennessee. With a little digging, any of the elders could connect the same dots I did." His answer didn't lessen the fear tightening her chest like a vise-grip.

"I'm sure Chance is fine. He can take care of himself." Lilith glanced up in surprise as Cohen appeared to read her mind. Of course, his insight shouldn't shock her. Sensing her emotions told him plenty.

"What is so important about this infernal book?!" Nicci surged to her feet and began pacing again. The woman's ponytail swung from side to side, and her eyes darted to the end of the alley every time she reached the corner.

"There are legends, but I don't know what's fact or fiction. My grandfather believed it was worth circumventing the council, which is one hell of a gamble. He wouldn't make such a dangerous play unless he had proof of its value. As for the other elders…" Cohen leaned his head against the stone and released a sigh. "All of them want it, but I honestly don't know why."

"I can't imagine my uncle hiding a secret recipe to ultimate power in his diary. None of this makes sense." Lilith frowned and rubbed at her pounding head as her breaths became more rapid and shallow. After concentrating on deep, calming breaths, she tried to sift through what she knew.

"Duncan's research journals referenced the Voynich Manuscript several times, but only in connection to Mary, Ashcroft, and his family. Sure, it may hold details…" Lilith paused while attempting to assemble an answer that didn't involve Cohen's lineage.

"What?" Nicci huffed in exasperation. "About his species? You may not have spelled it out, but I know he's not human or vampire, so drop the act." After a deep scowl, the petite detective began pacing again.

"Right… Well, I understand your kind not wanting the info to go public, but I can't imagine it contains anything useful."

"Possibly. Several council members, like Luminita, agree with you. They merely want to keep the cipher out of human hands and secure their secrets."

"Luminita said the information about Ashcroft came from Farren, and…what was the other man's name?" Lilith closed her eyes, trying to push past the throbbing headache.

"Helton." A guarded expression crept over Cohen's face as he spoke. "He might be responsible for these animated corpses. Not only is he brutal and the most dangerous after Farren, but his resume is littered with weird, occult-style experimentation. He is a power zealot, like my grandfather, continually chasing legends. Still, for them to attack one another and defy the council, they must know something more concrete."

Lilith rubbed her temples while struggling to focus on his words. *Come on. Keep it together.* "Tell me about Helton."

"Alexander Helton, his current chosen name. He's a bulldog with a hefty bite. He takes what he wants by brute force, and his desires are quite eclectic. However, he isn't all brawn. The man became infamous during World War II as a high-ranking scientist named Wolfram Sievers. He acted as the director of *Ahnenerbe,* a Nazi institution where they studied the origins of the Aryan race and the occult."

"He's a Nazi?" Lilith stared at him incredulously.

"No. Helton didn't care about winning Hitler's war. He took advantage of the resources the Führer provided and hid his experiments under the guise of prejudicial genocide."

Nicci came to an abrupt halt, her brow furrowing deeper as he spoke. "Wait. The *Nazi Bluebeard* Sievers? That's impossible. The Bavarian government tried and executed him. Besides, even if he faked his death, he'd be over a hundred years old by now."

Both Cohen and Lilith turned to Nicci, shocked that she not only recognized the name but knew details about his death.

Nicci caught their dumbfounded stares and explained. "Italy wasn't immune to the war. Dozens of my relatives died inside concentration camps. The story I never forgot was how the SS tortured my grandparents inside *Ahnenerbe.* Sievers not only oversaw their genetic experiments. He also liked to get his hands dirty. My grandfather survived, but my grandmother didn't."

Nicci turned her steely glare on Cohen. She refused to hide behind a benign smile and pretend he was providing full disclosure. "Well? How is that monster still alive?"

"My kind possess similar longevity to yours, so age isn't a factor, and a rope around his neck wasn't either. He merely took his experiments underground."

"How do you know all this? Who are you?" Nicci abandoned tact and professional courtesy, making her mistrust clear.

Cohen wearily held up his hands in surrender. "I'm at the bottom of the food chain in my world, so it pays to know whose boot to avoid. Knowledge is my weapon of choice. It allows me to play the correct roles to stay alive. Helton is one of the few I avoid more than my grandfather."

Lilith sighed heavily and leaned her head against the brick wall. "All the bad guys are coming out of the woodwork. First Ashcroft, then Farren, now an ex-Nazi straight from an Indiana Jones movie?" She gazed over at Cohen with a defeated grimace. "Who else is on this damn council? Freddy Kruger, Voldemort, and Leatherface?"

"You're not far off target, sadly. I should call Luminita and tell her what's going on. If Helton wants this bad enough to expose his work publicly, she may be in danger. After all, she is overseeing our little mission, and if he knows about the cipher, we are at the top of his most-wanted list."

"Fine. I'll grab a cab since I'm covered in the least amount of blood. Worst-case scenario, I'll flash my badge and commandeer a vehicle. Then, we head to my apartment. It's off the council's radar, stocked with supplies, and perhaps I can dig up some more info while we figure out our next move."

When no one protested, Nicci strode toward the street with a singular purpose until she reached the open sidewalk. For a moment, she stood perfectly still, inhaling deeply. Once she mastered her fear, she hesitantly peeked both ways before stepping out of sight, with her long, straight ponytail swinging behind her.

That's when Lilith realized she couldn't feel Nicci's emotions at all. Although the effects of Cohen's blood had been fading, they now seemed non-existent. Perhaps she hadn't noticed sooner because she read facial expressions and body language to accomplish the same thing.

"I think the side effects are gone." The thought spilled out of her mouth with no context, but he somehow knew precisely what she meant.

The immense relief displayed on Cohen's face held a touch of fear, which quickly spread. "That explains why you aren't healing." Yep. She missed that part. "It also explains why Farren didn't pick up on anything, which probably saved our lives."

"He's done that before, hasn't he?" When Cohen peered up in surprised puzzlement, she clarified. "Threatened someone you...care about." It felt odd to throw herself into that category, but what else could she call it? No matter how complex the situation, Cohen's desire to keep her alive superseded his survival instinct multiple times in the past hour.

Andrew mutely stared at her for so long that she wondered if he would answer at all. Then he sighed and reluctantly spoke.

"My grandfather attempted to teach me self-reliance through loss from an early age." His sky-blue eyes drifted to the cracked pavement, lost in a sea of ghosts.

"Loss? You mean he..."

When his tear-filled eyes rose to meet hers, the rare glimpse of raw pain provided the answer. No wonder the man failed at teamwork and harbored extreme trust issues. "That is why I hate him with every stitch of my soul."

"I'm so sorry. I don't know what to say…" She fumbled through the empathetic apology, but he appeared sincerely touched.

"None of that is your fault, but perhaps now you understand why I keep people at a distance?"

"Yeah. So…how's your ankle?" Not the smoothest transition, but he didn't seem bothered by the nervous change in subject.

He rotated his foot a few times and slowly stood up. "Healing. I think I can walk."

A scream echoed through the alley seconds before Nicci came tearing around the corner. "Shit! We gotta move! Now!" Her pint-sized voice demanded action, and her face was pale.

"What's going on?" Lilith slid up the wall, finding her footing despite the pounding headache and gut-churning dread.

"There are tons of them!" Nicci sprinted forward, snatched their arms, and shoved them toward the street. "We have to leave now!"

Then, the sound of running footsteps began rattling down the alleyway with a chorus of menacing growls. Lilith's heart thudded in her chest as blind panic took over. The dead-end alley left them with one choice—running toward hundreds of undead minions ready to tear them into bite-sized pieces and pray they could somehow escape.

Chapter 20

"**R**un!" Nicci screamed while they held Cohen between them and sprinted for the street. If they stayed in the alley, the monsters would tear them apart, and Lilith had zero desire to become a snack pack for the undead.

The trio came skidding out from between the buildings, and Lilith's heart plummeted as the world slowed to a crawl. Less than three blocks away, a wall of human, decaying flesh barreled toward them. The horde flooded the sidewalk with no end in sight—Hundreds, if not thousands, of corpses.

"How is it possible? Did they empty every cemetery in the city?" No one answered Nicci's rhetorical question.

Someone tugged Lilith's arm, but her brain seized, unable to process anything but their inevitable demise. All her bravado and determination from seconds ago evaporated like smoke at the sight of the endless zombie mob.

"Lilith! God dammit! Move your ass!" Cohen screamed in her ear and yanked her arm so hard he nearly pulled it from the socket. The sharp pain cut through her panicked haze as everything went from slow-motion to full speed.

The three of them raced down the sidewalk as her body screamed with fatigue. Lilith pushed harder, forcing her aching muscles into submission, but the footsteps pounded closer, gaining on them. They couldn't outrun them, not with Cohen's ankle.

Lilith's chest began to burn as if her lungs were filling with napalm, leaving her gasping for each breath. Fresh panic lit her nerves like Christmas lights as the realization hit her—the headache, the rapid shallow breathing, the foggy brain. She couldn't keep up the pace until she replaced the blood she'd lost.

Given the current circumstances, she could attack a random stranger or run until she passed out, neither of which would end well. She needed a plan, or Nicci and Cohen would die with her.

"We have to split up!" Lilith screamed the words between wheezing breaths. "Get Cohen out of here!" She shoved the two of them forward and ran for the first shop door she spotted, hoping to find cover.

Her body bounced off the locked door, knocking her to the ground in a bone-jarring jolt. *Shit.* She scrambled to her feet and moved down the row of doors, pushing, pulling, and pounding each one, all to no avail.

Finally, the lack of oxygen became too much, and she slumped against a door, sliding to the pavement while her vision blurred. As she curled into a ball, fighting for every ragged breath, she rallied her scrambled brain. She had risked everything on a gamble, and now she had no options left. The enormous horde of undead loomed a few feet away, and she could barely stay conscious between the lack of blood and the rising panic attack.

Suddenly, hands wrapped around her arms. Lilith threw out her fists with a scream as adrenaline flooded her body again. She refused to go down without a fight.

"Shit!" The blood-drenched zombie covered his face and yelped, making Lilith blink in shock. The others hadn't appeared to register pain, even when Farren's men emptied an entire clip into them.

With growing confusion, she glanced up to witness the seething mass of zombies running past her without a second glance. *What the hell?*

"Please! I'm sorry! I thought you needed help!"

Lilith stared at the man before her in utter bewilderment. Then she noticed the smears of pale paint and bright red splatter on his clothes. There was no stench of death, only the odor of coffee grounds and sweat.

"What the hell are you doing?" Lilith's exasperated snarl made the man hold his hands up in surrender as his eyes darted about wildly.

"I saw you fall and thought you were injured. I was only trying to help."

"No!" Her patience wore thin as an unfamiliar ache in the roof of her mouth caught her attention. When she ran her tongue over the area, she felt her petite cartilage fangs unfolding. *Shit.* "Why the hell are you dressed like this?"

"Uh…it's the annual Zombie Run."

"The what?"

"The Zombie Fun-Run, you know, for charity? We dress up and race around the city to raise money and awareness for the National Brain Tumor Society."

Lilith squeezed her eyes shut and sighed heavily. "Get out of here!" He wasted no time scrambling to his feet and running off into the writhing mob without a backward glance.

Despite her horrifying circumstances, she nearly collapsed in hysterical laughter. What were the odds of being attacked by the undead the night before Halloween and mere minutes before a Zombie Run crosses their path?

The world either had a sick sense of humor, or the enemy planned the attack to coincide with the event. Considering the forethought put into the murders in New Haven, she placed her bet on the latter.

As she mulled over the possibilities, the midday breeze brought the unmistakable scent of decay. Her eyes flew open while her head popped up like a prairie dog, scanning the enormous crowd. The runners shot by too fast, and there were so many of them. If actual monsters lurked in the mob, she'd never spot them until it was too late—most likely part of the plan.

The instant surge of adrenaline forced her fangs to click into place with a sharp pain that made her whole skull ache. Instinctively, Lilith covered her mouth. Like every other living thing on the planet, her body had limitations, and for the first time in her life, she had reached them.

The image of Spencer flashed in her mind—pale complexion, blood-shot eyes, head pounding, temper flaring, straddling the dangerous edge. Although his dance with the hunger demon hadn't caused his downfall, it was the first time Lilith witnessed someone so close to losing control. Now she faced the same battle and desperately needed a solution that wouldn't cost her humanity.

Sure, snacking on someone in the crowd would probably go unnoticed, but she couldn't bring herself to do it. She had never used her fangs for their intended purpose, and the thought of killing an innocent stranger sent chills rattling down her spine.

The smell of rot hit her again while she wallowed in her moral debate. It was closer this time, and standing in the doorway made her stick out like a sore thumb. If she slipped into the crowd, she'd blend in, but three problems existed with that solution.

First, if she ran while oxygen-deprived, it would worsen her symptoms and shred her control. Second, hundreds of answers to her first problem would surround her. Third, real zombies hid in the endless mass of bodies, and she'd never see the attack coming until it was too late.

As the wretched stench became more potent, she realized she no longer had time to plan. Either she ran and took her chances, or she waited for them to tear her apart.

Lilith sucked in as much air as she could drag into her lungs and forced her reluctant muscles to comply, pushing her way into the seething mob at an easy jog. It didn't last long.

The people moved too fast. They bumped and shoved until Lilith rattled around like a pinball, losing all sense of direction. She fought to maintain her small, even breaths and remain calm. Thinking about the killers lurking in their midst or how difficult it was to breathe would only make things worse.

Then, the odor became intense, making her and the joggers within proximity gag on the rotten air. The faces racing past turned, searching for the source before giving up and sprinting faster to escape. If only they knew the truth.

Every time Lilith glanced behind her, the runners whizzing by brought an overwhelming wave of dizziness, so she surged forward while attempting to ignore the bubble of panic burning in her gut.

For a blissful moment, the stink of decomp faded, allowing her to draw in a few ragged breaths, which scorched her lungs. She couldn't keep up the pace but saw no fire escapes or hiding spots to offer her a brief reprieve.

Then, something hit her shoulder hard, and she stumbled forward, barely able to stay on her feet. She peered up as a guy blew by her, dressed as an undead 80s jogger, complete with inappropriately tiny shorts. The asshole didn't even spare a backward glance, much less apologize.

While mentally labeling the man a total dick, decay surrounded her again, more potent than before. It permeated the air, causing Lilith's stomach to lurch as a cold sweat broke over her skin. On the plus side, people began veering to give her a wide berth.

Fear tickled up her spine, raising every tiny hair. Something horrible crept behind her. She pictured the rotting hands reaching for her, mere inches away. Once the monster had her in its grasp, it would rip her apart like the guys in the morgue. The thought made her chest ache as panic warred with her low oxygen levels and clenched her gut into a tight ball.

Something raked against her back, catching on her T-shirt, and Lilith squealed in terror. Without a single thought, she dove sideways. The mystery hand tore the fabric, and she skidded to the concrete on her hands and knees. Thankfully, the jeans offered more protection than a pencil skirt, though the fall left ragged holes in the denim and skinned her palms.

Immediately, she sprang to her feet and sprinted for the crowd's edge. As soon as she reached it, she whirled around. Sure enough, two people followed her lead, veering across the current. *Crap.*

Her mind flipped through her options in a panicked frenzy. Hand-to-hand combat wouldn't be effective, and she couldn't use her gun in a crowd like this. Besides, she only had two bullets left, and not even an assault rifle had slowed them down earlier.

Why couldn't they be *Night of the Living Dead*-style zombies, pursuing her at a listless amble? At least then she could outrun them…maybe. But no, of course not. Instead, they resembled the undead from *28 Days Later* with bronze medals in the fifty-yard dash.

Using her surroundings was her only viable option. As she scanned the area, she spotted a taxi SUV idling ahead. Perhaps she could jump in and hide until the traffic cleared.

As Lilith sprinted for the taxi, she glanced over her shoulder. The zombies were gaining on her, less than twenty feet away, which made slipping into the vehicle unnoticed an impossibility. *Shit! What now?*

Despair cascaded over her like freezing water, and her legs gave out from pure exhaustion. She stumbled, scraped her ankle on the curb, and crashed into the street next to the yellow and black SUV.

While straining for each breath, Lilith whipped around, watching the two corpses veer from the crowd only a few feet away. The half-caved-in head of the first corpse leaned to one side at a sickening angle. His Hispanic partner lacked most of his midsection, with tendrils of intestines dangling from the bullet-riddled abdominal cavity. That explained the gag-inducing stench. The only things that stank worse than perforated bowels were burn victims and soupy decomps.

The two zombies shuffled closer as Lilith backed up and grabbed the door handle—locked. *Shit! Shit! Shit!* She couldn't just sit there, resigned to her gruesome fate. With no other options, she rolled under the cab seconds before her attackers collided with the SUV. The bone-cracking force of their impact rocked the vehicle onto two wheels, nearly flipping it over.

Lilith curled into a ball, covering her head as the cab slammed back to the ground, the hot undercarriage crushing her left shoulder with a resounding crack. It took a second for the pain to register, but when it did, she couldn't hold back the scream or the tears that flooded her eyes.

Her fingers palpated along the shoulder joint and down her arm—dislocated with a possible humerus fracture. The immense pain made her lungs tighten, squeezing the life out of her.

"Hey!" a Middle Eastern voice yelled irately.

The two corpses ignored him, dropping to their knees, reaching, and scratching. Lilith inched farther away, gritting her teeth as the exposed bone of their fingers scraped across the asphalt.

"Hey, assholes! Get away from my cab!" The door opened, and a pair of scuffed brown loafers appeared, followed by the dangling end of a baseball bat. Leave it to a New York City cabbie to carry a weapon. For the first time since she'd left the alley, Lilith felt a tiny ray of hope blossom. A bat would be more effective than her pistol. If he disabled them, they couldn't chase her.

"Help! Please! They're on drugs or something. They're trying to kill me!" Lilith utilized her best damsel-in-distress voice. As much as she hated getting anyone else involved, she couldn't swing a glitter wand, much less anything substantial enough to help. The *vampire* needed a *human* to save her.

While watching the loafers, she winced against the searing pain throbbing down her arm to her fingertips. Naturally, the undercarriage hit the same shoulder with the bullet wound—Murphy's Law had demanded it. Her vision swam from the agony as bouts of dizziness threatened to pull her into unconsciousness. *Focus!*

The loafers stepped toward the zombies, who didn't seem to notice. The corpse with the partially collapsed head shoved his snarling face against the road. His soulless eyes fixated on her while his arms clawed their way closer. The other one hadn't figured it out yet and simply tore at the pavement, trying to dig through it. Each pass of his fingers sent splinters of bone flying, grinding down the phalanges with a spine-grating sound.

"Damn druggy assholes!!!" The bat raised out of sight seconds before a hard crack split the air. The Hispanic zombie's hands flew out as he fell on his side. When his head smacked into the pavement, Lilith noticed he now matched his partner with half of his skull caved in. The cabbie obviously harbored a deep hatred for drug users and had no problem murdering someone on the word of a stranger, not that she blamed him. New York was a dangerous city, especially for cab drivers.

The baseball bat rose out of sight again, and her glimmer of hope grew. Saved by a NY cabbie? Why not? He deserved one hell of a tip if she survived.

Before she heard the bat connect, the SUV jolted and rocked onto two tires again as something slammed into it with ferocious force. When the vehicle came crashing down, the undercarriage bounced hard against her broken arm. Her vision went black as pain exploded across her nerves, pulling another scream from her raw throat. The intense agony made her stomach lurch violently, forcing her breakfast out onto the road.

Once she quit vomiting, she realized someone else was screaming, and then the blood-curdling sound abruptly stopped. Somehow, the way they ended terrified her more than the screams themselves.

The baseball bat clattered to the ground, followed by the cabbie's body and then his severed head. No, not severed. The word sounded too neat and clean. Torn.

A length of spine dangled from the skull, surrounded by tattered skin and muscle. The vertebrae slapped against the pavement, flopping as it rolled to a stop by the cab. The scream frozen on his dark face made Lilith scramble backward with tears of terror stinging her eyes.

The burning tightness in her chest squeezed all the air from her lungs. Her vision blurred. She wheezed and gagged, unable to control the accelerated rate of her respirations. True panic set in when she couldn't drag in a single wisp of oxygen.

Her eyes snagged on the cabbie's arm resting near her, palm up, welcoming her to take what she so desperately needed. What remained of her conscious mind screamed in violent protest, but her cartilaginous fangs throbbed with an instinctual need.

She fought the impulse despite her ragged, ineffectual gasps. Suddenly, the SUV seemed to close in on her, the minimal space suffocating her.

Lilith wheezed in one last desperate attempt to breathe, her eyes fixed on the dead man's wrist, and then everything went dark.

Jenny Allen

Lilith opened her groggy eyes to find her fangs buried so deep in the cab driver's wrist that her normal teeth pierced the skin. Her whole body glowed with warmth, and she took slow, deep breaths that seemed almost lethargic.

For the first time in her life, she felt like a stranger in her body, disconnected, as if she had lost the war with her inner demon. It lay there, lapping lazily at the blood like a contented monster full after a meal. Beyond the calm, she was horrified, revolted, sickened. The sharp contrast evaporated the euphoric haze.

Lilith shoved the arm away like it was a rattlesnake poised to strike. The delicate fangs folded back against the roof of her mouth. As much as her moral center wanted to vomit up the blood, expel the demon, her body refused to comply. It was happily sated, once again able to function, and thrummed with vibrancy.

Her vision appeared sharper, and an oddly familiar melody echoed within the chaotic city sounds. Even the mind-numbing pain muted to a deep throb.

She knew the moral war shouldn't exist. Her body acted on instinct so she could survive. Besides, her undead assailants killed the cabbie. She hadn't hurt him, at least not directly. However, she *did* make the conscious choice to get him involved.

Her brain registered the stench of rot a second before bony fingertips brushed her skin. Reality crashed over her like ice water, forcing her to swallow the guilt. The zombies had nearly reached her while she battled her inner demon. She needed to act.

Lilith scrambled away from the grasping hands, her brain snapping into sharp clarity. She couldn't stay under the SUV. The monsters wouldn't give up, and eventually, someone would notice the headless driver wasn't staged. Civilians would get involved, call the cops, and perhaps even riot. In short, more people would die.

Luring her attackers away from the crowd was the best way to avoid the deaths of more innocent people. Thanks to her animalistic blackout, breathing wouldn't be an issue anymore.

All the zombies—she counted four—attacked the same side of the vehicle. Their lack of a combat strategy bolstered her theory of limited control. The ability to tell them *what* to do but not *how* to do it would explain the bodies in the morgue and why they removed the hearts in such a rudimentary way. Perhaps she could use the flaw to her advantage.

Rose of Jericho

Lilith crept out from under the cab on the opposite side, still unable to put any weight on her left arm. The blood enabled her to breathe, but it didn't fix her dislocated shoulder, broken humerus, or bullet wound. The deep gouges, muscle exhaustion, and concussions didn't help either.

None of it mattered, though. She needed to survive. Lilith scrambled to her feet and used the surge of adrenaline to propel her forward, dodging car doors as they swung open.

Once she hit a steady stride, she glanced back to see all four corpses chasing after her. More than a few times, the uncoordinated zombies slammed into open car doors and knocked each other into parked vehicles. They displayed all the grace of stampeding bulls in a liquor store. Thankfully, their lack of higher thinking slowed them down, allowing her to put much-needed distance between her and them.

Then Lilith's eyes snapped forward just in time to avoid another door by swerving to the left. However, her broken arm slammed into another car, and she crumpled from the sudden jolt of pain. Her vision swam, the world spinning on its axis, as the bone-deep ache made her stomach lurch. *You can't stop! Keep running!* After gritting her teeth, she stood, cradling her arm, praying the pain would subside to a tolerable level.

Suddenly, screams boomed behind her, lots of them. It had only been a matter of time before someone spotted the headless cab driver. In fact, with the traffic at a standstill and drivers emerging from their vehicles to investigate, she was amazed it had taken so long. Dispatchers would treat the first few calls to 9-1-1 as pranks, but eventually, they'd send a patrol officer to investigate. She needed to be far away from the scene before that happened.

As Lilith turned to run, a hand grabbed her arm, and she screamed while scrambling backward.

"Stop! It's me." Nicci's Italian-New Yorker accent brought tears of joy to Lilith's eyes. "We gotta move. Can you run?"

After a determined nod from Lilith, they sprinted through the traffic jam. "Where's…Cohen?" Lilith huffed the question between heavy breaths as they veered toward the sidewalk.

"We got separated. I didn't see…" Nicci didn't sound the faintest bit winded while Lilith gulped in air. If the trend of life-threatening catastrophes continued, she would need to step up her cardio workouts. What unsettled her the most was how practical the thought felt, as if she had already come to terms with her life being an endless nightmare.

"When I couldn't find him, I circled back for you. I heard screams and followed them until I saw you tearing ass down the street." At least she hadn't witnessed the limb-tearing corpses taking Cohen down. Of course, if anyone could escape relatively unscathed, it would be Cohen. The man had dedicated his life to self-preservation and had somehow survived having Farren as a grandfather.

"There's more...in the crowd, and...I'm pretty sure people are... calling the cops." Lilith panted for every breath, and this time, she couldn't blame it on a lack of blood.

Lilith's eyes widened as she spotted a line of people ahead, standing steadfast as other runners streamed around them. She glanced out at the street, hoping they could merge back into traffic, but the zombies from the cab had caught up and now ran parallel, ready to cut them off.

She peered over her shoulder and considered backtracking, but noticed several faces with the same dead, milky eyes behind them. Sure, they might be contact lenses, but she wasn't willing to risk their lives on that gamble.

As she continued to scan their surroundings, it finally hit her. The enemy was herding them, controlling their route, just like the thieves in New Haven. Haverty hadn't led them to a predetermined location. The corpses had herded them into a perfect ambush spot. That's why Haverty had resembled a shell-shocked vet with PTSD when they found him.

The fake he'd dropped may have distracted them long enough for Haverty to distance himself, but he had witnessed their gruesome deaths. If she didn't find a way out, Lilith and her new partner would star in the sequel.

Before she could come up with a solution, Nicci yelled, "This way!" and swerved down the side street, falling right into the puppet master's trap. Lilith followed, not only because she didn't have another viable option, but because she couldn't lose another partner.

As soon as they rounded the corner, Lilith's heart sank. She gazed hopelessly at the ten-foot brick wall, standing before them like a monolithic giant—a dead end. *No! It won't be our end!*

Lilith gritted her teeth with fierce determination burning in her belly and adrenaline pounding through her veins. Her mind focused on one thing—survival.

They scrambled around the alley, searching for some way to escape, but found nothing but a pair of locked doors. Lilith dug in and shoved the metal door with her uninjured shoulder, but it didn't budge. The thing probably had four deadbolts and a security rod.

Refusing to give up, Lilith spun around, analyzing every inch of the area, trying to formulate some sort of plan. That's when footsteps echoed off the brick walls. The tiny hairs on the back of her neck rose as she swung her gaze to the source.

A dozen or more corpses crowded into the alley's mouth, blocking their only escape. Then, they stopped, a wall of dead flesh, milky eyes staring straight ahead without any spark of cognizance.

"What are they doing?" Nicci's brow furrowed in confusion while she wandered closer to Lilith.

"They're…waiting." But for what? A knot of dread burned in her stomach as the decaying bodies stood perfectly still, like a line of gruesome scarecrows.

"Shit. I don't want to know. We need to find a way out. We can't count on anyone else showing up in time."

Suddenly, an idea sprang to mind. Calling Cohen's burner phone might get them reinforcements, at least enough for a distraction. Hopefully, it didn't mean endangering more lives, but she was out of options.

When Lilith dug in her pocket, her heart nearly stopped. She patted all her pockets frantically before squeezing her eyes closed, unable to contain her roar of frustration.

Somewhere along the way, she had lost her phone, her sole line of communication with Cohen and Chance. If he got her message about arriving at Haverty's apartment and she didn't answer his call, he'd haul ass back to New York…right into a damn trap.

"Here, give me a boost, and I'll help you climb up." Nicci studied the wall, unintimidated, despite it being twice her height.

"I can't…I'm pretty sure I broke my arm." Lilith's absent reply hovered in the air.

"There are some loose bricks six feet up…if we can get high enough, I can scale the wall and pull you over."

Once again, they both surveyed their surroundings for an answer. A dumpster sat against the adjacent wall a few feet away, and although the rusting hulk appeared fused to the pavement by age, it seemed like their only option.

"Come on. We have to try." Lilith ran with Nicci hot on her heels, quickly picking up on her train of thought. Lilith shoved her uninjured shoulder against the cold metal as Nicci pushed with all her might.

The metallic groan echoed like the death cry of an old dinosaur as the wheels slowly turned. The effort caused Lilith's muscles to pull at her injuries, sending searing pain down her nerves. Defiantly, she turned her scream into a ferocious roar and threw everything at moving the metal beast.

When the dumpster finally lurched forward, creaking and moaning, a surge of hope surfaced, but after a few feet, the hulk came to an abrupt stop. They both shoved hard, sneakers sliding across the crumbling pavement, but it didn't budge. Nicci backed up and took a running start, slamming her petite body into the dumpster with all the fury of a Valkyrie, but to no avail.

Despite the thunderous sound of the impact, the massive thing didn't move an inch. Nicci slid down the peeling paint, landing on the ground in tears as Lilith peered back toward the street.

The line of undead puppets stood in the same place with blank expressions, entirely motionless. Somehow, the sight scared her more than watching them tear limbs off anonymous henchmen. Perhaps because they represented inevitability, like a blazing neon sign flashing, *you're wasting your time…tick tock.*

Lilith felt like a firefly in a jar, beating against the impenetrable glass walls until it died. *To hell with that. I'm not giving up, not now, not after everything.*

"The wheel must be stuck on something. Come on, Nicci. Help me out." Lilith dropped down, the crumbled pavement biting into her knees. She ignored the pain and reached toward the front wheel to brush away chunks of asphalt as Nicci hurried to do the same.

"It's no use. This entire alley is a mess of rubble." Nicci sat back on her heels and slammed her fists against the metal, making the whole thing groan again. "We can't build enough momentum to force it over all this."

Before Lilith responded, footsteps echoed off the walls. Slowly, she peered around the immovable beast as the zombies separated, clearing a path for a lone figure. A throaty melody tainted the air with a palpable sense of unease, prickling over her skin like a thousand tiny thorns. *Peisinoe? No.* The low, guttural tones were different, like a tribal chant flowing past reverent lips, none of which fit the bombshell's style.

The mysterious person emerged from the crowd of corpses with her full lips parted in a terrifying mantra. Instant recognition shot down Lilith's spine, leaving her almost speechless. "No fucking way." She hadn't realized she'd spoken the words out loud until Nicci glanced at her in confusion.

"You know her?"

Lilith shook her head, her eyes never leaving the woman. Dead bodies surged around her like a flock of loyal sheep—the pied piper of corpses. "No, but I've seen her before."

A woman with mahogany skin speckled with dark freckles along her cheeks eased into the alley. She had an otherworldly grace as if her feet never touched the cracking pavement. Long, black skirts swished as her dreadlocks swayed to the rhythm of her cryptic chant. The tangled mass of necklaces around her neck tinkled like death bells decorated with charms, rough pewter pendants, and bits of bone that appeared human.

When Chance had spotted the woman behind Hickson's apartment, she'd appeared out of place in the Queens borough. Now she seemed at home, transporting them to *her* world as the gathering darkness crept into Lilith's bones. Although her logical brain knew it was merely the clouds passing through the afternoon sky, it felt like this mysterious villain summoned the night to fold around them.

As the woman moved closer, Lilith noticed an odd little plant cradled in her open palms like a precious jewel. What had Chance called it? The Rose of Jericho—a deceptive name. It looked more like a miniature tumbleweed than a rose, and the only glimpses of green stemmed from the base while the rest branched out, brown and shriveled.

The weird plant also confirmed the voodoo woman's presence at Tome and Hickson's apartments, most likely looking for the book, but how had she found Haverty's address? The man's extreme paranoia negated any chance of stumbling across it. Nicci had only found it because of police access to their files.

While Lilith's mind tripped over facts, the woman came to a stop, closing her lips as she stood tall. The abrupt quiet commanded Lilith's full attention. This woman possessed all the power, and she damn well knew it.

Lilith and Nicci weren't the only ones affected by the silence. The zombies slumped like empty husks or androids in the off position.

Lilith's eyes widened as a surprising thought occurred to her. Was it possible this woman animated corpses the same way Peisinoe controlled men? Did she serenade the dead to life? But how?

Commanding a mind, altering its perception of reality, she could wrap her mind around, but reanimating tissue and directing a mindless heap of flesh? No logical, scientific answer existed for how the woman accomplished her parlor trick, and Lilith refused to accept voodoo magic as an explanation.

Tension wrapped around them with thick tendrils as the woman stood still, her dark eyes studying Lilith. When her gaze swung to Nicci, the woman's head tilted to one side without a trace of recognition, and for a millisecond, her lips pursed. The expression told her Nicci wasn't a target, merely an unexpected complication. Unfortunately, Lilith knew how this assassin dealt with loose ends.

"To hell with this. I won't be responsible for the death of another partner." With grim determination, she planted her back against the wall and shouted at Nicci. "Climb up! Now!" Then she slid down, bending her knees to give the petite detective a starting point. If they couldn't both escape, she fully intended to give her partner a fighting chance.

Nicci rushed over with a business-like scowl fixed on her heart-shaped face. After planting her foot on Lilith's knee, she surged upward. Her fingertips immediately found grooves, and she stepped onto Lilith's uninjured shoulder.

The voodoo queen merely watched them, as motionless as her zombie horde, except for the slight lift of amusement to her brow. She displayed no signs of urgency or concern, which wasn't reassuring.

Then Nicci's foot landed on Lilith's dislocated shoulder, and her screams ricocheted off the buildings as she fought to stay upright.

"T'ere ease no point runnin'." The thick accent took her a few seconds to decipher, but it sounded familiar. Caribbean? French? It wasn't quite Cajun...

"You come wit me." Her low tone rumbled like a storm looming on the horizon, leaving no room for opposition.

Lilith tore her eyes away from the enigma and glanced up as Nicci lifted her foot, and the weight left Lilith's shoulder. The detective gripped the top as her shoes found grips in the brick. As soon as she hauled herself over, she turned and held out her hand. "Come on. You have to try. Give me your hand."

Unfortunately, Lilith didn't have a boost, and she somehow doubted a zombie would volunteer to spot her. Hell, even if both of her arms worked, she couldn't scale a ten-foot wall, and Nicci's tiny hundred-pound frame couldn't lift her weight. No, climbing wasn't an option.

"Go! Find Cohen and get help!"

Without a second glance, Lilith ran to the dumpster and grabbed a length of wood from a broken pallet. If they intended to take her down, she'd fight to her last breath. A howling laugh swirled around her, raising goosebumps across her flesh. The dark, eerie sound made her feel incredibly foolish and left her shivering.

"You cannot fight wit me." The woman cackled in deep tones, and her intense eyes glinted. When Lilith didn't surrender, she shrugged her shoulders before resuming her creepy chant.

Lilith's eyes snapped to the dozen zombies as life breathed into their still forms. Their chests rose, their heads lifted, and then their sightless eyes swiveled to Lilith in unison. The pops and cracks of degrading joints crept into her mind, conjuring images from her nightmares.

Then, the corpses began to move forward, some at a brisk walk, some with slow, lumbering steps. Lilith backed up, her eyes scanning each of them for weaknesses until her sight rested on one that was unable to walk. The left leg crumpled beneath him, useless, and tendrils of tattered flesh and intestines dangled from his midsection. What remained of his skin seemed leathery and decayed, marking him as the oldest of the lot.

Lilith watched in fascination as the woman strolled toward the immobile corpse, her full, dark lips frowning at his broken body. Then she shifted her plant to one hand and lifted a sliced palm to drip several drops of blood into the mouth of the unresponsive zombie. Amazingly, his leg straightened enough to support his weight, and he lumbered forward with an awkward gait. As fascinating as the development was, Lilith didn't have time to explore the implications. The rest of the horde was closing in.

Then, a rock flew, striking one zombie in the head hard enough to make it stumble. Lilith followed the trajectory to Nicci, still crouched on the wall, trying to assist without jumping down into the jaws of death. Lilith appreciated the sentiment, but backup would be more helpful.

"Nicci, go! Bring back help."

Reluctantly, the detective nodded, her long ponytail flipping over her shoulder before she dropped out of sight.

They were alone now—Lilith, the voodoo witch, and her zombie horde. The odds didn't favor her, but that wasn't a new occurrence, and she'd made it this far. No reason to give up now.

Lilith backed up against the wall to keep them from surrounding her, but that tactic alone wouldn't save her. If only she could get to higher ground and somehow stay out of reach. Then her eyes swung to the rusting dumpster.

After tossing her improvised weapon on top of the metal beast, she scrambled up the side, despite the bone-deep pain.

Once perched on top, her injured arm dangled uselessly at her side, so she tightened her one-handed grip on the wooden slat until splinters bit into her palm. Moments later, the deadly corpses surged around the rusting hulk, fists banging the hollow metal and exposed bone scratching the sides. The sharp, screeching sound flooded Lilith's ears until she couldn't hear anything else.

Despair and panic burned in her belly. Eventually, the corpses would find a way up and tear her apart. *No!*

How many times in the past few weeks had she thought, *"This is it. I'm gonna die"*? She had survived so far, and she still had reasons to live. She couldn't give up now.

As shriveled hands grasped the dumpster's lid, Lilith released a war cry that boomed off the walls and slammed the wood down on their fingers with all her strength. Splintered bones went flying as the bodies collapsed on the ground, but no screeches accompanied the crushing blow. Knowing her enemies couldn't feel pain chilled her to the marrow. Without some sense of self-preservation, the onslaught wouldn't end until their bodies physically stopped following commands.

With a lingering sense of doom, Lilith peeked over the edge and spotted the zombie that had killed the cabbie. He lay there, useless hands scraping the pavement, trying to move. The thing reached toward her, and the hand flopped back against his forearm, all the bones shattered.

As Lilith reeled from a sudden wave of nausea, his comrades trampled him while pushing forward, and the bone-crushing sounds gave way to wet, squishy noises as they crowded closer, reaching and straining, trying to grab her.

Suddenly, a hand swiped through her auburn curls, and she quickly jumped back from the edge while more hands reached for her.

Before she could plan her next move, the metal beast lurched up on two wheels with a violent jerk. Lilith dropped the piece of wood and latched onto the lid, praying her left arm wouldn't give out. Lilith's heart sank when her only weapon clattered to the ground. *Shit. They're going to push the dumpster on its side.*

After a moment, suspended on two wheels, the rusting heap crashed back to the ground. Lilith's chin slammed against the top, rattling her teeth. But the sharp pain racing through her left arm almost made her black out.

As she tried to catch her breath, the dumpster lurched upward again, tipping farther this time. Lilith screamed and kicked as hands grabbed at her legs. She caught one zombie in the chin, sending him flying back, teeth clinking to the pavement like Chicklets. Then, the metal hulk slammed back down with a thunderous bang that left her ears ringing. This time, the broken bone flared with such unbearable pain that she briefly succumbed to the darkness.

When her eyes fluttered open seconds later, she swallowed the acrid bile in her throat and tightened her grip on the edge, ignoring the burning muscle fatigue.

She needed a plan. The next shove would most likely tip the beast onto its side and leave her exposed. She didn't have a prayer of climbing over the side as it moved. Even without a broken arm, she wasn't a rock climber. If only real life mimicked the movies—a little blood, a latex body suit, and she could leap to safety, unscathed.

Being a true vampire meant enduring a laundry list of negatives with only two bonuses—a great immune system and semi-immortality. Of course, neither of them mattered if a zombie horde tore her to pieces.

The dumpster lurched up again, its metallic groan crawling down her spine as it slowly tipped further and further. Her fingers burned, and her injured arm pulled screams of excruciating pain from her lips as she hung on for dear life. Hands hooked in her clothing, another wrapped around her ankle. She refused to give up, struggling and kicking as the dumpster continued to tip.

When the rusting beast finally slammed onto its side with a deafening boom, the corpses fell backward from the jarring jolt. Lilith used the split-second opportunity by pushing off the metal hulk and sprinting through the disorganized bodies. Grasping hands reached out as she rocketed past, but none of them grabbed her.

The voodoo woman's dark eyes widened as Lilith barreled toward her. The chanting suddenly became feverish, and dozens of pounding feet echoed in pursuit. With a growl of determination, Lilith shoved her shoulder into the woman, sending her sprawling to the ground as she ran toward freedom.

Her eyes fixated on the street before her, and she wrung every ounce of energy from her muscles, pouring it all into reaching that one goal. The closer she came, the more her heart pounded with hope, and when her sneakers hit the sidewalk, adrenaline washed over her with a burst of euphoria.

She still wasn't home free. The gridlock eliminated catching a cab as a possibility. Doing so would only endanger more innocent people.

"Come on. There must be something." The newfound euphoria wore thin as she scanned the area while wandering into the sea of stopped cars. Then, her eyes caught a glimpse of moving vehicles through the alley across from her.

Without a backward glance, she used every remaining shred of adrenaline to propel herself down the dark pass-through, picking her way through piles of trash.

When she finally emerged on the busy street, she came to a screeching halt with her hand in the air, pacing back and forth, panting for breath, each muscle screaming in pain. To her dismay, cabs flew by, one after the other, and her panic rose again.

Lilith glanced behind her. Zombies swarmed around the parked cars. The voodoo woman calmly strolled with them, cradling her mini tumbleweed. The woman didn't care about staying out of public view, which made sense. On the night before Halloween, a small army of corpses running through Manhattan wouldn't raise an eyebrow, so why expend the energy to stay hidden?

"You gettin' in, lady?"

Lilith spun around to see a cab sitting in front of her with the driver's side window rolled down. The driver frowned, his middle-aged face a mask of impatience with anger brewing below the surface. She grabbed the handle, yanked the door open, and slid into the backseat as fast as possible.

"Where to?"

Lilith slammed the door shut and watched the horde as it thundered down the alleyway. "Just drive!" Her heart fluttered nervously as the first corpse stumbled onto the sidewalk.

"This ain't some movie, and I'm not a damn mind reader, princess. Where to?"

Lilith's frustrated mind tripped over the dozen addresses floating in her brain as four bodies raced toward the car. The others trailed

Rose of Jericho

behind them, with their puppet master bringing up the rear. The destination didn't matter if it put distance between her and the undead mob.

Lilith blurted the first address that popped into her head as hands hit the window. She scrambled across the seat, trembling and shaking. "Drive!"

"Damn kids!" The cabbie reached under his seat, and she thought about how badly that tactic ended for the last guy.

"An extra Twenty if you put this fucking car in gear and get us the hell out of here! Now!" More hands slammed against the car, making it rock as Lilith's fingers dug into the cheap microfiber. "Come on! Go!"

The cab launched forward, slamming her backward with the high-pitched squeal of nails and bone scraping the paint, and then… silence.

Lilith peeked through the rear window, watching the corpses mill around aimlessly. She didn't take her eyes off them until the vehicle turned a corner a few blocks down.

She had done the impossible…again. Perhaps her guardian angel took steroids with a side of Hulk-style gamma radiation. Whatever the reason, she had defied logic and escaped certain death.

Lilith leaned against the seat, closing her eyes in a silent prayer of gratitude. As her heart slowed to a normal rate and the adrenaline seeped away, her laundry list of injuries—broken humerus, dislocated shoulder, bullet wound, deep gouges, multiple concussions—throbbed and ached with increasing ferocity. She could sure use Cohen's healing abilities right about now. Cohen…hopefully, he was still alive.

Now there's a thought I never expected to have.

Chapter 21

Lilith stared through the cab window at the modest colonial house with a grimace. The brown patches in the once-green lawn heralded the coming winter, and the slate blue paint starkly contrasted with the brilliant white shutters and sparkling clean windows. Although the home resembled any other house on the block, the person who lived inside ignited a deep-seated fear in her belly.

When the driver had demanded an address, she had blurted out the first one that came to mind. Now that she'd arrived at the edge of Brooklyn, anxiety kept her from opening the door.

Desperately, she flicked through the laundry list of alternatives and dismissed each one. She couldn't go home, Chance's place, or her father's because Farren knew about them. Sure, the corpses might have killed Farren, but he wasn't the only one who possessed that information. Helton was still on the loose with his zombie queen, not to mention the other council members. Without the book or a way to find it, she was useless—another word for dead.

She could hide out at Nicci's, but she'd lost the address with her burner phone. Going to Solasta for medical help made sense, but if the demons weren't aware of it already, she didn't want to lead them there. Besides, the staff would ask a million questions she couldn't answer, and they'd start an official investigation.

With no one else to call and no other place to go, this was the only sanctuary that remained. Well, *sanctuary* might be a ridiculous stretch, but if this door slammed in her face—a distinct possibility—then she was out of options.

"Cross one bridge at a time," she muttered to herself.

"Don't forget the twenty you owe me. I don't know who those people were, but if the cops ask questions, I'll have no choice but to tell them what I saw." The cab driver shrugged into the rearview mirror, and Lilith realized the *law-abiding* citizen wanted a few extra dollars to keep his mouth shut.

Sadly, a flaw existed in his logic. Not freaking out meant he saw nothing significant. Besides, the police would never believe a bunch of rotting corpses attacked his car.

"I am the police, so I'd expect nothing less." Technically, she merely worked *with* the cops. She had never attended the Police Academy or worked the streets. Despite her badge and gun permit, she was just a contracted investigator, but the cabbie didn't need to know that.

"Thank you for your help and keep the change." Lilith leaned over the seat and slapped the fifty-dollar bill Cohen had given her into the man's outstretched hand.

"Cheers." The driver flashed a toothy smile, advertising the importance of dental health, and slid the bill into his lockbox.

Lilith inhaled deeply to steady her nerves and opened the door. For a moment, she stood still, studying the quaint family home tucked into a postage-stamp-sized lot. As soon as she closed the door, the cab sped down the street—no turning back.

When she paused at the front door and smoothed her t-shirt, she quickly realized making herself presentable was impossible. Half her shirt was wrapped around her bloody arm, her torn jeans were caked with dirt, blood, and god knows what else, and blood still trickled from the bullet hole in her shoulder. On top of that, bruised scrapes covered every inch of exposed skin, and even her auburn hair spilled out of her ponytail in a frizzy, blood-matted mess.

Worst of all, no one could miss the acrid stench of decomposing flesh. The foul odor radiated off her so strongly that it coated the back of her throat like dirt over a rotting corpse.

"What I wouldn't give for a shower or five. Well, only one way that can happen."

She bit down on all the excuses not to knock, gathered her strength, and rapped her knuckles against the bright red door. Once the sound reverberated through the house, her muscles twitched with an overwhelming urge to run. *I'm not ready. I can't do this.*

Rose of Jericho

While her mind rambled through the dismal alternatives again, the apprehension of what would come next held her captive, frozen in place.

When the door opened, her stomach seized violently. She stood there, panting, on the verge of a full-fledged panic attack with her eyes fixed forward, petrified.

The soft lines of the woman's olive skin wrinkled in confusion as more than a dozen emotions flickered across her face—disbelief, uncertainty, shock, anger, regret, guilt, sadness, shame, affection, fear, anxiety, disgust…. What if the woman slammed the door in her face? Where would she go?

"*Bonita*? What has happened?" The middle-aged woman rushed onto the porch and pulled her inside. No tones of anger or hatred infiltrated Gloria's Spanish-flecked voice, and contempt didn't tug at her lips. Instead, Lilith only witnessed concern mixed with the same nurturing instinct that forced her to eat gluten-free cookies and sit through painful blind dates.

At the funeral, rage had contorted Gloria's features while Lilith had taken everything the widow threw at her. After all, the guilt made Lilith believe she deserved no less, and when Gloria slapped her in a fit of anger, Lilith had thought she'd never see this warm expression on her best friend's face again.

As Lilith swallowed the lump of tears in her throat, intense relief flooded her body. "I am so sorry about Felipe…I…I miss…" Her voice broke, overwhelmed by sadness and shame.

Gloria came to a stop and turned toward her.

Shit. She hadn't meant to blurt that out and reopen the wound that had driven them apart. *Come on, idiot, say something else.*

To her immense relief, Gloria cupped Lilith's blood-splattered face, lifting it until she met the woman's eyes, which glowed with fierce sincerity.

"The friend you brought to Felipe's funeral was right. It was not your fault. You hear me, *Bonita*? *It was not your fault. You* did not drag him to Tennessee and put him in harm's way." The sympathetic smile lifted a tremendous weight from Lilith's shoulders, allowing her to breathe easily for the first time since the funeral.

Then, the friendly expression faltered, and Lilith braced for the worst. "Your father made that decision." A definite edge sharpened Gloria's voice as she shifted the blame. "But we can talk once I get you cleaned up."

Sadness chilled Lilith's heart when she thought about why Gloria could never confront him. Suddenly, she realized the council possessed her father's body, which meant she couldn't bury her father and put him to rest, even if she survived. He'd rot away in whatever dark hole the demons used to dispose of inconvenient corpses. The image brought fresh tears to Lilith's eyes as Gloria led her into the kitchen.

Once she helped Lilith into a chair, she shoved a warm cup of coffee into her hand while Lilith gazed at her surroundings. After spending every Sunday morning for the past four years sitting in the same chair with her hand wrapped around the same mug, the sunlit kitchen should have felt like home. Instead, it seemed like a glimpse into a past life, familiar but far away.

"Where are the girls?" Since they hadn't immediately pounced on her, Lilith was sure they weren't home, which was a stroke of luck. She didn't want Gloria's daughters to see her like this, especially after losing their father.

"Erica is at cheerleading practice." Gloria padded back over to the table with an industrial-sized first-aid kit, scissors, and a mug of coffee. "Sofia and Rose are both at soccer."

A soft chuckle escaped Lilith's lips at the normalcy of her answers. While Lilith, Chance, Nicci, and Cohen were running from demons and zombie queens, the rest of the world moved along—just another Saturday afternoon.

Of course, most people wouldn't consider cheerleading and soccer normal vampire activities, but reality strongly differed from pop culture. Without super-strength, they could play sports whenever and wherever they wanted, and the sun didn't set them on fire or make their skin sparkle. Although Erica probably wouldn't mind resembling a disco ball. Much to Gloria and Felipe's dismay, their sixteen-year-old daughter had plastered her room with Team Edward paraphernalia.

"I don't pick them up for a few hours yet, so we have some time." When Gloria leaned in with the scissors, her entire face scrunched, and she turned away. "What is that *repugnante* smell?"

"You *really* don't want to know. I wish I didn't." Lilith muttered the answer as Gloria fixed her with a skeptical stare and hesitantly set to work cutting off the mangled shirt.

"As soon as you are able, you are marching straight into the shower." Her stern voice left no room to argue, not that Lilith intended to object. She desperately yearned for the scalding hot water.

"*Diosdulce*," Gloria whispered the exclamation as she peeled the T-shirt off Lilith's skin. "I am no doctor, *bonita*." The woman sat back in her chair with a huff, staring at the apparent wounds—a dislocated shoulder, the dark bruise indicating a broken humerus, the gouged nail marks, and the bullet hole still weeping blood. Basically, her entire left arm was in rough shape.

Gloria's rounded face clenched in disbelief while her eyes roamed over the wounds, not knowing where to start. Then Gloria shook her head and tossed the scissors on the table, giving up the fight. "You need to go to Solasta."

"I can't. The people after me know about the lab in Tennessee, which means they probably know about Solasta. If by some miracle, they don't, I don't want to lead them to it. Coming here is enough of a risk. If I had anywhere else to go…"

The woman's eyes hardened as her fear turned into something easier to manage. She crossed her arms, eased into her seat, and stared at Lilith again. "Who is after you? Someone from Tennessee? Does it have to do with Felipe?"

"Fix me up, and I'll tell you…everything."

"Everything?" Once Lilith nodded, Gloria took a deep breath and rose to her five-foot-six height, full of false bravado. "What do I need to do?"

After two excruciating hours, an entire bottle of alcohol, and countless reassuring instructions, they finally finished. Lilith had blacked out from the pain a few times, but Gloria managed to tough it out and keep going.

Removing the bullet had proven difficult, but resetting her arm had been the most painful part for them both. It had taken Lilith twenty minutes to help Gloria work up the nerve to push everything into place, and it had ended with them both screaming like banshees.

When Lilith made it to the shower, she let the steaming hot water run over her for what seemed like an eternity as it washed away all the stench, grime, and blood. However, the anguish in her head wasn't so easily removed. Everything sat on her chest like lead weights, slowly compressing the life from her.

With Farren and his she-devil pet most likely torn to bits in the apartment of horrors, and another enemy possessing the book, she appeared to be out of options. No matter how hard she tried, she couldn't picture a scenario where they escaped the death sentence awaiting them.

After pulling on yoga pants and a fresh T-shirt, she padded barefoot into the kitchen with a towel wrapped around her unruly hair. Lilith came to an abrupt halt.

Gloria slammed a bottle of whiskey onto the table and poured herself a glass. Lilith could only stare slack-jawed as the matronly woman knocked back the generous shot, a view as rare as an albino elephant in the wild. Of course, considering the current circumstances, the woman had more than a few reasons to drink.

"Your father pulled you into something else, didn't he?" Gloria's teeth clenched, and her fingers tightened around the glass. When she twisted in her chair to stare up at Lilith, anger roiled beneath the surface. "First, he sends you to Tennessee to take care of *his* problems, then he drags Felipe down there, and now, here you are… showing up on my doorstep half-dead."

Lilith swallowed the sudden lump in her throat and sank back into her seat. How could she answer that question? True. The current situation directly resulted from her father's actions, but condemning a dead man wasn't helpful.

"Your father is out of line! I already lost Felipe. I can't lose you, too, *bonita*. The girls…" Gloria choked on thick tears, unable to continue.

Lilith stared at the scuffed tabletop, trying to summon the right words. She refused to provide her friend with a false sense of security. Reassurances might help ease Gloria's mind for a few moments, but ultimately, they would all be lies.

"Whatever he dragged you into, walk away. Let him clean up his own messes. You don't have to—"

Each word deepened Lilith's sorrow until her expression collapsed in utter devastation, stopping Gloria mid-sentence. Once Lilith felt she could trust her voice, she met her friend's eyes as she spoke. "What did Felipe tell you about Tennessee?"

Gloria's head tilted to the side in confusion, unable to connect the dots between her rant and Lilith's question. Eventually, she leaned back in her chair with her arms crossed over her chest. Clearly, this wasn't a comfortable subject, which made sense. Two days ago, the woman had buried her husband, the man she'd spent a century with, the father of her children.

"Felipe called me from the Marriott. He told me Gregor sent you to take care of some family business in Knoxville, but things became more complicated than he'd expected. You were in danger, and Felipe wanted to bring everyone home safe."

Then, she hesitated as if something new flashed through her mind, and her eyes sank to the floor while she processed the thought. "He knew." Her warm eyes flew up to Lilith in a moment of stunning revelation. "I heard the despair in his voice, but I didn't want to admit it. He knew Gregor dragged him into something he might not survive. He was…saying goodbye." Gloria dissolved into tears as Lilith's mind rambled.

Felipe had called after Gregor's heartfelt tell-all, which meant he had known the odds they were facing when he'd spoken to his wife. The thought brought tears to Lilith's eyes. Hours after Felipe had called Gloria, his worst fears had come true. Her partner had done the noble thing, drawing Ashcroft's focus to give the rest of them a fighting chance. Unfortunately, he'd paid the ultimate price.

While Lilith tried to shake off the haunting images from that infernal basement, Gloria's eyes hardened again. With a startling urgency, she shoved away from the table and paced the kitchen. Lilith didn't need Cohen's blood to sense the anxious wrath emanating from her body like heat from a torch.

"This is all Gregor's fault!" She glared at Lilith as she continued to move, her finger jabbing at the air to emphasize her point. "He *has* to stop this. We aren't cannon fodder for his personal war. You need to walk away before you end up like Felipe. Your father may be the only blood relative you have left, but he isn't—"

"Gregor's dead." The words unexpectedly spilled out of Lilith's mouth, and as soon as they did, Lilith finally believed it was true. No matter how many times she had replayed the scene or discussed the tragedy with Chance, Cohen, and Timothy, saying it out loud to Gloria made the truth inescapable. "This"—Lilith gestured at her myriad of wounds— "isn't his fault. It's mine."

The woman's mouth opened and closed. The anger leeched from Gloria's face along with the color, leaving her pale and shaken. She attempted to speak several times, stumbling over a few mumbled words before collapsing into the chair like a lifeless sack of bones. Her eyes remained locked on the tabletop, ashamed by the complex emotions preventing her from simply comforting her friend.

Lilith understood the conflict. Yes. Gregor had dragged Alvarez to Tennessee, which had resulted in his death. However, he was also a generous benefactor to their entire race.

Her father had initiated the cooperative system with the police to give their kind a modicum of safety. He had begun negotiations with the Elders to create a unified front, helping to decide the future of their race. Not to mention, Gregor and Duncan had founded the labs and blood banks that kept them alive and off the radar.

Did his violent past eradicate all the incredible things he had accomplished? When Lilith glanced up, she witnessed the answer in the downcast, teary eyes of her best friend.

"Gloria." Lilith reached out and tentatively grasped her hand. She waited until the woman eventually lifted her gaze. Despite Gregor's role in Felipe's death, she still mourned the loss of a friend and an irreplaceable pillar of their community.

Lilith swallowed the lump of emotions in her throat and focused on the things she needed to do. "I… I need to call my voicemail. Hopefully, I'll have some good news. Afterward, if you help bandage me up, we can discuss all this."

Gloria nodded as two tears splashed onto the battered tabletop. Without another word, she rose from her chair and wandered toward the living room, lost in her thoughts. As Gloria walked, her shoulders slumped as if the guilt and sorrow physically weighed down on them.

For the first time that day, Lilith found herself grateful that the side effects of Cohen's blood had disappeared. Her own emotions felt stifling enough without adding her friend's.

All Lilith could do was check her voicemail and pray that a miracle lurked somewhere in the digital universe.

Chapter 22

Lilith stared at the cream-colored phone hanging on the kitchen wall as if vicious teeth lined the thing. What would be worse? A dozen frantic messages or none? And who the hell still used a corded phone in this technologically advanced age?

The first time Lilith had come over for dinner, she'd asked Gloria about the bulky dinosaur. Her answer? They had three daughters, and one was nearly a pre-teen. Only allowing them to use the house phone enabled her to monitor their calls.

It also meant no text messages, Facebook, Instagram, Snapchat, TikTok, or any other social media hellscapes. The girls each carried kid-friendly cellphones with four buttons pre-programmed to call Gloria, Felipe, 9-1-1, and Solasta. Erica, who was now sixteen, threw regular fits about the overbearing limitations, but arguing with her mother proved as effective as yelling at the Great Wall of China.

While lost in the warm memories, Lilith's eyes drifted from the bulky phone to the living room. Gloria stood before the fireplace, gazing at photographs. Her fingers lovingly drifted over the glass as tears rolled down her cheeks.

Lilith clenched her jaw and concentrated. She couldn't keep distracting herself. The modicum of safety she'd found in her dead partner's home wouldn't last, and the longer she stayed, the more she endangered Gloria and her daughters.

Besides, Chance, Nicci, and Cohen still needed her, and she wouldn't abandon them for a false sense of security. Gregor had started the fight, but now it belonged to her. Although she couldn't see a way out now, if she gave up, their deaths were a certainty. She had to keep trying.

After a slow exhale, she grabbed the phone and dialed her voicemail. The robotic voice announced three new messages and two saved ones. Part of her felt relieved, but the rest dreaded the possible contents.

As the mechanical tones rattled off the first number, she jotted it down in case she needed to return the call. The first one was time-stamped about five minutes ago from a local area code.

"Hey, Lilith, I know you're still on bereavement for a few more days, but we picked up a case downtown on White Street." Her breath caught as soon as Detective Boyd mentioned Haverty's neighborhood.

"Multiple civilians reported FBI activity in a high rise, which uncovered a complete blood bath on the 11th floor. The weird thing is, there hasn't been any Fed chatter, except a single call asking the police to stand down while they take out a terrorist cell. As if that wasn't enough, the 9-1-1 calls about a murdered cab driver are even more…well…bizarre is the only way I can put it. Peters isn't very thorough, and…" Boyd paused, most likely due to a conflicted conscience. *"If you're interested, call me. If not, I'll see you when you get back."* Another pause. *"We sure miss you around here."*

Apparently, Peters left a lot to be desired—not surprising. The medical examiner in New Haven and Detective Vincent Peters had a lot in common. Both were burned-out, alcoholic, two-pack-a-day-smokers going through the motions on autopilot. At least the M.E. performed a thorough autopsy. Detective Peters only cared about clearing cases, regardless of the evidence.

Lilith hesitated, considering whether to call the station. Under normal circumstances, she'd take the lead to eliminate incriminating evidence and steer the investigation in a helpful direction. However, with zombies, a voodoo queen, and demons searching the city for her, playing interference on a case could severely shorten her lifespan. No. She had to leave things in Peters' incompetent hands and hope for the best.

The second message, time-stamped an hour ago, came from a number and area code she didn't recognize. Cohen's vaguely European timbre emanated from the speaker with anger and panic.

"What the fuck is going on, Lilith? Why the hell did you run off? I got separated from Nicci and tried to find you both, but nada. *This whole thing is a complete shit storm."*

The man's deep, ragged breath shook with fear. *"I called Luminita. She confirmed the German is in town. He flew in yesterday. He* must *be the man behind the…well, you know.*" It seemed Cohen couldn't bring himself to verbally acknowledge what he'd witnessed.

"*Call me as soon as you get this!*" A lengthy pause crackled through the speaker, making her wonder if he'd forgotten to hang up. Then he spoke in a rush of soft, almost humiliated tones. "*Please…don't be dead.*"

Cohen had survived. Somewhere past her immense relief, a tiny part of her wondered why she felt that way. If the man had never crossed their path, her father would still be alive, and she wouldn't be running for her life from logic-defying zombies… *No.* She couldn't make Andrew the scapegoat anymore.

His help had prevented Ashcroft and Spencer from succeeding and had spared Chance and herself a torturous death at the madman's vengeful hands. As dire as her current circumstances were, without the Durand, she'd be a pile of smoking ash in Tennessee.

After learning more about Cohen's past, she understood why he kept people at arm's length and played various roles to push people away. The information didn't make it easier to trust him, but she could no longer view him as an albatross dragging her down. In fact, she saw a bit of herself reflected in him. They were both fighting to survive the dark sins of their families.

"Shit." Lilith sighed at the old phone and dialed Cohen's number, which rang once before his aristocratic voice rattled through the receiver.

"Lilith? This better be you!"

"Hello to you, too."

"Thank fucking god!"

She couldn't help but snicker. "Getting religious on me?"

Cohen ignored her smart-ass humor and barreled forward. "What the fuck was that? Do you have a damn death wish? This isn't Scooby-Doo. We *don't* split up. Where the hell are you?"

"Brooklyn and I had no choice. I couldn't breathe, and I needed… I would have slowed you down. Without me, you and Nicci stood a better chance. Besides, I'm alive, so everything worked out. You said the German is in town?" She'd rather focus on relevant information than on her embarrassing vampiric needs.

"Brooklyn? Where exactly? I need an address!"

When he pushed for a precise location, her lingering doubts reared to the forefront. She refused to gamble with Gloria's life, so she avoided the subject.

"Andrew, calm down! I'm safe. Tell me where you want to meet, and I'll be there. I'm assuming you came up with a plan?"

Silence filled the line, and every passing second made her optimism fade a bit more. "I'm working on one. Luminita said Helton flew into LaGuardia, so I'm attempting to track him down. He's the key. If we stop him, we get the book, and when Chance returns with the cipher, we'll be free of the council. You can return to your quiet life, and I can go back to mine."

My quiet life. The remnants of her existence no longer resembled anything she recognized. That life had ended in soul-twisting misery. So, what would her new life look like?

"Lilith?" Cohen's inquisitive voice pulled her back to the present.

"Yeah."

"If you're somewhere safe, stay there, but please tell me where, so I can pick you up when I have a location. I need you in this fight." The sincerity in his voice eradicated her doubts, but someone else could be listening.

Lilith glanced into the living room as Gloria held onto the mantle, wiping tears from her eyes. She couldn't put her best friend through anything else.

"I'm visiting a friend. I needed someone to patch me up—"

"You're hurt? What are your injuries?" The abrupt questions sounded clinical, demanding a report on her viability.

"You witnessed the bullet wound and gouges. A vehicle dislocated my shoulder and fractured the humerus. I have a dozen scrapes and bruises, *and* I added to my collection of concussions. You know, typical Saturday."

"You got hit by a car?"

"Kinda." Technically, the car slammed on top of her, but close enough.

"Okay." Cohen released a long breath, probably rearranging his plans based on her injury report. "Sit tight. I'll call you back at this number when I find him. I understand you wish to protect your friend, so think of a place nearby where we can meet. Also, I should speed up your healing."

"What? No. I'm not doing that."

"You won't be much help if your arm is in a damn sling. Besides, it's not like sharing my blood will make things worse at this point. They can only kill me once. I need you at your best, okay?"

Rose of Jericho

Theoretically, his statement was inaccurate. Ashcroft died several times before he'd stayed that way. Of course, he was an abomination. Still, the possibility existed.

"I'll take your stunned silence as a yes."

Before she opened her mouth to argue, he hung up.

The sudden stillness stifled her blind panic, allowing her stiff muscles to unclench one at a time. They had a plan, at least part of one, with a clear enemy, a light at the end of the tunnel, a way out. Now, all Cohen needed her to do was wait patiently for their next move—not her strong suit.

Lilith picked up the cream-colored dinosaur and re-dialed her voicemail to hear the last message. After skipping past the first two, the robotic voice announced a timestamp around four hours ago. *Odd.* Her cell hadn't rung.

Then she realized four hours ago they had arrived at Haverty's apartment. The call must have come through while her phone had been on silent.

A warm, Cajun-flecked voice rumbled through the speaker like a balm for her soul. Her throat clenched, tears welled in her eyes, and her fingers tightened around the clunky plastic. *"Cherie, I'm sorry I missed your call. I'm sure you're still dealing with the perp's apartment, but I wanted to give you an update."* He paused and said a muffled goodbye to someone before his rich voice filled her ear again.

"I'm leaving the lab with the tin and the samples you wanted. I know I said I'd sleep first, but…" Another pause with a whoosh of doors opening and closing. *"I can't rest knowing you're in New York with Cohen, especially after what happened in New Haven. I mean…I trust Timothy, but…"*

He released a heavy sigh, and she knew he was running a hand through his hair. *"I don't like how we left things and, well…Damn, I miss you."* The soft silence allowed her a second to revel. Despite everything, he still needed her. *"I'm heading straight back. Don't worry, I'll be fine once I'm back in New York."*

She couldn't contain the Cheshire cat grin crossing her lips as she hugged the phone to her ear. She wanted nothing more than to dismiss his fears, shake off the horrible nightmare, and jump into his arms. But what if the nightmare had scarred her for life? What if she never recovered?

"Lily." Chance's voice returned with a commanding edge. Something was wrong. The tone of that solitary word said everything.

"*I need to cut this short,* cherie. *I have company.*" Lilith heard someone barking orders in the background. "*I love you.*" His voice sounded strained, as if he were running or jumping. Gunfire crackled over the speaker.

Lilith jumped, and the phone clattered on the kitchen tile. She quickly snatched the handset, but only heard the dull beep signaling the end of the message. For a moment, she stood there, frozen, as her world spun on its axis.

"No!" she screamed, clutching the phone so tight her knuckles turned white. A thousand scenarios raced through her head at a million miles an hour. Had Farren sent his men? Was Sievers, Helton, or whatever the German called himself, behind the attack? Had someone else made a play for the book? Was Chance still alive? Were these people holding him, or did he get away?

Fear hummed through her body, making her fingers shake as she redialed the number. The call went straight to voicemail. *No!*

She stubbornly clicked the button and dialed again, but nothing changed. The fifth time she reached the robotic beep, all her words caught in her throat, and she slammed the handset into the cradle so hard the wall rattled. *Not Chance. I can't lose him now.*

Lilith furiously wiped her cheeks while she tried to think. *I have to do something...but what?* Chance left the message four hours ago from Tennessee, and she had no idea if he was even alive. The outcome of the gunfight had already happened. She couldn't change it now.

She smashed her palm into the wall before collapsing against it in tears. She was so tired of being powerless to save the ones she loved. Then a hand touched her shoulder, and she nearly jumped out of her skin.

"Lily, *bonita,* what's wrong?" The soothing tones of Gloria's voice were so inviting that she fell against her shoulder, emotionally exhausted.

"I don't know what to do anymore."

"Tell me, *bonita.*" The matronly woman pulled back enough to give Lilith a firm, yet sympathetic frown. After a deep sigh, she told her all about the message from Chance while continuing to stare at the phone.

Not only did she desperately hope it would ring, but she also wanted to avoid the judgmental stare now that her feelings about him were obvious. Thankfully, Gloria stayed on task and didn't verbalize any reservations about her blossoming relationship.

"Call Solasta. They'll give you the number for Goditha. Perhaps the guard can tell you something."

"Yeah!" For a split second, Lilith smiled brightly, but then her face became a mask of frustration. "No. They might know about Solasta and be monitoring calls. If you knew the full story…"

"Surely there is someone you can call." Gloria didn't push for information. She merely tackled the immediate problem, which kept Lilith on task, focused, and able to breathe.

Call. A thought clicked into place like a cog connecting with the rest of the machine. She flashed a hopeful smile and kissed Gloria on the cheek. "You're brilliant!"

Lilith grabbed the phone, called her voicemail, skipped to the first saved message, and jotted down the number. Then she hung up and dialed while mumbling a prayer under her breath. *Please pick up!*

"Hello?"

"Nicci?" Relief flooded her body. Another tragedy averted. "Are you okay?"

"Lilith?! Damn, girl. I thought you were worm food. Yeah. I mean, well, I'm fine, considering. I got away and phoned in an anonymous tip to the station. I thought perhaps a police presence would scare 'em off. Are *you* alright?"

"Injured, but okay." She sucked in a deep breath before barreling onward. "I need a favor. Considering recent events, I have no right to ask, but I *need* your help."

The line went silent for a moment, and the gut-twisting guilt made Lilith feel like the most selfish person on the planet.

"This shit is serious, an actual threat, and not only to you. This affects all of us and needs to be handled. It's my job, so stop asking for favors and tell me how I can help."

Lilith sighed in relief, finally able to exhale after the awkward silence. "I can never thank you enough, Nicci."

"There'll be time for that later. So, what do you need?"

"I got in touch with Cohen. He's tracking down Helton, who recently arrived in New York City. In the meantime, I need the phone number for Goditha Labs in Knoxville, Tennessee."

"Goditha? Yeah, sure. Give me a second." Several clicks on a keyboard echoed through the phone before her New York-Italian accent returned. "You ready?"

"Yeah." Lilith scribbled the digits while juggling the huge receiver on her shoulder.

"So…uh…isn't Goditha the lab that Dev…" Nicci didn't get far into her attempt at Chance's last name before giving up. "Your security guy went to?"

"Deveraux, it's French Cajun, and yeah, he drove down last night." Lilith's voice sounded depressed, even to her.

Unsurprisingly, Nicci picked up on the somber tone. "I'm assuming things didn't go well?"

"Something happened, but I'm not sure what. Chance left me a voicemail that ended with gunfire. I'm hoping the guard at Goditha can tell me what happened. If he's hurt or worse…" Sudden tears clenched Lilith's throat, while she tried to figure out how to finish the sentence.

"Do you want me to call?" The valiant offer meant Nicci understood her partner was worried about more than a few scraps of paper.

"No. I'll handle it. I need to know."

"Okay. Where are you? We need to be ready when Cohen calls, and I have weapons." Judging by the eager tone of her voice, Nicci didn't take defeat well, and probably viewed running away as a moment of weakness. Now she seemed impatient to not only settle the score but prove herself.

"I'm at a friend's place." She exchanged a significant look with Gloria, who nodded, giving her permission. She stifled her mistrusting nature, gave Nicci the address, thanked her again, and hung up.

For a few seconds, she simply stood there, staring at the numbers, crippled by the possibilities swirling in her head. When she lifted the phone and attempted to dial, her fingers shook so badly she couldn't hit the buttons. She flexed her hand to steady her nerves, but Gloria gently removed the phone from her tight grip.

"I need to make this call." The words barely squeaked past the growing lump of dread wedged in her throat.

"Take a minute. You're shaking all over." Once again, Gloria was right. If Lilith called in a raving panic, the guard probably wouldn't take her seriously.

"Let me dial for you."

Lilith nodded and handed Gloria the flowery piece of paper while she took several deep breaths, bracing herself for worst-case scenarios. When the line started ringing, Gloria handed her the handset with a supportive smile.

"Goditha Research Laboratories, Security Officer Fontaine. How can I direct your call?"

Despite her best efforts, the image of his predecessor, Richard Coffee, sprang to mind—pinning Ashcroft to the furnace, the madman's talons tearing through Coffee's guts, skin melting on the hot metal, entrails dangling to the floor. After forcibly shaking off the horrific memory, she concentrated on the present.

"Lilith Adams. Security code A10978…"

"I'm sorry, but that code is no longer recognized. If you believe this is a mistake, you need to—"

"I know. I initiated the emergency protocol last night, but I have a question about the man I allowed to use my access, Chance Deveraux." The unnerving silence only made her trembling worse.

"I believe that falls outside the parameters of lab security. What is your question?"

"He left me a voicemail while leaving a few hours ago, and I heard gunfire…" She couldn't bring herself to verbalize the implied question.

"Yes…" The man paused for a significant amount of time, which did nothing to calm her nerves. "An SUV entered the premises as Mr. Deveraux headed outside. We had no scheduled deliveries, so I followed him out. Four men in tactical gear emerged with assault rifles and opened fire."

Lilith's heart leapt into her throat as she imagined a scene like her experience in New Haven.

"Mr. Deveraux took down one assailant before I moved close enough to shoot. I provided cover fire, taking down another gunman while Mr. Deveraux escaped in his car."

"So, he got away?" Unmistakable desperation rang in her voice.

"Yes, ma'am, but the last two assailants chased after him in their SUV. I also found his phone in the parking lot. What's left of it, anyway. I'm not sure if he dropped it or destroyed it on purpose in case they apprehended him."

The glow of hope dimmed. She had no way to discover what happened after he'd left Goditha or to contact him if he was still alive.

"I recorded the license plate, but these men were professionals, so I doubt it will lead you anywhere. Sorry I can't be more helpful."

"Thank you for the report, Officer Fontaine. I appreciate the information. If Mr. Deveraux shows up again, will you have him call me at this number?"

"Absolutely, Miss Adams."

Lilith hung up and sank into her chair while attempting to unravel the puzzling events. Although SWAT henchmen fit Farren's M.O., he couldn't be behind the attack at Goditha, and she now doubted he played a role in New Haven.

Farren had displayed genuine shock when he realized Timothy took Chance's place. Besides, if the psycho had known about Chance's mission, he would have immediately held it over their heads. Perhaps he'd stationed a team there for surveillance. He could have connected the same dots as Cohen, and he had possessed an endless supply of anonymous mercenaries. The man either bought in bulk or used a placement service.

No. When it came down to it, Farren had enjoyed attending to things personally, especially when it gave him an opportunity to hurt Cohen. He had used the henchmen as backup, retrieval squads, or minions to handle mundane tasks, like eliminating Haverty. They were tools that served a purpose. That ruled him out of the attack in New Haven, but not necessarily Goditha if he'd wanted his men to bring back Chance alive.

Honestly, none of it mattered to her. She only cared about Chance and his odds of survival. Hopefully, he had ditched the men tailing him and was halfway back to New York City by now. Although she refused to officially acknowledge the alternatives, the thought of him dead on a Tennessee road ate at her insides like slow-acting acid.

Gloria leaned across the table and softly squeezed Lilith's hand. "I think it's time to talk."

Slowly, Lilith raised her eyes to Gloria's sympathetic face, knowing the woman was right. Gloria needed to know everything because Lilith's presence put her and the girls in danger.

Besides, she couldn't accomplish anything else until Cohen called, so she may as well lay all the chips on the table.

Lilith took a deep breath and began her story right at the beginning, when she left New York City with Chance in search of her uncle.

Chapter 23

"*Hositaputa!*" Gloria's eyes went wide with disbelief when the story ended. Lilith had never studied proper Spanish, but the strong blush indicated her response wasn't meant for polite dinner conversations.

Gloria's hands hovered over the makeshift sling before her trembling fingers tied the last knot. For a moment, she merely stared at the Monster High sheets she'd used to splint Lilith's broken arm, unable to say anything else.

If Lilith lived long enough, she owed Sofia a new set of sheets, but that wasn't the reason for Gloria's catatonic stare. The truth was a lot to take in, and she hadn't held anything back.

At first, speaking the words proved difficult. But once the dam had broken, everything had gushed out—Ashcroft, Mary, Miriah, Duncan, Chance and their relationship, her nightmares, Gregor's murder, Cohen's family, the siren, and the voodoo queen, all of it. Dumping all those secrets had felt liberating, like cutting the cords on a suffocating corset.

"I never thought creatures like the Durand existed." Gloria cracked a smile and rolled her eyes as a thought occurred to her. "It's ironic to hear a vampire say such things."

Comments like that explained why they had become best friends. On the surface, the two women existed in very different worlds.

Gloria played the dutiful roles of a detective's wife, a mother of three, and a middle-class suburban homemaker. Lilith was a twenty-seven-year-old forensic examiner who lived alone, liked sweet cream in her Folgers, and had suffered through so many horrible dates that she had contemplated writing off the entire male species.

Something deeper connected these seemingly incompatible women, and it didn't stem from their heritage as vampires. They shared an ironic view of the world, which sparked intense intellectual debates and hilarious conversations. Those moments of kinship kept Lilith coming back every Sunday, even if it meant enduring failed attempts at match-making—the primary cause for her lackluster dating history.

"So, how do you think this woman is controlling dead bodies?"

"The million-dollar question." Lilith stared into her coffee mug, dredging up every detail to make sense of what she remembered—the creepy tribal chant, the corpses responding to her changes in pitch or words, the way they stood like vacant husks when she'd stopped singing.

"I could be imagining the connection, but I think she was serenading the dead." Then another thought occurred to her. "One of the zombies struggled to follow her commands, like the body was too degraded. The woman cut her palm and fed him blood. Afterward, the thing walked straighter and moved with the pack. He even appeared more...fresh."

"Do you think the blood controls them? Perhaps everything else is just for show." Gloria lifted a curious eyebrow, prompting Lilith to explore every possibility.

"No. She only gave blood to one of them." Lilith rubbed her chin and sank into the chair, mulling over what she knew about the Durand.

"Maybe she had him around longer, and the effect was wearing off?"

Lilith carefully considered the theory until she remembered Haverty. "No. I don't think so. She animated a body in another room, moments after Berman killed him." Then, a remote possibility took form in her mind.

"The Durand possess mind-altering abilities, which I witnessed in Tennessee. Ashcroft was an abomination, with the ability to control people. Peisinoe is an anomaly capable of overriding someone's perception with her voice. What if this woman is another genetic variant of the Durand?"

"Even if you're right, controlling a living person is a lot different from bringing the dead back to life."

Lilith frowned at the inaccurate description. "She doesn't bring them back to life. There is no awareness, only an empty shell, like remote-controlled robots made of rotting flesh."

Gloria shivered and cupped her hands tighter around the warm coffee mug. "So why the blood and the weird plant?"

"The tumbleweed may not be important. Chance said people commonly use it in voodoo rituals involving the dead. The blood, though..." When the last piece clicked into place, she saw the bigger picture.

"Shit." Gloria glanced up at Lilith's exclamation with excitement. "Cohen's blood contains healing elements. Perhaps the blood regenerates enough tissue to accomplish basic tasks—movement, grabbing, tearing, biting. She can't restore higher brain functionality, which is why reasoning and intellect are absent. They follow literal commands in the most direct way possible."

"I don't know if I'm more comforted or more terrified by that." Gloria leaned back in her chair, trying to picture it before shaking her head. "On second thought, I shouldn't dwell. If all this is correct, do you think Cohen knows what she is?"

"In my gut? No. The shock on his face, the terror...appeared genuine. However, he isn't always forthcoming with sensitive info about his race."

"From the story you told me, he hasn't lied when it truly counts."

Lilith frowned as she reviewed the entire saga. Everything fell into the categories of underhanded, sneaky, and misleading. When push came to shove...she couldn't believe Cohen would withhold information about a voodoo queen on the loose, especially with so much at stake. "You're right."

"So, what can we do?"

Lilith released a sigh that nearly turned into a maniacal laugh. "I have no clue. I'm so lost, Gloria. The enemy has the book, Chance is MIA, and I don't even know if I'm right about the cipher's location. All I can do is hope Cohen finds the German." Helpless doom settled over her shoulders like a lead beam as she turned her coffee cup, staring at the creamy concoction inside. If Cohen came up empty...

"I remember when you were a rookie, fresh out of college, with Felipe walking you through procedures. You were always a fast learner, obsessed with details."

Although the abrupt subject change surprised her, Gloria's happy nostalgia became infectious, creating a warm bubble of familiarity. Suddenly, it felt like a normal Sunday, and the council, Cohen, the zombie queen, and the undead horde all seemed a million miles away.

"Six months in, you caught your first genuine case—the death of an immigrant vampire down at the docks. Do you remember?"

"Of course." *How could I not?* In six years working with Major Crimes, it was one of three cases involving their species. It was also one of the hardest to solve. An unknown, unregistered vampire died on the docks with only scant bits of evidence to go on.

The rope fibers buried in the ligature marks on his wrists and ankles had indicated the assailant bound him before death. Salt water had covered the body, but the M.E. found none in his lungs, which meant he hadn't drowned. The only trace on his clothes matched the dock where they'd found him. However, one thing had stood out—the missing patches of skin, cut in a perfect square, on his left shoulder and right pectoral muscle.

She had stared at the file for hours every night. Vamps weren't typically territorial, and identifying the victim had proven difficult. In desperation, she'd begun researching human signature killers, fanatic zealots, even supernatural conspiracy theorists, and had found nothing.

That was when she'd first questioned joining Solasta as a forensic investigator. Not because her position had held no merit, but because she'd doubted her abilities. It didn't matter if the vampire community had someone to advocate for them if the person couldn't perform the job.

"Felipe found you in the records room one night, poring over thirty files on your hundredth cup of coffee."

Lilith couldn't help but chuckle. "Yeah, I hadn't slept in...three days at that point. The file clerk snapped at me a few times for requesting so many files, but I couldn't let it go."

Gloria nodded with a soft smile, which held a dash of sadness. "Felipe worried about you so much, *bonita*. He knew if you didn't step back and gain perspective, you'd burn out before you truly started. Did Felipe ever tell you about Pope, his first partner?"

"Mark...no. Matthew Pope, right?"

When Gloria nodded again, Lilith dredged up what little she remembered.

"I think his father worked as a big-shot lawyer for Pharma-corp. I don't know much else. Alvarez didn't like talking about past partners." Lilith couldn't stop the sudden grin as she reminisced. "He said it felt too much like telling his wife about his ex-girlfriends."

A rich boom of laughter infused the room with a glowing warmth. "That's my Felipe. You're right about Pope's father. The man is also an OCD perfectionist, the one trait he'd shared with his son."

"Ahh." Lilith saw Gloria's line of logic. An OCD detective driving himself nuts, like she had with the dock case. Still, it didn't truly translate to her current situation. This wasn't a case. She was merely trying to survive a superior organization during a deadly coup while stuck between the warring factions.

"Well, Pope caught his first and only vampire case about a year into the job. They later proved the crime was nothing more than a mugging, but Pope was convinced the murder had involved the vampire community. He lost perspective and couldn't visualize the crime outside the context of his own world. Matthew kept pushing and prodding in places he shouldn't until someone stopped his investigation. Felipe found him hanging from the rafters in his loft apartment—a staged suicide. If the man had stepped back and inspected the evidence without the supernatural angle, his death could have been avoided."

Lilith sighed heavily, but before she opened her mouth, Gloria continued. "You suffered the same issue with your dock case. You latched onto the idea of an elaborate serial killer. After all, who else would kill a vampire and take patches of skin as a trophy?"

Lilith frowned and settled into her seat, reluctantly acknowledging Gloria's point. She'd been so obsessed with the case that Alvarez had gone to Gregor, hoping her father would talk some sense into her.

"Until we discovered his enormous debt to a local loan shark and discovered he had two distinctive tattoos where they'd removed the skin. The shark figured removing them would make an ID more difficult, especially for an undocumented immigrant."

"Because we remain hidden, we must consider mundane answers to questions, *bonita*."

"I understand, but this…"

"Is different?" Gloria lifted an eyebrow and stared at her like an expectant teacher. "This situation may be more complex, but you are behaving like Pope, rushing from one danger to another, pushing headlong into disaster with no perspective."

"I'm not choosing this!" An edge of defensive indignation rang in her voice, which the woman across from her ignored.

"Why didn't you call for backup before raiding Haverty's?"

Lilith blinked as her mouth hung open for a second, blindsided by the ludicrous question. "This isn't…they couldn't… This is *not* a case."

"Why? Because it's personal? How is this not a vampire community concern? Isn't this precisely why Solasta positioned you in the police department?"

Lilith sank into her chair, as every single injury began to ache, a bloody reminder that Gloria was one hundred percent correct. If she had treated this like a normal case from the beginning…

"Damn it. You're right. I did exactly what Farren wanted me to do. I kept everything secret and, in return, only gave him more control. Shit. Why didn't I see it?"

"Because he killed Gregor."

"What?" Lilith's eyes flew open with a mixture of shock, horror, and anger.

When Gloria continued, her voice grew softer, hesitantly testing the waters. "That is why he killed your father."

"I'm not following. He killed Dad on a whim. It wasn't planned." She frowned at the sudden leap in logic.

"*Bonita*, from what you told me, Farren is a manipulator. He murdered your father to make it personal, to scare you into secrecy, and to leave you unfocused. He didn't want you turning to outside help because he is afraid of our kind, and what we could do to him."

"Ashcroft." Lilith whispered the word as the pieces finally clicked. "He's scared of what Gregor did to him. I thought he desired the power, but something Cohen said about his past. Farren takes pride in his race and wants to keep it pure. If so, he would view Ashcroft as an intolerable abomination."

"Good, and who disagrees with him?"

Lilith silently contemplated the question for a moment. "If Farren tried to keep the book away from the council, then they are all suspects." Lilith buried her face in her palms as a dull roar crept up the back of her neck. "Why aren't you a detective?"

Gloria flashed a warm smile, patted Lilith's hand, and stood to cross the kitchen for more coffee. "Aww, *bonita*. I have no desire to chase bad guys. I merely watch after my girls."

Then she glanced down at her watch, as if suddenly remembering something. "Speaking of which, I need to pick the girls up and drop them off at Olivia's house. Erica agreed to take her sisters trick-or-treating. A bunch of them are carpooling to Grand Central Station. It's funny…even though Erica and I are constantly butting heads, she seemed excited about handling her sister's costumes, and taking them downtown."

The abrupt interjection of normal life felt completely foreign. Usually, Halloween was the one holiday Lilith braved the crowds to celebrate because of one simple truth—she loved costumes. Of course, designing them was infinitely more fun than the actual parties, but that had never stopped her.

Last year, she had created an elaborate cabaret girl costume, which had earned her several awkward dances, eight phone numbers she never intended to call, and a wretched cup of coffee at an all-night diner. This year, she merely hoped to see another day.

"Stay here, Lily. Rest and re-group. I'll help however I can when I return." Gloria flashed a half-hearted smile as she tugged on a thick, gray sweater that was two sizes too big. "I realize the circumstances appear dismal, but...I'm glad you're here." The warmth in her eyes accomplished more than the lukewarm cup in Lilith's hands.

"Thank you. That means a lot." Although her eyes watered, Lilith refused to break down again. As long as she drew breath and still had things to fight for, she wouldn't give in to despair.

Gloria nodded and grabbed her ancient, battered Coach purse. The sight of the faded blue bag brought a sense of nostalgia that made Lilith laugh.

"When are you gonna retire that thing? I mean, seriously. How many times have you sewn the handle back on?"

Gloria clutched the purse close with a proudly defiant stare. "Four and it doesn't matter. Felipe insisted on buying me this over-priced contraption, and I told him that at the price he paid, it better last forever. I'm going to ensure it does. Besides, I love the silly old thing."

Lilith suspected she was talking about Felipe more than the once-blue, tattered leather bag. Her husband should have been by her side forever, or at least longer than the damn purse, but that possibility no longer existed.

Ashcroft took more than a life in the basement of Phipps Bend when he'd sliced Alvarez's throat. He had killed part of the woman who loved Felipe, and now she carried the remnants of her heart in that purse, hoping the thing would come back to life if she kept it close. Then again, perhaps hauling her memories around in an old purse helped keep the past alive.

Either way, Lilith was in no position to judge. She was only maintaining a tenuous grip on her own sanity at best.

Chapter 24

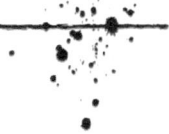

Once Gloria left, Lilith wandered into the living room, pulling the warm memories around her like a security blanket. Her olive eyes scanned the line of picture frames above the fireplace before fixating on a family portrait dominating the center.

They all appeared so happy, even Erica, a rarity for the rebellious teen. Felipe stood proud with his arm around Gloria's shoulder while Rose sat on her lap and Sophie stood by his side. The man's broad smile possessed all the warmth and humor she remembered, and she tentatively traced the glass with tears in her eyes.

"Miss you, partner. Wish I had your help on this." A heavy sigh escaped as she stared at the photo that embodied their quiet, happy life, now torn apart forever. His murder created a gaping hole in their lives that no number of guilty apologies could fill.

As she stepped back from the mantle, she thought of all the family and friends she had lost, each one leaving a cavernous wound. How many more before nothing remained of her? Perhaps it was already too late.

What if her nightmare about Chance didn't stem from Peisinoe and her threats? What if she had nothing left to give, and that was her subconscious clueing her in? Or perhaps the nightmare came from her crippling guilt for enjoying something while surrounded by so much tragedy.

A blaring ring erupted from the kitchen, making Lilith jump. After swallowing the lump in her throat, she ran for the ancient wall-phone, praying to hear Chance's voice. She couldn't handle another loss, especially not that one.

On the third ring, she snatched the receiver and balanced it on her shoulder. "Hello? Chance?"

"I was so wrong. So damn wrong." An almost unrecognizable voice rattled through the speaker, worn and defeated. Every tiny hair rose on end as the sense of impending disaster crept over her.

"Cohen? Is that you?"

"Run, Lilith. Go!" Although his voice became stronger and more familiar, it didn't soften her blooming panic.

"What? You told me to stay put until you located Helton. What is going on?"

"Don't argue! I don't care where you go but leave! Now!"

Dread hovered in the air like a violent twister waiting to destroy her. The last time Cohen had made a panicked call like this, things had turned from bad to worse in a matter of hours.

"You *have* to give me something here." The words emerged thin and shaky as she prayed for him to shout *Just kidding!* and dissolve into inappropriate laughter. Neither happened.

"I swear to all that is holy, I will follow your ass to hell and kick it for the rest of eternity if you don't shut the fuck up and run! It's not Helton! Are you listening? It's not the fucking German! He's dead!"

Lilith's gut seized with a sudden cramp of fear, turning her blood ice-cold, but before she responded, a loud slam echoed from the front of the house.

"Did you hear me? I said the German is dead! I chased him down and found him torn to fucking pieces in his hotel room. We can't trust anyone, and I tracked your location through this phone number! Run!"

Each breath became a struggle as the heavy receiver fell from her hand and dangled by the curly cord. While inching backward, her eyes fixated on the archway leading to the living room, hoping to see Gloria and her battered blue purse, but knowing she wouldn't.

Lilith forced her clenched muscles to move as her gaze drifted into the vacant room. The front door stood wide open. Blood pounded in her ears, drowning out the screams emanating from the swaying phone.

Suddenly, a face growled in the kitchen doorway only a few feet away. An instinctual shriek escaped her throat as she scrambled backward, tripped over a chair, and lost her balance. The arm sling prevented her from breaking the fall, and she landed awkwardly on her hip while her mind stuttered. *No! This is not possible. It can't be possible. Dear god, no!*

Rose of Jericho

She backpedaled along the slick tile in terror as her father's corpse lurched toward her. The once steel-grey eyes sat milky and vacant in their sockets, while his mouth hung open in an animalistic snarl.

The smooth skin she remembered now displayed sickening splotches of blue and purple—the hues of early decay—and the bullet wound above his left eye oozed a dark substance each time he took a step forward. It was a scene straight from her nightmares.

"This can't be real! Did I fall asleep? I don't remember lying down..."

As fear and logic battled for control, Gregor's hollow shell broke into a run and lunged for her. When the dead man's nails brushed her skin, certainty hit her like ice water to the face. *This is real. This is happening. Shit!*

After stumbling several times and slamming her broken arm into a cabinet, she made it to her feet. Dizzying waves of nausea accompanied the agony shooting up and down her arm, but she ignored it all. She needed to escape, get out of the house, run!

In one swift motion, she turned and started for the back door, but something stopped her short. She winced at the iron-clad grip around her ankle and stared back in horror at Gregor's corpse, his face vacant, devoid of any emotion, like Chance in her nightmare—no recognition, no cognizance, no soul.

This is not Gregor, she reminded herself. Her father was gone, and only an empty shell remained, following the lyrical commands of a voodoo witch. *This is a clump of rotting flesh, and nothing else!*

When the hand tightened with excruciating strength, the pain derailed her train of thought. Her logical mind recognized the truth, but she still hesitated, unable to fight back—the exact reason the voodoo woman had used this particular cadaver, no doubt. She had brought it with her, all the way from Farren's courtroom, to ensure victory. *No! I can't let it end like this!*

Lilith squeezed her eyes shut, envisioned the anonymous zombies from earlier, and kicked as hard as she could over and over. Tears cascaded down her cheeks as she screamed to drown out the bone-crunching snaps and squishy sounds filling the air each time her foot connected.

Once she broke free, the momentum sent her crashing to the floor. Bare bones scraped against the tile, inching closer, but she refused to look. She couldn't handle witnessing the damage she'd inflicted, whether or not it was her father.

Instead, she got to her feet and almost collided with the back door. Anxious hands slipped and trembled over the lock as a gurgling moan rattled behind her and crawled up her spine. *Don't look back. Run.*

The phrase repeated in her head until the lock clicked, and she wrenched the back door open. Then she came to an abrupt stop as she stared into a pair of ocean-blue eyes lit with smug satisfaction.

"Well, well. Fancy meeting you here." The melodic lilting tones slid across her brain like red-hot razor wire. *No! The bitch died! I saw them surround her, heard her screams! She has to be dead!*

In a blind panic, Lilith whirled around to run back through the house, but Peisinoe snatched her hair. "Oh, no you don't." With a violent yank, the siren spun her into the door and grabbed her by the throat.

"See, now…if you had played by the rules…" Peisinoe tilted her head to the side, her platinum blonde tresses spilling over a shoulder. "I could have kept my promise." While she spoke, a wicked grin slowly curled her lips until it reached her eyes.

Desperate, Lilith clawed at her hand, then tried to pry her fingers back, as the world spun on its axis. She choked and gasped but couldn't break the banshee's hold with only one working arm.

"Tell me, kitten, where is your hunky bodyguard?" The hand relaxed enough for Lilith to draw in a huge gulp of air, quenching her burning lungs.

In a moment of déjà vu, Lilith mumbled incomprehensible words and gulped in another deep breath. If she could catch the vicious bitch off guard like she had with Spencer, perhaps she still had a chance.

"Aww. Are you hurt?" The sadistic woman's mouth transformed into an insincere pout as she leaned closer. "Let me help you find your voice." Peisinoe's eyes hardened, and her fist struck Lilith's broken arm with brutal force.

A blood-curdling scream ripped through the air as Lilith's vision went black, and her legs buckled. Only Peisinoe's hand clutching her throat kept her upright, which cut off her air supply, making her dizzy and light-headed.

"There, there, kitten." The siren stood her back up and straightened the makeshift sling. "Tell me where your bit of man candy is." The way she batted her long eyelashes made the request seem innocuous, as if asking her best friend for a guy's number, but it ignited a flame of rage in Lilith's stomach, which burned white-hot.

Rose of Jericho

Without any warning, Lilith slammed her head forward, resulting in a thunderous crack. The vicious headbutt to Peisinoe's face made Lilith lose consciousness briefly. When she came to, seconds later, the siren's gargled groans filled Lilith's ears like sweet music.

She opened her eyes to see Peisinoe doubled over, cradling her bloody nose. It wasn't enough.

"Fuck you, you tone-deaf bitch!" Lilith screamed as she snatched the woman's Marilyn-esque curls and thrust her knee into Peisinoe's face with all her might.

Instantly, the siren went limp and collapsed on the patio as Lilith collapsed against the door. The entire world spun as a tidal wave of white noise filled her head. If she'd managed to escape a concussion before, she sure as shit had one now, but the threat wasn't over. *Come on! Run! Keep moving! I need to get to the back gate!*

The inner pep-talk kept Lilith going, and she stumbled across the patio like a drunk, banging into everything and swaying from side to side. A chanting voice reached her ears, making her skin prickle. The voice didn't belong to Peisinoe. The siren was still unconscious. No, Lilith recognized the low, guttural tones—the pied piper of the dead.

Logically, her father's animated corpse meant the voodoo queen must have been close by. But the sound still set her teeth on edge and summoned memories of that infernal alley.

While her heart beat against her ribs like a caged rabbit, she sprinted for the gate to the high fence and grabbed the latch. She tugged and pulled, but to no avail. The heavy door sagged on the hardware, making it impossible to open without lifting the gate with one hand while sliding the bolt with the other. Working the mechanism required two hands.

When she attempted to raise her left arm, the pain became overwhelming after a few inches. The break was bad enough *before* Peisinoe slammed her fist into it. Now, her arm seemed utterly useless and probably needed to be reset.

The ominous chanting grew louder, closer, making her panic swell to a fevered pitch. She tried again to reach the latch, but the piercing pain quickly won out, and her arm collapsed before her fingers brushed the metal.

With a determined grimace, she tore off the sling, grabbed her left wrist, and, after several panting breaths, shoved her hand on the latch despite the excruciating agony. Once she lifted the gate with her right hand, she poured every ounce of concentration into pulling the bolt.

For a moment, her fingertips twitched, but then went numb and refused to close.

The chant reached a crescendo, making the air appear darker, coiling about her like a deadly tentacle. Footsteps sounded from inside the house, several sets, padding across the kitchen floor. *I have to get out of here!*

Lilith forced her focus back on the crucial lock, the one obstacle between her and freedom. As hard as she tried, she couldn't hold the bolt tight enough to make it move. Desperate tears burned her eyes. Lilith dropped her useless arm and tried to grip the bolt handle with her teeth. The thing jiggled but wouldn't slide.

The footsteps reached the patio, leaving her no options, no brilliant plan. She couldn't run back through the house now, and she couldn't escape the backyard and its high wooden fence. After a heavy sigh, she recognized defeat and put her back to the gate. All she could do was face her enemies.

The voodoo queen's full skirts swished into view as she wandered out of the house. Her deep, chestnut eyes stared intently at Lilith, and she continued her fervent refrain to the odd, brown plant cradled in one hand. Four corpses flanked her, each in various states of decay, and still dressed in their funeral suits. Thankfully, her father wasn't among them.

Lilith glanced out at the small yard, praying a last-minute plan might spring to mind, but Rose's slide sat too far from the fence. The only escape routes were a gate she couldn't open and a fence she couldn't climb.

Her only hope for survival hinged on the voodoo woman's master wanting her alive. Hoping someone kidnapped her was a dismal thought, but it beat being torn into bite-sized pieces.

"I told ya. Dere is no runnin'." The woman's raspy voice hovered in the air like a dark omen before seeping deep into Lilith's bones. Then the zombies lurched forward and stood on either side, cornering her. Their milky eyes stared, never blinking, vigilant but lifeless.

While calmly approaching, the voodoo queen dug into ta pouch hanging at her waist. "And dere is no fight-tin wit me."

Something about the sheer certainty of those words aggravated Lilith's rebellious nature. She hunched down, tensing every muscle, waiting for the woman to move closer. If she launched off the gate and knocked the puppet master down, she could make a break for the house, hopefully before the zombies grabbed her.

Rose of Jericho

Before she put her plan in motion, the woman brought her palm up to her lips and blew a cloud of dust into Lilith's face. The powder scorched her eyes, nose, and throat, inducing violent coughs as she doubled over, gagging for breath.

Finally, she fell to the ground, clawing at the grass, as her chest became painfully tight. The earth beneath her vibrated, and she managed to open her eyes enough to see corpses on the ground. Then, hands the color of mahogany reached for her, and the world melted into black again.

A sickening thought trickled through her brain before she fully lost consciousness. *When Gloria comes home, she'll find my father's mutilated corpse on her kitchen floor, assuming I left enough for her to recognize.*

Chapter 25

Somewhere, a voice called Lilith's name. The sound came from far away, like an eerie whisper at the end of a tunnel. When she tried to open her eyes, it felt like sandpaper lined the lids. She stopped for a moment, listening to her surroundings—the faint whir of air vents, but nothing else.

Once she creaked an eye open, only inky darkness filled her vision. The impenetrable blackness only deepened, quickly becoming stifling, oppressive.

She squeezed her eyes closed through hot, angry tears, refusing to participate in another hellish nightmare. She couldn't handle seeing her undead father, Alvarez, Miriah, Spencer, Duncan, or any of them. Why did her brain torment her with all the people she couldn't save, as if she should be punished for surviving?

A drawn-out groan, reminiscent of a heavy door opening on unused hinges, echoed across the room. She waited, anticipating footsteps, movement, skin-crawling moans, something, but the room remained silent as a tomb.

Then she tried to move, and discovered the restraints across her chest, upper arms, wrists, thighs, and ankles combined with the coolness of metal at her back. She instinctively fought against them, which only resulted in teeth-gritting pain flaring down her left arm.

Once the bone-deep ache receded, she craned her head toward the patch of black where the sound had originated. Her eyes darted everywhere, searching the darkness. Nothing magically appeared, and no other noises rose from the unsettling silence.

Am I dreaming? This doesn't feel like a nightmare, but neither did the last few dreams. What if I never woke up from the dream about Chance and Peisinoe?

What if he couldn't revive me? Since that moment, things had delved into true madness—zombies, her father's corpse, a voodoo queen with magic powder—what if none of it was real? What if this was her own personal hell?

Lilith closed her eyes, taking small, deep breaths to quell the panic threatening to consume her. The philosophy didn't matter. Either she dealt with the problems in front of her, no matter how insane, or she bet everything on waking up. That was a risk she couldn't take.

In the past two weeks, she had wasted too much time freaking out and not enough taking action. If she had moved with purpose, shaking off the tragedies and setbacks, perhaps she'd be in better shape with a few less bodies piled on her conscience—easier said than done. She may not be human, but she shared the same inherent emotional responses.

Okay. Focus on something constructive. If she didn't keep her mind busy, she'd rattle apart at the seams, over-analyzing every square inch of her life. With a heavy sigh, she dredged up what she could remember from Gloria's house.

Peisinoe and the zombie puppet master had found her, but how? Only one person had the address and betraying her seemed unlikely for Nicci. Wait. Cohen said he'd tracked her burner phone, but if he turned her in, why warn her? Either the council possessed information on her former partner, or they had forcefully obtained it from Cohen.

Of course, there was a more concerning question. Why had they both shown up at the same time? Were the warring factions hot on each other's heels, or were Peisinoe and the voodoo chick both working for the same person?

If so, who was pulling their strings? Farren? But why hire thieves with a sophisticated plan to steal the book, *and* a brutal zombie queen to make a mess of things? Why attack his own men at Haverty's?

Perhaps he'd wanted to throw off suspicion, an elaborate charade to muddy the waters. Their entire race appeared to enjoy manipulation, so why should he be any different? Although Farren's shock had appeared genuine when the zombies attacked, Cohen had been certain Peisinoe would never cross her master. If that was true, Farren had to be the culprit, didn't he?

None of it mattered. Whoever had orchestrated the living-dead comeback didn't do so to make friends. They'd taken her alive, which meant they wanted something she wouldn't give willingly, and the story wouldn't end with her walking away. No one knew her location. There was no rescue coming, no cavalry riding in to save the day. She was alone, helpless, hopeless, condemned.

A soft clattering, like small clay pots tapping against each other, knocked Lilith out of her spiraling thoughts. She wasn't alone, after all. Although her heart sped up, she kept it in check by lying still and staring into the darkness toward the subtle noises. The faint echo of bare feet padded across the tile, accompanied by the soft rustle of fabric, which grew closer with each step.

When the sounds stopped, she felt eyes studying her, which seemed impossible. Nothing could see in complete darkness. Of course, yesterday, she had believed reanimated corpses were merely fiction. Hell, two weeks ago, she'd have committed anyone who told her the Durand were real. The world around her kept expanding faster than she could comprehend.

A hiss slithered through the air a split-second before a lit match pierced the darkness, forcing Lilith to squeeze her raw eyes shut. The brilliant red light danced against her eyelids, flickering in and out until it became a steady flame.

She peeked one eye open, and the candlelight overwhelmed her retina. After a few tries, her vision adjusted and drifted up to a mahogany face splattered with freckles staring down at her.

No! She refused to let fear overpower logic, so instead of dissolving into a puddle of helplessness, she absorbed every detail of the woman's face. The candlelight made her appear younger, perhaps mid-twenties to early thirties. The smooth skin held only vague hints of creases around the eyes, but displayed deep frown lines, indicating a life of hardship.

Then the woman turned to the side, either unaware or unconcerned by the prisoner studying her. An enormous scar ran from one eye to her ear before blazing a trail down her jawline. The ragged and puckered edges represented an angry badge of tragedy typically hidden by her dreadlocks.

If this woman was an abnormal Durand, like Peisinoe, why did she have a scar? For that matter, why had Ashcroft? In Goditha, she had watched in horror as he regrew half his head without a trace of the damage. So why had Gregor's torture left scars behind? Was it the type of instrument, the powerful emotions tied to the act, the addition of salt? Another riddle about the Durand that may never be solved, at least not by her.

Jenny Allen

The voodoo woman moved the candle to a metal instrument tray, and the light flickered off an array of scalpels with a malevolent glint, making Lilith's pulse race. Her mind flashed to Miriah's corpse, covered in hundreds of precise torments made by similar instruments.

Ashcroft is dead, and this is not Phipps Bend, Lilith reminded herself once again. *Yeah, this is a new nightmare, starring the queen of the damned and a torture tray. No.* The gleaming, modern instruments didn't fit the scene, the woman's M.O., or her Marie Laveau vibes. She used her undead minions to tear apart her enemies, never dirtying her hands, especially not with something as up-close and personal as surgical tools.

A quiet chant fell from the woman's lips as she swayed, and the light hit something bulky and white swinging from her neck. At first, Lilith's eyes couldn't make sense of the thing, but the image finally clicked—a human mandible, cleaned and bleached, a souvenir from New Haven. The jawbone shone ghastly white against her dark clothing, like a ghostly remnant, floating in thin air.

Lilith turned away from the grotesque sight and searched within the limited candlelight. When the woman chanted, the dead came out to play. This time, there seemed to be no corpses ambling to surround her. Lilith only spotted the edge of another table and a few darker shapes on the floor. Nothing moved.

Then the voodoo woman pulled on a leather string and retrieved a blackbird's wing from the folds of her skirt. The chanting rose in pitch, her dark eyes closing as she fanned the air over Lilith. The resulting breeze prickled each tiny hair along her body, making her painfully aware of her lack of clothing.

After angling her head, she gazed down at the black bra and panties—the only garments that remained. The bandages on her forearm and shoulder appeared new, and someone had set her broken arm again before wrapping it tightly. They wanted her alive... for the moment.

"Where am I?" The reluctant words croaked from Lilith's sore throat in a gruff whisper, but still seemed shockingly loud in the silent room. The woman ignored her, continued her chant, and fanned the bird's wing toward Lilith's feet.

"How long have I been unconscious?" Although Lilith hoped for some speck of information, she didn't expect a response after the blatant dismissal of her first question.

"Eight hours. De powder is po-tent." Her thick accent made the sentence nearly indecipherable, but when Lilith's dazed brain finally caught up, her eyes widened.

Eight hours. A sudden cascade of realizations struck her. By now, Gloria would have returned home to find Gregor's mangled corpse on her kitchen floor. Nicci would have shown up at the Alvarez house, looking for her. Cohen had probably left a hundred voicemails, each more desperate than the last. Chance...

The eerie creak of rusted hinges resonated through the air, disrupting her spiraling thoughts. As the door opened, the widening sliver of light revealed someone strapped to the neighboring table, a male someone. Although only the stomach and hips became visible, she realized it wasn't Chance—No lily tattoo, a slimmer build, and fine curls of blond body hair.

"Isadora!" Peisinoe's commanding voice boomed through the room as her voluptuous silhouette filled the doorway. "What are you doing?" Purposeful footsteps resounded with the hefty click of high heels until the siren's Marilyn-esque face popped into view. The bandage saddling the bridge of her nose and the black eye made Lilith smile despite her better instincts.

The voodoo woman ignored the question as she continued to chant and swing the wing over Lilith's chest. In a frustrated huff, the siren stormed closer, heels cracking against the concrete. When she reached the table, she spotted the grin on Lilith's face and stopped short.

Before Lilith knew what was happening, the siren's palm struck her left cheek, leaving a sharp sting. "Wipe that look off your face." The words oozed like venom, full of contempt and hate, which only made Lilith's smile brighten. Whoever controlled Peisinoe's strings still wanted her alive or the siren wouldn't have settled for a mild bitch-slap.

The monster's chilly eyes narrowed, and she leaned in close enough to be intimidating, while staying out of head-butt range. *Guess she'd learned her lesson. Pity.* "The boss may want to keep you breathing, but they didn't feel the same way about your little bodyguard." The vicious grin she flashed made her mouth resemble a knife slash as Lilith's world fell away.

"I had such plans." The bombshell sighed heavily as Lilith tried to wrap her mind around what she was saying.

Chance is dead? No, he has to be alive. Our story can't end with him dying hundreds of miles away. The siren is wrong. She has to be. But why would she lie? No. She has to be lying.

"Such a pity. I intended to torture him until he became a gibbering mess, then I would have chained him to the floor and let him gnaw off his own limbs, just like your uncle."

As Peisinoe pulled back to revel in the shock and horror, Lilith descended into an abyss of desolate thoughts. The siren had flagrantly used details of Duncan's death that she shouldn't know.

Sure, Farren possessed information about Ashcroft's death and Gregor's crimes, but how had she found precise knowledge of what had happened in that basement? Her words sounded like an eyewitness account, but from whom?

Had she forced every detail out of Gregor? Unlikely. Cohen? Had he betrayed us after all? Her gut said no. She couldn't picture him confiding in his grandfather or the banshee bombshell. Coffee and Whitmore had never made it out of the basement, and if Chance had been killed in Tennessee, the siren had nothing to do with it. That only left her... *So, where is the flaw in my logic?*

"Isadora, the boss instructed you to keep your mumbo-jumbo bullshit away from this one. We can't let anything contaminate the ritual."

The voodoo woman—apparently named Isadora—stopped chanting and glared at Peisinoe with a huge helping of contempt. *Dissension in the ranks.*

"*Feminduolou, bouzen.* Aye makin' tings aight wit Baron Samedi. He's none too 'appy."

The siren's eyes rolled dramatically as she tilted her head from side to side. "Blah, blah, blah." She snatched the bird's wing out of Isadora's hand and shoved it against her chest. "The boss said no! You want to chit-chat with your crazy ass god, do it with the other ones."

The other ones? They had more prisoners. Lilith tilted her head as much as the restraints allowed but couldn't spot anything recognizable beyond the meager cone of light.

The voodoo woman picked up her candle and stormed away, skirts swishing like an angry tide. "*Mwen pral tranch gòj ke fanm la ak pipi sou nanm li.*" As Isadora moved, she mumbled in another language, and although Lilith didn't understand the words, they didn't contain a friendly apology.

"You forgot your miniature tumbleweed." Peisinoe closed her finger and thumb on a leaf and held the thing up like contaminated garbage.

Isadora reappeared, grabbed the plant, and cradled it against her chest lovingly. "Dis is no tum-bull-weed!" She spat the contemptuous words like verbal knives, a sentiment Lilith understood.

"Dis is a resurrection fern. Tis da Rose of Jericho!" Isadora directed her attention to the little plant, coddling the precious thing. Chanting tones moved through the air like something sacred or evil, perhaps both. "Gives life ta dose dat 'ave no soul left in dere husk. Let's me sing to dere body."

The bombshell maintained her bored expression but shifted her stance. The voodoo woman made her uncomfortable, and the goose bumps traveling up the siren's pale arms confirmed it. "Yeah, okay. Whatever. Take your creepy plant and stay away from this one."

Then Peisinoe strolled toward the open door and paused with her hand on the knob. "They will be here soon with the cipher, so get your kicks while you can. The ritual will start once they arrive."

The siren closed the creaking door as Lilith's heart fell into her stomach. *They have the cipher. Could Peisinoe be bluffing about Chance? What if he is here somewhere in the dark?*

"Chance?" She knew Isadora was still in the room but didn't care. "Chance!" she screamed and pushed at the restraints, ignoring the blazing pain in her left arm. *Come on. Please answer me. Prove the bitch is a liar and answer me!*

"Wat you callin' for, you?" The voodoo queen's deep voice rumbled from the darkness.

"Chance Deveraux. Is he here?" She hadn't expected the woman's help, but what did she have to lose?

"Deveraux? Dat sounds like creole name, dat does."

"Yes. It is. He's from Breaux Bridges, Louisiana." If she kept the woman talking, maybe she'd say something useful. "Do you know it?"

"Dis is my first time off de island. Wat dis creole man look like?" Isadora's face loomed into view again with genuine interest. Lilith couldn't tell if answering the question would make him a bigger target or if the woman honestly wanted to help.

"Tall, brunette, leanly muscular build, light tan..." She couldn't believe she was giving a missing person's description to a voodoo queen who raised the dead. It seemed too surreal to be true.

Lilith followed the candle flame as it bobbed across the room and whispered "Please be Chance" repeatedly.

"Dis one?" Isadora gripped a handful of hair and Lilith's heart raced as the woman jerked the man's head back. As soon as the light revealed his face, she released a sigh tinged with relief and despair.

"No. That's not him."

The dreadlocks bounced as Isadora shrugged. "He is de only brown 'air." Then she released Timothy's head, letting it slump down between his shoulders again. He was unconscious, but alive. One less corpse to weigh on her conscience. Of course, the night was still early, and he wore a thick metal collar around his neck, *just like Duncan.*

Calm down. This doesn't mean he's dead. Maybe they stashed Chance somewhere else, or perhaps he escaped the attack in Tennessee. The guard at Goditha stated he drove away. He could have lost the cipher before he fled. Peisinoe fed on misery, so lying to cause devastation wasn't outside the realm of possibilities.

"Your accent is thicker than his, and you mentioned an island. Where are you from?" Under different circumstances, Lilith would never initiate small talk with the woman who raised her father's corpse and tried to kill her with it. However, filling the void with polite conversation kept her mind from spiraling into a chaotic multiverse of possibilities.

"I come from de island, me. Haiti. I am Isadora Heno, child to Baron Samedi. Dey tell me you are *vanpir.* Dat true?" Her face loomed into sight again, black eyes studying her with skepticism. "You no look like a *loogaroo,* you." The woman waited, expecting an answer, but Lilith had a difficult time interpreting her thick accent.

"I don't know what a *vanpir* or a *loogaroo* is. Can you tell me?" She flashed a nervous smile, hoping she didn't offend the deadly woman.

"*Vanpir.* You steal da blood, drink it." Her eyes narrowed suspiciously, as if asking her to clarify, provided solid proof that Lilith couldn't be what they claimed.

"Vampire. Yes." Without warning, Isadora shoved Lilith's top lip and drew the candle closer.

"Lies!" Her dark face scrunched into a snarl. "I no fool." An intense hatred burned in her eyes that scared the crap out of Lilith. Then she pushed Lilith's face away from her before turning toward the door. "Dey tell me I crazy. Now dey play tricks and laugh at Baron Samedi!"

For a second, Lilith hesitated, uncertain if being a *vanpir* would help or only put her in more danger. After all, Isadora was the closest thing she had to an ally in this place. The voodoo woman hated Peisinoe, and her boss didn't appear to value her religious beliefs.

"Wait! I can prove it." She opened her mouth as much as possible, and the woman inched forward until she held the candle so close that the heat caressed Lilith's skin. After an agonizing moment of performance anxiety, the cartilage fangs clicked into place.

Isadora jerked back. "Dis true!" She stared at the fangs with a mixture of shock and fright. "*Loogaroo*! De devil canno have my blood!" As she backed away, venom seeped into her words. The woman capable of animating an army of corpses to tear the world apart was scared of a vampire? *Damn.* Revealing herself probably hadn't been the smartest move.

"I don't want your blood, and I don't deal with devils." *Unless you count the Durand.*

A headache began throbbing in the back of her head as the woman mumbled heatedly. *Wonderful! I'm on Isadora's bad side because Haitian superstitions made the woman racist.*

"Come on. I'm not the one you should be scared of…"

"Lie wit your devil tongue, you." In the blink of an eye, she snatched a scalpel from the table and pressed the blade to Lilith's throat, making her heart skip a beat before racing in her chest. "No sweet talkin', *loogaroo*."

The sharp blade bit into her skin, and a drop of blood trickled down her neck. "Farren will be mad if you kill me." She took the risk, speaking slowly to avoid slicing her throat.

Isadora snorted with a twisted smile. "Farren? Wat name dat be? Your devil god?"

A confused frown immediately furrowed Lilith's face. "The man you and Peisinoe work for—Farren."

Cackling laughter split Isadora's face as she tossed the scalpel aside. "Stu'pid *loogaroo*. I no work for Farren, me."

Lilith's gaze followed the candle as it bobbed away. Then Isadora bent down, illuminating the corner. There was Cohen's grandfather, propped up against the wall, unconscious with a thick iron collar around his neck.

"I work for no *man*!"

All the pieces clicked into place, and her gut turned ice cold. Suddenly, she knew their enemy's identity.

The door screeched, echoing through the room, and Lilith stared at the silhouette, shorter than Peisinoe's. Only two questions ran through her mind. *Why* and *how many people would die in this room because of it?*

Chapter 26

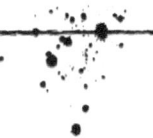

"*C*rin. Sorry to keep you waiting. I swear the traffic in New York gets worse every year." The petite woman spoke with a much softer Romanian accent than the first time they had met. It was only a soft lilt on her fluid speech instead of dominating her broken English. *Fucking demons and their acting.*

The curvaceous silhouette paused in the doorway. "Peisinoe, if you please."

Harsh fluorescent bulbs flickered to life overhead with a high-pitched hum, dousing the room in unforgiving light. Lilith blinked hard several times, trying to quell the sensation of hot pokers stabbing her eyes. When she managed to take in the anonymous white room, she realized it closely resembled a morgue—fitting.

After glancing at the improvised leather straps pinning her in place, her gaze moved swiftly to the other table. Cohen was similarly restrained, his eyes closed, mouth slack, but his chest moved rhythmically. For a millisecond, she wondered if Cohen was innocent or playing a part, but the memory of their last conversation made her dismiss the thought. Cohen had no idea who his friend was.

High heels clicked closer, a more hollow sound than Peisinoe's heavy stilettos. Then a hand smoothed through Lilith's hair, making the bile rise in her throat. "*Crin*, don't worry. I do not intend to kill you. I just need something from you."

Lilith swung her head around to glare at the elvish woman. "Where the hell is Chance, you psychotic bitch?!"

Luminita raised her delicate eyebrows in surprise as her hand hovered in the air like a lost bird. "You don't understand." The woman ignored the question. After Luminita's shoulders fell in disappointment, she held up Duncan's infamous book.

"I thought a woman of science would appreciate the power contained in these pages." She waited for the dawning epiphany that never came before sighing again. "I suppose it isn't pivotal for you to comprehend what I'm doing."

As the petite Romanian strolled away, she placed a slip of paper inside the open book and began reading. How did she recognize the cipher, much less know how to use it? She had her hands on Duncan's book for...what...eight hours at most?

Lilith had never voiced her theory about the blank papers to Cohen, so how had Luminita figured it out in record time? Cohen probably wasn't the Romanian's only resource. However, the ease of use, the familiarity, indicated first-hand knowledge, but how?

"What don't I understand? Why you created a monster to raise the dead so you could secure my uncle's diary?"

The woman's laugh tinkled like evil jingle bells, bright and tinny. "*Created?* Oh, *Crin*, you give me far too much credit. I only found Isadora. Of course...if I had Gregor, none of this would be necessary."

The causal, absent-minded tone didn't fit the context of her words. It sounded more like a lecture on leaving early to avoid rush-hour traffic than explaining the merit of Gregor's life. The way Luminita thoroughly dismissed the true value of her father grated Lilith's nerves. How dare she reduce him to mere inconvenience?

"So why kill him?" Lilith spat the words with every shred of hatred looming inside.

The woman came to a stop as the muscles in her back tensed beneath her white blouse. "I did not kill your father. Farren alone is responsible. He murdered him to render this book useless and keep you under his thumb, but he's blind and unimaginative."

When she turned around, her glare was fixed on the unconscious man in the corner. "If he wasn't such a short-sighted bigot, your father would be alive, and all this would be...simpler."

"What the hell are you talking about?" Lilith frowned, unable to follow her train of thought.

"Peisinoe, translate the first steps." Luminita gingerly placed the text in the siren's hands, once again ignoring Lilith's question. "When you have it, wake Andrew and keep him lucid. We must follow the ritual precisely."

Lilith's mind whirled with a litany of questions. What were they doing? What ritual? Why did they need Cohen? Why would her father make a difference? What part did she play in all this?

If Duncan had possessed a magic formula, surely someone would have uncovered it by now. As far as she knew, the book only contained research on Ashcroft's family, the story of Mary's death, and Gregor's revenge. Suddenly, everything clicked with a sense of dreadful certainty, making Lilith's gut turn ice-cold.

"Oh, my god! You're trying to recreate Ashcroft, aren't you?" Panic flared through Lilith's nerves like lightning. "You want to turn Cohen into that...thing?" If Luminita didn't succeed, Cohen would suffer an agonizing death, and if she did... "Does he know what you're planning to do to him?"

The insane woman swung around with a defensive snarl. "He is the *only* one I trust to stay loyal if the ritual works. I don't expect you to understand our relationship. I don't need your permission, only your blood." That's why the Romanian wanted Gregor alive—Not for his first-hand account, but his blood, which had transformed a Durand before, and theoretically, could again.

"You *cannot* do this! You weren't there! You didn't see what Ashcroft became! He drew his power from the excruciating agony of others. For fuck's sake, he tortured Duncan's daughter right in front of him to satisfy his hunger for vengeance. Do you really want Cohen to become a monster?"

The Romanian stormed around the table to tower over Lilith, signaling an end to the polite conversation. Frustration pinched her soft face into something older, perhaps even ancient. "I know everything about Ashcroft Orrick! Do you honestly think I am that stupid?" Her eyes hardened when she saw the answer on Lilith's face.

Luminita stood taller, straightening her white blouse in a motion so similar to Farren's that bile rose in Lilith's throat. Then her eyes glinted as her lips curled into a smug grin. *Shit.* Openly gloating meant Lilith wouldn't like whatever came next.

"Who do you think sent Ashcroft after Duncan and forced the county to sell Phipps Bend so he'd have a safe place to work?" Lilith's eyes widened as the words sank in. *Dear god.*

"We forced Duncan to spill everything...eventually. Then *you* showed up."

We? God, that meant Luminita helped Ashcroft torture Miriah and Duncan, or at least been present. She'd wanted his secrets, and Lilith and Chance interrupting Ashcroft before he found the tin had been the only reason she'd failed.

"All was going to plan, but you...*you* were too much of a temptation. Once he ran into you in Madisonville, he became obsessed with his stupid vendetta! The fool got himself killed, lost the cipher, and turned Duncan into a mindless animal. *Useless!*" After slamming the table, her sharp eyes returned to Lilith.

It was all Luminita's fault. Everything that had happened, all the deaths, every shred of misery, had all occurred because of this woman's psychotic inferiority complex.

"He was never following your plan. He was a monster who only wanted pain, death, and destruction. His lackey, Spencer, called my father and reported Duncan missing. That's why I came to Tennessee. They lured me there and left enough breadcrumbs to ensure Gregor would follow. He didn't give a shit about your *greater purpose,* and neither will Cohen if you do this to him."

"No." She calmly rejected everything with one clipped word, firmly planting her flag in the world of denial. "Ashcroft was an evil man before Gregor turned him." She moved to Cohen, running her fingers over his short blond hair.

Her voice became soft and loving as she continued. "Cohen is a good man. He will not follow the same path. He will form a new race... a better one."

"Said every person with a Napoleon complex and power. You are spouting the mantra of the truly psychotic. Do you hear yourself?"

The petite woman waved a dismissive hand and chuckled, entirely unfazed. "All visionaries are painted as lunatics by their peers."

Lilith stared at the ceiling hopelessly. The woman thought she was doing the right thing. "Why not try it on yourself? Why Cohen?"

Luminita refused to turn around, much less respond to her questions.

A sarcastic laugh bubbled free as Lilith relaxed against the table. "Yeah, you are *so noble*, such a *visionary.* You want to start a master race of demons, but you're too cowardly to do it yourself. Instead, you're going to risk Cohen's hide, make *him* suffer for *your* crazy dream."

"Do you have the first step, Peisinoe?" A slight tremor emerged in the Romanian's voice, and Lilith couldn't tell if it came from fear or anger.

"Gregor began by carving names into his body, those the Orricks had killed." Peisinoe strolled closer to Cohen, her hand slipping over the instrument tray with a malicious glint in her eye, but Luminita grasped her hand and pulled it away.

"No. It is *my* responsibility. Sit and give me directions." A disappointed pout formed as the siren stepped aside.

"This is ridiculous! Torturing Cohen won't make a difference! If you feed him my blood, he'll either die, stay the same, or become like Ashcroft. Ritualistic torture won't magically transform him into an abomination."

Luminita swung around and pointed the scalpel at her with a clear threat. "Rituals *have* power! They change the unchangeable. They create." Flickers of pain appeared on the woman's face but disappeared just as quickly. "More exists in this world than your narrow mind can comprehend, *vampire!*"

"You're delusional." Lilith's eyes bounced between the insane woman and the scalpel blade, poised to strike.

"No! I've tried before and failed. Duncan's account *must* be the difference. The ritual *will* work!"

"Before? What…What is going on?" Cohen interrupted, his groggy eyes fluttering open. After several seconds, he focused on Luminita, and his lips curled into a sleepy smile. Once his brain caught up, the happy expression vanished, and he strained against the straps, confused.

"What the hell is going on?" The bewilderment in his voice quickly transformed into panic and disbelief. Sadly, things were only going to get worse for him. The only person he had trusted intended to either torture him to death or turn him into a monster. No number of apologies and explanations would make that okay.

Lilith had a sinking feeling that even if Cohen survived, this…would break him.

Earlier, when he'd hinted at his dark past, a small sliver didn't believe the incredulous story, but now, she pitied Cohen without reservation. The man had survived every malicious thing his grandfather had put him through, only to end up here.

"Shh. Sweet Andrew. This is for us both." When Luminita moved to stroke his hair again, he jerked away and glared at the blade in her hand.

"What the fuck, Luminita?" Cohen's hands clenched into useless fists as his stare moved to her eyes, searching for some reason he could understand.

The woman averted her gaze and glanced at Peisinoe. "Give me the first name and location."

"Mary, in capital letters across his chest, just beneath the collarbones." Peisinoe's lips curled into a sadistic smile while she relayed the instructions from her perch on the counter. Then she casually thumbed through the next few pages, as if perusing the latest Home & Gardens.

With a resolute nod, Luminita lowered the scalpel toward Cohen. He squirmed and screamed, but the restraints kept him fixed in place as she aimed for his chest.

As soon as the blade sliced through the skin, he shrieked, making Luminita hesitate for a brief second. "Gag him."

Isadora appeared and shoved a rag into his mouth to stop the screams. But the fabric only muffled the horrified shrieks of agony when the Romanian continued to drag the blade in a downward stroke.

"How did you find Ashcroft?" Lilith didn't care about the answer. The question was merely a distraction so Cohen could get his bearings before they carved him up. It was the least she could do.

After all, most villains crave a long-winded speech. Although plenty of critics complained about the common movie trope, recent experience had taught her they happened more often than not.

The compulsion to prove their actions were for the greater good often seemed irresistible to zealots like Luminita. Then again, perhaps they only wanted to gloat, shine a spotlight on their brilliance. Whatever the reason, she doubted Luminita would be any different. Even Ashcroft had given his little rant before he died. In the end, they all just want to be heard.

The petite woman paused for a moment, her delicate hand hovering in midair. She let it fall to her side but didn't turn around. If Lilith had been the only one in the room, she probably wouldn't have answered the question. Luminita put no stock in her opinion, but Cohen was listening, and she wanted him to understand.

The Romanian glanced over at the siren. "It is my business to find things. I found Peisinoe, trained her, and gave her to Farren. She's been a very useful spy."

So, she hadn't turned Peisinoe against her master. The siren had been on her payroll the entire time, which explained why she'd appeared so loyal to Cohen's grandfather. Whatever leverage Farren thought he had, it probably wasn't what had kept her subservient. The siren had stayed at his side by choice, on a mission.

That's how Isadora had ambushed Farren's robbery attempt. Peisinoe had given them the time, place, descriptions, names, everything except Haverty's info. Farren had played that card close to the vest.

Once the Romanian had positioned herself as liaison for Lilith and her group, she could stay one step ahead of Farren and get a lead on the cipher without raising suspicion. She'd known they would go after it because the cipher was their only leverage.

While Lilith continued to connect the dots, Luminita nodded toward the voodoo queen, who fanned her blackbird wing over Timothy with whispered chants. "I discovered Isadora on the island of Haiti fifteen years ago. She was a 13-year-old orphan, and the men of her village sliced her face with ragged knives, attempting to remove the *demon* riding her."

"Okay, you're the demonic island of misfit toys, but how did you uncover Ashcroft? Cohen told me there were no records of his family."

Luminita considered her for a moment, most likely trying to decide if she should continue to indulge Lilith's questions. Then she glanced at Andrew, who continued to watch her intently, waiting to hear her explanation.

"Helton and I have been researching obscure branches of the family tree, so to speak. The interconnected age of electronics has put us at a disadvantage. It is only a matter of time until humans discover our existence, and we need to be ready when they do." Her eyes never left Cohen's, imploring him to understand her intentions.

"Helton caught wind of an impossible anomaly from a reporter, but the blood sample disappeared. So, we tracked down the *patient* and tied up loose ends." Her tone made it perfectly clear that she was responsible for the deaths of the reporter and doctor connected to Ashcroft.

"So, you found Ashcroft and what? Offered him prime real estate in crazy town?"

The woman's eyes turned icy as she rounded on Lilith. "Scoff all you like, but I am attempting to turn the tide. If I unlock Ashcroft's secrets, we won't have to hide from humans. We won't be subjected to their cruelty, their rules, their bigotry. Instead, we can dominate them, put them at *our* mercy for change. It is the only way we will survive what's coming."

"Let me guess. You have the final say on who survives? Guess Helton didn't make the cut, huh?"

"He was siphoning off samples to run his own experiments. I couldn't trust him, so I used Ashcroft to track down Duncan and extract the information I needed. When the German uncovered the truth, he threatened me, and I defended myself. I am not some murderous dictator."

"Really? I don't think Helton and the dozens of people you executed would agree. You don't give a shit about your race surviving, or protecting abominations like Ashcroft, Peisinoe, and Isadora. They are nothing but tools for your power trip."

The elvish woman's jaw clenched, and her hands curled into fists. "I won't debate ethics with a vampire! I know your kind all too well." Her lip curled in disgust, betraying an obvious bias either against Lilith or her entire species. "Dishonor, deceit…cowardice. Your childish lectures have no bearing. Isadora, gag her!"

Dammit. She'd let anger tip her hand and lost the opportunity to spare Cohen a few more moments of agony. On the other hand, she couldn't stand another minute listening to Luminita brag about gathering genetic anomalies, experimenting on innocents, and murdering everyone who got in the way, all in the name of world domination.

"You're worse than Farren, Ashcroft, any of them!" Lilith spat the venomous words and fought the straps while Isadora stalked closer. A rag that stank of patchouli and sweat moved toward her mouth, but uncertainty lingered on Isadora's face, which caught Lilith off guard. She couldn't fathom why the necromancer suddenly appeared uncomfortable. Was she afraid the vampire would bite her?

Unfortunately, Isadora regained her resolve while Lilith stared at her in confusion. The woman shoved the rag into her mouth, making her gag.

"You cannot compare me to him!" Luminita jabbed a delicate finger at the corner where Farren lay unconscious. Apparently, Lilith had scored a direct hit to the villain-rant button.

"That monster ordered the execution of Andrew's parents because they coddled him too much! His son and daughter-in-law were murdered because he hadn't agreed with their parenting style! Andrew was only seven years old!

"After that, the madman ordered the death of anyone the boy got close to—friends, teachers, lovers—*everyone*. Farren called it '*teaching him independence*'. Utter bullshit! The sick bastard simply enjoyed torturing him. A lifetime of guilt, pain, and loss is all he's ever given his grandson.

That is his legacy, and once I am successful, all of it will finally end. I may cause Andrew physical anguish now, but I'm giving him power, strength, immortality—a true future! Don't you understand that?"

Luminita searched her face for acknowledgment or approval of her noble plan.

Lilith merely stared back, horrified by Farren's list of crimes and the insane woman's fanaticism. Cohen already endured more than anyone should, and now...

Luminita stepped closer, looming over Lilith with cold, piercing eyes. "You and Mr. Deveraux complicated things. You're almost more trouble than you're worth." Then she traced the scalpel down Lilith's forearm with only enough pressure to break the skin. Lilith groaned behind the disgusting rag but refused to give her the satisfaction of a scream.

"I want you alive...for now. Only you carry Gregor's blood, and you're the purest vampire on this side of the country." No wonder she'd been so interested in Chance's heritage. The woman had wanted a contingency plan.

Ocean-deep eyes traveled from the cut to Lilith's face, while her voice became chillingly sinister. "How I take the blood is up to you. If you keep arguing, I'll remove body parts instead of using an IV. Now. No more distractions." Luminita tapped the flat of the blade against Lilith's forehead while flashing a delusional smile that bordered on friendly. The severe change was like watching someone with multiple personalities change back and forth with a flick of a switch.

Were all the Durand master manipulators or just straight-up insane? Perhaps decades and centuries of consuming the emotions of others warped their minds. The concept wasn't that far-fetched. A few days of sensing everyone's feelings had put a serious dent in Lilith's sanity. How could a person handle a lifetime or more of that and remain a functional person?

Was it too late for Cohen? If she couldn't figure out a way to stop Luminita, it would be...one way or another.

Chapter 27

Luminita stood over Cohen, resolute, inhaling deeply as she lowered the scalpel toward his chest. Panic widened his hazel eyes while he bucked and squirmed in a pointless attempt to escape. The first prick of the blade brought fresh tears as his head rolled to the side. She pressed deeper and dragged down in a smooth motion as he screamed behind the rag.

Lilith squeezed her eyes shut, unable to stomach the grisly scene. According to her father, he had visited every horror imaginable on Ashcroft over a matter of days until his pulse had become too weak. That's when he'd attempted to turn him and prolong his suffering.

Luminita intended to recreate those events the way Duncan recorded them. Unfortunately, her uncle obsessed over details, and judging by Ashcroft's scars, Gregor hadn't exaggerated his deeds. While Lilith tried not to think of her father in Luminita's role, each muffled shriek from Cohen etched itself inside her skull. Then they stopped.

When she opened her eyes, the Romanian still hovered over Cohen while he panted around the gag. Lilith hoped to see sorrow, regret, or even hesitation in Luminita's face, but she remained determined.

As Cohen turned toward Lilith, apologies flooded his sky-blue eyes, and for the first time since they'd met, she had no doubts about his sincerity.

"Next name and placement!" Luminita barked the words with impatience. The violence made her uneasy, but didn't shake her conviction, at least not yet. Lilith prayed that the woman's resolve crumbled while Cohen still had a pulse.

"Margareet along the left ribs."

Cohen leaned his head back and clenched his teeth on the fabric, bracing himself. Slicing into his side would be ten times more painful than his chest, and he knew it.

Lilith worked at the restraints and tried to catch the gag with her shoulder. If she pulled it out enough to get her tongue behind it, perhaps she could say...something to stop her. Nothing she'd said so far had made a difference, but she had to try.

The screams became deafening, even muffled by the rag. They ripped through the air with each letter she carved into his flesh. The cries briefly stopped when he inhaled, which should have been a blessing.

However, several times during those short-lived moments, Luminita nicked a rib, producing a horrendous sound Lilith wished she could scrub from her brain. The resulting shrieks of agony made bile creep up her throat. Each time, she forced it back down so she wouldn't drown in her vomit—another drawback of being gagged.

Luminita continued, growing more tenacious with every name— Finlay, Gregor's eldest, down the right ribs...Mirren, his youngest son, across the stomach...Bridget, Duncan's wife, below the sternum... Emma, the unborn baby, over his heart.

By the last letter of Emma's name, Cohen's red-rimmed eyes leaked tears, and only weak murmurs escaped. Shock was starting to set in.

"Stay with me, Andrew." Luminita swatted his cheek a few times as his eyes rolled without focusing. He couldn't take what lay ahead. Ashcroft already possessed ten times his strength when Gregor... *No.* She didn't want to imagine her father inflicting this level of depraved torture on another person, not even the man who had slaughtered their family.

"Next!" the woman shouted angrily.

"He smeared salt into the names."

The Romanian scooped salt from a bowl on the tray, hesitated for a split second, and shoved her palm on the carved letters. The poor man arched and convulsed as endless blood-curdling screams echoed through the room.

At first, the woman flinched. Lilith could only imagine how potent his agony felt beneath Luminita's palm. Despite that, the woman dug into the bowl again.

Finally, Lilith caught the cloth with her shoulder and pulled enough to spit out the gag. "He won't make it! You're killing him!"

"De *loogaroo* is right. Baron Samedi be wantin' dis one soon, Miss."

"Isadora! Stop your nonsense and silence that woman's damn mouth. Peisinoe, next!" The snarled words oozed past her gritted teeth, and the siren hesitated, allowing the tension between her co-conspirators to thicken.

"Miss. Baron Samedi is none too 'appy. No time to take offerins from dose in town. He be needin' his gifts for de deeds you ask or Kalfu will ride us all." *The hearts—Isadora used them as tributes.* That's why the cadavers from New Haven were missing theirs.

"Silence!" Luminita's sea-blue eyes hardened with cold ferocity. "I did not ask your opinion!"

The voodoo queen stood tall as she fidgeted with her charms. "No, miss! Dis is not right." The long dreadlocks swayed with each vehement shake of her head, unable to look away from Cohen's bloody body. "De torture is Kalfu's work. You condemn dat man for de same ting." One hand swept toward Farren before nervously caressing the bleached jawbone hanging from her neck.

Before Luminita said a word, Peisinoe's melodic laugh cut through the room like a hot knife. "You must be joking, you fucking swamp rat. You take hearts and jaws from humans as offerings to your imaginary best friend, and suddenly you're queasy?"

The rage contorting the Haitian woman's face gradually transformed into a snarl of contempt. "I end 'em quick like. I take de offerins after dey pass to de utter side! Baron Samedi is real, *sòsyè*!"

"Right..." Peisinoe rolled her eyes with a patronizing smirk. "You and your fictitious god are such humanitarians."

Isadora's dark eyes narrowed to dagger points, fixing on Peisinoe as she stepped forward. When she spoke again, the words slithered past her lips in deep, hypnotic tones. "He is real, and he be comin' for you. No salt or ritual will save you. I see de mark on you..." One slender finger rose, and time slid into slow motion as she pointed at the siren. For a brief second, Peisinoe's sharp smile faltered.

"That is enough! Your Baron doesn't give you power. Stupid child! Hold your tongue or I'll cut it out. Peisinoe, give me the next step!"

Isadora gathered her skirts and stormed off, muttering under her breath. When she reached Farren's corner, she cradled the precious fern and stared daggers at the Romanian. If Luminita didn't control herself, she'd lose all her motherly kudo points with the voodoo witch and find herself on the wrong side of a zombie army.

Apparently, Isadora wasn't totally onboard with the master plan. Dissension in the ranks might be useful if Lilith hadn't been strapped to a damn table.

With the excitement over, Peisinoe returned her attention to the book with a triumphant grin. The woman devoured pure chaos, no matter the source. After witnessing Luminita chastise Isadora, she lounged on the counter like a cat with a belly full of cream.

"Let's see. Mary, Margareet, Finlay, Mirren, Bridget, Emma…rub with salt…oh, yes, here we go. Ouch!" Her vicious blue eyes swung to Lilith. "Damn." The siren whistled and raised her perfectly plucked eyebrows. "Remind me not to get on your dad's bad side." Her cupid's-bow mouth curved into a devilish smile that overflowed with venomous glee before she continued. "Oh, wait. He's dead."

"Fuck you!" Hatred seared up her spine, as an overwhelming desire to wrap her fingers around the bitch's throat made her fists clench.

"Enough games! Read the next step. Now!" While Peisinoe was enjoying the show, the Romanian's patience was wearing thin.

"Alright." Peisinoe sighed, as if being lectured by a teacher for talking in class. "It says here he made slow, purposeful cuts to Ashcroft's face in a crisscross pattern. It refers to a picture with directions on how to interpret it…" She flipped the page, and her eyes lit up while she scanned the image.

"The first cut extends from the midpoint of the right lower eyelid to the chin, but he left the eye intact to witness the punishment for his crimes." Peisinoe stared at Lilith with a spark of sadistic glee as she shivered overdramatically.

Horror twisted Lilith's insides. She paled, tearing her gaze away to lock eyes with Cohen. The panicked expression told her the poor man was already praying for death to release him. If only she could grant him some peace. Maybe she still could.

"Wait! There is a problem with your ritual! It won't work."

The Romanian paused with an impatient snarl. "What now, vampire?"

"Ashcroft practiced the dark habits of a Rogue for years, perhaps decades, drawing power from pain, which made him much stronger than Cohen."

The woman did not appear interested in her observation and turned away.

"Well, what about intention?"

Luminita craned her neck to peer at Lilith with a suspicious glare. "What do you mean?"

"Gregor and Ashcroft harbored a deep hatred for each other beyond any reason. My father…" Lilith forced the bile down and pushed herself to continue. This wasn't about her or her late father. This was for Cohen.

"Gregor enjoyed torturing him and only gave Ashcroft his blood in hopes of prolonging his torment. Hell, the monster probably used my father's sorrow, anger, and madness to heal in between cuts. This will not work."

"No. You are wrong." The words didn't ring with certainty this time, but Luminita still reached for the instrument tray.

"Andrew." Lilith caught his gaze again, trying to give him something to focus on, a center. "Breathe, Andrew. Stay with me. You can survive this. I am so sorry."

Although the words seemed ridiculously inadequate, Cohen nodded, focusing intently on her instructions. Tears cascaded down his cheek as he swallowed hard and braced himself. The scalpel glinted inches from his face, but his terrified eyes stayed locked on hers, refusing to acknowledge the blade.

"You do not have to do this! You can stop! I know you don't want to kill him." Lilith broke eye contact to plead with Luminita in sheer desperation. She couldn't let this happen. No one deserved it.

The Romanian stared at the names carved into Andrew's chest with misty eyes. For a moment, Lilith thought she had finally gotten through to her. The hope was short-lived. Luminita's teeth clenched in steely resolve, and her hand tightened around the scalpel.

"No! Don't!" Lilith's screams fell on deaf ears as Luminita snatched Andrew's jaw and stretched his neck, pinning him in place.

Lilith squeezed her eyes shut while the sound of metal scratching bone clawed at every nerve. Seconds later, Cohen's shrieks erupted with so much force the gag flew out of his mouth. Her useless fists clenched, and she wept as the man's suffering permeated the air so thick it became palpable even without the Durand abilities.

When his cries ended, Cohen went limp, and his eyes rolled back in his head. He panted for ragged breaths as Lilith watched helplessly. *God.* What Duncan must have endured, watching this happen to his daughter. No wonder he had become a mindless beast.

"Slice from the right upper eyelid to—"

Jenny Allen

Without warning, the whole building shook as dust rained from the ceiling. The tables rattled, instruments clinked onto the concrete floor, bottles rolled and shattered, and then, the fluorescent lights blinked out, plunging the entire room into darkness. Everything froze, and only Cohen's murmured groans broke the silence.

A struck match hissed to life, and a glow came from Farren's corner. The candle bobbed toward Luminita, casting Isadora's speckled face into sharp shadows. Despite the rage tightening her eyes, she handed the candle to the petite demon.

"Light more candles, so I can continue."

"Dey are for ritual, not your torture!"

"Isadora." The cold, calm tone in Luminita's voice sent chills down Lilith's spine. "This *is* a ritual. Light the candles, go see what happened, and *then* you can take your offerings for Samedi from the male vampire." It appeared Luminita had realized her mistake and changed tactics, offering Timothy as a consolation prize.

However, her realization seemed to come too late. Isadora stood still as stone with an offended scowl.

"Please, Isa. I helped you when no one else would, and now I need your help."

Unfortunately, the personal plea swayed the Haitian, and she moved about the room, lighting candles until it reached a warm twilight. Then the voodoo queen stalked to the creaky door and pulled it open. Her eyes landed on Luminita with cautious uncertainty before throwing a baleful glare at Peisinoe. She disappeared into the dark hallway without another word, the door screeching behind her.

"Repeat the previous instructions." Fierce tenacity infused the words, a tone Lilith recognized.

The Romanian had risked everything on her plan. She'd double-crossed the Council, kidnapped their most influential member, and had another one torn apart. After that, she'd betrayed and tortured her only loyal ally. The psycho had crossed lines, taken leaps of fucked-up faith, and now she had to finish what she'd started. It was her only prayer of survival.

Peisinoe brushed the dust off her powder-blue dress and shook her platinum curls before complying. "Right upper eyelid to the brow and diagonally to the hairline. Then from the right tear duct across the nose to the left corner of the mouth."

"Nita, please." Andrew sobbed with gut-wrenching sadness. "You can end this. Please, I don't want this. Let me help you. This isn't the only way…"

Tears gathered in Luminita's sea-blue as her fingertips traced the bleeding gash across Cohen's almost handsome face with tenderness. "Andy, my sweet boy…"

A ragged sigh of relief escaped as he closed his eyes, every muscle relaxing under the simple touch of affection and remorse. "I forgive you, Nita. Just let me go."

With a sudden movement, she snatched Cohen's jaw and forced his head against the table again. Andrew's eyes flashed open in shock, and he tried to shake his head.

"No! You will thank me when my work is done. This is for us. This is our future!"

Lilith squeezed her eyes shut again, digging her nails into her palms while Cohen's nightmarish cries filled the room. Bile rose in her throat as the coppery scent of blood tainted every molecule of air.

"Repeat the same pattern around the left eye." The siren sounded bored, as if merely relaying furniture instructions.

A lot of monsters inhabited the building, but Peisinoe was the most dangerous. She had no purpose, no mission. The bitch simply craved disaster and caused as much pain as possible for sheer pleasure. She didn't care about Luminita's experiments, and her loyalty was temporary at best. If she had double-crossed Farren, why wouldn't she do the same thing to the Romanian?

"What about Isadora? What is going on out there?" After a tremendous effort, Lilith spoke with submissive concern, hoping for a distraction. Cohen succumbed to the darkness, alive but unconscious, and she wanted him to enjoy the blissful peace before the psycho continued her work.

The woman paused with the blade poised over Cohen. "Peisinoe, check on Isadora." She muttered while pinching his eyelid and dragging the scalpel up to his hairline, waking Cohen and drawing fresh screams.

So much for distracting her. Although…forcing Peisinoe out of the room would be a decent consolation prize.

"You're taking orders from that blood-sucking bitch?" The rebellious words dripped with venom while the siren glared at Lilith.

Luminita stepped back, dropped the scalpel on the table, and dragged an arm across her forehead to wipe away glistening beads of sweat. The click of her heels echoed in the silence as she strolled over to the siren, wiping her hands on a cloth, and took the book.

Peisinoe merely stared at her in confusion.

The Romanian was in no mood for her insubordination. Luminita stood tall and snatched the siren's throat in a ferocious grip that elicited a squeak of pain. The woman's seemingly delicate fingers tightened, and she dragged Peisinoe off the counter and down to eye level.

Lilith couldn't hear the conversation, but judging by the tightening muscles in Peisinoe's face, it put her in check. What kind of threat would scare the siren into submission when one melody from her could kill everyone in the room? That was the truly terrifying question.

Once Peisinoe appeared properly chastised, Luminita shoved her away with surprising force and stalked back to the table. "Nothing but bickering children."

Peisinoe didn't so much as mumble a retort under her breath. Instead, she complied with the Romanian's orders. Her heavy heels clacked on the tile, and the door opened with an eerie creak. A faint glow lit the hallway, most likely from emergency lighting.

"The power must be out in the whole building. I can't see a thing." She stepped through the doorway and leaned out, checking both directions before turning back to Luminita. "The guards are—" A few loud pops echoed from the hall, interrupting her.

Peisinoe pouted in confusion as she took a step back into the room, holding her shoulder. When she pulled her hand away, crimson covered her palm. The moment of disbelief hung in the air, slowing time until her mouth opened in a shriek so powerful Lilith thought her head might split open.

The scalpel clattered to the floor an instant before Luminita collapsed. The Romanian covered her ears as the scream grew louder, curling into a fetal position. Lilith would have enjoyed the sight, but Peisinoe's voice pierced through Lilith's skull in blinding anguish, and she couldn't do anything about it.

Lilith bucked against the restraints as the world spun. Bile flooded her throat, making her cough and gag on the acid. The shriek tore through her like red-hot knives, slicing her brain to pieces. She couldn't even feel the blood trickling from her ears. Every inch, every cell was consumed in endless waves of torturous agony.

Desperate for any shred of solace, Lilith tilted her head to cover one ear with her shoulder. She spotted Cohen staring blissfully at the ceiling. Whether under the siren's spell or death's, at least he had a moment of peace.

The banshee screech went an octave higher, and the air pulsed with brutal force, hitting Lilith like a 30-foot wave of churning metal. After an excruciating pop, the world spun into darkness.

Chapter 28

An incessant ring tore through every cell in Lilith's brain. The shrill sound became so deafening she couldn't hear her own agonized screams, and the leather straps kept her from covering her bloody ears. Instead, she was forced to endure endless waves of disoriented nausea, which almost dragged her back into unconsciousness.

Once Lilith quelled the instinctual panic, she focused on deep breaths while the siren's shrieks reverberated off the walls. After a few moments, the dizziness slowed, and she bravely opened her eyes. Weak candlelight flickered through the spinning room, and she fought down the rising bile. As she began to close her eyes again, something moved in her field of vision.

A dark form on the floor twitched as she tried to focus past the swirling colors and lights. Considering the person's size and placement within the room, it had to be Luminita. The shadow crawled past the shrieking banshee with something clutched in her hand—Duncan's book, most likely.

Then the room whirled faster in dizzying spirals, ending the split-second reprieve as the screams reached a fevered pitch. Flickering lights and darkness spun around her. It felt like she was falling, drowning in the depths, unable to tell which way was up, and eventually, it dragged her back into oblivion.

A grumbling noise broke through the silence with all the comfort of a horror movie, startling Lilith out of incoherent dreams. She had no idea how long she had been unconscious this time—two minutes, two hours, two days?

When the garbled sound broke through the din again, it almost reminded her of a voice that was too distorted to understand. It was as if she were deep underwater, straining to hear the world above the surface. She turned her head toward the noise, hesitantly opening one eye despite the dread clamping down on her dry throat. She had witnessed too many horrific things in this place to expect it to change now.

The door still hung open, but before she made out anything else, the room spun out like a bad acid trip. All she saw was an empty doorway. Luminita was gone. She squeezed her eyes shut again, wincing from the searing pain still tormenting her brain as the shrill buzzing persisted.

Although each experience of Peisinoe's voice had varied slightly, this seemed different, like the aftereffects of standing too close to an explosion. The high-pitched ringing blocked out other sounds. Hopefully, it didn't mean permanent hearing loss.

When she opened her eyes again, the room appeared darker with slight flickers, as if the candles were drowning in melted wax. The encroaching darkness surrounded her, closing in. *Don't panic.* She kept whispering the mantra in an endless loop, hoping it would dissipate the looming sense of doom—it didn't. Luminita, Isadora, and Peisinoe were out there…somewhere.

Then a garbled voice shouted right next to her ear, the hot breath moving over her skin, and it nearly stopped her heart. The voice spoke again, but it was a muted mess of sounds, formless and indecipherable. It reminded her of the old cartoons when Charlie Brown's parents spoke.

Lilith blinked a few times, trying to focus on the flickering light while she teetered on the edge of consciousness. Continuously struggling to avoid the comforting arms of oblivion almost felt unnatural. If she simply let go, slipped away, all the pain and suffering would disappear with her.

No. She dug her nails into her palms until she drew blood. The crisp pain from the crescent-shaped wounds gave her clarity, something to concentrate on. The spinning room slowed, allowing her to focus her vision, but when she turned her head, no one was there. Whoever had shouted in her ear had either disappeared or never existed. Perhaps her traumatized mind was playing tricks on her, toying with her remaining shreds of sanity.

Then, a sudden tug at her ankle strap sent a jolt straight up her spine, and her eyes snapped open. The diminishing light reduced the person to a shadowy silhouette as formless as the voice. However, the odds of this being a rescue were slim to none.

Real monsters with deeply personal grudges lurked in the darkness, and no one else knew her location. She'd rather die fighting than allow any of those crazy lunatics to drag her off, especially Peisinoe. Without someone to yank the siren's leash and bring her to heel, the bitch would discover every conceivable way to punish Lilith for humiliating her multiple times.

Lilith's first instinct was to lash out, but the straps didn't provide much leeway. However, when her ankle popped free, the chaos roaring in her brain settled into a calming lull, and she stayed still. Working without two senses meant she had better odds if she concentrated and chose the right moment to attack. Assuming she didn't pass out first, which remained a possibility.

The restraint popped off her right wrist, and she rotated the joint, flexing. The strap across her upper arm disappeared, followed by the one constricting her chest, and she continued to wait patiently. *When they lean over to release the left side, I'll make my move.*

With her dominant hand free, she could remove the last few restraints without assistance if her muscles cooperated. Thankfully, she had a built-in weapon. After closing her eyes, she focused intently.

The cartilaginous fangs clicked down from the roof of her mouth to extend past her incisors as the weight of a body leaned over her. *This is it.* If she didn't strike now, she'd lose the element of surprise. She opened her mouth wide and came inches from stabbing her petite fangs into the bastard's throat when a familiar scent stopped her cold.

The shock came first, freezing her in place as she tried to identify the scent. Her aching, ravaged brain couldn't connect the dots at first. Slowly, the smell conjured images of warmth, safety, home. Then it clicked. Her fangs folded back as tears of joy flooded her eyes.

The voice rumbled again, louder this time, but no less garbled.

"I can't hear anything. Peisinoe…the siren…" She thought she spoke the words out loud but couldn't be certain.

The tugging sensation stopped with her left wrist, thigh, and ankle still secured. A dozen scenarios buzzed through her mind while she waited for what seemed like an eternity. When she tried to catch a peek, the dizziness returned, forcing her to squeeze her eyes shut again.

Then something wet touched her lips, and she jerked back, slamming her head into the metal table. Fireworks exploded behind her eyes and seared through her traumatized skull. After all the hits she had sustained in the past two weeks, it'd be a damn miracle if she avoided permanent damage.

A hand smoothed over her hair with a gentle caress, coaxing her into complacency while the liquid met her lips again. This time her body acted on instinct, opening her dry mouth to let the fluid roll over her tongue. The strong, coppery notes surprised her as they pinged off her taste buds in an explosion of flavor. It was like drinking electricity or pure energy, and she had never tasted anything so incredible before... No. She had *once* before—Cohen's blood.

The world started to come into focus like the sun burning away a thick fog. It finally stopped spinning like a hellish merry-go-round. Then the sounds and voices gradually lost their garbled echo, as if she were moving toward the water's surface. Unfortunately, the thick stench of blood, urine, and feces also became more acute, coating the back of her throat.

As the incessant ringing receded along with the violent pounding in her skull, she realized her broken humerus and bloody gashes had also begun to heal. If only her blood had the same effect on Cohen. He was in far worse shape, and she felt guilty for taking anything from him.

A Cajun-flecked voice rumbled beside her ear, and even though she barely made out the words, an overwhelming sense of relief washed over her. She hadn't imagined his scent. He was here. Right here.

"Did you miss me, *cherie?*"

At first, she couldn't speak as her throat clenched on joyful tears. After nodding, she swallowed hard and took a deep breath as Chance went to work on the remaining restraints. When she tried to help, her shaking hands fumbled with the straps, but couldn't work the buckles.

Finally, she gave up and relaxed against the table with a dozen questions swirling around her head, but she dismissed them all. In the end, she didn't care how he found her. *Chance is here and breathing. He's alive!*

As soon as he tossed aside the final strap, she flung her arms around him—no nightmare-induced hesitation, no fear, no apprehension. Her entire body shook as she clung to him, afraid he might evaporate at any moment, a figment of her traumatized imagination.

Instead, his arms circled her waist, drawing her closer, surrounding her with warmth as he buried his face in her neck. "I thought I lost you." The whispered words brought a rush of heat to her skin as tears fell on her shoulder.

Lilith pulled back to study his face, her tentative hand caressing his cheek. "I thought the same thing. You're really here?" She held her breath, searching his eyes for some sort of confirmation.

A tear rolled down his cheek as he cradled her face. "Yes, *amour de ma vie.*"

Then, his lips crashed against hers in an explosion of emotions. The passion and desire they poured into the kiss shot through her like a streak of lightning, igniting a hunger for more. Cohen's blood craved the energy as it sang seductively through her veins, shredding all logic and circumstantial awareness.

Abruptly, Chance broke the kiss, ending the animalistic trance, and pulled her against his chest. Lilith contentedly listened to his heart race like a rabbit on amphetamines. *He is really here.*

"It'll be okay, *cher.*" The words lacked confidence as if trying to convince himself it was true. Then, he placed a feather-light kiss on her forehead and moved back to see her eyes. That's when she sensed the tension, fear, and relief humming over his skin like an oil slick over water.

"Are you okay?"

She tried to answer, but the words caught in her throat, so she settled for a nod.

"We don't have much time. Can you walk?" The practical question burst the private bubble of serenity, and the real world roared to life with pops of gunfire and distant voices. Either Chance had brought back-up, or there was a mutiny in full swing, maybe both. Things were about to become very messy.

When she nodded again, still not quite trusting her voice, Chance unclasped his tactical vest, tugged off his black T-shirt, and shoved it into her hands. "Put this on."

Lilith glanced down at her bra and panties with sudden embarrassment. Somehow, she had forgotten about her lack of clothes. She immediately slipped the shirt on, grateful for any scrap of fabric. *Can't fight evil in your underwear.* She'd heard that somewhere once.

Jenny Allen

"And you'll need this." He pushed a 9 mm with a tactical light fixed to the barrel into her hand before his hazel eyes locked on her again. "I'm going to help Timothy, and we'll get out of here, okay?"

When she nodded, Chance stood up and snapped his tactical vest back in place. Then her vision shifted to the other table, reminding her that Tim wasn't the only victim who required help.

"Wait. We need to help Cohen first. He's in terrible shape and—"

"What?" Chance frowned in disbelief. "He almost got you killed...again." The roiling anger she sensed from him wasn't subtle. "No, Lily. He caused this mess, and he doesn't deserve our help." Without another word, Chance turned away, stalking toward Timothy.

"You're wrong." He froze in place but didn't turn around. "Cohen isn't—"

He cut her off with the hand signal for silence as his face turned toward the door.

When she followed his eye line, she only saw weak light emanating from the hall. She didn't hear footsteps or voices, didn't feel any shifts in airflow, didn't smell anything past the odors in the room. So, what had put him on alert?

While attempting to make as little noise as possible, she slid one hip off the table, her bare foot reaching for the tile. However, the moment she put weight on it, the pins-and-needles sensation ravaged her legs, nearly forcing her to whimper. She turned, supporting as much weight as she could with her arms, and gingerly lowered her other foot to the ground. The prickling numbness became unbearable, and she bit down on her lip, drawing blood to keep from crying out.

Her nervous eyes flickered to the doorway. If someone burst in with guns blazing, she'd be a goner. Until the paresthesia wore off and her legs woke up, she couldn't force her muscles to move.

The doorway still sat empty as Chance crept forward, heading for the wall, gun held loose at his side. She still couldn't see or hear anything that would put him in full bodyguard mode. *What am I missing?*

Then she felt it—a mixture of fear and exasperation emanating from outside the room. *How had he sensed that before me? I just drank Cohen's blood, and it's been a week for him. How is that possible?*

With careful movements, she lowered herself to the floor as her brain snagged on one thought—*what if Luminita wasn't bluffing at the hotel?* What if she knew something about Chance, his heritage, and the effect from a Durand's blood? If the Romanian died, Lilith and Chance might never know the answer.

Rose of Jericho

A metallic thwack pulled Lilith back to the present. She stayed low and scrambled around the table to investigate. Chance gripped the door handle, staring down at the boots of someone on the ground. The henchman probably hadn't expected a door to the face.

As she began to move, alarms rang down her nerves. She sensed several people now, and they weren't stealthy. Boots raced across the tile, heading toward their room.

"Stay." In the blink of an eye, Chance slid into the hall and slammed the door behind him.

Shit.

He wanted her to stay put, but how could she do that? She already thought she had lost him once tonight, and if he died now...

No. He's right this time. The cramping spasms in her legs barely allowed her to move, and her arms shook so much she could hardly grip the gun, much less aim it. In her condition, she was a liability, and he was better off on his own.

Of course, that didn't mean she had to sit around and do nothing. Other people still needed her help.

After a moment of indecision, she scrambled over to Timothy. Sure, Cohen was in horrible shape, but she couldn't move him by herself. When she reached Tim, his pulse beat strong beneath her fingers, and his chest rose with deep breaths—unconscious, but alive.

The iron collar and accompanying chain attached to the floor were a problem, and randomly finding a key seemed unlikely. She needed something to pry him loose...something long, thin, metal. Her keen eyes darted around the weakly lit room until they caught on an iron poker among other miscellaneous tools. It appeared Luminita had prepared for every conceivable scenario. For once, Lilith was glad the woman had been so thorough.

After a few attempts and several broken tiles, she pried the chain off the steel loop with a loud clank. The sound didn't stir Timothy, not that she was surprised. He slept through the yelling, gunfire, and blood-curdling screams. However, a few sharp slaps to the face did the trick.

As soon as he opened his eyes, Lilith shoved the fire poker into his hands. That's when she noticed his forearm, the one the zombie had bitten during the attack in Haverty's apartment. The skin was smooth and unblemished. Luminita must have healed him in case he was needed.

"What's going on?" Tim's words were thick and almost slurred.

"We're getting out of here."

"Wait. What?" He rubbed his groggy eyes and gazed around the room in confusion while Lilith limped over to Cohen. "Where are we?"

"Someplace we don't want to be. I'm gonna need your help." She pushed two fingers against Cohen's carotid artery, saying a prayer under her breath. "Come on."

A weak pulse throbbed beneath her fingertips. Relief washed over her as she shook his shoulders, and his eyes rolled behind the sliced eyelids.

Blood was everywhere—welling from his eyes, trickling down his ruined face, puddling on his chest, dripping to the concrete. Her father doing this to someone he despised was hard enough to swallow, but how could Luminita carve up someone she claimed to love?

"Andrew! You need to wake up!"

He only responded with a few incoherent murmurs.

Crap. "Tim, can you help me carry him once I remove the straps?"

"Yeah, I think so." While Timothy got to his feet, her shaking hands went to work on the straps.

Muffled pops sounded from outside, setting Lilith's heart racing. Her eyes locked on the door as her fingers fumbled with another restraint. No matter how hard she tried to pick apart the sensations from the hall, she couldn't tell which one was Chance. It was like picking someone out of a lineup based on the color of their soul while peering through a wriggling mass of pain and fear.

With a frustrated scowl, Lilith tore her eyes away from the door. Staring holes into the thing wouldn't help Chance or anyone else. With renewed purpose and laser focus, she attacked the remaining buckles one by one.

"Lilith." The raspy voice almost made her jump out of her skin. When she glanced down, Cohen blinked, unsuccessfully trying to clear the blood from his eyes. A ragged murmur passed his lips as his muscles twitched in pain.

"Relax. Close your eyes and don't talk. You're okay for now, but we need to move you."

"I just w…thank you." Speaking appeared to take a considerable effort. Each time he opened his mouth, the thin clots on the nearby incisions broke open, oozing fresh drops of blood. No matter how much pain he had directly or indirectly caused her, Cohen didn't deserve this.

Lilith swallowed hard on a lump of tears and forced a faint smile. "Thank me when we're out of here." Doubt crept into her voice, but he didn't seem to notice.

The door creaked as it swung open, catching Lilith's attention. When she grabbed her gun and aimed at the door, she kept her arms from shaking by sheer will.

"Lily! We have to move now!" Chance raced into the room with wild panic in his eyes. He stopped short when he saw Timothy awake, free, and ready to bash his head in with a fire poker. "Tim. You alright?"

While Chance was distracted, she unbuckled the last strap and eased it away from Cohen's bloody torso, but not fast enough.

"What are you doing?" Chance rushed over to the table with a scowl.

"We need to help—"

"No, we don't! I am not risking my neck or yours to protect *him*. Come on." He grabbed for her wrist, but she danced out of reach. When he glanced back at her in confusion, she met his eyes with an unyielding stare.

"I am *not* leaving him! He's innocent—"

"Innocent?!" Chance stepped closer, looming over her with every inch of his six-foot-three height. "He gave away my location. Those were Luminita's men waiting for me in Knoxville. He nearly got me killed, and you ended up strapped to that fucking table. He has been playing us the whole time. He's done nothing but lie, Lily! If you save him now, he will only bring more death to our lives."

"Luminita betrayed him, the only person he trusted. He had no idea, Chance. Look at him and tell me he wanted this!" Tears filled her eyes as she recalled Cohen's desperate pleas for Luminita to stop.

Although Chance's expression softened, he could never understand, not really. He hadn't been there to witness the person Cohen loved like a mother slice him open. He hadn't heard the scalpel nick the bone beneath, or the shrieks of agony as the blade cut deeper. Those sounds…would bring fresh torments to her nightmares.

Chance stepped closer, dumbfounded by her reaction. Then he finally took a good look at Cohen, and his eyes widened in shock. Apparently, he hadn't paid much attention when scooping up Cohen's blood to heal her.

"What the hell happened?"

"Help me get him up first." Lilith moved to slide her hand under Cohen's shoulders but jerked back after one touch.

The man's entire body was a dark vortex of emotional and physical anguish, spiraling into nothingness, and the blood she had taken from him craved the darkness. She felt drawn to it, pulled toward the swirling mass of tortured memories that prayed for oblivion. Ashcroft had tormented his victims for a reason—power. It was sick, twisted, and disgusting, but also exhilarating.

After gritting her teeth, she shook off the hypnotic pull and moved forward to try again when Chance laid his hand on her shoulder.

"*Cherie*, you don't have to do this alone. Let me help."

She turned and smiled up at him with tears of gratitude. "Thank you."

After a lot of winces, groans, and yelps, they finally maneuvered Andrew into a sitting position. He still couldn't open his eyes properly, but at least the bleeding had stopped. Unfortunately, she couldn't say the same for the deeper cuts on his torso.

Chance stared at the slices, reading the words before his eyes drifted to Cohen's face. "*Cher Dieu*, what did she do to him?"

"Luminita is trying to recreate Ashcroft. That's why she wanted Duncan's book—to reenact Ashcroft's torture. She believes that is the missing component in her experiments. It gets worse."

Chance pulled his gaze away from the names carved into Cohen's flesh to meet her eyes. "How?"

"She worked with Ashcroft, helped him torture Miriah and Duncan. *She* was his silent partner, the one who purchased Phipps Bend."

His expression hardened as he swung his stare to Cohen. "And he knew nothing about any of it? I find that very hard to believe, Lily. I know you want to trust him, but—"

"I was here. I witnessed the shock and disbelief. Cohen didn't ask for this. He merely trusted the wrong person." Lilith stared up at Chance, begging him to understand. When everything sank in, his conflicting emotions buzzed across his skin like static electricity.

For some reason, he still hesitated.

"Whether or not you believe me, if we don't get him out of here, what's to stop Luminita from continuing her sick ritual? What if she succeeds?"

He studied Cohen's face, weighing his options. She'd won the moral debate, but he knew taking on the liability would put their lives at risk.

"We can't leave him. Not after—" Her voice broke with fresh tears.

Chance gripped her shoulder and waited for her to meet his gaze. "It's okay. We'll help. Tim, can you carry him while I take point?"

While Tim hurried forward obediently, Chance moved around the table and pulled her close for a moment. "That's why she wanted you? To turn him?"

She merely nodded and snuggled into his chest, pulling his warmth around her. She couldn't explain why, but for some reason, his observation embarrassed her.

When he stepped back, he tilted her face toward him. "Are you sure you're okay?"

"Honestly? No. I feel like the universe has gone mad and nothing makes sense anymore."

With tears in his eyes, he tugged her tight against him again and rested his chin on her head. "I know, *cherie*. Things are completely screwed up, but as long as you're alive, I'll get us out of this. We'll figure it out. I promise."

For one selfish moment, she closed her eyes and accepted every word as absolute truth. She was wrong. There was still one thing in her life that made sense.

"Okay. We need to leave." She wiped her eyes one last time, stepped away, and helped Tim get Cohen off the table.

"Wait!" A commanding bark from the corner took them by surprise, but Lilith recognized the voice—one that would haunt her forever.

Before anyone else moved, Lilith snatched her pistol and stormed across the room. As soon as Farren's face came into view, her hatred surged until it gnawed at her insides, clawing its way to the surface. What if she just gave in? Let her monster take control? Did she really want to waste an opportunity for vengeance?

"Don't stand there, staring. Get me out of this thing!" Farren's fingers tugged at the thick metal around his neck, making the chains tinkle against the tile. Lilith stood still, eyes locked on him like laser targets as her hand flexed around the 9 mm.

"Leave him to rot, *cherie*. He's not worth our time or bullets." Although Chance's hand slid over her shoulder, her eyes remained fixed, burning holes in the man who had killed her father as casually as he'd swat a fly. The one who had wanted to kill her to torment his grandson. She couldn't walk away and leave him to an uncertain fate. He deserved to die.

"Lily, this wouldn't be self-defense. It would be murder, and you're not a killer." The words rang true, but she still seemed unable or unwilling to turn away.

"Release me, now!" Even though Farren's voice boomed with authority, it felt hollow and empty. "I'm your only ticket to freedom. Get me out of here, and I'll make sure the council doesn't hunt you down."

Outrage and fury exploded inside her like a violent backdraft in a building fire. Even chained to the floor, he had the audacity to threaten them. No matter what he claimed, they would never be free as long as he drew breath. The man had betrayed his fellow council members, and when he lost everything, she knew where he'd place the blame.

"Lilith." Chance's soft voice filled her ear as his breath tickled across her skin, easing the pounding in her head and leeching the anger away. "He's powerless now. Without resources, he won't be able to hurt us." As soon as the words left his lips, she knew they were true. "Let's go, *mon cherie*."

She nodded while swallowing the lump in her throat and let the gun fall to her side. As much as she wanted to put a bullet in his head, she wasn't a cold-blooded killer like Farren.

While she prayed that he'd die along with his hollow threats, Tim supported Cohen's weight and ambled closer. Farren's attention quickly turned away from Lilith, searching for a new ally.

"Wait! Andrew! You can't leave me here. You are my grandson. You're one of *us*!"

Lilith laughed wholeheartedly at Farren's desperate plea. The monster never considered Cohen a true member of the Durand, and he destroyed every positive thing in his grandson's life, forcing Andrew into the arms of a madwoman.

As she turned to follow Chance, Cohen leaned away from Tim and snatched the gun out of her hand. Before she registered what happened, a gunshot ripped through the air like thunder. She whirled around to see Cohen standing there, shaking, smoking gun raised, and a determined expression pulling at the cuts on his face. She followed the trajectory to a bullet hole above Farren's left eyebrow and a splatter of red against the white tile.

"I was *never* like you!" His hysterical scream contained a visceral pain they all felt. The incisions near his mouth opened again, but he swallowed the cries threatening to break loose and stood still. His eyes remained locked on his grandfather's corpse as tumultuous emotions tore him in a million directions. He wasn't the only one.

Lilith couldn't tear her eyes off the wound, which was identical to the one that had killed her father. How was she supposed to feel? Relieved, vindicated, sick, afraid, sympathetic—they all swirled in her brain as everyone stood silent, not daring to speak a word.

When she forced her gaze away from Farren's body to meet Cohen's blood-soaked eyes, he pushed the gun back into her hand. "Luminita may be bat-shit crazy, but she was right about Farren. I couldn't let him hurt anyone else." Beneath the tears in his voice, lived a resolve hardened by decades of emotional torture. Farren's legacy of anguish, manipulation, and murder was finally over.

She nodded and cast one last glance at Farren to ensure he was truly dead.

"We need to go." Chance's voice emerged soft and tender as he slid a hand over her shoulder again.

Lilith nodded. "Let's get out of this hellhole."

Chapter 29

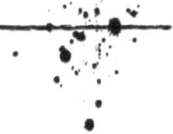

Chance took point with his AR-15 aimed and ready when they entered the dimly lit hall. Lilith and Timothy supported Cohen's weight between them while he bit down on murmured groans. Despite their best efforts to take slow and easy steps, every motion tugged on the deep slashes in his torso. The task took considerable effort, especially with her brain screaming for her to run. *Fight-or-flight* hormones flooded her body, making her pulse race and muscles twitch.

Weak emergency lights and exit arrows cast the barren hallway in an eerie glow, illuminating the neutral walls and white tile floors with splashes of red and yellow. Black plaques sat vacant next to each closed door, their anonymity only adding to the creep factor.

Although the place was in decent shape, the tiny hairs on Lilith's neck still stood on end with flashes of déjà vu tightening her chest—Phipps Bend, sneaking through the dark to evade the evil clutches of a psychotic villain. Their current situation wasn't much different.

Ashcroft and Luminita were two sides of the same coin, but she had something Ashcroft didn't—powerful allies. Lilith was reasonably sure Luminita and Isadora would focus on escaping, but Peisinoe held a grudge. The vindictive siren lurked out there in the dark somewhere, waiting to strike, and Lilith had no idea how to take her down.

As they picked their way past a dozen guards dead on the ground, Chance scooped up an assault rifle and passed it to Tim. For a moment, she considered grabbing one herself, but she'd never fired a rifle before. With the recoil, she would probably hit everything *except* her target. Too bad she didn't possess an instinctual knowledge of weaponry like every hero in the movies.

As they neared the first corner, Chance held up a fist and pointed without glancing back. Thankfully, Timothy interpreted, steering Lilith and Cohen until their backs met the wall. Once they were in position, Chance held up his clenched fist again before creeping forward. Then he crouched down as his muscles tensed, like a panther ready to pounce, and waited.

The place remained as silent as a tomb. Lilith nervously glanced behind them, searching the dark for shifting shadows. Although she didn't spot any movement, thick splatters of blood covered the floor. The trail they were leaving was glaringly obvious even in the dim light, like glow-in-the-dark breadcrumbs.

Her gaze shot to Cohen. His head rested against the wall, eyes half closed. The fragile clots covering his lacerations had broken. The names now bled at a steady pace. If hypovolemic shock hadn't set in yet, it would soon. Cohen was dying right in front of her, and she couldn't help him.

Even if they had time to stitch his wounds and stop the bleeding, it wouldn't be enough. As deep as Luminita had cut, she probably nicked an organ or perforated his bowel, both of which were deadly. If she closed the incisions, the blood would only pool inside. He'd still bleed out.

A compulsive need to save him overcame her. Not only because they had endured something horrible together or because she empathized with him. He was also their only shot at escaping the death sentence from the council. It was a shamefully selfish priority, but still a valid concern.

Without the book and cipher, reporting Luminita's crimes was their sole bargaining chip. With Farren and the German dead, only Cohen could corroborate their story. Otherwise, it was her word against Luminita's, and she doubted the testimony of three vampires meant much to a tight-knit clan like the Durand.

They had to get Cohen out and fast, but the maze of sterile hallways and locked doors stood between them and freedom. The morgue-style chamber and continuous tile floor indicated an old medical facility. There couldn't be *that* many in New York City. Who was she kidding? The post-Obamacare world contained an empty physician's office, skilled nursing facility, or health insurance building every few blocks. Besides, they might not be in the state, much less the city.

Rose of Jericho

A flickering shadow moved up ahead, and Lilith held her breath, eyes locked on the corner. A crackle of electricity popped seconds before Cohen slumped against her with his full weight. She glanced back, expecting to see Timothy. Instead, she faced a guard with a tactical knife and a stun baton. Time froze as her eyes roamed from the open door behind the mercenary to Timothy, twitching on the ground. *Shit.*

While Lilith raised her gun, the man snatched Cohen as a shield and pressed the blade to his throat. He refused to give her a clear shot, unlike the helpful villains in the movies.

"Drop the gun and kick it down the hall."

Obediently, she let the pistol clatter to the floor, held up her hands, and used her foot to slide it across the tile. A split-second later, she sensed Chance behind her with his assault rifle aimed.

"You too. Lose the weapon." When his demand went unanswered, Lilith glanced over her shoulder, hoping he had a plan or at least a better shot, but his face held no discernible expression.

"Or you'll do what? Slit his throat?" With slow, purposeful steps, Chance moved around Lilith, putting her behind him. "Three problems with that scenario—your boss wants him alive, I couldn't care less if he dies, and if you kill him, I'll shoot you before his body hits the ground. So, how about *you* drop the knife?"

"The mission failed. My orders are to clean house. No witnesses."

"Not exactly making a strong case here. Where's my incentive if you plan to kill us anyway? Drop your weapon and I'll let you walk away."

The man's hand tensed as he defiantly stared down Chance, but Cohen's face caught her attention. He was smiling. Considering the situation and the deep slashes on either side of his mouth, it was a disturbing sight.

"Idiot. They trained you better than this." Beneath the broken and raspy voice lingered a confidence she didn't understand. Then both his hands shot up, grabbing the assailant's arms with an iron-clad grip.

The knife breached the skin, and blood welled around the blade, but Cohen didn't seem to care. His eyes met Lilith's, silently telling her to run before he threw his weight backward and knocked the man to the ground.

Chance took advantage of the distraction to drag Timothy to safety. After a few sharp slaps, Tim opened his groggy eyes, disoriented until he spotted Cohen and the guard. "Jesus. What the hell is he doing?"

Although blood trickled down Cohen's neck from the fresh slice, the silent scream frozen on the man's face was more horrifying. The color leeched from Tim's skin when Cohen's grip tightened.

He's drawing on his energy, just like I did to Humphries in Phipps Bend.

Before she fully processed the thought, the drywall above them erupted in a shower of shrapnel and dust. The shots sent Chance, Lilith, and Tim skidding around the corner. She screamed Andrew's name, but only heard boots stomping down the hall. *I can't let him die now! We still need him!*

When she tried to turn back, Chance looped his arms around her waist and pulled her in the opposite direction.

"Run, Lilith," he screamed over fresh pops of gunfire. She opened her mouth to argue, but then sensed a blast of frustrated anger emanating from four...no, five men. *Shit.* The mercenary wasn't bluffing. Someone wanted this place scrubbed. It didn't matter who pressed the reset button, Luminita or the council, the result would be the same if they didn't act fast.

"Come on." She stared at the corner, trying to force Cohen to appear by sheer will. Without him, the Durand would kill them all, and if she attempted to save him, the henchmen would shoot her. As the gunfire grew louder, her entire body froze with indecision.

Before she made a choice, Chance stepped in front of her, looming inches away with a calm intensity in his hazel eyes. "Lily. I need you to run. He's dead."

Whether or not she liked it, Chance was right. She couldn't wait any longer. *Damn it.* After a final whispered prayer, she took off down the hall while Chance provided cover fire. Her bare feet slapped against the tile, but the sound drowned in the chaotic shots from half a dozen assault rifles.

When they rounded the next corner, a bright exit sign pointing left doused the area in brilliant red. The immense relief that flooded her system almost made her knees buckle. *We are so close.*

With renewed vigor, she sprinted forward, passing Tim as she raced for the next turn. Leading the pack dressed only in her T-shirt wasn't the best idea, especially since she didn't have a weapon, but the instinctual need to escape defied logic.

A few feet from the exit sign, a familiar sound erupted, sending chills down Lilith's spine. Every muscle seized with paralyzing fear and sent her crashing to the floor. The ominous clicks of heavy heels echoed off the walls as time slowed to a crawl. She scrambled backward, panting for each breath while panic took over.

No. Not her. Shit. Lilith opened her mouth to warn Tim and Chance, but she couldn't utter a single word. Terror cinched her throat tight, blocking all sound.

Peisinoe's round face loomed into view like a scene straight from her nightmares. As she sauntered forward, a toothy smile of glee stretched her lips. There was no one to restrain her, no master to tug on her leash. With Farren dead and Luminita in the wind, the monster had complete autonomy.

Lilith clawed desperately at the tile, trying to get on her feet and run, but her muscles refused to comply. The siren's lips parted in a delirious expression, savoring the dread emanating from Lilith like she was tasting a fine wine.

"Alone at last."

Lilith forced her panicked muscles to move, shot to her feet, and raced toward Chance and Timothy. "Run!!!" Even as she screamed the word, she knew it was too late.

The shrill note Peisinoe released stabbed into Lilith's brain like a white-hot poker, sending her to the floor again. She waited for the siren to kill her with one final scream, but the monster's voice settled into a hum, like a buzz-saw in the next room.

At first, Lilith stared in confusion. Why was she holding back? Why not finish her?

The satisfied grin of triumph widened as the siren stalked toward her…and kept going. When Lilith turned to watch, she spotted the blank expressions on Chance and Tim. Everything clicked as her heart plummeted. She couldn't move, speak, or even breathe as all the trauma from her nightmare roared to life before her eyes. But this time, it was all real.

For a moment, Peisinoe scanned Timothy, weighing his usefulness. "Stand her up and hold her."

Tim moved forward without hesitation, breaking Lilith's trance of terror. She scrambled to her feet and tried to run, but not fast enough. Tim's arms clamped around her like iron bars and swung her back to face the monster.

The siren's gaze slithered over Chance's body with a possessive hunger that twisted Lilith's insides. All she could do was watch as Peisinoe unclipped his tactical vest and tossed it to the ground.

"There. That's better. Luminita was a clever minx, making me think you were dead. She didn't want me distracted."

As Chance stood still, vacant, devoid of personality, her delicate fingertips skimmed his chest. Plain, old-fashioned hatred burned in Lilith's stomach, growing hotter each time she touched him.

"Ah...Karma." Peisinoe walked her fingers over his shoulder as her eyes swung back to Lilith. "If you had played Luminita's game like a good little minion..." She lightly guided his face towards hers and smiled as she studied every line.

"Actually...I prefer things this way. Fuck Luminita." Peisinoe flashed a malicious grin and leaned on tiptoe to whisper into his ear.

In a sudden movement, Chance shoved her away and drew his pistol, but Peisinoe recovered quickly. With one powerful shriek, the gun clattered on the tile, and he fell to his knees. Then she stalked toward him with a sneer and yanked his head to the side.

"Hmm. Smart little insect, but not good enough." She plucked the black buds from his ears and tossed them aside. "Frequency-reducing, I assume? Can't storm the castle with earplugs." The lilting melody of her voice forced the truth, and Chance nodded as his eyes swung to Lilith. For a moment, they held an apology, but when the siren hummed, everything recognizable ebbed away into the ether, leaving nothing cognizant behind.

"Now, where was I? Oh, yes." With one delicate finger, she guided Chance to his feet and whispered in his ear again. This time, a blush crept over his cheeks. Peisinoe's teeth nipped his earlobe, but her attention rested solely on Lilith, drinking in her tearful reaction.

The gut-wrenching scene replayed in her mind, even after Lilith looked away. Logically, she knew Chance had no control, that the reactions didn't belong to him, but her heart didn't care. The blush on his cheeks still felt like a punch to the gut.

The sharp click of stilettos echoed off the bare walls, moving closer. Although Lilith's body screamed "fight", she stood limp in Tim's arms, resigned to what came next. She recognized the unavoidable fate awaiting her and couldn't witness that level of betrayal again.

Of all the times she thought she was about to die, she'd never felt so defeated and heartbroken. This wasn't just the end of her life. The inevitable act would leave Chance a tortured, empty husk who prayed for death. How long would Peisinoe make him relive this moment? A year, a decade, a century?

Fingertips caressed her cheek as his familiar voice whispered in her ear. *"Cherie."* Her eyes flew open and stared into Chance's hazel ones with their flecks of green. How was it possible? Did he find some other way to fight off Peisinoe's influence? The razor-sharp tone of her control still buzzed through the air, but there he stood with a familiar smile full of affection.

"Chance?" The hesitant question escaped her raw throat as he brushed the hair from her face.

"Shh," he breathed as he leaned closer, his lips barely grazing hers in a trembling kiss. When he pulled back, his expression of sheer love was so captivating that she didn't notice blush-pink nails curling around his arm.

Then the light in his eyes slipped away like grains of sand through her fingers. Little by little, he became less like himself, and her heart sank into the icy depths of hopelessness. The siren appeared over his shoulder, studying her, memorizing every ounce of pain.

"Good boy." She ruffled his chestnut hair affectionately, and he nestled into her hand like a faithful dog.

Stupid! I should have known better. Cohen flat-out told her no one resisted the monster when she took control, but Lilith had still fallen for the brief illusion of hope.

"Fuck you, you jealous, soulless, pathetic bitch!" Lilith snarled the words through gritted teeth as her rage became too intense to contain. She hovered on the edge, about to erupt in an explosion of fiery hatred that would leave only ash behind.

A melodic laugh filled the air like acid rain as Peisinoe grinned. "Now there's the feisty bitch! It's no fun if you roll over and play dead. I like a challenge." Her smile stretched impossibly wide as her blue eyes practically radiated with glee.

"You know, when I had Cohen under, he told me some fascinating things. I hear you had a dream about me." As Lilith paled, her insides trembling, Peisinoe whispered in Chance's ear again.

"Chance, please…don't listen! I love you. Don't do this." Lilith begged, hoping that he'd miraculously snap out of it, but his hand kept moving toward her. "You know me, you know us…please."

"Oh, kitten. I may own him, but he's awake in there. Beg all you like. I prefer it. When I release him, these memories will break his mind in delicious and irreversible ways. Every beautiful moment will turn toxic until all he remembers is this."

Lilith swallowed the lump of tears and threw her shoulder against Timothy's arms, trying to break the bear hug. Unfortunately, he held her as securely as the straps on the table. The man didn't even flinch when she kicked his legs. There was no escape.

Soft fingertips traced the collar of her borrowed T-shirt and then brushed against her pale skin. Even though her brain screamed in protest, her body craved his touch, melted beneath its warmth.

Come on. Get your shit together. This is not Chance. Just like the corpse in Gloria's kitchen wasn't my father.

If they couldn't escape the fate that awaited them both, she could at least diminish the bitch's enjoyment by not taking the bait. So, Lilith averted her eyes and focused on a single tile on the floor.

Flutters of heat followed his fingertips as they danced along the delicate features of her neck, but she stayed resolute. As she concentrated on memorizing each crack in the tile, she let her body go limp.

While Tim leaned forward from her dead weight, Chance's hand caressed her neck, fingers slipping around it. She expected a throat-crushing grip, but his hand tightened only enough to show possession.

"Do you want to kill her, my pet?" As Peisinoe's voice slithered past her lips, the hatred boiling in Lilith's veins seeped into her bones.

"Yes, of course, my love." Although he spoke with the same deep tones, it wasn't Chance. The warm flecks of his Cajun accent had disappeared. He sounded robotic with no real emotion attached to his words. He was nothing more than a ventriloquist dummy with Peisinoe speaking for him, or at least that's what Lilith repeated to herself.

"Why?" The unexpected question caught her attention.

"Because she's weak." Despite her resolution not to react, she glanced up at his face, surprised by his answer. Why would he say that and not some automatic response like *because it would please you* or *so we can be together?*

Because I refused to participate. That's why? Stop falling for her shit.

"Go on." Now that Lilith was watching the show, despite her better instincts, Peisinoe rested her cheek on his arm and dragged her nails up and down his bare chest. Once again, her eyes remained fixed on Lilith.

"She runs away and forces others to fight for her, to die for her." His fingers flexed around her throat as his eyes narrowed. "She risks the lives of people she loves to save a monster like Cohen."

Lilith stared at him in utter shock. *Does he really think that, or is she playing me? Come on. You know the answer.*

The siren caressed the stubble on his cheek as her eyes shifted to him. She drew his face toward her, and his eyes lit up as a lethargic smile replaced his scowl. For a moment, Lilith struggled to breathe, and it had nothing to do with the hand choking her.

Peisinoe nudged his lips with hers while Lilith's stomach lurched. "Squeeze." When she whispered the word, he pulled her close for a deeper kiss.

Lilith squeezed her eyes closed, choking on a lump of heart-rending betrayal as tears rolled down her cheeks. Her face burned hot, pure hatred consuming every inch of her. It blocked everything else out, even the growing pressure of his tightening hand. Her throat closed, the air hunger set in, but it only inflamed her rage.

With a sudden burst of desperation, Lilith coiled her legs and jumped up with every ounce of remaining strength, cracking her head into Tim's face. The resulting crunch indicated a broken nose. He didn't release her, but his hold loosened just enough.

She took advantage of the wiggle room by kicking Chance in the kneecap. He howled in pain as his choking grip vanished. Then Lilith dropped her weight, catching Tim by surprise, and slid out of his arms.

Amid the ensuing chaos, she scrambled past Chance and lunged at Peisinoe, aiming for her throat. But before she reached her goal, an arm slammed her into the tile with bone-crunching force.

While Chance kept her pinned to the floor, Peisinoe hovered over her, grinning like a fat cat with a belly full of cream. "I love it when you fight." As her lips parted, Lilith pressed her face against the cool tile, waiting for the inevitable shriek that would scatter her hopes like ash in the wind. Whether she died from the scream or Chance killed her, the result would be the same. At least she'd fought to the very end, not that it mattered.

Suddenly, a harsh gagging sound broke the controlling hum, and Lilith twisted to see Peisinoe's blue eyes wide with shock. The hand pinning Lilith down vanished.

The siren clawed at her neck, trying to remove the strap constricting it. Lilith seized the moment. She shoved her hands against the floor and tried to stand. Her bare feet slid on the tile, but she managed to get to her feet and back.

"You okay?" Nicci's New York-Italian accent was the most beautiful sound Lilith had ever heard.

The strap around Peisinoe's neck jerked backward, forcing the bitch to the ground while she struggled for air. Lilith skirted around the monster. Meanwhile, Nicci shoved her foot into the demon's back and pulled the belt tighter.

Without a second thought, Lilith snatched Nicci's gun from the holster and circled back to stand in front of Peisinoe. The siren's eyes filled with panic, fixating on the gun and showing true fear for the first time.

As she stared down at Peisinoe, a hatred more intense than she'd ever experienced burned through every pore. Yes, Farren murdered her father. But the siren's particular brand of sadism had not only made Lilith powerless, it had set fire to everything good left in her life…for mere fun.

With a surge of venomous spite, Lilith shoved the barrel against Peisinoe's temple. "You wanted the feisty bitch."

The siren attempted to respond, but when her mouth moved, only garbled noises emerged.

Every ounce of her wanted to pull the trigger, erase the siren's power, destroy her threats with one bullet. So why wouldn't her finger move? The digit twitched, her grip flexed, her arm shook, but she couldn't squeeze the trigger.

Something Chance had said kept echoing in her head. *Lily, this wouldn't be self-defense. It would be murder, and you're not a killer.* Could she cross that line? Would she ever come back from it if she did?

"What's the play, partner? Gag her?" Nervous energy bounced off Nicci's skin as she kept the leash tight.

Lilith didn't answer. Her focus remained locked on the face of evil, one that would haunt her dreams no matter what happened next. Her arm stiffened with resolve as hatred, vengeance, and righteous fury coiled around her.

This is self-defense. If I don't kill her, she'll use Chance to kill me. Maybe not now, but one day. She knew the monster wouldn't slink into the shadows never to return. Peisinoe would seek payback and destroy countless lives in the process.

A small smile crept across Peisinoe's lips, growing larger by the second. She knew Lilith wasn't a cold-blooded killer, and each moment that passed made her more confident in her assessment.

"Lilith?" Nicci sounded uncertain, but never let her grip on the belt falter. "We gotta make a decision here."

Suddenly, something hardened inside Lilith. "You're right. This ends now."

For a split second, the siren's lips parted in shock, then Lilith squeezed the trigger. Blood splattered the white tile as the deafening bang echoed through the building. Peisinoe's body went limp, her head flopping to one side as blood poured down her platinum-blonde curls.

It's over. But it didn't *feel* over. Lilith stared at the 9 mm in her blood-splattered hand and tried to breathe through the suffocating emotions swirling around her.

Nicci shoved the body away like a sack of garbage and rushed over to Lilith. "The perps are all dead or detained, and your friend Cohen is down the hall. He's in rough shape but stable. Are you hurt?"

When she didn't respond, Nicci changed tactics. "She didn't give you a choice. Not really." With a gentle touch, Nicci reached for the gun and slowly pulled it out of her shaking hand.

"Chance left his mic on so we could stay in touch, and I heard everything." When she glanced up at Nicci's face, she saw tears in her warm brown eyes. "I'm sorry the earplugs didn't work, and I'm sorry I didn't get here sooner."

Chance...

After swallowing the sudden lump in her throat, she turned, petrified of what might happen next. Would he judge her for killing an unarmed monster? What if she still felt betrayed by actions beyond his control? Could they ever recover? Her mind raced in a million directions before her eyes rested on Chance, still kneeling on the floor.

"Lily..." His sorrowful voice emerged in a haunted whisper as he stared at his hands. "I...I couldn't..." He choked on tears while his shoulders sank in defeat. When he met her eyes, his gaze immediately fell back to the ground, ashamed and unable to forgive himself, much less ask her to. "I would never..."

The dam holding back all her emotions burst, and everything rushed over her at once. When the tidal wave finally ebbed, the fear, heartache, and anger dissipated, leaving behind a compulsive need to erase that look from his eyes. She still recognized the beautiful soul buried beneath the guilt and shame.

Lilith skidded to the ground and wrapped her arms around him, trying to infuse him with all her warmth. As he attempted to pull away, she gripped his face and forced him to look at her. Although some sliver worried about seeing that vacant expression, her doubts evaporated the moment their eyes met. The truth shone like a beacon in the night, but how could she make him see it?

Telling him it wasn't his fault, that Peisinoe controlled him, was pointless. He understood that better than anyone, but still couldn't shrug off his actions.

With tears in her eyes, she rested her forehead against his. "I know. I love you, Chance, for who you are in here." Her finger tapped his chest. "She couldn't touch that or change it. She only imprisoned it."

A heartbreaking sigh escaped his lips as his arms circled her waist, clinging to the idea of absolution.

"She made me say those things, forced me to…I swear. I tried to fight…" His voice broke as his eyes squeezed shut against memories that would forever haunt him, and she pulled him closer, trying to thaw the icy fear in his gut.

"Chance, you don't have to explain."

He lifted his head to search her eyes frantically. "I don't think you're weak. You are the strongest person I've ever met, and you were right about saving Cohen. Leaving him to die would make us no better than the Durand."

The bold sincerity in every word erased the tense fear still clenching her body. All her feelings wedged in her throat, cutting off any possible reply, so she kissed him while tears rolled down her cheeks.

"Um, I hate to interrupt, but can we get out of here before something else knocks me out?" Lilith turned to peek at Timothy, mopping the blood off his face. After the last twenty-four hours, the poor guy needed to be put on concussion protocol as much as she did.

"Sorry about your nose, Tim."

His broad face frowned in genuine confusion. "What?" He stopped, his jaw clenching in sudden frustration. "You know what? Never mind. I don't want to know. I just want to go home."

Strange. Chance remembered every excruciating detail, but perhaps it had taken more effort to dominate while leaving an active consciousness. It made a certain sense. Achieving the delicate balance would be more difficult than assuming full control. If so, the siren wouldn't have wasted the energy on Tim. He was merely a convenient tool.

"Same here." Lilith got to her feet and offered Chance a hand. His hazel eyes stared at her hand like it represented a lifeline from the mire of guilt and failure, an unexpected way back into the light.

Rose of Jericho

After the night terror in New Haven, she hadn't been able to get close to him, much less touch him. However, after the nightmare came to life in vivid and violent ways, she had done everything possible to comfort *him*.

She couldn't explain why a dream had traumatized her more than reality. Perhaps the night terror had allowed her to work through things faster, or maybe her subconscious recognized the man who had tried to kill her wasn't Chance, no matter how much he'd looked like him.

A soft smile pulled at the corner of his mouth as he gripped her hand. He didn't need the help, but the gesture meant everything. Once he got on his feet, she stood on tiptoe and stole a quick kiss.

A blush crept over his cheeks before he flashed a lopsided smile and dragged his hand through his chestnut hair. The familiar combination felt so much like the Chance she loved that her eyes misted with tears.

"We really should go." Nicci's tone thrummed with nervous energy, eager to put distance between her and the building of horrors.

"You're right." Lilith bent to pick up Nicci's gun and cast a glance at Peisinoe's lifeless face, splattered with blood. Part of her expected the siren to pop up like some horror movie villain, coming back for one last scare, but nothing happened. Peisinoe was dead, and Lilith had pulled the trigger. Somehow, that fact didn't instill the sense of absolute joy she'd expected. Freedom came at a cost. Hopefully, it was one she could live with.

"Come on, partner." Nicci patted Lilith's shoulder and pulled on an encouraging smile. "I'll take control of the scene while you three help Cohen to an ambulance."

"Thank you, Nicci." Lilith pulled her into a tight hug, unable to properly express the depth of her gratitude.

"You can thank me later with a bottle of red wine and the full story." After a wink, Nicci took off and jogged toward the exit while Chance stepped up beside Lilith.

"I know you don't trust him, but Cohen isn't to blame. None of this would have happened if Gregor had let Ashcroft die six hundred years ago. What Luminita did…" The deep well of emotional trauma cut off her words.

"You're right. I don't trust him."

Lilith turned in frustration, but he squeezed her hand and continued. "But I trust you. Let's go help the demon."

Tim and Chance followed as she turned away from the exit and headed back into the bowels of the eerie building. When she rounded the second corner, she saw Andrew on the floor, propped against the wall. Although the slices on his face had healed into puckered, red scars, the deeper cuts on his torso still oozed blood, and he seemed impossibly pale. *Shit.*

Lilith raced over and pressed her fingers to his carotid artery, searching for a pulse.

"I'm still alive, thanks." The hoarse whisper caught her off guard, and she nearly jumped out of her skin.

"Damn it!"

Cohen raised an eyebrow at her outburst and then winced in pain.

"I meant for scaring me, you ass."

"Please, contain your jubilation for my survival. It's stifling." Although the aristocratic sarcasm was no surprise, it lacked his usual confidence and superiority, as if he were merely playing the part everyone expected. A ragged cough left him groaning as the names across his stomach bled a little more. "Can you help me up?"

Chance and Tim flanked Andrew, got him to his feet, and supported his weight between them. "We got him. Lead the way." Her eyes lingered on the tight smile Chance wore. He didn't like helping Cohen, but he was doing it for her, not him.

After mouthing a silent *thank you* to Chance, she led the way back toward the exit.

When Lilith faced the hall with Peisinoe's body, a mix of relief and shame left her conflicted. She gave the corpse a wide berth and tried to concentrate on the exit instead of the moment she squeezed the trigger. *I had no choice. It was self-defense.*

"Stop driving yourself crazy, *cherie*. She didn't give you a choice." Chance echoed her thoughts as he left Cohen with Tim and slid an arm around her shoulders. After pressing a kiss into her hair, he guided her forward. "I can tell you with absolute certainty that she intended to…"He paused as guilt and self-disgust oozed from every pore. "…do horrible things. She didn't want me to…kill you. If you had let her live, she'd have spent the rest of her life tormenting you."

Deep in her bones, she understood his logic, but only nodded absently. The siren was one more thing piled on top of a mountain of decisions, making her question her sanity. She agreed the bitch needed to die, but the cold way she had pulled the trigger on an unarmed, restrained person reminded her too much of Farren.

Rose of Jericho

Chance shoved the exit door open to a sea of flashing lights, and Lilith held up her arm, shielding her eyes as EMTs sprinted toward them. They descended in a rush of voices, and someone tugged her away from Chance. Instinctively, she whirled around, searching the chaotic mess of bodies and lights for him, but a young man threw a blanket around her shoulders and guided her away.

"We need to treat your injuries."

"I'm fine. I don't need—" Her voice faltered when they approached an alley engulfed in flames. The black skeleton of a car sat at the epicenter, and she suddenly remembered the explosion that had rocked the building, quite a distraction. Hopefully, it wasn't Tim's car.

Then something dark caught her eye, and she wandered closer, but the EMT steered her back toward the ambulance.

Lilith whipped around and held up her hands. "I said I'm fine. I'm sure there are people who need your attention, but I'm not one of them."

The guy sighed heavily—clearly not the first time he'd heard that argument—and gripped her arm, refusing to back off. "Cops are the second-worst patients, behind doctors. Give me ten minutes and you can—"

She shook off his grip and frowned. "I understand, but maybe you shouldn't manhandle the victim of a violent crime. Now, fuck off." While the EMT stood there shell-shocked, cheeks red with embarrassment, she stormed toward the alley for a closer look.

Bright orange light flickered off a mound of black, but her sensitive eyes couldn't make sense of the shape. She bent down, grabbed what felt like a shoulder, and turned the thing over. Isadora's lifeless face, smeared with blood, stared sightlessly at the night sky with a bullet hole in her forehead.

When she followed the line of her outstretched arm, she found the little fern lying on the ground. The bottom still displayed a vibrant green, but flames danced across the top. Lilith scooped up the miniature burning bush and extinguished it.

"Odd little thing, aren't you?" With no real idea why, she placed the plant into Isadora's palm before running her fingers over the woman's eyelids. The simple change made her appear more at peace, and the woman deserved that much.

The voodoo queen had survived a hellish existence, ostracized and maimed by her own people until she put her faith in the wrong person and realized it too late, like Cohen.

Jenny Allen

"Why do people bother to trust anyone?"

As she stood, her eyes scanned the crowd. When they fell on Chance, who was dodging the same over-eager EMT, she found her answer.

People trust because of fear. The fear of misunderstanding the tortured soul within a beast, of never experiencing something beautiful, of wasting away in solitude. Their collective existence, human or not, was a habitually brutal leap of faith. If people stood still and refused to jump, life would pass them by, leaving them alone with those fears. When it came down to it, everyone wanted companionship, to belong, even a monster like Luminita.

Chapter 30

A full moon bathed the winding path in cool light, leaching the colors until only muted shades remained. Lilith gazed at the trees as their branches swayed and creaked in a crisp breeze tinged with the scent of snow. The night was peaceful while she tugged her wool coat tighter around her. It was hard to believe a place this tranquil existed amid the hustle and bustle of New York City.

As she turned down a row of tombstones, she glanced at the armful of red roses stained purple by the moonlight. Her black flats crunched on the frost-covered grass until she stopped before a recent grave. For a moment, she stood still, staring at the headstone while she sifted through all the things she wanted to say.

Lilith bent to brush the dirt from the marble, her fingers lingering on the chiseled letters. A soft sigh escaped her lips with a cloud of vapor as she pulled a single rose from the bouquet and placed it on the bare ground.

"I miss you." A tear streaked down her cheek while she caressed the cold stone. "I'm sorry for everything. I should have visited sooner, but…" She faltered as every reason became nothing more than a weak excuse.

"Gloria and the kids are doing well, considering." She smiled as she read the carved words. *Felipe Alvarez, Loving Husband and Father.* An unearthly silence settled over her, as if he stood there, waiting for her to say what was really on her mind.

"I should have listened to you…when I was a rookie. If I had… maybe I could have avoided making the same mistake. I was so focused on dad that I didn't see the big picture until it was too late." She hesitated, forcing her chaotic thoughts into coherent sentences.

"That first night, when Gregor sent me to Tennessee...I knew he was lying. He was holding back vital information. I knew it, Felipe, but I trusted his judgment. I should have confronted him and forced him to tell me everything. If I did, we could have ended this whole thing before it began, and you wouldn't be...here."

She swallowed hard and wiped the icy tears from her cheeks. "I'm sorry. You deserved better." She caressed the headstone one last time before rising to her feet. "I'll look after Gloria and the girls. You have my word."

With a reluctant sigh, she returned to the moonlit path, still cradling her armful of roses. A glance at her watch told her people would begin arriving in a few minutes. She didn't have much time left.

On her way further up the hill, she stopped to place a rose at the graves of Duncan, Miriah, Malachi, and Spencer. Her cousin wasn't born a psychopath.

Once upon a time, Spencer had been nothing but a wide-eyed boy who loved uncovering history, especially when it pertained to art. With a soft smile, she recalled a lazy afternoon when he had bored her with a million facts about his antique teaspoons. Ashcroft had twisted that once-innocent soul into something unrecognizable and evil.

When she checked the time again, a pained sigh escaped in a puff of condensation. *It's time.* She couldn't delay the inevitable any longer, and if she didn't show up soon, they'd send out a search party. *You can do this.*

As she crested the hill, some distant part of her mind hoped she'd gaze out at more peaceful trees and tranquil gravestones. Instead, she spotted a group of people huddled around a heater, and beside them sat a gleaming gray coffin topped with white lilies. She didn't want to say goodbye to her father. She wasn't ready for a life without him.

From her vantage point atop the hill, she watched a line of cars begin to arrive. Each vehicle paused long enough for people to climb out before pulling away. They came from all over the country, and a few even made the journey from overseas.

She'd wanted an intimate funeral with Chance, Timothy, Ray, Gloria, and her girls. However, his company's board members insisted on a public, practically political affair to minimize the stock impact. Then there were the other Elders.

The ostentatious display gnawed at her insides. She hated watching strangers show up to mourn a man they didn't know and had probably never met face-to-face.

Rose of Jericho

While she mulled over the injustice to her father's memory, a tall figure exited the growing crowd and moved toward her at an easy stroll. The tension eased from her muscles as she walked down the winding path to meet him with a relieved smile.

"Everything okay, *mon petite cherie?*" The soft rumble of his Cajun-flecked voice wrapped around her like her favorite blanket. She nodded as he slid his arm around her shoulders and hugged her close. When she rested her cheek on his black Peacoat, she closed her eyes and wished they were curled up on the couch at her apartment. He'd been staying there ever since they'd escaped the medical building on Homelawn Street.

Chance had claimed he didn't want to leave her alone until they received word from the Council. However, two weeks had passed without a single peep except for Cohen's call about the now-closed FBI investigation on the *terrorist ring* they had taken down.

Of course, he also worried about Luminita reemerging with the book to finish what she had started. The monster was out there somewhere, plotting and licking her wounds, but one day she'd try again. The extent of her fanaticism and the things she had already sacrificed wouldn't allow her to give up.

"Ignore them, Lily."

She glanced down at the crowd gathering near her father's casket.

"You aren't obligated to shake hands with strangers or put on a performance. Just say goodbye to your father. Then we'll run away to my place tonight and avoid the reporters."

"Reporters?" She frowned and peered up at him.

"They started arriving outside your building right after you left. They're setting up camp—all vying for an interview with the daughter of New York's most powerful and reclusive businessman." Chance rolled his eyes, but anger and frustration clenched his jaw. "They won't find you at my place."

Lilith shook her head, grinning at the thought of his loft disguised as an abandoned warehouse—the perfect security system. "Not unless they're also hunting for dead hobos."

Chance pointedly ignored the dig. "And…" Although his hazel eyes glinted with pride, a mischievous grin pulled at his lips. "I packed a bag for you before I left since I'm incredibly considerate."

She quirked an eyebrow and stared at him with suspicion. "Chance Allen Deveraux, please tell me you included actual clothes in that bag."

When his impish grin only broadened, lighting his handsome face, she laughed. "Really?"

"What?" The innocent smile he adopted didn't suit him one bit, but this was what she loved most about him. On the darkest day of her life, he still managed to make her laugh and forget about the heart-rending task ahead of her, even if only for a minute.

After shoving him playfully, she started toward the waiting crowd as Chance jogged to catch up. When he matched her stride, his fingers interlaced with hers, filling her with warmth. Thankfully, she no longer felt the trippy effects of Cohen's blood. Unlike the first time, they had lasted longer than a few days, but then Ashcroft had nearly bled her dry. Still, they had dissipated after a week.

Halfway to the gravesite, a man emerged from a black town car, and Lilith stopped dead in her tracks. Moonlight shimmered off sandy blonde hair as he stood tall, straightening his suit with one hand while the other clutched a thick leather-bound packet of papers. The man searched the crowd until his sky-blue eyes rested on Lilith and Chance with a sigh of relief. He appeared uncomfortable—a word she never thought she'd associate with him.

"What is he doing here?" The underlying animosity in Chance's voice was understandable but unwelcome.

As Cohen made his way toward them, she turned to face Chance. "Hey." When he didn't take his eyes off the demon, she reached up and guided his stubbled chin down until he met her eyes. "Please, don't pick a fight. We are here for Gregor, and if Cohen's here, he has a reason." After taking his reluctant sigh as an agreement, she kissed his cheek and walked down to meet Cohen.

"Hi...I know this isn't the best time." Everything about him seemed different—the quiet voice, the hunched shoulders, the humble sadness lingering in his shifty eyes. Every mannerism emphasized the stark contrast to the arrogant aristocrat she knew. Of course, being tortured by the only person he loved was bound to transform him. At least the scars on his face had faded to pale symmetrical lines.

Lilith pulled on a smile that she hoped appeared more welcoming than nervous. Although she was glad to see Cohen, the possible reasons for his presence scared her. "Thank you for helping with the FBI and for keeping my father out of it...again."

His gaze fell to the ground as guilt tugged at his lightly scarred face. "It was the least I could do after what you did for me." He took a deep breath to calm his nerves before staring at the bundle in his hand.

"I won't take up much of your time." When his sky-gray eyes rose again, a million things filled them, none of which he seemed able to voice. "I wanted you to know that I took Farren's seat on the Council. I dispatched a team to track Luminita, but they haven't found any useful Intel yet. I also convinced the remaining Council members that a cooperative relationship with you…"

"Cooperative?" A palpable skepticism infused Chance's voice as he stepped up behind Lilith.

Cohen's eyes shot up at the sound of his voice, and he swallowed hard on his words.

"What does that mean, exactly?" Chance prompted.

"In the future, we may need each other's help. The world is becoming a more difficult place to hide."

"So, basically, they won't hunt us down, and in return, we are at their beck and call like eager lapdogs?"

Cohen bristled, and for a moment, she thought they'd resort to another pissing contest or start cursing each other in French. "No. *Cooperative.* If you need our assistance—"

"We don't need anything from the damn Council."

Lilith turned, placed a hand on Chance's chest, and looked up at him, pleading with him to understand. "Please, stop."

He opened his mouth to say something, but she pressed her finger to his lips.

"I know, believe me, but not tonight. Let me speak to Cohen alone. Then we'll bury my father and hide out in your apartment as long as no homeless drunks attack us before you unlock the freight elevator."

The sarcastic comment almost made him smile. Instead, he dragged a hand through his chestnut hair and peered over her shoulder at Cohen with a deflated sigh. "You're right. I'll check on Gloria and Tim." As his hazel eyes fell to hers, he brushed a stray curl from her face. "Be careful, *mon cherie.*"

"I'm just going to talk to him. He's not going to attack me, especially not in front of two hundred witnesses at my father's funeral." She stood on tiptoe and kissed him, her lips lingering there as thrills raced down her spine. Chance wrapped his arms around her, hugging her close for a moment, before reluctantly walking away.

His stare fixated on Cohen as he passed, and Andrew found the gravel path so fascinating that his sky-gray eyes didn't rise until Lilith stepped closer.

"I'm sorry about Chance—"

"—Who has every right to be angry." He finished her sentence while his eyes drifted to the flowers in her arms. An awkward silence settled over them as if he'd lost his place in a speech that he had rehearsed a hundred times.

"You didn't have to come all the way up here. A phone call would have been okay." Sensing his obvious discomfort, she offered a sympathetic smile, hoping it might put him at ease.

Instead, he nodded absently and chewed at the inside of his cheek.

"Is that for me?" She switched tactics and pointed at the bundle in his arms.

For a moment, he stared down at the huge file as if he'd never seen it before. Then his scrambled thoughts clicked together. "Yes. It's, uh… a peace offering." After clearing his throat, he met her eyes again. "I wanted to come in person to pay my respects and to give you this." The indicators of shame and regret in his expression seemed completely out of place somehow.

Lilith shifted the bouquet of roses to one hand and accepted the leather folder, which contained more pages than *War and Peace*. "What is it?"

Cohen straightened, his hand smoothing his tie—a flicker of his old self. "That is every record we have on you, your family, Ashcroft, and…Luminita." The strength in his voice faded as the last name left his lips. "It's everything I could find that pertains to you in any way."

Lilith stared at the leather-wrapped pages, some of them yellow with age. "The originals?"

The nod held a hint of his familiar stiffness. "I can't guarantee the other council members don't possess private information or copies of these files, but this is all I could access. I know this doesn't…" His words trailed off as his internal thoughts overcame him again.

"Andrew, you don't owe me an apology. You didn't know what was coming." As Lilith gazed at the fine white lines that marred his almost-handsome face, she wondered if they'd heal or become permanent reminders of Luminita's betrayal.

"I should have." Cohen snarled the words in a moment of self-loathing. "Over thirty years and I never even questioned her broken English. I should have discovered Luminita's true ambition. If I'd dug deeper into the Phipps Bend records…"

"Believe me, I've scrutinized every decision I've made that led to this moment. I have regrets, things I wish I had done differently, but we all did what we could. You needed *her* to survive Farren and his sadism. That is not something you should apologize for, and it's not your fault she took advantage of that."

When Cohen nodded again, he turned to face the ever-growing crowd below, putting his back to her. "Thank you. I wouldn't have survived the table, much less anything else, if you hadn't been there."

Without another word, he strolled down the moonlit path, his shoulders slumping forward. To her surprise, he walked past the cars and slipped into the mass of people who waited to pay their respects.

She glanced down at the bundled papers with fresh curiosity, but it would have to wait. With a heavy sigh, she made her way down to the gravesite and skirted the milling crowd. She kept her sights locked on Chance, who stood with Gloria and her daughters Erica, Sofia, and Rose. Sixteen-year-old Erica gazed up at the six-foot-three Cajun, hanging on every word as he finished a story that had Gloria grinning from ear to ear.

Before she could reach them, Ray Valinski, the final member of Gregor's security team, stopped her to extend his condolences. Then Tim swooped in, wrapped his arms around her, and hugged her tight.

"I'm so sorry, Lily. I never should have let him stay in Tennessee alone."

Lilith patted his back and softly kissed his cheek before pulling away. "None of this is your fault, Tim. I'm grateful for everything you've done for me and Chance. You are a great friend."

Tears welled in his warm brown eyes as he pulled her into another hug and wept against her shoulder.

"Aww, Tim." After squeezing him tight, she stepped back and smiled up at his kind face. "I'm glad we finally got to know each other."

He wiped his eyes and nodded somberly. "If you need anything…"

"Thanks, Tim."

As she resumed her journey through the crowd, a few guys from the police department, including Detective Boyd, stepped forward to shake her hand and say a few words. Before she got much further, Nicci rushed up for an awkward hug.

"Here, let me take those." To Lilith's relief, Nicci scooped up the enormous leather file.

"I have something for you." Her partner flashed a bright smile, shifted the papers, and dug into the pocket of her little black dress. When her hand emerged, it clutched a small decorative tin with faded paint. The familiar sight brought tears to Lilith's eyes.

Nicci handed her the box, and Lilith's fingers traced the top before popping it open. Inside lay the tiny portraits of Duncan, Bridget, Gregor, Margareet, Finlay, Mirren, and little Mary. Her misty eyes flew up to Nicci in shock. "How did you—"

"Well, I convinced the FBI they weren't relevant to the case, so they cleared them from the evidence locker for me. I sent the blood sample to Solasta but thought you might want these." The sympathetic smile she wore brought an embarrassed flush to Lilith's cheeks.

"Thank you…for this, and everything else. I meant to stop by the precinct, but…" The endless whirlwind of detectives and phone calls with FBI agents had been bad enough. Then, Solasta had refused to reinstate her as a forensic consultant until a therapist declared her fit for duty. On top of that, the meetings with Gregor's business partners, accountants, and lawyers had consumed the rest of her free time.

"You're my partner, but Chance is the one who deserves your thanks. When I arrived at Gloria's…" A shadow passed over Nicci's typically buoyant expression. "If Chance hadn't tracked me down and warned me about Luminita, I may never have found you."

"I have to ask. Why did you think to check property purchases?" It was the one question that Chance couldn't answer, and not knowing had nagged at the back of her mind.

"Honestly, because of Phipps Bend. When I read the file on Tennessee, I started digging into the sale. Like those checks, the money led through a half-dozen shell companies."

"Okay…" Lilith still couldn't see the leap in logic.

"Well, when Chance called, I searched each company for property sales or leases in New York City. I can't explain why I made the mental connection between Luminita and Phipps Bend. Perhaps it was because the setup for the sale was so similar to the checks for the thieves— different companies, but the same shuffle. Anyway, I figured she needed someplace local to stage the massive attack at Haverty's apartment. I got lucky. I only wish I had gotten there sooner."

"I'm lucky you have amazing instincts." Lilith squeezed her shoulder, and Nicci's gloomy frown melted into a reassuring smile.

"Maybe you can return the favor someday." With a conspiratorial grin, Nicci stepped back into the cluster of cops.

Before Lilith took another step, Gloria, Erica, Sophia, and Rose engulfed her in a group hug. The outpouring of love warmed her to the marrow. They clung to each other in the chilly fall night until someone coughed behind her.

Rose of Jericho

They untangled themselves with tears in their eyes, and Lilith reluctantly turned. The funeral director stood before her with a compassionate yet expectant expression.

"Are you ready, Miss?" The balding man wrung his hands as his beady eyes scanned the growing crowd. Holding a funeral at night was an uncommon practice, especially with so many people in attendance, which explained his nervousness.

When she nodded, the skittish man rang a brass bell, and the dull roar of a hundred conversations fell to an eerie silence. Every eye turned to her. Embarrassment burned her cheeks as if someone had thrust her into the spotlight of a packed theater naked. For a moment, she forgot how to breathe under the weight of those unrelenting stares.

Chance grabbed her hand and gave it a lingering squeeze. A rush of strength seeped into her bones as he leaned close to whisper. "None of these people matter. You're here for Gregor, and no one else, *amour de ma vie.*"

"I love you, too, handsome." She kissed his lips with a grateful smile before facing her father's casket.

As she moved forward, her fingertips brushed the steel-gray coffin, which gleamed silver beneath the full moon. Lilies cascaded over the top, blazing white, a stark contrast to the scarlet roses she placed beside them.

Then she stared down at the battered tin in her hands, and for a while, she forgot the looming crowd behind her, lost in a sea of memories. They all flashed through her mind—the apology on Gregor's face when he'd died, the tears he had shed while confessing his past, the voicemail full of hope and promises, the proud smile he'd worn at her graduation, the mugs of hot chocolate he'd made on cold winter's nights, riding his shoulders beneath the full moon...*one just like tonight's.*

"Ms. Adams wishes to say a few words before you pay your respects." The funeral director's booming voice dragged her back to the present, and she wiped the tears from her eyes.

When she turned around, the words froze in her throat as an ocean of anonymous faces stared back. Some appeared bored, impatient, or confused, but only a few displayed genuine sadness. *What am I supposed to say to a bunch of strangers?*

Her frantic eyes scanned the crowd to find familiar faces. First, she spotted Cohen, who stood with Nicci and the guys from the precinct. Timothy and Ray close by, both wearing supportive smiles.

Then her eyes caught sight of two familiar people at the very back—her uncle Aaron and his son Michael. Goosebumps raced over her flesh as she stared at their emotionless faces. Although they were blood relatives, they possessed less warmth than the snow-scented wind biting her skin.

Lilith forced her gaze away from them and finally found solace in the faces of her true family—Chance and Gloria. Her eyes never left them as she spoke.

"My father was not always a good man. A time existed when most people would have justifiably called him a monster..." Rumbling murmurs sparked through the crowd, but Lilith kept her focus, and with an encouraging nod from Chance, she continued.

"A wise person told me once that it doesn't matter who someone used to be. All that matters is who they are to you." A small smile crossed her lips as she gazed at Chance, narrowing her focus to his handsome face.

"To me, Gregor was a generous father, a prolific philanthropist, a loving friend..." Lilith paused to swallow the lump of tears in her throat. "He was my entire world, and when he died, I thought my universe went with him. But in those final days, he taught me a lesson. As long as you draw breath, you can build a new world and change the narrative.

"Life is not a game of luck, and its sole purpose is not survival. Life is an excruciating ballet of experiences, a world of mediocrity filled with people who want to be heard. So, this is my message to you. Create the world you want around you. Find the people who hear your voice even when you can't, and never let your love for them be mediocre. My father believed in redemption, second chances, and it's never too late to write a new story."

Lilith turned away from the attentive audience and caressed the chilly casket. Tears flooded her eyes as she said goodbye, not only to her father but also to the person she was less than a month ago.

As warm hands circled her waist, she relaxed into them and let the weight on her heart slide away. Although she'd miss her old life, the future held potential. Her existence hadn't ended with her father. It had merely transformed to become something new.

"That was truly beautiful, Lily. Gregor would have loved it." Fresh tears misted her eyes as Chance tenderly kissed the nape of her neck. "I hope so."

The crowd began forming a line, aimed toward them, and all her anxious embarrassment roared to the surface.

"Do you want to get out of here, *cherie?*" As his warm breath tickled over the fine hairs on her neck, she considered the prospect of spending the next two hours with an endless parade of strangers telling her how sorry they were for her loss.

It was time to let go of the past and leave her guilt with the dead. She hadn't shared the true lesson she'd learned. It wouldn't have made a good eulogy, and only a select few would have understood.

The truth Lilith had uncovered was that surviving trauma didn't matter if the resulting guilt and hatred poisoned what remained. If she allowed that, life would become nothing more than a painful stay of execution, an excruciating form of suicide. It wouldn't be easy, but if she truly wanted to live, she needed to embrace her new life and shed the past like a second skin.

After Chance and Lilith ducked past a few businessmen discussing stock prices, they broke free to the moonlit path lined with trees. Once she escaped the oppressive crowd, Lilith could finally breathe. She stopped at the hill's crest and cast one last look at the casket below with a firm resolution in her mind.

She would not follow in her father's footsteps. Revenge only led to more pain. It solved nothing.

Instead, she'd spend her life creating the world he had always wanted for her. A world she would fearlessly fight to protect.

To be continued in
Book 3, The Lotus Tree

About the Author

Jenny Allen (Deardorff), award-winning author of The Lilith Adams Universe, was also published in University journals and spent time as a reporter and photographer for the Chattanooga State College newspaper. Allen studied forensic science, Nursing, Psychology, and extensively researched world myths and history. She applied all this into a thrilling supernatural universe featuring the Lilith Adams main series, as well as the Draga & the Savage Novella series.

Her background as a published photographer and award-winning artist helps her visualize scenes, contributing to her unique style of vivid imagery. However, the emotional depths of her characters is what stands out to most readers. Mental health awareness is a passion project to Mrs. Allen and infuses that with every aspect of her writing.

Born on a Royal Airbase in Lakenheath, England, she left the U.K. at age nine to travel the United States and Germany. In her sophomore year, she began writing poetry after the suicide of a close friend. She later graduated to short stories and narratives until, in 2002, she wrote her first novel, Lilith in London, which was never published but still exists as 432 handwritten pages. Over twelve years, it underwent a metamorphosis, eventually becoming her first published novel, Blood Lily.

Currently, Mrs. Allen (Deardorff) lives in York, Pennsylvania with her husband, Eric Deardorff, and their two sons, Kaidan and River. When not working as a full-time RN, she is expanding on the Lilith Adams Universe and completing art commissions, as well as editing and formatting for fellow indie authors.

"Writing has been a tremendous benefit to my mental health. It's provided me a way to trap certain issues in the paper and allowed me to work through them in a safe space. My characters have grown exponentially since the first book, and I'm excited for the continuing journey!"

Suggested Reading

These are some of my favorite Authors!

Jennifer Saviano
Saviors MC Series

An intense slow-burn MC Romance/Thriller series with all the emotional depth and trauma response. Clever, bold, and endearing!

Avanne Michaels
The Beta Series and much more!

A gifted author in the Omegaverse realm who deals plenty of emotional trauma. Why choose at its best!

Desie Marie
Whiskey & Weights

A delightful Polyamory novella debut with female empowerment and positive plus-sized representation.

Trisha Wolfe
The Hollows Row
Trilogy & More!

Extremely smart and twisted dark romances that are absolutely addictive! The obvious research and exceptional writing bring the characters to life in every book.

Samantha Moran
Dealings in the Dark,
Bound & Betrayed

Supernatural, demonic possession horror at its finest! The intricate mental health questions woven into these books, especially the second one, are brilliantly handled.

Kelsey Humphries
Heartlanders Series

These audiobooks are a must-have for rom-com lovers. Voiced by Paige Reisenfeld & Ryan Lee Dunlap, these quirky books make us anxious introverts/extroverts feel seen & deliver heart-touching stories.